A

Casualty

of

Perfection

by Renee Sellers Bennett

Author of
Hearts Immersed Within:
Recipes, Reflections and a Side of Relish

A
Casualty
of Perfection

A Novel

Renee Sellers Bennett

Disclaimer

This book was written as a work of fiction. The names and characters are of the author's imagination. They are used fictitiously and not to be interpreted as authentic. The geographical locations that are depicted have inspired the author to fictitiously promote their relevance and charm. In no way is the resemblance to actual events or persons, whether living or deceased to be construed as anything but a coincidence.

ISBN 978-0-578-50307- 3

Acknowledgement

This book would not have been possible if not for my wonderful family and friends. A special thanks to Katie McDonald, Jan Hauser, and Heather Bennett who have believed in me and given me love, support, and encouragement. Thanks to those that have believed in me and have given me love, support and encouragement. A special thanks to my friend who sat at my kitchen table after reading the book and spoke of my characters as if they were acquaintances. She was fully vested in their lives and I knew then that I had accomplished what I had set out to do. The ramblings of my heart are penned to entertain, enlighten and empower women to fully appreciate the beauty of womanhood. The wonderful watercolor on the cover is my imagination transcended to the fingertips of Darika Stevens, who with the stroke of a brush has brought my book to life. Kudos to Katrina Bennett, my technical guru extraordinaire. Finally, to the one who believed in me the most and will forever be in my heart.

Dedicated to My One True Love

Ronnie

Chapter 1

The doorbell rang as Cynda had just drifted into a fitful sleep as she was inclined to do these days. She jerked herself half awake and felt her head bobbing like the red and white cork attached to her fishing line. In her semi-slumberous state, she was watching it from the banks of her childhood. "Daddy, I think there is something on my line," she whispered.

The sound was relentless and penetrated the layers of her sub-consciousness to the realization the doorbell was ringing. She rose up on one elbow, now fully awake. No one was expected she thought, at least not now. She strained to hear the response from Dane as he opened the door. She heard the familiar voices of her sisters Suzanne and Marcy, subtle in their mutterings, their words too faint to distinguish.

"It is rude to speak about someone else in their presence," Cynda demanded from her room in her weakened voice, but with enough inflection, that they knew she was not to be dismissed as if she wasn't even there. "I will be there in a minute, so change the subject," she said with the same tone, and no one dared, not even Dane to question her ability to make her way the short distance down the hallway to greet her visitors, even though she could not possibly have the strength to rise and greet them. At least that was the impression Dane had given her sisters. He certainly was not inclined to argue with Cynda given the situation at hand. Heaven help anyone who was willing to dispute her word. She was supremely confident in her request and the walls between them echoed her telepathic thoughts.

Both of the sisters looked at one another with raised brows and under the guidance of Dane made their way to the living area to wait. And wait they did for at least a half

1

an hour after hearing the sound of the bedroom door quietly being shut.

Cynda lay there for at least five minutes, working up enough strength to push the blankets aside. As she did, a film of perspiration covered her upper lip, and then what had been the hairline on the back of her neck broke out in sweat. She managed to swing her legs over the side of the bed, and in doing so, raised herself in a sitting position. Her head felt heavy and she paused for a few moments to regain her composure. Once she stood up, she began to lose her sea legs and felt a renewed strength to begin the task at hand; commitment to excoriate the vision she knew her presence would make in her current state. It was a sad state of affairs, she thought, as she began her mission.

It was her room, solely hers. It had been since she moved in it some weeks ago. She had always liked it. The decorations had been carefully chosen to make her guests feel as calm and peaceful as the sea green walls that rose up to meet elaborate white dental molding. The plantation shutters added the look and feel of the lowcountry to the room and she kept them open every day, open to the world outside, as she watched from her personal prison. Under any other circumstances, its lowcountry persona would have been quite tranquil.

The white furniture felt airy and the linens were white as well, mixed with a khaki leaf motif on the bed coverlet. There were splashes of color in the room and the deep pink chaise lounge made an appealing presence with its one pillow that sported an exotic bird, its plumes vibrant. Who would have ever thought that her guest room would serve as her private escape? From what, she thought, as there was no escape from her fate.

Cynda took several precarious steps and was soon standing at her dressing table. She slowly lowered herself to rest on the stool and took one look in the mirror; then she

2

stared at the reflection of someone she did not recognize. The image had an eerie look of familiarity, but the eyes that were once as green as the emeralds in her jewelry box had no luster or sparkle. They were dull and lifeless as they glowered at her from their hollow surroundings. The once high cheekbones that gave her the exotic look that had made her so striking now served to pronounce her thin and haunting presence. Then there was her hair, or the lack of it. She stared at the few strands that she had left and they seemed to mock her. There was not enough to brush.

Cynda slowly began the ritual that she had repeated through years of practiced confidence. She started by applying creams, foundation and blush. It was a ritual that she knew all too well. She could do it in her sleep. But this time, there were no eyelashes to enhance, no brows to brush with her wand of magic. She took the pencil and drew brows as best she could without looking too exaggerated. The other tools of her artistry lay there among her cosmetics, now void of purpose. She cradled the mascara wand and the expensive brushes that she had taken so much pride in possessing and threw them in the trash. Striking the bottom of the pink metal trash can with finality, the sound was magnified and a fleeting moment of regret dissipated as quickly as it came.

Cynda looked over to the blank face on the Styrofoam mannequin head that rested on the table. She wondered what it would be like not to be required to show any expression or feelings, just existence. Isn't that what she had been doing as of late, just existing? She lifted the wig from the Styrofoam and gently set the head back on the dressing table with care. She spoke to the expressionless face in a facetious manner and said, "You are no better than I am Missy; you have no eyebrows or eyelashes either." Taking the wig and gingerly arranging the hair as she held it in one hand, she shot back at the mute head again and said, "Besides, I paid enough for these locks that matching brows and lashes should have come with them," laughing in spite of herself.

The wig sat precariously on Cynda's head. Suddenly, she did not have the strength to adjust the errant locks into place, much less style them. She took a deep breath and sat there thoughtfully for a few minutes. What was the use, this effort to project an image of someone who was still chic and beautiful, still trying to take a stab of perfection? She had her pride and she would never relinquish it, she thought, not even to the two people who would probably see right through her charade. She resumed her efforts to place the wig on properly and after a few minutes of adjusting it, she was pleased with her success, at least as much as possible.

Then for the final touch, the lips. Cynda reached to get a lipstick color and looked at the selections with concern. The reds were much too dark, too stark against her now sallow complexion. The pinks were a safe choice and she sorted through the array of shades. She chose a medium color, not too light, not too dark. As she reached to remove the cap, she stopped to read the name of the color. *Perfect Pink*; now that was a shock. Cynda almost laughed out loud at the irony. She tried to remember purchasing the lipstick and wondered if her *Perfect Pink* was an omen of a perfect day. She decided it was a good sign as she twisted the cap from the tube and applied the color in the skillful manner that she had done hundreds of times. There! She was finished. The image stared back at her and she leaned closer to examine in detail the finished product in the mirror. She was somewhat pleased with her effort, but as always never quite satisfied. Oh well, she did not have the strength to expend any more energy on her appearance.

Cynda moved to the dressing room with the attached closet to inspect the few items of clothing that she had moved there a few weeks earlier. The selection was sparse, but the items had been chosen well. The turquoise and pink shift was light and airy and floated over her body as she pulled it over her head. Her dress was almost complete. She just needed to add some earrings and a piece of jewelry; nothing flashy, just one of her favorite costume bracelets. The entire exercise had taken more out of her than she had expected. She took a few steps to the chaise and dropped ceremoniously in an upright position, cradling the cushion under one arm as if her lounging were a planned event.

At that moment Cynda decided that a change in plans was in order. She reached over to the table beside the lounge to pick up a well-placed Waterford bell. It had been her idea to place it there when she had moved into the room, a way to summon Dane without causing any undue stress or strain on her already taxed body. The tinkle of the bell began its soft and melodious strains, not very loud, but loud enough to achieve a response. She heard a tap at the door and answered in a most precise and whimsical manner, "The Queen is holding court upon her chosen throne. Please enter my sisters with the respect you would accord royalty." The door opened for her subjects to enter and she smiled at them, though their visit was unexpected, but welcome. Their momentary state, akin to jet lag, had not had time to subside as they had ridden from Atlanta, but they were anxious to see their sister. Dane left the room immediately, excusing himself to run an errand. The reason for his mission was not a mystery as the sisters nodded in silent agreement. It is sister time and the French Canadian is on sacred ground.

Neither one of the siblings was prepared for the vision of their sister. Cynda's carefully orchestrated appearance did not erase the telltale signs of the ravages of her disease. It had been some months since they had seen her and they were startled at the image before their very eyes. Suzanne stepped over to the chaise finding enough space on the end to sit down, but not before bending down to give Cynda her customary hugs and light kisses on the cheek. She was the baby sister and had no qualms in showing her affection to the *One* she had always admired. Marcy followed suit, but hovered over the chaise, contentiously crossing her arms over her chest. She rubbed her right hand back and forth from her elbow toward her shoulder. She seemed unsure how to approach the sister who had always been somewhat aloof. Now the illness seemed to add to the distance. Marcy reached down and gave her sister a perfunctory kiss. Cynda gave her a look that seemed to direct her to find a more comfortable posture; Marcy then leaned against the bedpost at the foot of the bed.

"So, what do I owe the honor of your presence? I did not expect you today," Cynda asked pointedly.

Both sisters scrambled to speak at once, but it was Marcy who blurted out the purpose of their visit in one provocative sentence. She explained, "We are here to give you wonderful news, plain and simple. You are going to be healed! We could not wait another day to share the good news with you."

She flung the words as swiftly as possible. Marcy felt a sense of smugness that she had been the one to make the monumental pronouncement. Yet, she could not help but have an overwhelming and foreboding feeling as she looked at Cynda with her crown of purchased locks, painted brows and the absence of eyelashes. The careful attention that Cynda had exercised on her appearance could not hide the state of her declining health.

"So, who do we have here?" Cynda responded. "Helen Keller, the miracle worker," she added, trying to keep the conversation in her lighthearted comfort zone she had created for herself when this nightmare began.

Suzanne was quick to respond, intuitive and sensitive to the matter at hand. She did not want to give

Marcy the opportunity to destroy the confidence they both hoped to build in Cynda in their efforts to share their good news. She quickly reached for Cynda and touched her on her arm, cringing as she felt the absence of flesh on the bone and tried to hide her reaction. She appealed to Marcy in her diplomatic manner by saying, "It's true Cynda. We have had many churches praying for you, as well as family and friends. Marcy and I have gone to a healing service at her church and we received peace about your healing. We have also brought a vial of healing oils with us and want you to participate with us in our own healing service."

Her delivery was subtler. Suzanne looked at Cynda with imploring eyes, waiting for her response. It was a very long moment before Cynda answered, as she tried to digest this newest revelation and to grasp its meaning. She certainly wanted to believe what they had to say and with her Christian upbringing, the statement was certainly not foreign to her ears. She was never far from her Christian values, even though she had chosen not to exercise them as faithfully as she could have done. Had she not prayed and prayed for God to heal her from her abomination? Could this be the answer to her prayers? Maybe God did want to heal her; maybe these sisters of hers were heaven sent.

Cynda said as a matter of fact, "This is too much for my mind to undertake right now." She followed up with her effervescent attitude by adding, "I have a great idea; let's have a picnic."

The tension in the room was so thick you could cut it with a knife. Suzanne looked at Marcy, who looked mortified that Cynda had not seemed to take them seriously. She had the urge to admonish Marcy, but the pleading in the violet blue eyes caused her to cease her mission. Their delayed reaction came at once as both sisters nodded in agreement. Neither one could imagine a picnic at this moment, but an unspoken understanding passed among all three of them.

Cynda had told herself that she would not lose control of her situation, nor pander to the morbid reality of her circumstances. Her control would last as long as she had her faculties, both physically and mentally. Had she not been told that after the last round of chemotherapy, she would begin to gain her strength back? She was determined that it would happen. With that thought in mind, she directed her sisters to the kitchen.

Cynda made her way across the room, summoning all the strength she had acquired while resting on the chaise. She ambled into the kitchen, finally sitting down at the table. She issued orders to both Suzanne and Marcy as they opened cabinet and refrigerator doors at her command. If either sister had any reservations of Cynda's mental capacity, they quickly dissipated. She had them both preparing sandwiches and lemonade from her well stocked kitchen pantry. An assortment of cheeses, crackers and homemade pickles completed the fare. They were not surprised at the efficiency of the area, and Cynda's mastery of putting a picnic together at the drop of a hat, even if they were doing the work.

They packed the food in a basket of sea grass crafted by the Gullah people of the low country and prized by their sister. They both marveled at its craftsmanship, knowing the timeless construction that had been passed down from generations of the Geechee. Under the guidance of Cynda's instruction, their task was complete. They placed the basket on the table in front of her. No one had bothered to ask where the picnic destination would be. By this time, Cynda's strength was quickly waning and she was mortified at the prospect of admitting defeat. She looked at Suzanne and instructed her to retrieve a butter yellow tablecloth from the small buffet in the kitchen.

The sisters looked for Cynda to give them the next order, both anticipating her disclosure of where they would be traveling. Neither could have guessed the destination, not in a million years. Cynda stood up and motioned for the sisters to follow. Without hesitation, they left the kitchen and moved deliberately toward the front door. Cynda's stride did not falter as she moved down the hallway away from the sisters, directly to her bedroom. Suzanne and Marcy looked at one another and followed suit. They watched as she climbed into her bed and pulled the bedding up around her legs. She sat Indian style, as a child in anticipation.

"Suzanne, please spread the cloth on the bed. I am getting hungry."

Suzanne unfolded the butter yellow square of fabric that was embossed with spring flowers. She spread it over the white comforter with khaki leaves and wondered if Cynda had taken leave of her senses, as she knew the value that she had put on her bed linens. Cynda signaled for the basket and their presence on the bed. The sisters all managed to congregate as though they were on a grassy knoll, and the tension of the moment gave way to laughter and camaraderie. Once again the spell had been cast on her sisters without her really trying. The *One* that seemed to mesmerize those around her. It was a subtle tactic of hers, one which helped to camouflage her true demeanor.

No mention was made of the healing service from any one of them, but an air of tension hung over the three. Cynda's enthusiasm had begun to wane. Suzanne noticed it first and nodded at Marcy to follow her lead in packing up the picnic basket. In deference to Cynda, Suzanne asked her to guide them in the process. She carefully placed the healing oil on the bedside table.

"Leaving this for you; just rub it on your temples when you pray at night," Suzanne said nonchalantly.

"There," Suzanne thought, "Our healing service may not have been well received, but Cynda will have that vial staring her in the face," she silently applauded herself for the idea.

The visit reached its own conclusion as the picnic was put away and the kitchen returned to its former state of affairs, immaculate.   When the sisters returned to the bedroom, Cynda was sound asleep. Suzanne and Marcy quietly retreated from the beautifully appointed room, a grim reminder that the guest room was now a symbol of flawed perfection, its persona imitating peace and tranquility. Both knew that in that room, there was a battle with a ruthless enemy that frightened both of them out of their wits. What they did not realize, there was another enemy that was much more ruthless. It had controlled Cynda all of her life and had controlled her very soul.

Chapter 2

Suzanne reached over and flipped the lock open on the passenger door of the 1974 aqua blue Volkswagen Beetle, she had affectionately named *Hug Bug*. Suzanne had found it rather comical as they drove down Interstate 16 in Marcy's SUV with a trailer hitch dragging a precocious little Beetle sporting its own trademark - a pink wreath on its grill. The honks and thumbs up from other vehicles became a counting game on the long drive. Suzanne had owned the Beetle since she had graduated from college. She had held on to it as if it were a member of her family. The car had been treated like a baby and she had kept it in mint condition. The saddle colored convertible roof matched the immaculate interior. It was her pride and joy. They had pulled it the nearly three hundred miles to the outskirts of Savannah.

Marcy gingerly slipped into the limited space afforded by the car and lamented her decision to allow Suzanne to talk her into bringing *Hug Bug* with them on the trip. It seemed like a good idea at the time to bring the Bug along with them as an alternative to riding in her large SUV everywhere they went. "It will be so much fun riding around the island, and think of the gas we will save," Suzanne had said. Once again Marcy had been a sucker for the pleas of her little sister and those mysterious violet eyes that never seemed to grow old.

As Marcy gained entrance to the passenger seat, she was met with the familiar hot and humid air. It was so stifling that both sisters promptly exercised their arms in a rowing motion as they manually rolled the windows down. Suzanne simultaneously flipped the air conditioner lever to high. Thank God for the air-conditioner, Marcy thought. As they backed out of the driveway, she also had second thoughts of spending the greater portion of her summer at the beach with temperatures already hovering around the ninety-five-degree mark. After all, it was only early June.

"Okay, little sis, I know that I was probably overly optimistic about the heat and humidity down here not being so bad, but I have to admit I am beginning to dread the coming weeks. Not to say that I have any reservations of rescuing our sister," she said.

Suzanne put the gear in drive and sped quickly away from the house in an effort to create a cross breeze. Her mind was already analyzing the visit with Cynda, but first things first. She needed to set the record straight. When you were smack dab in the middle of the road to menopause and on the verge of becoming an empty nester, the term 'little sis' just didn't fit, at least not in her book. She hated being called by that name. She had struggled all of her adult life to be her sister's equal. The two of them were in this effort together, and she was determined that Marcy recognized her as an equal partner. Their older sister had never been a part of their sisterly competition.

"Marcy, you know how much I hate being called that silly name, and if the truth be told, I have always been more mature than you, even before reaching the grand middle age. I do however; relish the title of 'little'. But let's focus on Cynda. I really thought she would chill out some with this illness of hers." Suzanne could not bring herself to use the "C" word.

"In fact," Suzanne said as both simultaneously rolled their windows backup as the air conditioning had kicked in, "she just needs to let her hair down."

"Suuuue, what did you just say?" Marcy screamed at her. Suzanne knew that Marcy only called her that when she was really upset and quickly corrected herself.

"Marcy, you know what I mean. Of course I did not mean that literally. We both talked about this before we came down here. Cynda just needs to lighten up. We have always known how uptight she can be."

"Yeah, and we also know how she can change the conversation to suit herself. Did you see how smooth she was in getting us to steer the discussion away from our healing service?" Marcy said.

"Yes, and not to mention her production of the picnic," Suzanne added.

"Look, I am all for having a little fun to lighten the air, but once again she was able to exercise her control of us in that pristine kitchen of hers. I am shaking in my boots, wondering if we put everything back in the right place. I wonder how old that yellow tablecloth was? Classic mid-century I would say."

"It must have been from the fifties or the sixties for sure," Suzanne replied.

"It looked as if it was in excellent condition no doubt, but I am afraid that when she washes it, the fringe will unravel completely. Can't you just see her peeking in the machine to find a huge ball of lemon fluff?" Marcy continued as she failed to suppress a giggle.

Now it was Suzanne's turn to admonish Marcy.

"That's not funny Marcy. She's sick and I'm sure that sort of thing might just unravel her. Uh-oh I did not mean to say that! It's just that I have so much sympathy for her that I cannot see any humor in her situation."

"I am going to remind you of the pact we made before we started on this journey. We are here to do everything we can to make Cynda's life more comfortable, but we will not do it at the expense of depriving ourselves of the much needed humor that we desperately need in this situation. Otherwise, we will fail. And if you ask me, Cynda needs lots of laughter. She looks as if she has been cooped up in that little prison of hers too long. We have got to get her out of the house even if it is only for a ride in the car. And Suzanne, I do believe she can be healed."

Suzanne chose not to respond to her sister, and the two rode in silence to the cottage located on *Tybee* Island, a short drive from the glaring truth of a sister with the big "C".

Chapter 3

Cynda woke from her short lived rest feeling somewhat energized, although it was a brief respite from her constant weakened condition. She had to remind herself where she was and the events leading up to her slumber. She eyed the vial of healing oil on the nightstand and thoughts of the visit from her sisters caused her to reflect on their purpose. So far she had avoided the whole mess of dealing with her illness by pretending it was not real. Unfortunately, it was not merely an obstacle to overcome in her perfectly planned current life. When faced with the reality of her situation, she had made the decision to carefully tuck her successes and failures away for future examination. Isn't that what one does when the inevitable demise of one's existence is glaring at them with imploring eyes?

It was not that Cynda wasn't glad to see her sisters, humble in their intent to save her. Their innocent resolve was more of an ultimatum for her to search her heart to finally face the ghosts of her past and have final peace whether in this life or after. She began to contemplate her life, visiting those long ago days growing up with her sisters that brought her mixed pain and pleasure.

Memories surfaced that had transpired while she was on the brink of puberty. Lawrence and Lydia Brooks, had given her the name of Lucinda Ophelia, better known now as "Cynda". It was 1957 and the twelve-year-old lay in a prone position, her head suspended over a shampoo bowl and resting on the well trained hands of Miss Edna. It did not matter that the hairdresser took great pains to exercise gentleness throughout this process known as a permanent wave. The smell of the permanent solution had permeated the air with a relentless odor that almost suffocated her. Cynda was miserable.

Cynda she was recovering from the "rinse" that had brought a sense of short lived relief as the warm water oozed over her scalp. Once again the pungent odor of the wave solution was resurrected like the smell of damp earth after a summer rain. She lay, literally, in the hands that would soon issue the next tortuous step in the process of "the permanent wave" that she did not want, much less desire; nor had she been willing to sacrifice all for the sake of her mother's idea of beauty.

Miss Edna reached down and draped a towel around Cynda's head, supporting the back of her neck; in a swift and deft manner, she gave the lever of the chair a jerk, which sent Cynda reeling into an upright position. Cynda looked up into the face of her torturer, the woman who by no stretch of the imagination sported horns or looked as she was a spawn of the devil himself. Instead she saw the outline of a perfectly styled bouffant around a kind and gentle smile and eyes that crinkled from behind the large lens of amber colored glasses.

"Are you okay Lucy?" Miss Edna said in her southern drawl as her sing, song voice contradicted any comfort Cynda received. Miss Edna began to pat the towel against the curlers that clung possessively around the tendrils of hair. Cynda did not dare correct Miss Edna for calling her Lucy.

"Yes ma'am'," Cynda squeaked out in response, determined in her resolve to be brave as her tender head was taking the abuse from the well intentioned soul. She thought it was not Miss Edna's fault whose duty was to put some curl in her straight as a board hair. Instead Cynda considered her mother's plight. How many times had she heard her mother bemoan her locks that were 'as fine as frog's hair'? The stylist had promised her mother she could remedy that little problem.

"You are such a good little girl," Miss Edna purred as she continued the abuse on Cynda's head; finally, the repetitious act ceased. She began to survey her target with one eyebrow raised as she looked quizzically for Cynda to respond. Then she raised the other eyebrow for a more pronounced facial gesture, as she peered from over the top of her glasses to inspect Cynda's face. It held no trace of the discomfort that Cynda felt, as she had become an expert at hiding her true feelings at a tender age. Her green eyes could flash as brightly as the only traffic signal in town on go. She did not betray her predicament with those eyes that would someday become her secret weapon against friend and foe. They looked serene and calm as they peeped up over her slightly crooked nose at Miss Edna.

Not waiting for a response, Miss Edna continued her questioning, "Now how old are you?" She then turned to her partner and said, "Clarice, she must be about eleven or twelve. I remember when she was born. Lawrence was beaming from ear to ear when he came down to John's to get his ears lowered." She turned back to Cynda to explain, "Getting one's ears lowered means getting a haircut." She grinned at herself as she made the age old comment that had hung around the shop as long as the plastic Norman Rockwell clock that hung dangerously over the shampoo bowl.

Cynda eked out a belated answer, taking somewhat of a deep breath as she responded with, "I am twelve and a half years old," placing emphasis on the half as if it made a big difference in her age. She smiled to herself at the comment about her daddy being so proud when she was born. She held that close to her heart with sacred fondness knowing it had been spoken in the confines of the little brick building that housed both a beauty and barber shop. Barber John was on the other side of the building working magic with his shears, exercising a surety of his own expertise in the execution of grooming his customers.

Beneath the hair curlers that formed around her head like a helmet, Cynda sighed in relief as Miss Edna finally announced that it was time to put her under the dryer. The idea never occurred to Cynda to admit to the purveyor of beauty that her head hurt. Cynda had not given Miss Edna any indication that she was unusually "tender headed". For Cynda to confess her state of affairs would have been perfectly understandable. But she did not, no more than she would correct her elder for calling her Lucy when she had already shortened her own name to "Cynda" just after entering third grade, tired of being called anything from "LuLu" to "Lucy Goosey". Didn't everyone in town know her chosen name by now? After all, if you blinked, while driving, you were in another jurisdiction.

The decision to change her name had been easy enough when her own mother had agreed with her. After all, she had always been called Cynda at home; the shorter version of Lucinda, was easier to say, especially when she was in trouble. She decided that her mother must have felt that she had owed it to her for hanging such an old fashioned name on her in the first place. What had she been thinking and how had her sisters Suzanne and Marcy escaped such a fate? They had "normal" names. Marcy was five years younger than her and Suzanne was three years younger than Marcy. Cynda had decided that her mother realized her antiquated choice of a name for her was a mistake.

It had been a long process, this business of having a permanent wave, and Cynda had made her mind up to be brave, for most important was her desire to please her elders, something that was taught and expected in her family. But for Cynda, the desire ran deeper. She wanted to be perfect and set her course for achieving this early on in her short life, not knowing that she was heading for many disappointments and on occasion - disaster.

At this moment Cynda was heading for her first experience of sitting under a hair dryer, which upon later examination for her was a calamity. The very notion of it sent a thrill of excitement through her very being. She was finally on her way to what she thought was one of the first steps to the threshold of womanhood. Maybe this whole experience would be worthwhile after all, she thought.

Cynda had made up her mind just exactly how she would sit and which magazine she would read with her legs crossed just so while under the dryer. She fervently hoped that Miss Edna had a copy of the current *Teen* magazine that she had seen at the drugstore, but had been too shy to pick up and peruse. The clerk, Miss Roberts, customarily made the rounds in the small store to keep merchandise in order, and heaven forbid if she caught Cynda with something she thought might be inappropriate for a child.

Cynda stood in anticipation as Miss Edna adjusted the pink hair dryer dome that looked like a rocket positioned to launch. Miss Edna had a small booster box in her hand made of the same pink vinyl of which the seat was constructed. Cynda cringed at the sight of it. All hopes of her looking like a "lady" were dashed at the vision of her feet dangling from the seat. She may as well be in a high chair.

Miss Edna ceremoniously signaled Cynda to have a seat. She did not ask her to choose a magazine, but instead she handed her *Highlights,* a children's magazine. Oh she liked the magazine well enough; the puzzles and exercises were designed to sharpen the mind of the children who read it. It was one of her favorites, but not on this day. Miss Edna pulled the dome down over Cynda's head and she found herself engulfed in a blast of warm air. She raised her voice to just below shouting to say to Cynda, "Okay Lucy, time to set your curl."

Cynda had enough of this Lucy business. She was appalled at how she must look hanging from the dryer like a pink Popsicle on a stick, especially since she was just about as thin as a stick. Her skinniness had been the source of snide remarks since day one of first grade. Forget the teasing she had endured of her name.

Miss Edna ambled over to the timer and gave it a turn. The next thirty minutes seemed like hours. Cynda was not expecting the warm air to whistle through her ears and give her an instant headache. She found herself not being able to even look at the magazine, much less work any of the puzzles she had discovered inside. Instead, she placed both hands over her ears, pressing the lobes protectively to keep the warm air out.

When Miss Edna discovered Cynda's predicament, she apologized and brought over a handful of cotton balls to put in and around her ears. "Here hon, you should have told me your ears were hurting," Miss Edna exclaimed in her sweetest voice. Cynda took the cotton and packed it in her ears, but the sneaky warm air found a way into them and an aching head. Finally, it was over. The jangling of the silver timer was as welcome as the last bell of the school day.

Miss Edna lifted the dome and checked for dryness by taking one of the curlers out. "There, you are done," she declared as if she were speaking to a chicken she had just removed from the fryer - a true southern expression. In Cynda's case, it was the final phase of her torment. "Let's get those curlers out and see what a beauty you will be!" she proclaimed.

Cynda once again found herself in the same chair where she began the process. She recalled the cutting and then rolling process and how she had held the thin wrappers that were placed between the curler and her hair. She had felt rather important in being given the wrappers to hold for Miss Edna and was ready to hand them to her as needed. She had complimented her over and over on how quick Cynda was to have the papers ready. It had been her finest hour in this process of disappointment. Now she was back in the chair again. She would soon discover just how deeply disappointed she would be.

After removing all of the curlers from Cynda's hair Miss Edna took her fingers and pulled them through the curls that were formed like cased sausages all over her head. She suddenly turned Cynda away from the mirror and declared, "Let's make your new look a grand surprise." She then turned to Clarise who was finishing her customer with a final twist to the *blue* curl that wound its way possessively around her customer's ear.

Cynda had contemplated *blue hair* before as now she found herself studying it once again. Bluing of the hair was a common practice for the elderly women of the community she had learned after grilling her mother. Bluing she learned helped to reduce the appearance of yellow in gray and white hair. Go figure, Cynda decided.

"Clarise, don't you agree?" Miss Edna repeated her question.

Clarise was in the throes of a haze of hairspray that promised to hold the customer's set in helmet head fashion for at least a week. She seemed to be oblivious to the pointed question, but realized that her partner was speaking.

"Sorry, Edna, what did you say?" Clarise replied.

"I said, don't you think that I should make Lucy wait to see her hair, until I am completely done for a grand surprise?" she repeated once again with more enunciation.

Clarise looked at Edna, who like Cynda chose not to correct her partner in using the wrong name, but said in a conspiratorial manner, "Cynda, what do you think?" making sure her tone was gentle and emphasizing Cynda's name.

Suddenly, the implication of her camaraderie placed Cynda in the sacred ranks of womanhood and a complacent kinship. Although the reference to Cynda's actual name seemed to go right over Miss Edna's head, she looked at her pensively, as she grasped for an answer tempered with compassion, afraid that she might offend her if she gave any other response and replied, "Let's go for the grand!"

It was not until some twenty minutes or so later that Cynda's hopes for a new look crumbled into a million pieces. Miss Edna slowly turned the chair around and waited in anticipation for accolades as she said, "Ta-da!" Cynda's mouth opened, then closed quickly shut as she searched her mind for an appropriate response, one that would be acceptable and complimentary; one that would be just a *little pink lie* or at least that was what her mother had called them, "a white lie with a little pink cotton candy coating," she had said when teaching her girls how to spare feelings.

Cynda remembered well her mother's conversation as she had explained a *little pink lie* to her and her sisters. She began with the statement of "Let's identify first what a *white lie* is," and continued with "The primary reason in telling a *white lie* is to purposely spare someone's feelings. On most accounts, that can be anyone – your family, your neighbor or maybe just the mailman if you feel inclined to do so. Ordinarily, you would not, under any circumstances, tell a lie, unless it falls, of course, into that category. Then, you must give consideration to the outcome; for example, you avoid the truth to keep from causing embarrassment to the other party. A little sugar coating can and will be used in most cases, which then makes the deviation from the truth a *little pink lie*, especially if told in the South by a Southern Lady," she was careful to describe.

At that moment, it came to Cynda, her mother's words as clear as the ringing of a bell, "Probably the one lie that warrants the utmost discretion is the one used when discussing a woman's hair, especially when she had just had it *done* or *fixed* and you are convinced it is less than flattering." Except in this case, Cynda would be sparing the feelings of the purveyor of beauty.

Cynda's lips moved, but she did not feel connected to the words that spilled from her lips, "Oh, I just love it! It is just beautiful." She had said it. She had accomplished the terrible deed, her first real *pink lie*, and to an adult! Yes, she had passed over that threshold today, but not in the way she had expected. She just hoped that her friends at Luxomni Middle School had a lesson in the art of telling *little pink lies*.

It took all of the resolve to be kind that Cynda could muster to get through the arrival of her mother and her declarations of how wonderful Cynda's hair looked. She had left her in the tender care of Miss Edna and Miss Clarice and they both preened at the compliments, as she forced smiles on all of them. By the time she left the little red brick building, Cynda thought her face must have looked as plastered as the smiling face on the red and yellow bread wrapper at home in the cupboard - except the fact that the smiling face on the wrapper portrayed a girl with beautiful curls, unlike her hair that looked like a fuzzy balloon.

Cynda followed her mother to the pink and white nineteen fifty-four Pontiac. Ordinarily she would feel like royalty as she took her place in the front seat with her mother, a place she had sanctioned as her territory in her father's absence. She had never missed a chance to send a gloating glance in her sisters' direction. However, this time she took her seat without even looking back. Instead she sat as still as the angelic figure that graced the cemetery on the corner. They pulled away from the curbing and the little red brick building, and its fluorescent sign that glowed in mocking approval. The Pontiac high-tailed its pink and white chassis down Main Street under the guidance of Lydia Brooks and her mastery of the steering wheel.

Cynda held her breath and waited for the comments that would surely come from the two sisters that she adored and of late, tolerated. Marcy spoke first. She said, "Cynda, your hair looks nice," unable to hide the giggle that practically jumped through her words as she raked her own mop protectively.

Cynda's face was as stoic as the Pontiac Chieftain ornament that adorned the hood of the car. She remained rigid in her stature, facing forward with a blank expression, deep in thought, wondering how she was going to face her friends at school. Their mother remained silent, sensing her displeasure. If she thought Cynda's hair looked anything less than beautiful, she never indicated it. Not a shred of disappointment showed in her face. She was like that, loving but in a distant way, never revealing her deep emotions. Ignoring her sister, Cynda finally looked over at her mother and said, "How do you really like my hair?"

Her mother replied, "Cynda, it looks so stylish and fashionable"

Stylish and fashionable? There was her answer. She was waiting to hear, pretty or beautiful, not 'stylish and fashionable'. It was a habit her mother had of being painfully honest with the ones she loved. Her mother seemed to forget the lesson she had taught her girls about *little pink lies*. Boy, could she have used a little sugar coated *pink lie* right now! She suddenly envisioned the pink cotton candy from the county fair and realized if her hair were pink, she would have something in common with it. She quickly redirected her mind to what she was going to do when she got home to remedy the helmet of hair.

Cynda felt a little tickle on the back of her head and turned to look into the big violet blue eyes of her little sister Suzanne, who looked up at Cynda with her sweetest smile and said, "I like your hair Cynda".

Cynda could not resist Suzanne's honesty and sweetness and replied, "Thanks, I will be sure that mother does the same for you when you are twelve," unable to resist a jab at her mother.

Lydia Brooks was never one to admit a mistake, unless she was unduly forced. She certainly would not allow that to happen, especially where her daughters were concerned. Had it not been in Cynda's best interest to have one of the stylish permanent waves that were the rage, she asked herself? All the young girls her age were getting one, unless of course they were lucky enough to have naturally curly hair.

Lydia could feel the seed of doubt plaguing her mind by this time and wished she could assure Cynda how pretty her hair looked without revealing her true feelings. She felt responsible for insisting on the *perm* without really giving her daughter a voice in the matter. Wasn't that what mothers were supposed to do, she reasoned? Cynda's thin and fine locks had always been a battle for her and now that she had begun to style her own hair, Lydia was just trying to help.

Finally, Lydia resigned herself to say, "Cynda, I think your headbands will add to your new style, and surely make it easier to fix your hair in the morning before school."

Cynda gave her mother's comment some consideration and did begin to think about the headbands that she had in every color to match her outfits. Yes, that was the answer to the fuzzy balloon that was attached to her head. She would just wear one every day, but not around her hair, maybe over her eyes!

The reflections of her first permanent wave left her in a melancholy state and Cynda found herself smiling, which was rare these days, especially when she was alone. What would she give now to have some of her own hair back? She would even settle for the fuzzy balloon effect. She turned her attention again to her sisters' visit. They were in town for a few summer weeks and she already felt smothered by the thoughts of their vigil. She had her good days and on those days, she longed for her freedom. She wanted to be able to drive wherever the roads would take her, away from anyone and everyone. She valued her quiet time and was secretly glad that they were not staying in her home.

There was another secret she was not willing to share. It was her reluctance to visit *Tybee* Island. How could she tell them? *Tybee*, sweet *Tybee*. Her thoughts caressed the name of her sanctuary of sand, salt and wind. Although she had avoided its sweet embrace over recent years, it would always hold her heart. Once upon a time, it had renewed her spirit and saved her life. Why, oh why, had she suggested her sisters rent a cottage on *Tybee* Island for their visit? The question hung in her universe.

Suzanne and Marcy rented the cottage on *Tybee* Island at her suggestion and were well pleased with its charm. They made it clear before their arrival that they planned to visit Cynda almost daily. They had also made it clear that they did not want to intrude on her privacy. The short drive over to Wilmington Island to see her would be a minor inconvenience, they had lamented, since they would have access to the beach for the summer as a bonus. Wilmington Island, where Cynda and Dane resided, was an extension of Metropolitan Savannah; however, there was no beach access. They lived in an exclusive neighborhood with access to the waterway which fed into the Wilmington River and surrounding waterways. She and Dane were also members of the prestigious *Savannah Yacht Club*. It was all very nice, but her heart was by the shore.

The hours spent with her sisters today, in the absence of Dane, had been precious and somewhat surreal. In the past, it was as if they all were going through the motions of companionship, avoiding substance in their relationship with one another. It had always been that way she thought. Cynda knew that in their presence, Dane would quietly excuse himself as he had done today and make excuses for the many 'errands' he seemed to have to run. It was an unspoken relief among the three who teetered on the realities to be discovered. She wondered what the dynamics would be like for the summer weeks ahead. There were only so many so called errands that Dane could run.

Cynda was glad that he was still gone, so she would have some time to think more about her sisters' visit. She wished desperately she could have been closer to them. She loved them dearly, but there had always been a void in her relationship with the two. Her life had taken a different turn early on when she got married right out of high school. She had lived away for such a long time now, causing an even greater void, just from the nature of distance.

Who was she kidding she thought? She had never made the effort to solidify relationships because it took too much from her. She had never let her guard down with her private feelings, not even with her own family. Besides, it was a well-known fact amongst them that Cynda was a private person. She had always been and she was not going to change now – especially not now. She did not want to feel vulnerable, even to her own family. What she did want was to feel anything but despair.

Chapter 4

It was a bright and sunny day and the words "it's gonna be a bright, bright, sunshiny day" were playing softly in Cynda's head. She could not resist thumping her fingers to the tune against the arm of her chaise. She had been outside most of the morning and was feeling much stronger. She did not know if the idea of her sisters' impending visit was responsible for her renewed energy. What she did know was that it was going to be a good day. She could feel it in her bones. Suzanne and Marcy would be arriving soon and after yesterday, she woke up feeling drawn to their companionship as never before.

She heard the sliding of the screen door behind her and looked up to see Dane who was dressed for boating and wearing a smile. She had recently noticed that her once doting husband was obviously running short on his charitable patience where she was concerned. Since her sisters were in town, he would be relieved of the constant care that he had been giving her. It was something they had discussed. It was just a fact. She was glad for him. He needed a break and come to think of it, she needed one too.

Dane leaned down to plant a conciliatory kiss on her forehead as he reached the chaise.

"Have fun with the girls," Dane said.

Suzanne and Marcy had always carried the title of "girls" and they still giggled like a pair of adolescents who were on the brink of puberty. Marcy had just turned the big 50. Suzanne was knocking on fifty's door. Cynda accepted his kiss as a truce between them, even though there had been no ill words spoken. She was in such a lighthearted mood today that she reciprocated with a clasp of his hand.

"Don't stay out there too long, Dane. You know how much the sun drains you. By the way, did you pack plenty of water?"

"Yes, mother dearest," Dane chided.

Terms of endearment, Cynda thought. Those phrases had always been routine and she missed their banter. The thought turned her mood sour for a moment. She did not feel like matching his wit with sarcasm. She chose instead to drop his hand with resignation.

Cynda said in a quiet tone, "Be safe."

Without a reply, Dane turned on his heel and headed for the dock that was just behind their home on the waterway. It was his favorite thing to do, boating; hers, too. She watched as he cranked the motor and moved slowly and seamlessly through the water. He was adept at commandeering the vessel and had taught her as much. The craft disappeared from her sight in a haze of brightness.

Cynda returned her attention to her last statement. Be safe. How much did she crave that one thing? Safety. It was elusive to her. How long had it been since she had felt really safe? Weeks, months, maybe a lifetime?

She had to admit it to herself. It had been building for months, this tension between her and Dane. His once patient nature had turned to irritation, and sometimes he was downright nasty. The time and attention Cynda had always given him had diminished because of her illness, and of course, it was beyond her control.

In the beginning he had been kind and supportive, but as time had marched on the ramifications of her illness had become apparent. Their world would be forever changed. Nothing could ever be the same and what lay between them had become a great divide. Cynda had been defiant at first in her quest to remain as normal in her routines as possible. However, her treatments had robbed her strength, forcing her to finally give in to her illness. She began to tire more easily and her attention to the man she loved began to wane. Shamefully, Dane was less than receptive to her lack of devotion. He appeared to be lost and afraid. Consequently, as the days passed, he had become more and more distant to her.

The turning point had been when on one of Cynda's good days, she decided to cook one of her specialty meals. She had showered and gotten dressed early in the day; taking care of her appearance as usual. Dane was out working on his boat, and she elected to take his Lincoln down to the seafood market to get some fresh crab to make crab cakes. She was only gone for about thirty minutes, leaving a note for him in the kitchen.

When Cynda returned, Dane was sitting quietly at the kitchen table poised to admonish her for leaving without first consulting him.

"So when did we start leaving the house without first checking with me?"

Cynda looked at him with her flashing green eyes, and responded as she ceremoniously put her package on the kitchen counter, "Since when do I need your permission?"

Dane just gave her an exasperated look as he shook his head and said, "From now on, you need to tell me when you are going somewhere; you know I worry."

"Do you really?" Cynda asked Dane in a pleading voice.

"You know I do; nothing has changed in the way I feel about you. You are still my 'green eyed girl'."

Something inside Cynda felt hollow as she looked into Dane's eyes searching for answers. Somehow his words did not fit his actions. She had conceded that he was just afraid, so with her own broken wing she tended the wounded.

Always good at rallying, she defied defeat and gave him a half smile as she said, "Crab cakes at high noon and you better not be late."

Dane retreated to the backyard to work on his boat and as Cynda watched him leave, her smile faded. She began the laborious process of preparing the meal, which in the past had been a cinch for her. She looked around the small, but sufficient kitchen and wondered how many more times that she would be able to complete the task of preparing what used to be a simple meal for the two them.

Her beloved kitchen of sunny yellow, chosen because the color had always made her feel happy and warm, but did not seem to generate any warmth on this day. It was almost as if it reminded her of what she would or could not have very soon. She reached for the yellow mixing bowl with the Dutch ladies embossed around the top of it. The bowl had always been her favorite, her longtime friend. She looked at the crock of utensils that had helped to fashion mere ingredients into creations of divine cuisine by her own hands. Many of the utensils had wooden handles that had been painted a bright red. The red had begun to fade on some of them and the paint was chipped in places, a reminder of the imperfections in her life. She suddenly realized their imperfections were endearing and wondered if Audrey would appreciate them someday when she was gone, or if she would toss them out in favor of something new. She could not imagine Dane wanting anything to do with her kitchen. She knew the answer, before the thought even entered her brain. "Oh Audrey, what did I do to fail you?" she had asked herself. "Daughters are supposed to be your friend forever," she muttered to herself.

Before long, she finished her crab cakes and as always, she kept her word; lunch was served promptly at twelve noon. She called for Dane to join her. He sat down at the table Cynda had set for the two of them. She had cut some fresh flowers from the beds planted outside the front door and had arranged them in a simple white vase. She had decided to conserve her energy and had refrained from using cuttings from her flower garden close to the dock.

Cynda never failed to use linens and fresh flowers. It was her trademark. If none were available, she had an amazing talent for using fresh greenery, cut and arranged as if an artist had been at work. In fact, she was an artist in her own right and Dane had always taken great pride in her for that.

When Dane arrived, the two of them served their plates. Somewhere between the senseless conversation and the quiet sounds of nothing, Cynda saw for the first time, just how much Dane was removed from her. He was certainly sitting before her, but absent. It was in that moment that she realized that he was gone. Her perfect husband and her perfect life was gone - for in her mind, there was nothing more personal than eating a meal with a captive audience. Not just any audience, but her love for over twenty years.

Their mealtime had always been special, not because of the time and devotion she put into its preparation, but in her mind the actual consumption of a meal was sacred. Their meals had always been an intimate affair sitting across from one another where eyes met in conspiratorial conversations and on occasion, a battleground. There was no chance to take the high road if something unpleasant surfaced.

On this day, he seemed as if eating with her was a chore and he did not finish the meal that she knew he loved best. It was as if her illness had seeped into his body and stolen the spirit that she had loved. She awaited its return patiently. How had they come to this impassable road? She did not want his wounded spirit to remind her of the situation. After all, she had believed him when he had pledged his faithful love to her, for better, for worse. Could it get any worse she had asked herself?

She admitted the truth that day. She had seen it clearly. It was written all over his face. He was a coward and she would have to face the end alone, at least emotionally. Coward. That term seemed familiar. Had she not been a coward herself when it came to facing the friction with Audrey? And long ago, after her own daddy had died so suddenly, cowardice had been her companion for a while. Then, accepting nothing less than her own perfection to conquer the world, she had won on some levels, but had lost sight of her daddy's wisdom.

It was her day of reckoning and that is when she decided to move into her own room, using the excuse that she wanted to prevent disturbances in Dane's sleep. She cited her restlessness and tossing and turning like the choppy seas plus the never ending trips to the bathroom as evidence. And so it seemed that she had become just a shadow of existence for him.

Dane in turn readily accepted her suggestion. It was as if she had given him a deserved pass for his actions. After the move, he began to make his morning rounds to bring her breakfast and then found something to do around the house as had always been his practice. Yet, there was a more profound withdrawal from her and his spiritual absence continued to cut her like a sword. She had tried to ignore it and sometimes wished that she had never left their bedroom, blaming herself somehow for his actions. And now that her sisters were here, she knew that even without their acknowledgement, they felt it too in their short visit.

She wiped the plaguing thoughts from her radar and instead sent her antennae up in search of some good vibrations. Suddenly, she could not wait for her sisters to arrive.

It would be a few hours before her sisters appeared. In the meantime, Cynda could not help herself from reflecting on her relationships. This time it was about her volatile relationship with her daughter Audrey.

Audrey had always had a mind of her own, strong willed, much like her father. At thirty-five years old, she was still single and independent, however, not financially. She lived on the graciousness of her paternal grandparents, taking jobs that provided no advancement. She was currently living in Atlanta with a live-in boyfriend. Cynda did not approve of the arrangement; however, she really did like Lane. He reminded her very much of her easy going father; that itself was a big plus. He seemed to be climbing the corporate ladder and had a bright future.

In earlier years, Audrey had begun her rebellion of sorts immediately after Cynda had divorced her father, Brock. Unlike herself, Audrey was not a pleaser. She danced to the tune of a different drummer and Cynda's tune never seemed to play in her ears. Without a doubt Audrey had a love and respect for her mother stopping just short of the daughterly devotion that Cynda craved.

Just as thoughts of Audrey began to pull her down into the abyss that she resisted like an epidemic, she heard the screen door sliding open and quickly terminated her visit to unpleasantness, thankful for the sound of its presence.

Chapter 5

The girls had arrived. The air smacked with drama, not unusual when the two got together and now there were three in the mix. Without a greeting Marcy dragged an iron chaise beside Cynda and ceremoniously plopped down like a splatter of fresh paint. She reeked of vitality as she instantly peeled her shorts away from her hips and pulled her t-shirt over her head to reveal a sleek black bathing suit. It was flattering and the shirring served to hide her expanding midriff. She was lean and lanky otherwise. Her watery blue eyes and page boy locks of brunette, accentuated a heart shaped face. She was HOT.

Suzanne was in a modest two piece with boy-cut legs, its style reflecting the essence of who she was – quiet and unassuming. Her straight faded blonde hair was not so stylish but it suited her and framed a more vibrant pair of violet blue eyes. She too found a chaise and pulled it over to the others, stretching her long legs to their sinewy length as she delivered her greeting to Cynda with a chatty "hullo".

Marcy echoed with her own brand of greeting "Hey ya'll". Cynda was not sure if it was a greeting or the lead in to comic relief.

"I am as hot as a two-dollar pistol. I just don't know how you have been able to tolerate this heat all of these years Cynda, especially while in the throes of menopause. It is just too much for me. Thank God you have the pool. I don't know how you could survive without it!"

"Yes Ma'am, it has been a lifesaver. I have never hesitated to use the pool night or day, suited or unsuited if you know what I mean."

Suzanne looked surprised at this revelation, not because it was so shocking, but the words had been spoken by the guarded one.

"I didn't know you had it in you, Cynda," Marcy said as she eyed her for more details of the mischief that had just been revealed, but not expecting much.

"There's a lot you don't know about me," Cynda responded quietly and pensively, not giving the sisters a hint of what she was implying.

Marcy responded, "I am as transparent as a negligee, big sister. I have no qualms about sharing the juicy details of the joys of menopause, sordid as they might be to hear," without a breath she painted a vivid picture of how her morning routine prior to arriving there played out.

"Let me just give you girls a rundown of how my day started. I'll just say that I was on brink of hysteria before I could finish what started out to be a simple pedicure that I could not seem to work in my schedule before leaving Atlanta. Big mistake. Before my bath, I decided that these babies could not go another day in the public eye," she said as she eyed the ruby red toes that looked as if a five-year-old had been practicing on them.

"I had just gotten out of the shower and was still scorching hot, even after drying off. I had no intention of wrapping myself up like a pig in a blanket, so there I stood in my birthday suit mind you, contemplating my little piggies. I gave my towel a toss and propped one foot on the side of the garden tub and performed a balancing act with my other foot planted. I then proceeded to trim my toenails. I forgot my 'readers' but they were within my reach. Without them, I was headed for amputation. I grabbed the glasses and planted them on the end of my nose and began to butcher my nails. I was pretty successful in the jagged edge technique; however, I don't think I could get a job at Nails N' Such down the street," she giggled.

"Just as I began applying the polish, my lack of estrogen sent me into one of my usual private summers. I was beginning to feel the heat rising even in my state of nakedness. My forehead, nose and back of my neck broke out in a geographical pattern of perspiration and soon my glasses fogged up. After repeated attempts to wipe them free of the reoccurring fog and finish smearing a single coat of polish on the last little piggy that went to market, I surrendered," Marcy sighed as she cocked one eye at the cartoon toes.

It was like a dam had broken. The laughter coming from Cydna began with a smile that crescendo into a 'cackle like a hen' as their Mama would have said. Marcy and Suzanne both stared at her as she continued hysterically. There was nothing to do but join in, not quite sure if Marcy's little piggies were the source of their hilarity or the vision of her nakedness. What was even more bizarre, they were taken aback at this odd behavior from the sister that seemed absent of humor, at least over the last twenty years.

"Can't you just see Mama in that same predicament with her toes hanging over her claw foot tub, professing to an audience of none that the shower was just too hot," Cynda said.

She continued, "The one who never even acknowledged what menopause was or that it even existed? I suppose she could have used a disclaimer of ignorance to justify her lack of acknowledgement of it. What was wrong with that generation? Did they expect the wrath from the Testosterone King to descend upon them and give them a full grown beard if they admitted to its existence?"

Marcy mocked her deceased elders in a sarcastic reply by adding, "I know Aunt Sally had a penchant for those hair removal commercials, as if anything could have really stopped the growth on her chinny-chin-chin."

"You are right about that! I don't think I ever heard Mama or Aunt Sally mention the word menopause in my life. It was as if that by sheer acknowledgement, they were accepting the demise of their womanhood or maybe just their sanity," Suzanne chimed in.

"Well, I certainly second that emotion. I continually have brain freezes while the outside of me is licked by the flames of hell," Marcy said as she proceeded to wipe the sheen of perspiration from her upper lip.

Cynda added her own tale. "I remember Mama being so appalled when Aunt Sally came sailing in one day wearing her peculiar behavior like a cape, declaring 'I fell off the roof today'. Mama looked at her in horror and I guess I did also. She looked fine to me and she certainly was walking around as if she had not suffered any physical damage. Mama was shaking her head at Aunt Sally and raising her brows. At that point, we had not had 'the talk'. It wasn't until later that I found out that Aunt Sally was talking about her monthly cycle."

The very idea of their peculiar Aunt Sally was overshadowed by another unflattering quality. She had been one of the most sanctimonious women that Marcy had ever met. She started to remind her sisters of that, but refrained.

Cynda added in a more serious manner, "Mrs. Lydia Brooks was certainly a product of generational influence. She was the epitome of proper etiquette; that she was, God rest her soul. And you know, Aunt Sally could really push her buttons." The sisters all agreed in a conspiratorial manner in their shared and thoughtful silence.

The camaraderie of sisterhood continued throughout lunch and the rest of the afternoon. The day ended much too soon when Dane began his approach to the dock in the boat. The motor was reduced to a slow humming noise, but it broke the reverie of companionship.

The sisters gave their regards to Dane and left the two, promising Cynda an outing the next day if she felt well enough for a little trip. They made plans to be there around ten in the morning in hopes that her continued energy would sustain her for their arrival.

Chapter 6

"Well that was a revelation," Marcy exclaimed as the two cruised down the quiet residential street leading them away from their sister.

"What," Suzanne asked, "We've talked about this before, and Mama being tight lipped about menopause. She wasn't much more informative about the birds and the bees. Remember we both had to watch *A Summer Place* with Troy Donahue and Sandra Dee about a girl getting pregnant out of wedlock. By the time Mama and I watched it, the movie was nearly twenty years old."

"No, silly," Marcy said, "I was talking about how relaxed Cynda was and how she went on and on about Mama and Aunt Sally and their generational nonsense. Can you believe that Aunt Sally swore she had never had a hot flash? I had never heard that one before. She told on herself though by her actions. I remember that she was constantly wiping her brow with that lace handkerchief with her initial in the corner. I can just see her now, daintily dabbing her forehead as if it were some required feminine act. How about mopping your entire brow with a roll of paper towel? That would be more like it."

"I thought it was a demonstration of worry over the three of us," Suzanne said. "We were a handful you know. Aunt Sally always thought she had some sort of obligation to help raise us after Daddy died; at least that is what Mama always said. She tolerated her out of respect for Daddy, I think. Mama never said a harsh word against anyone, but I could sense her frustration with Aunt Sally especially when she tried to make us walk with a book on our heads to train us to carry ourselves like a proper lady. I finally had to open the book and wear it like a hat for it to stay on my pointed head. 'You just have to overlook people sometimes, especially when they do mean well' Mama would say," Suzanne continued with her perspective.

Marcy decided to change the subject back to their sister.

"Did you see the change in Cynda when Dane got home? She made a complete about face. I was thinking all afternoon about her situation. She will probably never go to a healing service with us or allow us to perform one on her. If she would just use the healing oil on her own, I would feel better. Maybe you could hint around to her to do it, Suzanne. She has a soft spot for you and she will not think you are trying to boss her around."

"Well, sure, I could do that, but I have been doing some thinking on my own," Suzanne said.

"If we could have Cynda to ourselves with no time constraints, maybe, just maybe, it would help her to heal; instead of withering away in that house day after day. I think a change of scenery would help tremendously. I think she would be more receptive to living life again."

"I totally agree, but our hands are tied. I think we made the right decision by renting the cottage. We certainly did not want to impose by moving in for the summer weeks as Cynda had originally grudgingly suggested. I would have felt so uncomfortable in Dane's presence under those circumstances. He has become so distant around us, and I am sure Cynda senses it too," Marcy responded emphatically.

"That's just it. We can't make any headway with Dane around all of the time or wondering when he will show up from his never ending errands. I have a proposal. Why don't we invite Cynda to spend the weekends with us over on *Tybee* Island? We can present it as a plan to give Dane a break. That way Cynda will not think we are trying to run her life and I guarantee you that Dane will agree – maybe reluctantly, but silently thankful."

"You are genius, little sis!"

"I have told you to stop calling me that, even though I am beginning to like the title more and more. I am not so little anymore," Suzanne implied as she grabbed her mid-riff and pulled out a handful of flesh.

Marcy looked at the slender woman who had never had a problem with her weight. She kept herself physically fit and was equally as pretty with her violet blue eyes that were her asset. She knew that Suzanne was on the brink of menopause herself and she decided to vow an alliance to her deceased Mama. Marcy would not tell her that besides the hot flashes, the weight seemed to creep upon a body like a ghost in the night. No, she would let her little sis find that out on her own. No sense bringing up that little tidbit of information.

Just then, Suzanne steered the Beetle through the narrow street that led them to the little white cottage trimmed in yellow. It puffed its last breath for the day as it slid into its designated spot. They found their dwelling to be a welcome reprieve from the low country heat as both were silently mulling over the idea of Cynda as their guest.

Marcy began to consider the ramifications of inviting Cynda over for the weekends. Sure, there was plenty of room as there was an extra bedroom, she told herself. And of course, the three would have to share two bathrooms. She had no idea how much *stuff* Cynda would bring if she agreed. It was worth the risk of getting Cynda to use the oils in a healing ceremony wasn't it, she asked herself? What was more important would be the opportunity to get to know the sister that the two had always admired, yet who had remained a mystery for most of their lives. Yes, Suzanne was a genius; she had to admit, at least this time.

Chapter 7

Cynda and Dane had a light supper of chicken salad and fruit that he had purchased at the local supermarket. It was cool enough to dine on the patio and the atmosphere was much more relaxed when the two were able to have the diversion of the sounds of nature. The rhythm of the gurgling water snaking its way through the marshes and the orchestrated cicadas in unison were welcoming as the sun began to set. She appreciated the tempo more now than ever. There wasn't a need to worry about mosquitoes, as the pool and patio area was covered with screening.

After dinner, the two retired to the living area as their routine had dictated for a number of years. Cynda found it hard to concentrate as she perused her magazine. Nothing interested her anymore. Her thoughts kept going back to her visit with her sisters.

The earlier conversation with her sisters about their mother and Aunt Sally had conjured up memories that had made her realize that she held the keys to their past. Not just hers, but theirs also. She wondered if Marcy and Suzanne also felt as robbed as she with the untimely death of their father. Cynda had never discussed it with them. It had been too painful, even years later. Marcy had only been eight and Suzanne an innocent five years old. Maybe she should have made the effort, Cynda thought.

Cynda retired to her bedroom. Dane was already asleep and she left him there in his recliner as she often did. He preferred to wake on his own, protesting if she tried to assist him on his way to his bed. She decided to lie on the chaise when she entered her room and soon the memories of her father opened like a floodgate. As they rushed through the tethers and slid themselves into her guarded consciousness, their presence screamed to be recognized. She could feel the tightness in her chest as she remembered the days that led her into forced adulthood sooner than she was ready.

It was not long after her permanent wave debacle that the days ahead for Cynda became difficult. She did not dismiss the sideways glances and quiet whispers she received from some of the students at school. Even her best friends did a poor job of feigning approval of her new hair style. The headbands helped, but they were only a slight distraction from the helmet that graced her head. The boys were the worst, making no excuses for their snide remarks.

Cynda felt betrayed by her own mother. It did not matter that she had good intentions. Cynda had to agree with her that her hair had a mind of its own. Now, it was worse. The hairs on her very head had defied the permanent wave, shamelessly into helmet formation.

Cynda remembered vividly, one night in particular, after the repeated remarks and teasing at school had tested her endurance. Although Cynda had just drifted to sleep after battling a few hours of tossing and turning and dreading the next day, she had found some comfort in knowing that as long as she was awake, she would not have to start a new day. Somewhere between dreaming and reality, she heard her daddy's voice.

Down the hall in her parent's room, Cynda heard the pleading of her father's voice to her mother.

"Lydia, please get up and help me. You know that I would not ask if I were not hurting really bad," her father pleaded.

It took a few minutes for Cynda to realize just how late it really had gotten. She turned over to eavesdrop on the conversation. She knew that her mother had gone to bed at ten o'clock, even though her daddy was not home. That knowledge coupled with her own troubles had contributed to Cynda's inability to fall asleep.

"It is eleven o'clock and I told you not to go out to play basketball tonight," Lydia said, "And besides that, it is freezing cold outside!" she added.

The bantering back and forth was not uncommon with her parents, as the frequency of her daddy's recreation basketball games had become routine in the fall and winter months. She had heard her mother admonish him hours before with her usual frustration, "Lawrence not another night. It's a school night, for Christ's sake."

Her father had given Lydia another one of his sad sob stories earlier of how he would have been glad to have been an alternate, but Frank had sprained an ankle and he could not let the team down. Her mother once again had been cajoled into feeling guilty about him letting the team down and had conceded with her blessings. Of course, deep down, Cynda sensed that her mother really did not mind and was rather proud of her daddy; after all he was one of their star players.

"Lydia, you know it is the only thing that will bring the swelling down and relieve some of the pain," Cynda heard her father saying, only this time, he seemed to be begging. But, by this time, her mother's patience was wearing thin. Cynda waited on pins and needles for her mother's reply, wondering if one day she would just let him have it. She had never heard her mother as much as raise her voice to her father. Her mild mannered voice penetrated the lingering silence.

"Just why did you not get one of your buddies to take care of you?" her mother said rather sternly this time. She softened a bit when she added further, "You know there comes a time, Lawrence, when you have to grow up and take some responsibility for your actions. Playing basketball for the rest of your life is not really an option; one of these days you are going to get hurt really bad. Your girls are getting older and they need to see some maturity. Grow up Lawrence."

There was no answer from her daddy, just silence and then the sound of him walking down the hallway. Cynda heard the front door open and her father go outside. She lay there for a few minutes and wondered where he was going and what he could be doing outside in the cold if he were really hurt.

Cynda got up from the comfort of her warm bed and slowly crept down the hallway, so as not to disturb her mother. She found her warm winter coat hanging by the front door, glad that she had not taken it to her room as she usually did. She slipped on her shoes and crept outside to find her father. She looked around the garage and did not see him anywhere. Then she heard a low mumble from just across the lawn. Cynda moved closer to the mumbling and it turned into a rant from her father as he spoke to himself.

"This is just great. I can't see anything!"

She saw the upper part of his body rising up from the edge of the embankment just over their property line. Then he disappeared from sight. She crept over to the edge of the embankment, being careful that he did not see her. The earth was barren of any grass and the color was red - covered in the red dirt that was native to Georgia. The winter rain had created valleys and indentions in the dirt and it had softened, so he was having trouble getting and keeping his balance.

Her daddy laid the flashlight on the ground that he had in his hand. It cast an eerie light on the soil and it glared back at him with red eyes. He began to thrust the small spade into the earthy matter, deftly removing its outer shell. He dug for a couple of minutes longer, and then put the spade down to use his hands as his tool. They seemed to cradle something of value that he brought from beneath the earth. Cynda in her innocence wondered if he were digging for gold.

Her daddy seemed to squeeze the object and then put it in his pocket. He reached for the flashlight that

45

illuminated the mysterious earth; as he did Cynda approached her daddy so quietly that she startled him. He quickly pointed the flashlight in her direction. She covered her eyes as the light blinded her eyes.

"Well, hello Lucy, what are you doing out here?" her daddy said. "I thought your mother had a change of heart and had come to rescue me from my own self," he said as if wounded. "You should be sleeping. By the way, if your mother finds out you were out here, she will add contributing to the delinquency of a minor to her list of my shortcomings," he said softly.

Her father's voice was music to her ears and even more so when he called her *Lucy*, the one and only person whom she would allow to call her by that name. He seemed to embrace it as it rolled off of his tongue, *Lucy,* an endearment that Cynda cherished. When she was *his Lucy*, she felt confident and secure.

Cynda approached her father pensively, wondering still what he could be doing out here in the cold and dark night, pondering what he might have put in his pocket. She was a bit apprehensive and began to wonder if he was going to scold her for following him outside. He motioned for her to join him.

She was careful as she placed her steps strategically, trying to hug the embankment. The vision of the illuminated red earth was fresh in her mind and its aura had mystified her. She joined her daddy rather quickly and he reached out to steady her as she did so. She could not stand the suspense any longer.

"Daddy, what are you doing out here?" she asked pleadingly.

He looked at her thoughtfully and for a moment forgot that his nose was on fire with pain. He was beginning to feel somewhat dizzy by this time. His hands felt frozen and numb, but his heart sensed that her presence at this late hour meant something was wrong with his Lucy.

It was not a surprise to him as he had seen her struggle with her individuality. Cynda was relentless in her strive for perfection both at school and at home. She had confided in him that she had been teased time and time again, not only for her thinness, but her precious little nose. The nose that had a slight bump on it, the one he loved as he looked past it into her piercing green eyes. It was a bond they had always shared – his intuitive nature of her and her complete adoration of him.

"Well, Lucy, I might ask that same question of you," her daddy said as he placed his arm around her shoulders and brought her close to his chest.

Cynda looked up at him and said, "I was having trouble sleeping and woke up when I heard you and mother arguing."

He gently pulled her away from his chest and said, "Not a real argument Lucy, just a little disagreement. You know how much your mother hates it when I am late getting back from a basketball game. She really doesn't mind, not deep down in her heart. Sometimes I just think she plays the part because she feels it is her duty as a mother to act like she does not approve. It's her way of showing that she does have a stake in the time the ball games take away from you girls. Actually, I think she is really proud of me," he said, confirming to Cynda what she had already guessed.

Cynda looked up at her father and said to him, "So why are you out here? You still did not answer my question."

He said to her, "Looking for a little healing."

Cynda replied, "Daddy, if you need to ask God to heal you, you should not have to go outside in the cold. You have always told me that I could pray anywhere."

Her daddy looked at her with merriment in his eyes and said, "Yes Lucy, you are right, but this time I am not out here to pray. But, I am here to take a little bit of God's hidden treasure to help in healing my swollen nose."

At that moment, both of them realized just how cold they both were as Cynda began to shiver and he wrapped his arms tight around her. She could feel not only his warmth but his strength. She felt secure in knowing that her daddy was her champion and those nasty kids at school did not matter at this moment.

"Lucy, let's finish this conversation in the house, as we better get you to bed since you have to go to school tomorrow," he whispered in her ear.

The two of them climbed precariously back up the hill and walked arm and arm into the house, Cynda reeling from the cold and giddy at the same time. Her mind was fixated on the hidden treasure with healing power in her daddy's pocket. She wondered if it could heal the hurt she was feeling from today's fiasco at school. Not a chance, she decided; feelings were different, not exactly something you could even touch for she was wise for her twelve years.

Cynda sat at the aluminum kitchen table with a silvery blue Formica top. She was tracing patterns with her finger on the table, pretending not to acknowledge what her father was doing. She held her breath as she watched her father remove the object he had placed in his pocket. He closed his hand around it and walked over to her. He slowly opened his hand to reveal a grayish image that was soft and pliable, rather sticky.

"God's healing powers are in this clay, only from the red dirt of Georgia," he proudly proclaimed. He broke a piece of it and laid it on the table, rolling the remainder of the clay in his hand into a ball, and then patting it flat. Next he took the clay and placed it on the bridge of his nose, gently rubbing it as it molded quite nicely. Cynda looked at him and thought he looked rather comical standing there like a clown. However, she did not laugh as she heard the pride in his voice as he was giving her a life lesson, one that she was grateful to be in his presence to hear.

He took the remaining piece of the clay and rolled it into a ball and placed it against his chest and pressed it flat, saying, "It will even heal a broken heart, if you have the courage to believe in yourself, even when others do not." She sat there stunned at his statement, trying to digest the impact of what he was really saying. Surely, the clay could not make the hurt she was feeling go away, and did he somehow know just how miserable her day had been?

Cynda looked at him quizzically and wondered as she said, "Is your heart broken Daddy?"

He answered instinctively, hearing the pleading in her voice that told him that he was right about her being troubled, "If you are speaking about your mother's and my little argument, no. Nothing is ever perfect, not even when you love the perfect one for you. No, my little Lucy, my heart is not broken; hearts get broken every day, but they will heal. It just takes courage. Never forget that. Sometimes, it takes longer than other times. Remember, words can be powerful, but only as powerful as you allow them to be. It's your choice," he said, as he sensed something was amiss, but wanted her to confide in him at will. He reached for the last lump of clay. He gently rolled it into a ball and pressed it into her hand.

"Keep this to remember tonight and the secret of the healing power of the red clay of your Georgia home. It's just a little ball of courage. Keep it to know that God will heal a broken heart. All you have to do is have the courage to believe. And another thing. You will always be perfect in my eyes. You just have to believe in yourself," he reassured his little perfectionist, in hopes she would listen to his words.

Cynda took the clay and touched it to her heart, mimicking her daddy's earlier actions, somehow forgetting the earlier pain of her day at school. Witnessing the look of relief in his daughter's eyes, he then kissed the top of her head and signaled for her to go to bed, but not before hugging her one last time. Brushing back the wayward tendrils that now fought to cover her eyes, he quietly said, "I like your hair." He released her with a glimmer of understanding in his eyes and the unnecessary words hung in the air like a caress.

Cynda seemed to float back down the hallway to her room, being careful not to wake her sister as she slid into bed beside her. She lay there, holding the clay in her tightly held fist, cherishing not the clay, but the feeling of redemption from the hurt. Tomorrow would be her day. She felt renewed and empowered. She would not allow the boys at school to gain any satisfaction when they teased her, especially one boy in particular.

Cynda drifted into a restless sleep, but not before placing the treasured clay into an empty pill bottle that she had kept in a drawer beside her bed. She emptied the bottle of some coins that she had been saving. Somehow it seemed the perfect home for her new treasure with healing power. Tomorrow, she would silently be Lucy, confident in her resolve to conquer her insecurity. Tomorrow she would have courage.

Cynda had no idea how much those precious moments with her father would impact the remainder of her life. For the short few months ahead, she became braver than ever before when facing the challenges of growing up. Then the hands of fate snuffed out the life of Lawrence Brooks and her world changed forever. On that day her childhood as she knew it ended. She would never shake her need to strive for perfection; however, she would forever rely on her courage to face her many disappointments and her much needed validation from others.

Chapter 8

Suzanne was awake first the next day. She was thankful for her space upstairs as Marcy's soft snoring had been a bone of contention on previous trips. She swore that she did not snore. Suzanne had threatened to record her on more than one occasion.

Suzanne's idea of having Cynda stay with them at the cottage kept her from sleeping very well the night before. She lay in the queen sized bed and looked around at the wallpaper that had seen its better day. The sea foam and tan striped pattern was dated. She thought a fresh coat of paint would give the room a cheerful look and a much needed facelift. Oh, well. Not her worry. She could tolerate the room for the next few weeks and go back to her own brand of dated. Her husband Steve had always worked hard and they were able to make ends meet rather nicely, but remodeling their home had not been a priority.

The children were on their own now and she had successfully removed herself from intruding into their lives. Both Bradley and Richelle had graduated from the University of Georgia and had good jobs. She was now on the road to the next phase of her life. Neither one of her children was serious about anyone, so planning a wedding was not on the horizon. Suzanne secretly wondered if Cynda was a bit jealous that her children were University of Georgia graduates. Cynda's first husband Brock shared that "elite" status as Cynda did not.

Suzanne had not remained idle after her children's graduation. She worked in the Methodist Church preschool program in her area and was off for the summer break. Steve was supportive of her summer hiatus at the beach and her effort to renew her relationship with her ill sister. His only condition was that he visit a couple of times. He traveled randomly to South Georgia and would extend his travels down to Savannah. She would miss him dearly, but her resolve to spend time with her sister and help in any way made her dismiss the homesickness that was already welling in her heart just thinking of him.

Suzanne made her way to the kitchen focused on her coffee fix. Marcy soon made her grand entrance gliding toward her morning coffee ritual, preempted by what appeared to her sister to be a haze of extended slumber. She was guided by eyes that peered expectantly at the amber colored liquid gold that would slowly extinguish her lethargic state. Suzanne watched as her sister cradled her coffee cup and silently walked across the room toward where she was sitting. Marcy planted herself on the beige couch that had absolutely no personality.

Suzanne had always viewed her inanimate surroundings in terms of inspiration. At this moment she certainly was not inspired. She believed that sometimes surroundings had more influence on attitude than the people who filled a space. In this case, the boring personality of the couch seemed to explode at the moment compared to the occupant who rested in the depths of its beigeness.

Marcy's blurry eyes finally began to focus on Suzanne, who waited for her to speak. Suzanne's patience was running thin and she blurted out what had been on her mind last night and all of the morning.

"Let's get the ball rolling right away. It is already Thursday and I think if we can convince Cynda of our plan, we could make this thing happen by the weekend."

Suzanne kept on with her reasoning of why they should act on their proposal today while visiting with Cynda.

"Today would be perfect, since we have already told her we want to get her out for a change of scenery. Once we leave her house, we can bring her over here to the cottage, you know, show her around. Maybe we could act as if the idea came to us while she is visiting. I know you like the room downstairs, but would you consider moving upstairs with me, just so she might embrace the idea more readily? I had not thought about it until this morning, the stairs might be a deterrent."

Marcy whose words were few in the morning considered the idea of moving upstairs for a few moments and agreed.

"You are probably right. We really do not know much about her limitations. Let's try to alleviate any roadblocks before they materialize," she said.

After pausing for a few seconds Marcy added, "Sure, I can move upstairs. That means we have to share a bath. Are you okay with all of my morning rituals?" she added hesitantly.

Suzanne knew her sister was referring to her array of *face paint*. She looked at the *Queen of Cosmetics* and wondered how she had ever been able to convince her husband Phillip to allow her the summer to spend with her sisters. He was rather possessive of her, but she could not visualize him coming down to visit even for a few days.

Marcy had a failed marriage early on and it had taken years for her to make another commitment. When she met Phillip, the attraction was instant. They had dated for a short time and Suzanne secretly thought her sister was as much in love with his success as she was the man himself. He was the golden boy in his company and had made a small fortune. Suzanne did not really care because she knew he really loved Marcy, and if it worked for them, then that was all that mattered. He was also the one who had paid for the cottage for the two of them, an act far beyond his normal capability of generosity given his financial status. You might say he was as "tight as Dick's hatband". Suzanne was just thankful for the time that both of their husbands had afforded them to spend with Cynda. That was worth a fortune.

Marcy and Philip had decided against children, since they were both in their forties when they married. They had their dogs and that was enough, at least it appeared so. Both Marcy and Philip had showered her own children and Cynda's daughter Audrey with expensive gifts. As frugal as Phillip was, when it came to his nieces and nephews, his generosity knew no bounds.

Audrey had been spoiled from both sides of her family. Her paternal grandparents were of the Brookhaven elite in Atlanta and she lived partially from a trust they had established when she was just a baby. Suzanne had learned that tidbit of information from Audrey herself and it appeared she would someday receive more as her father, an only child, did not have any more children.

Cynda shared little personal information about Audrey with her sisters, but they knew the relationship was volatile at times. Audrey periodically showed up at both Marcy and Suzanne's homes for a little family time, especially since her grandmother, their mother, was gone. Audrey had adored her "Mimi" and likewise, as she was the firstborn grandchild. They all laughed and called her "the chosen one". The grandmother-granddaughter relationship did not bother Marcy or Suzanne as they both felt no jealousy. Actually, they were thankful for the time Audrey had spent with her "Mimi". They knew how much their Mama had missed Cynda over the last years of her life. The miles that had taken Cynda away from her mother had been a source of emptiness, no matter how often her daughter visited. Their mother had lamented her sadness to them often. Audrey had helped to fill that void.

Chapter 9

Just a few short miles away, Cynda got up early and began the routine she had established since moving into the guest room. Dane had been in her room earlier with juice and coffee. It was hard to predict her appetite, so he had learned to wait until later to bring her breakfast. It was a task that he had readily undertaken and it seemed to be a peace offering each morning for him, as their evenings had become so strained and conversation reduced to a minimum.

Cynda decided to wear a colorful scarf around her head and elected to apply a bare amount of makeup. She dressed in khaki caprice and a long sleeved white blouse. The blouse had a tail on it that covered her bottom or her gluteus maximus, a term she liked to use to describe her butt. The sleeves on the garment covered her thin arms and gave her some measure of confidence that she looked presentable for the outing.

The task of dressing complete, she felt hungry. Cynda found a light breakfast of toast and soft scrambled eggs in the microwave but no Dane. She ate sparingly and then felt a burst of energy and hope. Yes, that was it. Hope. Today that feeling would be her friend as she silently vowed to enjoy the hours ahead with her sisters. Still no Dane.

She found him outside as she suspected. She heard a swishing sound down near the dock. Through squinted eyes, she saw him laboriously working on the boat, cleaning and shining it. He worked at it with a fever high pitch, just as he had always done.

As Cynda watched, she noticed today that he seemed to clean and shine the same areas over and over again. It was as if there were demons that drove him during the task. Perhaps there were. Cynda knew she had her own demons.   She gave Dane a short wave and called out to remind him of her plans for the day.

"Dane, the girls will be here soon and I am not sure how long we will be gone," she called to him expectantly.

The old Dane would have left the dock and given her a kiss on the cheek before she left. Instead, he gave her a cursory wave of acknowledgement and turned his back to her, driven to complete his task. She in turn walked back into the house.

Yes, Cynda had demons too. They resided in every room in her house. This morning they were in the kitchen. She walked over to the sink. Dane had left the dishcloth draped over the faucet and there was a faint trace of crumbs on the countertops. She found herself wiping the counters down and with finality; she placed the dishcloth neatly folded across the double sink divider. There she thought. That's better. Just as she had finished, the doorbell rang and her sisters entered through the unlocked door, before she could welcome them in.

"Well, look what the cats drug in" she said, making a casual observation of their dress. Neither one of them was appropriately dressed for a luncheon at the club, as Cynda had assumed would be their destination, her treat. In fact, her sisters almost looked grungy. Neither had applied make-up and hidden behind their matching large lens of tortoise shell sunglasses were two pairs of eyes that were swollen from sleep deprivation. Both had confessed to one another their lack of sleep at the prospect of Cynda moving in with them on the weekends. They agreed the idea was too much to absorb before bedtime and had both found themselves tossing and turning. The girls had actually counted the weekends of their summer trip and realized that there were only four, before they had to return to Atlanta. How could that be?

At that moment, both of the sisters could feel the admonishment in the tone of Cynda's voice and they turned their attention immediately to explain themselves.

Marcy was the first to speak, which was not uncommon. She said, "Well, we were thinking it would be nice to take a day of leisure out on *Tybee*. You will still be getting out of the house and maybe we could catch a few rays of sun. You could sit under the umbrella," she stuttered, "I mean, uh – I am sure you would rather not sit directly in the sun".

Marcy had put her foot in her mouth and before Cynda could have a chance to reply, Suzanne spoke up to say, "Yeah, we thought you might enjoy sitting by the water and I made a seafood salad, your favorite," she said coaxingly.

Cynda immediately noticed Marcy's reference of *Tybee* Island as just simply *Tybee*. It easily rolled off the tip of her tongue as if she were a native. It was the name the locals called the island. She felt somewhat possessive of her exclusive right to call the island *Tybee*, as if her sisters were intruding on unchartered waters.

"Well?' Suzanne said, "Please, pretty please," she reiterated with hands clasped as she pulled them to her rest under her chin.

Cynda was still trying to wrap her mind around a visit to *Tybee*. How could she avoid visiting there with her sisters making it their home for the summer? She may as well get it over with, she told herself. She reminded herself that if she was surrounded by family as a distraction, *Tybee* was just another beach. It had been her refuge when she fled from what she considered her greatest failure, only to gain the strength she needed to persevere - lost then found.

Cynda never could resist her baby sister, and when she heard the pleading in her voice, her ire was softened. She did, however, admonish them slightly by saying, "The least you could have done was to give me some warning. If you will notice, I am basically covered from head to toe. I was looking for some air conditioning at the club for lunch."

Cynda abruptly turned on her heel and went to her bedroom. The girls were both left with their eyebrows raised and a shrug of confusion. Were they being dismissed? They sat down in the living room, both contemplating their rebuttal, if Cynda refused to accompany them to the cottage.

After a few minutes, Cynda entered the room wearing a white eyelet jumpsuit with a fringed wrap placed across her sleeveless upper arms. Her head scarf remained intact and she had a sleek pair of Christian Dior sunglasses resting on the crest of her forehead. The wicker beach bag she carried in her right hand sported a plush turquoise towel fashionably hanging from it. Even in her darkest hour, Cynda's sisters saw a chic and self-assured woman facing them.

"Well," she said, "What are we waiting for?"

The two of them scrambled to their feet and made light of the situation by making a regal gesture for Cynda to lead the way. And she did. Cynda halted when she stepped outside and saw the mode of transportation the girls were traveling, fully expecting to see Marcy's SUV. It was Suzanne's Beetle backed into the driveway. The convertible top was down. Her look of surprise did not go unnoticed.

"Cynda, we need to let you in on a little secret," Suzanne said as she moved past her toward the car.

"You are the honored guest of this well-oiled machine a.k.a. *Hug Bug*," she said as she gave a quick look to gage Cynda's reaction.

Hug Bug, she responded genuinely, "what is the significance of the name, little sis?"

Suzanne weighed the reference to Cynda calling her "little sis" to Marcy's same salutation. It was endearing coming from her and she was not about to say or do anything to spoil their day.

"You know I have always loved my car like a child. In fact, it has officially become an antique this year. I recently began to realize something; it loves me back. Hear me out before you laugh," Suzanne said as she held up her index finger.

"Since the kids are now on their own, I have begun to be a little melancholy, you know the empty nest syndrome. So, I began taking the Bug out for a spin. The first time, I found it so liberating, Steve said he thought he was going to have to extricate me out from underneath the wheel. He found me in the driveway, listening to the oldies and singing to the top of my lungs. I swear to you and you know Mama taught us not to swear, it's like being transcended back into time when you take a seat. Just like unwrapping a surprise that makes you feel warm and fuzzy all over. That is when I compared it to being wrapped in a big warm hug," Suzanne reminisced as she spoke.

Cynda gave her strange words some thought as she considered the phenomenon of a car creating that much human emotion. Suzanne looked like a lovesick puppy as she continued with her raving, "It is something I can't explain. When I begin to feel empty and a little lost, driving it fills a void. It's like my baby," she said with a sigh.

Cynda wrinkled her forehead and responded with a question, "I can appreciate the sentimentality, but the comfort level seems to be lacking."

Suzanne laughed and said, "I admit, it is not a car you want to drive for an extended time. When I first drove this baby again, after driving a sedan, I thought I was in a bumper car."

Suzanne climbed behind the wheel and pulled the passenger seat forward, as she motioned for Marcy to climb in. Marcy found her place in the back seat and nodded for Cynda to have a seat in the front. The regal sister gingerly placed her derriere in the confines of a seat that hauntingly whispered its welcome. Secretly, she was sure of it.

Suzanne put the car in drive and began to ease down the driveway. She turned onto the quiet residential street and the car lurched forward. Soon the wind started its dance, dipping and diving, teasing their spirits as they picked up speed on the open road. All three felt the exhilarating experience of the elusive hugs of which Suzanne had reverently spoken. The feeling seemed to be contagious as they were lost in thought and showered in tranquility.

Both Cynda and Marcy considered Suzanne's reasoning for naming the vehicle *Hug Bug*. It certainly seemed to make sense as they basked in the euphoric state. When Cynda had climbed into the aqua blue Beetle, she decided immediately that she was ready for a new adventure. She might just get Dane to buy her one! Wait, what was wrong with her, she thought. Had she left her senses?

Chapter 10

The short drive to the cottage was filled with mindless conversation about the weather and the traffic. When the three of them arrived there, Cynda was the first to exit the car. Marcy and Suzanne were amazed at how quick she was able to climb the three steps to the door of the cottage. Thank goodness they were able to find it so close to the beach and on ground level.

Once inside, Cynda gave an appraising look to the combination living room, dining area and kitchenette. It had a grouping of mirrors that ran horizontally along the wall of the dining area, creating a larger effect. Both sisters held their breath as Cynda's assessment of the room was clearly a high priority at the moment as far as Cynda was concerned. They saw her eye the ceramic seashell that held a clump of dusty greenery and rested in the center of the glass top dining table. She turned her attention to the dining chairs that were rattan and sported sea foam green and salmon colored cushions of assorted seashells. It certainly wasn't the Taj Mahal, but Cynda wasn't in a position to criticize. After all, she was here because of the good graces of her sisters.

Marcy spoke first and said, "It's a little dated, but comfy and we are just a few steps from the beach."

They were both shocked when Cynda responded by saying, "It's lovely, rather quaint."

They invited her to see their rooms upstairs. The two had moved Marcy's belongings on the second floor earlier that morning. After the short tour, they returned to the first floor. Cynda noticed the doorway to the third bedroom and asked, "What is there?"

Suzanne looked at Marcy for an indication of how the two of them should proceed.

Marcy responded quickly, "Oh, just another bedroom. Let's go ahead and pack our lunch and go down to the beach. What do you think?"

Cynda had the feeling that something was amiss, but she did not indicate that to her sisters; instead she agreed by saying, "Sounds like a good idea to me. I am ravenous for some of that seafood salad!"

The sisters went into the kitchen and packed a wicker picnic basket with plates and utensils. They loaded the cooler with the salad, fruit, water and wine coolers.

"Woo-hoo!" Cynda acknowledged, "I haven't had a wine cooler in a little while. Today is my lucky day."

Marcy and Suzanne both suppressed their grins as Cynda turned to examine a container on the kitchen counter that was molded like a fish. It had kitchen utensils spewing from its mouth.

"Unique," she managed to say as she proceeded to exit the kitchen into the seating area.

Along with the couch that had no personality, there were two chairs that virtually screamed to be recovered. They were made out of a madras plaid of salmon and sea foam green and looked as they belonged in a college dorm room.

Cynda sat down in one of the plaid chairs and waited for her sisters, making no comment about the décor. She fixed her eyes on the boat that was sailing above the couch in sea blue waters and framed with whitewashed boards. The scene was serene enough, but she failed to find it relaxing. Instead, she perused the entire seating area, and then her eyes rested on the closed door again. She thought it awfully strange that Marcy had not taken that room for her own, knowing her like she did.

Cynda's idle thoughts were interrupted as her sisters began to shoo her out the door toward the beach. It was a reversal of roles for her. Had she not always been the big sister and been in charge? Today it felt good to take a back seat, she decided, as she followed their orders.

Chapter 11

The three sisters sat on the beach in their own little sorority of sisterhood, Cynda under the umbrella reading her magazine and joining the conversation sporadically. Marcy and Suzanne both were slathered in sunscreen, deliriously hoping that the level thirty would protect their fair complexions, but tan them enough to keep the blinders off of everyone they met. It was an ongoing joke about their fair complexion. They were convinced their mother had an affair with a bleach salesman. Their father's dark skin had been passed along to Cynda, who shrugged her good fortune off as just being lucky. It was one of things that was not important to her.

Cynda had just put her magazine down when a group of girls and boys in their early teens who were sitting adjacent to them began cat calling and whistling. A young girl around the same age was quickly walking past them. It was obvious they were discussing the young lady among themselves and snickering behind her back. Cynda watched as the girl joined a couple more girls. The other girls had on modest bathing suits just as she did.

Watching them, she felt the bile rise in her throat as a familiar but suppressed memory engulfed her for that moment. She hated it when some memories surfaced that she wanted to forget. Suddenly she felt the need to share with her sisters the child she had been long ago.

"Hey, did you see that?" Cynda said looking over the top of her magazine.

Suzanne responded in a confused manner, "What are you talking about?"

"That young girl over there," Cynda pointed.

"She was being taunted by those arrogant jerks sitting in that group. I think they were making fun of her bathing suit. I have a mind to go over there and jerk a knot in their tails!"

That got Marcy's attention. When had she last heard that statement? Not since Mama had scolded her for allowing Phillip to take a trip without her. She told her in no uncertain terms, "If he were my husband, I would jerk a knot in his tail." Her Mama had been convinced he was "up to no good." Marcy had been quick to defend his actions by telling her that men needed some bonding time with other men, just like women needed women. For Heaven's sake, Marcy had thought, what would I do on a fishing trip?

Cynda began to speak to them in a conspiratorial manner, "Have I ever told you girls the bullying I had to endure in middle school?"

They both were taken aback and sat up and circled the wagon. Not for one minute were they going to miss the opportunity to delve into the mind of their empress of a sister. This was a golden opportunity.

"Do you remember the time that Mama had me get that awful permanent?" Cynda said.

Both Marcy and Suzanne nodded at the same time. How could they forget the months of walking around their older sister on eggshells? Even Suzanne who was not quite five at the time could remember.

"Well, I exercised great patience in my endeavors to ignore the snide and whispered remarks about my hair. Then it happened. It had been a few long months since the debacle at the beauty shop."

Marcy felt a stab of regret as she too had been snarky toward her older sister.

Cynda went on to say, "The remarks were sweet tempered with a bit of "smirking" on the side from my few friends. Of course Rosemary was my staunch supporter and raved about my hair and used the "fashionable" word. Unlike Mama, coming from her, it was acceptable."

"I was on the verge of turning thirteen and the remnants of the permanent wave still clung to my hair. You could not possibly remember, but I was a skinny little girl whose body had refused to plunge into puberty as most of my friends had already done. It was beyond my control and that was something that I abhorred. I was constantly reminded of my state of affairs as the girls in the class with the curvier shapes received the attention of the boys. On one hand, I wanted desperately to preserve my childhood, but at the same time, I wanted to embrace the march into full-blown womanhood. Mother Nature was not cooperating - oh no, not in the least."

Well, that was a revelation! Marcy and Suzanne sat there with mouths open listening to the sister that they had always thought was a goddess. It was hard to visualize the sister of theirs looking anything but exotic. Then she told them the story of their daddy and his injured nose; he had given her the ball of clay and told her she was perfect in his eyes and that she must believe in herself. She also told them it was not until much later that she realized that he wanted her to know that the standards of perfection she had set for herself had nothing to do with how she was accepted by her peers. She ended the story by telling them that their daddy told her how important it was to have the courage to believe in YOU, even when others do not.

They listened intently, both trying to absorb every detail of their daddy's words, groping for a morsel of inclusion. Both witnessed vicariously the wisdom of a man they had called Daddy for a short time in their lives. They were both able to embrace a father's love in a way that they had never been able to experience it in the past. Their full course meal had left them hungering for more, especially dessert. What Cynda did not tell them was that she still had that vial of clay in her nightstand at home. Neither did she reveal her periodic checks to see if it were still there, never opening the lid.

This is getting juicy, Marcy thought. They just shook their heads in amazement of their sister. Cynda continued, "The next day after Daddy gave me the clay, armed with the knowledge that I was perfect in Daddy's eyes - the most important man in my life - I was empowered."

"For the most part, I was just ignored by the boys in my grade making my anonymity somewhat easier to endure, but no less painless. However, there was a boy and you will remember him well, who would not allow me to fade into the woodwork. I had steadily worked to master avoiding confrontation with him by getting to my seat quickly in the classroom when we changed classes. Then, I would be the last to leave my desk. He was responsible for much of my humiliation. You know his name. Clive Fincher.

Both Marcy and Suzanne were startled to learn the bully was Clive Fincher. He was Cynda's good friend throughout middle and high school. At least they both thought so. They remembered he had a head full of rusty red hair and freckles that seemed to multiply as fast as his toothy grin appeared. The two were perplexed, but encouraged their sister to continue.

"But he was your really good friend all of those years. I don't get it," Suzanne remarked.

"I will get to that later, but let's finish the story," added Cynda.

"He always cracked a despicable joke. His jokes never seemed to fall on the shoulders of the confident; rather they fell on the weaker sex, most specifically me. He chose his audience and timing well when he was up to no good."

"I had just left my classroom and was walking toward the water fountain, unaware of the eminent meeting

67

with Clive. I knew it would come, I just did not know when. He had made it his goal to antagonize me daily."

"Just to let you girls know; I had made my own assessment of Clive. I knew he had low self-esteem. How many times had I heard Mama say, "If you can't say something good about someone, don't say anything at all." I wondered if Clive's mother had echoed those same words to fall on deaf ears. I also wondered if the laughter from his audience made up for the fact that he was truly unhappy or if the satisfaction from their laughter made him forget that his father had left home for good. On this day I tried to remember that as he approached me."

He said to me, "Hello, Cynda. Just wanted to know if you are in training?"

"I gave his question some serious thought and wondered for a brief moment if the torture that day had been replaced by sincere interest, since tennis season was about to begin. I had hardly allowed the thought to enter my mind, as the sound of Clive's own reply came swift and ruthless."

"Of course you are in training; why else would you wear a training bra?" Clive said and beamed at his comment.

This was getting to be really interesting. The sisters had been the targets of the wrath of Cynda on more than one occasion. They almost felt sorry for Clive and what her reaction had been.

Cynda continued with her story, waiting a moment for the effect. Then she said, "The crowd in the hallway starred in stunned silence waiting for my reaction. My face had to have turned every color of red in Elizabeth Arden's palette of lipstick."

Cynda looked at Marcy and said, "I am sure you could name most of those."

Marcy agreed by puckering her crimson lips and then allowing her bottom lip to rest in a pout.

Cynda continued with her story, "I could feel the warmth of my face as the temperature began to rise and the parchment of my mouth as it began to dry. I swallowed my pride and chose not to use the phrases that filled my mind. Instead I answered him with a question of my own."

I said, 'Clive, did you say that to make me feel bad or are you trying to make yourself feel better?'

"What I did not tell you was that just the day before Clive had humiliated me in the worst kind of way. His deliberate trip from his brown and white bucks had sent me sprawling into the hallway. I did not accuse him of the shameful deed, but I knew full well that it had been him. My lack of acknowledgement, through silence, had obviously spurned him to become more brazen with his words."

Both Marcy and Suzanne immediately felt an overwhelming sympathy for this sister who had always been their idol. They were anxious to hear his response.

"Clive stood frozen in his tracks as if the words that I had said turned him to stone. His face became a contortion of conflicted emotions. He neither answered nor did he make any effort to acknowledge my response. He turned and walked down the hallway, leaving a shocked crowd to walk away mumbling amongst themselves, trying to figure out what had just happened."

"I had wanted to hurl a lifetime of insults at him that I had heard about redheads. Instead I remembered my own broken heart and did not wish to inflict that pain on anyone. I remembered Daddy's wise words of the healing power of the red clay and realized that it was not the clay, but Daddy's advice to use courage to conquer my fears. Yes, even to heal my broken heart. Clive could not or would not hear those words from the father who was absent in his life."

The silence that followed was only interrupted by the gentle waves of the sea, applauding Cynda's heartfelt concern in the face of her own despair.

More words of wisdom poured from her rise of defeat, "I felt victorious as I walked away, but a quiet sadness entered my heart as I felt compassion as I had never known for the very boy responsible for my pain. It was as if I sensed a camaraderie that I could not understand. It was the last time that Clive made me his prey and he became more subdued in his efforts to gain an audience at the expense of others."

"Let me tell you that being ignored by the opposite sex brought me a quiet resolve of how I would then handle the future. In high school, I spent quite a bit of time reading and absorbing knowledge of human nature at every opportunity. I wanted to be in total control of my own destiny as far as bullies were concerned. I made that commitment to myself."

Cynda did not stop there as the floodgates continued to pour with powerful insight.

"That night after the confrontation with Clive, I took the clay from the bottle and allowed the smooth texture to be molded in my hands and thought of Daddy's wisdom. I was perfect in his eyes and I realized that the thought of his presence in my life would be enough to sustain me," Cynda said as her eyes became moist with tears.

Both of her sisters were also moved, and the warm moisture that streamed from their eyes bore no shame. The eloquent words that Cynda spoke framed a picture of humanity. Neither one of them could find the words to respond.

Suddenly Suzanne blurted out, "Oh, Cynda, we never knew how tough it was for you. And I thought I had it hard in middle school. When I was in the annual talent show, I won second place to a girl who skated across the stage and was lip syncing, "I've got a brand new pair of roller skates, you got a brand new key!"

The tension in the air was broken and suddenly all three of the sisters began to laugh once again, uncontrollably. When they gained control, there was an awkward silence before Cynda suggested they return to the cottage. As the three of them walked back in companionable silence, Marcy and Suzanne reached into the closets of their childhood, sifting through their own memories of a redheaded Clive. Marcy realized that Cynda's compassion had transcended her own pain as far as she was concerned. They had just had a rare glimpse of her very soul.

It was an eye opening moment for the sisters. It had been a painful loss for all of them when their daddy had passed away, but now they witnessed a more profound effect of his death. Their sister had been older and she had been cut deeper as she had been on the verge of puberty. Neither asked how Clive had become her best friend. Both had their ideas. Hopefully, that would come another day. Pandora's box was now open - hopefully.

Chapter 12

After the middle school revelations had been scattered on the shore like jack stones, the three sisters had picked them up and digested them in their own manner. Once they settled into the cottage, they were drawn to the kitchen like a moth to a flame. Somewhere in their psyche, it just seemed right to congregate there. The therapy they found in the presence of a few kitchen appliances and a fish that spewed its contents of assorted spatulas was a phenomenon.

The kitchen had always been the location of many of the Brooks family discussions. Many times the examination of the family tree provided much food for thought. Today would be no exception. The sisters all hungered for more of which neither one could assimilate consciously. Their Mama had given more good advice over a hot stove than anyone of them could count. She had also churned family problems as heartily as she had churned their butter into a malleable substance of sheer joy. As they gathered together, their relaxed conversation shifted once again to the past and to a familiar character. They began reminiscing about their younger days with their Aunt Sally.

Their Mama's only sister's eccentricity and her regular appearances in the Brooks' home, especially after their father had died, was a topic they all enjoyed. Aunt Sally made it her business to make the girls her business. Needless to say, she overstepped her bounds quite often. Their mother had always been diplomatic where Aunt Sally was concerned, but there had been times when their Mama's patience had worn thin.

Cynda reminded them about Aunt Sally's trips to the dentist.

"You girls probably don't remember this, but when Aunt Sally went to the dentist, she raided the complimentary basket of toothpaste and filled her purse. Then she would go around giving it out as if she were the tooth fairy."

"No, she did not!" Suzanne said as a statement of disbelief.

"She sure did. In fact, she took offense if you did not accept her gift and called you 'rude'."

The stories went on and on and the hour was getting late. The pleasant reverie set the stage for the conspiratorial plan into motion.

Without a thought, Suzanne asked Cynda pointedly, "So, we were thinking it would be a wonderful idea if you would consider spending the weekends with us out here at the beach. We have an extra room with its own bath and it is downstairs."

Marcy and Suzanne held their breath as Cynda's earlier puzzlement about the spare room now made perfect sense to her. She thought for a moment and then said, "Well, I don't know what to say. I certainly don't know what Dane would say either," Cynda said emphatically.

Marcy tag teamed Suzanne's proposition. She said, "We only have four weekends for our summer trip and we could spend more time with you if you were here. We thought we could prepare some gourmet foods and maybe get some tips from you, if you feel up to it. At least you could teach us some of your techniques."

"Yeah," Suzanne said, "You could sit right over there on that couch with no personality and direct us."

Cynda raised her eyebrows about the comment regarding the couch, looked in its direction, then back at Suzanne and said, "I think you have something there. It sure does not look very stimulating."

"You know what I mean. It's dull and boring and it would never be that way if you were sitting on it!" Suzanne added.

Cynda looked at her and began to see a sister she had not known existed. In fact, she liked this spunky little sister of hers, even if she spoke out at inopportune times. Yes, she liked her very much. The idea of spending time with her sass was beginning to take root.

"I certainly don't know how stimulating I am. I will have to think about it; yes, give it a lot of thought. I am not sure Dane will be up for the idea. You know, he really doesn't know how to take care of himself."

"Well, it's time he started. He is seventy-five years old. If he can't scramble an egg or make a piece of toast for breakfast, something is wrong! Look, he is twenty years older than you and he has been around the block. Don't you think he can manage on his own? I know he can make a sandwich. Surely he could grab dinner out or go to the club. In fact, he could dine with us in the evenings if he would like," Marcy declared.

"Let's just not get ahead of ourselves ladies, one step at a time. I have to admit, today has been wonderful and I already feel pretty darn good. Not to spoil the party, but we should go, Dane may get worried."

"We hate to be so pushy, but today is Thursday already and tomorrow begins a new weekend, sooooo – how about a decision by tomorrow?" Suzanne said with her fingers crossed behind her back.

"Let's get me back home and we shall see."

The three of them climbed into the Beetle, all of them lighthearted, eager to see what tomorrow would bring. Cynda was lost in thought on the way home as her sisters sang with the oldies. She insisted on taking a back seat, literally in the backseat of the car. It felt good. Her sisters sang as loud as they could within the confines of the *Hug*

Bug, innocent of the unexpected intrusion into Cynda's soul.

Chapter 13

The *Hug Bug's* engine slowed to a purr as its driver turned into the short driveway to rest at an idle. The pale pink stucco rose from the perfectly manicured lawn like the great Phoenix bird from its ashes, serene and elegant. It was surrounded by an emerald green carpeted lawn. Sago palms were placed in strategic areas, their fronds hanging in perfect symmetry. Variegated pink and yellow lantana surrounded the foundation of the house, in impeccable unison with the soft pink oleander on either side of the driveway. The appearance transcended perfection.

Inside the Beetle, the mood had become almost comical. Cynda had snapped out of her reverie to join her sisters in their contagious antics, even going as far as neck dancing to the oldies. Her sisters hid secret smiles as they helped her unload and escorted her to the door.

"See you tomorrow, ten a.m. sharp," Marcy said as she opened the front door for Cynda to enter. Suzanne leaned over and gave a quick brush of her lips on her temple and said, "Bye-Bye; your castle awaits and we will be your humble servants."

Leave it to Suzanne to be the ambassador of goodwill. She had always been sweet and kind. Cynda was beginning to be addicted to her endearment with a touch of sass. She suddenly could not wait to spend more time with her sisters. Why not start tomorrow? If she was not happy staying the entire weekend, she could always return home. In fact, she could just stay one weekend. Maybe that would satisfy them. Maybe that was all she needed, to get away for just one weekend. What could it hurt? Now, she just had to convince Dane.

It wasn't hard to find Dane. He was having his evening cocktail out on the patio. He was startled when she walked through the door, as if he was in some sort of trance.

"Hi Dane. How was your day?"

"It was good. I went to the club today and hit a few balls. How about you? Did those sisters wear you out at the mall?"

"Actually, we did not go to the mall."

Dane looked puzzled. He said, "So where did you girls go? I assumed you went to the mall, since you girls did not make an appearance at the club."

"To the cottage for a tour and then we went to the beach. Suzanne made some awesome seafood salad and we took a picnic down by the water."

"That's nice, but when did you decide that *Tybee* was worthy of your presence? Although I am glad to see you get a change of scenery. Are you sure that you are up to that kind of thing? I mean, you have been pretty weak lately."

Cynda avoided his reference to *Tybee* as she always had, being careful not to reveal her true affection. She countered, "Well, I have been doing some thinking. Some of that weakness is probably caused by inactivity, I have to admit. In fact, the girls have made a proposition to me."

"And what would that be?"

"They want me to spend weekends for the rest of their summer trip with them at the cottage," she said once again, avoiding referencing *Tybee*.

"Nice offer, but when did you become so chummy? I know you love your sisters, but you have never expressed any great desire to spend a lot of time with them. In fact, I have gotten the feeling the daily visits would get to you a little."

"Today was an eye opening experience for me. Maybe a change of scenery is just what I need. In fact, the girls are starting to grow on me in a way that I never thought possible. I felt lighthearted and carefree, even singing and dancing in the car. And for once, I did not care if the neighbors saw me."

Dane was thoughtful for a moment. He then nodded and said, "It's your decision. You know I only want what is best for you."

And in her heart of hearts she knew it was true. Dane had always been thoughtful and caring and she did not doubt his love and devotion. What Dane could not handle was his fear. It was high time he faced it she thought. Maybe the time on the weekends away from him was just exactly what he needed, too.

The two of them had a quiet dinner that Dane had picked up from the club. Afterwards, they settled into their respective routines of watching T.V. and reading. Both entertained thoughts about how their lives apart would be, even for just the weekends. The two silently agreed that their recent compulsory routines that held them captive in the pale pink stucco fortress were far more menacing to their bond than any disease.

Chapter 14

Marcy and Suzanne arrived at the cottage after a late dinner at the local pizza joint named *Lust for Crust*. Marcy thought the joint was appropriately named as she found it to be some of the best pizza she had ever eaten. Suzanne seconded that emotion.

The topic of conversation over dinner detailed the plan for Cynda to join them at the cottage and how it would play out. After debating the issue, they both decided they had a fifty-fifty chance that their sister would concede. The *Hug Bug* crept slowly back down the narrow street and the dark pavement was illuminated with hope. It was the night of the summer solstice and there was a full moon. The enormous moon rose up from the spires of trees that laced their fingers with one another in unison. It cast its glow in an air of superiority, reigning light over the entire cottage like a shroud. The single bulb that glowed over the doorway of the cottage cast a spidery reflection of the palms that waved in the light summer breeze as to welcome them home.

"Look, it's a sign," said Suzanne.

"Where do you see a sign?" Marcy said as she strained to see where her sister was looking.

"The moon of course, you silly woman; its brightness is an omen. There'll be bright and sunny days ahead, and I just know it. Cynda will be right here with us," she crooned with the look of a lovesick schoolgirl.

Marcy unknowingly agreed with Cynda as she marveled at the strong, but sensitive woman her baby sister had become. She was definitely the peacemaker in the family who looked at life through rose colored glasses and a pink haze of reality. The moon was in cahoots with the fairy godmother that predicted success with such clarity she thought.

Marcy could only reply, "I think you're right. I think you're right," believing her own words.

Once inside in their exhausted state, the two dropped unceremoniously into their respective plaid chairs and welcomed the respite. They had both decided upon moving into the cottage that the chairs were the comfiest. Furthermore, the chairs were not a target for disparaging remarks regardless of their dated appearance, unlike the couch with no personality.

Tomorrow, that would change if Cynda moved in for the weekend. They would have to take turns residing on the couch, allowing their sister the comfort of Madras affection.

Marcy rose from her chair and walked across to the vacant room, turning to look at Suzanne.

"Let's take a look at the room through Cynda's eyes and make sure that it will meet her approval. I want your input as I am sure you have an opinion of its persona. Do you think she will like it?"

"Now that was a million-dollar question. Do you really think the room could ever meet her high standards? Stop it right there. Let's not make it about the room and focus on the fun we are all going to have with one another. She sure seemed to catch the fever earlier when we suggested our plan," Suzanne said and as she refused to allow the seeds of doubt to plague her. "We have to stay positive," she implored.

They both stood in the vacated space that Marcy had left as neat as she had found it. The décor had not been a problem for her as she found it to be rather quaint and somewhat vintage.

Suzanne made a slow assessment of the room and wondered why she had not seen the attraction of it when they had arrived. She had always deferred to the wishes of her older sister, choosing neutrality and flexibility, and in doing so immediately chose the room upstairs. The larger bathroom in the cottage connected to this fascinating space that did indeed have a personality in her mind.

"The room is enchanting," Suzanne sighed as she made her appraisal. Why had she not even noticed its enchantment when she helped Marcy move out, she asked herself.

She eyed the celery green walls which were the backdrop to a white rattan headboard shaped with curvy detail. The bed was dressed in a stark white coverlet that met a pink and white striped dust ruffle. Pillow shams of a soft pink batiste sported pink flamingos that pranced across them in traditional fashion, one leg up, one leg down. Pink cording outlined the cases that provided a custom finish.

A matching chair of a pink and white stripe covering sat in the corner, facing an ample sized television on a stand. Nothing else seemed remarkable unless you could consider the iconic vintage seashell speared and mounted, a treasure.

The rattan dresser was void of adornment other than a jewelry box that was covered with shells and a matching tissue holder. The mirror above it reflected a double window from across the room that looked out over the sand dunes that blocked the ocean view. They danced in the moonlight waving their open arms of welcome to the sea beyond. The wooden blinds were open and allowed the light to envelope and spill its vitality over the room.

Yes, Cynda would love this room, Suzanne thought.

"Enchanting," she gushed as she found the entrance to the bathroom, moving toward it as she spoke.

The bathroom was of light green tile with matching sink and commode. The tempered glass shower doors hid a worn combination tub and shower of the same light green. A single pink wooden flamingo with its foot raised and resting on its dais sat on the back of the commode, marking the only color in the room. The room was of ample space with a white rug on the coordinating tiled floor.

"By the time Cynda gets her toiletries in this bathroom with her passion for pink, this dose of greenness will be toned down considerably," Suzanne said as she eyed the white curtain that covered the single window that hung high above the commode. It was like a ray of light in a sea of green.

"Hopefully the enchantment of the bedroom will overshadow this uninspiring bathroom," Marcy said as she stepped back into the bedroom.

Suzanne followed her older sister back into the room that she had forfeited when they arrived. They both stood there looking at it with anticipation.

Suzanne chose a name for the room, *Enchantment*. That would stick, she decided. She would make sure that Cynda was aware of its name, before she was ensconced into the overwhelming vintage cha cha cha of marching pink flamingos. More than anything they both hoped Cynda would choose temporary residence in the room, and in doing so, her presence would bring the enchantment of true sisterhood to their door. They hoped.

Chapter 15

Back on Wilmington Island, Cynda stood in the private sanctuary of the room that now illuminated her personality. The lovely guest suite filled with her personal possessions had lost its luster.   Designed to make its occupants feel warm and welcome, she stood resolved that "welcome" had been lost.

The previous few weeks had been as pleasant as conceivable given her condition. Her last round of chemo had left her weak and the room had served her well for much needed rest. She could not believe that only a few days ago she thought she may never leave her bed. She embraced her renewed energy.

Now this plan of her sisters, an adventure of sorts. Not too risky she told herself. She had to do it, she realized, or her demise would be eminent. Was this exuberance she was feeling a beginning of her healing? Secretly she had been rubbing her temples with the healing oils each night when she prayed.   Her decision was made.

The next morning Cynda packed her Louis Vuitton luggage with enough clothes and make-up to last her for the summer visit. She decided that she could leave her clothes there and transport her make-up and toiletries when she returned home on the weekends. It wasn't that she had great hope for the plan to work but she just wanted to be prepared, just in case.

After two hours of packing, repacking and contemplating her decision, Cynda was ready, at least as ready as she would ever be. She prayed for her sisters to arrive soon or all bets may be off. She argued with herself that her decision was too risky, but what did she have to lose? Maybe more than she had bargained for. She looked at the clock; it was nine fifty-five a.m.

Just as Cynda zipped and closed her bags for the last time, repeatedly checking to see if she had left anything out, the doorbell rang. Her heart jumped into her throat, but she slowly picked up the bags and moved toward the door. It was much more taxing than she realized and she wondered if she was making the right decision. Instead, she sat them down and called Dane for his help.

When the sisters stepped inside the house, to their astonishment, Cynda stood ramrod straight. She had suitcases sitting at her feet looking like two lazy brown doggies at rest after a satisfying meal. A coral colored turban rested on her head that matched her blouse, adorned by sapphire blue jewel toned buttons. Her slacks were of a matching coral gauze-like material. She looked as regal as she had always done. To their pleasure, a smile was reaching from the corners of her perfect coral pink lips.

Marcy was the first to speak.

"You look gorgeous. I can't wait to see what Louis is holding in those puppies at your feet."

"I second that emotion. Oops! There I go again, speaking from lyrics of a song. In all seriousness, it looks like you're in," Suzanne said leaning down to grab one of the bags.

It was a habit Suzanne had started long ago to speak from lyrics of songs, at any opportunity she could. Her gamut of music titles ranging from classical to country, and somewhere in between, had garnered her a reputation. The use of lyrics had worked effectively many times, especially when she sought to diffuse a situation. Today it helped to create a relaxed atmosphere. Both sets of eyes were on Dane now as he leaned over to give Cynda a tender kiss on her temple to bid her goodbye for the weekend. She reacted in like kind. Was there stiffness in Cynda's manner as she completed the act? Her sisters both sensed it. Dane did not seem to take notice.

"You can go with us," Suzanne teased.

"I am afraid not this time; thank you very much," Dane said as he shook his head and dropped his chin to peer over his reading glasses. "You ladies might just put me to work. I have done my time at the beach."

"We are just a phone call away," Marcy said in an amiable voice. She picked up the other piece of luggage and made a comical face feigning a struggle as she tugged on its handle.

"Likewise," Dane said.

And just like that the sisters followed one another out the front door, with its three vertical windows in offset order. This would be the beginning of a plan that neither sister had anticipated, but relished in its preliminary success. It was a start. They had their sister in tow. The outcome of her healing would remain to be seen, but this was a step in the right direction.

Chapter 16

Both Marcy and Suzanne had agreed on the way over to pick up Cynda that they would begin the weekend with fun and laughter. They began their hilarity as soon as Cynda stepped outside her front door, her eyes becoming transfixed on the mode of transportation.

"By the way Cynda," Marcy said, "looks like you dressed for the occasion, a little contrast going on there with our *Hug Bug*."

Cynda hid her smile, acting more interested in how she would manage placing her luggage in the Bug. She marched out to the car. Her two sisters succeeded in placing one of her Louis Vuitton bags into the trunk and then wedged the other one in the back seat. They left just enough space for Marcy's slim frame to compress itself into a spring form position like a jack in the box. Suzanne decided to remedy that situation by lowering the convertible roof.

Cynda's coral gauze bottom met the passenger seat of the *Hug Bug* as she placed her oversized matching coral sun glasses on the bridge of her nose. The coral and sapphire blue combination of her dress was stunning, but the glasses were a little over the top. She quietly waited for a reaction from the others, as she had purposely worn the glasses for fun.

The two companions held their silence until Cynda pointedly asked, "How do you like my glasses?"

Marcy immediately cleared her throat and stuttered a bit as she spoke, "Nice, really nice."

Suzanne shook her head in agreement as their sister suppressed a smile. Then she could not contain herself as she burst out laughing and said, "I am not sure which is more comical, my glasses or your feigned approval of them," pretending to be cynical.

Cynda had broken the ice for them. They joined her in making facetious comments as they took turns wearing the glasses to the beach. It was a good feeling for Cynda to take charge of something, anything, even if it was setting the tone for a trip that she previously had reservations about. In that moment, Cynda felt normal again. Yes, she had made a good decision.

Marcy took a vote while they were slowly leaving Wilmington Island and before the conversation could be drowned out by the unrestrained winds around them. The subject was what the three of them would eat for lunch; whether they would pick up some fast food or just eat a sandwich back on the island. They were all in agreement to drive directly to the cottage and get Cynda settled in to her room.

They arrived windblown and sated from the drive. Marcy unfurled her accordion body from the back seat and stretched like a newborn baby. They quickly unloaded Cynda's bags as she stepped out and moved toward the front door. When she rounded the corner of the car, she suddenly noticed the wreath on the grill of the car and said, "What is the meaning of this hideous 'creature' clinging for dear life on the front of your car?"

Suzanne had removed her wreath when they had first arrived on *Tybee* Island to fluff it up. She had forgotten to reattach it until this morning. Apparently Cynda had missed it when they had loaded the vehicle and come to think of it, Marcy thought, Suzanne had backed in the driveway.

Before she could get an answer, she persisted, "I guess I can kind of understand the concept behind *Hug Bug*'s name. But, really Suzanne, this is going a little too far," she said with a dismissive frown.

Suzanne did not reply. There were some things that did not justify an explanation. She liked her wreath. It was a rebellion of sorts, a way to say, "This is who I am! Get over it." Besides, the "hugs" felt even better once she attached the wreath to the grill as if it were a royal crown. When Suzanne did not respond, Cynda gave the wreath a second thought. She realized it made a statement. It was loud and clear. "Have the courage to believe in YOU, even if others do not." She could hear her father's words reverberate in her ears from long ago.

Cynda looked at her sister and quietly said, "Courage becomes you."

Chapter 17

Neither one of her sisters had given Cynda a hint of how her room had been decorated. They held their breath as she entered the cottage and proceeded to the room in question. She held her breath too, then released it when she entered the quaint space that exuded charm and something she could not put her finger on. Cynda did not have a chance to contemplate exactly what she felt when she entered the room. Her little sister chimed in with her own descriptive persona.

"Isn't the room just enchanting?" Suzanne bubbled as she placed one of the suitcases on the bed.

"I have named it Enchantment," she declared as she flitted around the room pointing out its attributes.

Cynda tried to suppress a smile, but the corners of her mouth began to twitch and she offered a nervous giggle and her obvious approval.

"It is just lovely," she admitted.

"We hoped you would like it. By the same token we also know that you will add your own special touch. You might want to bring some personal things from your house next weekend," Suzanne said hopefully, trying to keep the nervousness from her voice.

"Let's just take one day at a time. Right now I would like to unpack my suitcases and make myself comfortable. Let me see what Louis has in these puppies," she winked as her hands found the release on the latches.

Marcy and Suzanne took this as an opportunity to leave the room and allow Cynda her privacy.

"Let get that lunch started," Marcy said as she lightly touched Suzanne of the shoulder, guiding her out of the room and into the kitchen.

Once they left the room, Cynda gingerly lay down on the coverlet, kicking off her sapphire blue espadrilles in the process. She stared up at the stippled ceiling and the imperfections of the pattern that were not really obvious, unless closely scrutinized. Being here with her sisters was somewhat frightening as the past began to unravel and the suppressed memories suspended in time during the period of their father's passing began to surface.

It had been soon after that last confrontation with Clive and the eerie feeling of their solidarity that now triggered Cynda to revisit the memory of that day. How she had somehow felt pity for him when she finally called him out had been beyond her. In fact, she had not felt as victorious as she should have felt. Later it all made sense to her. It was just before her fourteenth birthday that they received the news. Lawrence Brooks was found dead at his desk at work. Her world would be forever changed.

When the news finally sunk in, Cynda experienced a deep and final sorrow for the man who had made her believe in herself. She clung to her memories like a life raft, fearful that if she did not hold on tight, they would be gone forever. She had wondered if Clive felt the same. His daddy had abandoned his family by choice, but her daddy's life had been snuffed out by sudden death. Clive at least had hope of seeing his father someday.

A new school year had begun and the excitement of being in high school had waned before it had begun for Cynda. She had even dismissed the change in her body that had suddenly taken place. The loss of her father superseded any satisfaction she might have experienced in her new transformation. Six weeks had passed since her daddy had died and the stark reality of his death stared back at her with despair; disguised as her mother. Cynda found her at the kitchen table with pen in hand, staring at the stack of bills before her.

Lydia Brooks had never paid a bill in her life. In fact, she didn't even know how to balance a checkbook.

Her eyes were transfixed on the sea of papers that lay before her, but her mind was a million miles away.

Why? Her mother had asked herself that question over and over again, but the answer never came. Lawrence had left her financially comfortable, but she would have to budget her funds. Thank God for that, because she had not worked since before they had married. Now, she would have to learn to pay the bills, manage the money and a family, all with no emotional support. The past few weeks she had been going through the motions of life and the emotions of coping with death, something she had not counted on or bargained for. Cynda looked at her mother's disheveled appearance and the papers that mirrored her image. She sat down at the table grasping for words of encouragement, uncomfortable in her new role as nurturer.

Cynda had been forced to grow up in a great hurry these last few weeks and her mother's dependence on her was something she decided would not be something she would accept. She needed her mother now more than ever and Lord knows, Suzanne and Marcy needed her even more, Cynda worried to herself. Her daddy was gone and their special relationship, too. She would not allow the strong and independent woman that her mother had always been slip away. Sure, her father had always worked and had taken charge of the bills, but she knew the backbone of the family sat in the chair before her.

Cynda had seen her strength as her mother quietly guided her father to her will and his unabashed willingness to follow her lead. Cynda had to take some action that would snap her mother back into existence and thought she knew the very thing to do just that.

"Mama, the time has come and I need your help," Cynda said.

Her mother looked up from the array of papers, totally caught off guard. Cynda had seemed complacent since her father had died and her Mama had found some comfort in that. Lawrence had always been able to say the right words to make Cynda happy and to soothe her hurt feelings. How could she ever make up for his absence and fill the void for her, she thought? The relationship between father and daughter was beyond special; it was extraordinary.

"Well, Cynda, what is 'the time" that has come? Your birthday has come and gone already."

Her mother had to admit that she felt a spark of interest that Cynda actually needed her. After all, her perfectionist daughter emanated independence.

"I need a bra, mama, a real bra," Cydna said.

It was the words that she needed to hear. She knew that Cynda had waited patiently for her time to blossom and suddenly the thought of focusing on a new phase of her daughter's life gave her a spark of hope. It had not gone without notice that Cynda had recently "outgrown" her training bra and her curves were much more pronounced. Not only did Cynda project herself as a poised and mature young lady, her curves were obviously more pronounced. What she did not notice was that Cynda had suddenly outgrown her childhood.

Subsequently, Lydia Brooks not only shopped for bras for Cynda, she spent hours shopping for a new wardrobe also. She purchased outfits that flattered and accentuated her daughter's new figure. It was as if she was possessed and the shopping sprees drove the demons from her. It was a side of her mother that Cynda had never seen. Her mother seemed to be living through her vicariously and it frightened her just a bit. She was afraid that she would disappoint her mother and she strove even more for perfection. She wanted to make her mother happy and never let her down.

Clive Fincher and Cynda had reached an unspoken truce. It was as if that somehow her pain had transcended itself to Clive and he bore some of it for her. She was grateful that he was her ally, even though he never voiced his intentions; at least not right away.

Chapter 18

Cynda's reminiscing came to a halt as her sisters called her to the kitchen for lunch. She could not shake the thoughts of how she had been forced to grow up in a hurry. She knew now that the impact their father's death had not been as devastating for her sisters as it had been for her. At least, there was no hint from either one, not yet anyway.

Suzanne called softly to her, "Do you want to join us or would you like us to bring you a tray to your room," she said sweetly as she peeked around the corner.

Cynda immediately rose from her lethargic state, reminding herself that she would push herself to join her sisters whenever possible. In fact, she was in a rather jovial mood, which surprised her, as visiting her past usually had the opposite effect.

As the three sisters munched on a light lunch of chicken salad melt, cucumber salad and sweet iced tea, memories of their childhood began to unify them in a way that neither one of them imagined.

It was Suzanne's idea. She challenged her sisters to share a story of their childhood, in hopes that they could get Cynda to open up Pandora's box again.

Cynda was thoughtful for a moment and then she shocked her sisters.

"Did I ever tell you that I thought I would never be able to break out of the prison of a training bra?" she said.

"I just walked in the kitchen one day and demanded Mama to give me her help. When Daddy died, she was in a sad state of affairs. I was at the point of asphyxiation from my starter bra! I told her that I needed a real one, and it was like the idea instantly transformed Mama."

"Mama's response was overwhelming to the point that for the next few weeks, I wondered if I had unleashed a demon. She not only bought me several new bras, she was on a tear to buy me as many new outfits for high school as her *Rich's* charge card could stand!"

Both of her sisters found the statement amusing and were surprised at their sister's sense of humor in referring to her "prison break." But the next statement changed their demeanor.

"Mama was so self-absorbed after Daddy was gone that she totally ignored all of us. You girls were too young to notice, I am sure, but I did notice. How could I not? I needed her too much," Cynda declared.

"We all needed her, but I was the only one who could voice it for us all."

Cynda became melancholy and shared how it felt to grow up in hurry and how she felt the burden to get her mother to pay attention to all of them. She also shared her uncanny wisdom to understand and appreciate the strength of their mother.

"You know Mama had a great deal of influence over our daddy. He always acted so tough, but deep down, he was just a cream puff. She had him under her thumb and he did not even know it," Cynda said, coming to that realization as she spoke.

Marcy and Suzanne sat quietly in awe of the revelation, a glimpse of the past that had not been theirs to own.

"Wow, it must have been hard to grow up in such a hurry," Marcy said.

"I must admit that I am a little jealous that you got to have Daddy a little longer than the two of us. As hard as it must have been, you are so lucky," she continued.

"Guess I never looked at it that way. I was always so angry and felt so cheated that we had lost Daddy that I could not get past it. I just tucked my pain away and chose not to visit the past. Now I feel a little selfish that I have never shared how special our daddy really was to all of us," Cynda said with regret.

The nature of the conversation had become more serious than Marcy and Suzanne had expected. Marcy decidedly changed the subject by commenting on the lunch.

"Suzanne you outdid yourself with the chicken and cucumber salad. They were both outstanding. I could take a bath in that sweet tea," she said as she took a deep swig of the sugary drink.

"Cynda you know that I will drive from Atlanta out to Luxomni, just to get a dose of Suzanne's sweet tea. Mama taught her to make it just like she did, and for the life of me, I cannot seem to get it right."

Suzanne and her husband had moved to Luxomni shortly after their mother had become too frail to take care of her home. She and Steven had been Lydia's rock until the day she had died. For that, her sisters would be eternally grateful.

Cynda nodded her head in agreement and took her own deep swill of deliciousness. As she sat the glass back down on the table, she noticed the parade of pink flamingos around the bottom half of the cylinder. There were scratches worn into the bodies and some of the feet were missing, but today she found their flaws were irrelevant, almost a sacrilege to replace them as she would have done in her own home. In the grand scheme of things what did it matter?

She turned her attention to what was beginning to matter more than ever, her sisters.

Chapter 19

The sisters had elected to go to the beach in the afternoon after a lazy morning. Cynda took a nap and they read and relaxed. Around four, they packed their paraphernalia and headed down to the beach. The air was hot and stifling as the three headed across the expanse of the sand and dunes to reach their destination. Both Marcy and Suzanne worried about Cynda's ability to walk the short distance, but silently held their concern, though insisting on carrying the gear. They arrived none too soon. The welcomed ocean breeze brought much needed relief to their encampment of chairs, umbrellas, coolers and various beach bags.

To their amazement, Cynda began to revisit their earlier conversation by asking her sisters, "Okay. I shared my story. Time for one of you to cough it up," she said as she threw some crumbled saltines to the seagulls that now circled precariously close to her umbrella.

"Marcy, you go first," Cynda said.

Marcy hesitated and thought for a moment, relaying a story that she decided would bring some more enlightenment from their sister.

"Do you remember the time that Clive Fincher came over to pick you up for school?"

"Which time? There were many." Cynda said.

"Ugh, you know the first time you rode in his car."

"Oh, the day he drove his sixty-two Chevy to school for the first time with all the windows rolled down and his sleeves rolled up? Yeah, I remember. I was the envy of half the girls in the class, even though Clive knew not one of them was interested in him. They just wanted the thrill of riding in his car. He knew it too. That's why I was his exclusive passenger right up until he started dating Sybil Slater. She flatly refused to allow me to ride with him after that. I just waited. The romance lasted a whole three weeks," Cynda continued.

"I had the biggest crush on Clive," Marcy blurted.

"And, it wasn't because of his car. I just found him so handsome!" she confessed.

"Who would have known?" Cynda said. "Clive would have been so flattered. You know back then he had no self-confidence."

"Speaking of that Cynda, how did you become such good friends with Clive after the fiasco in middle school?" Suzanne interrupted.

"Oh, that all transpired after Daddy died. I really needed a friend," Cynda confessed and then confided more of her true feelings.

"After Mama bought me the bras and new clothes, I felt more confident and certainly more mature. It was as if it happened overnight. The boys just started looking at me in a different light. In fact, some of them became tongue tied in my presence, and as for Clive, he was no threat. In fact, he became one of my best friends because of it. I guess you could say I used him to keep the unwanted advances away. Nobody dared approach me while he was around and that was often. To tell the truth, I might have looked like I was full of myself, but deep down, I was terrified of a relationship. I did not share all of my confidences with Clive, but I valued his opinions and sought his advice daily. Most of those conversations included his input of who wanted me to be his latest fling."

Both girls stared in disbelief at the story that Cynda had just relayed to them. Not for one minute had either one of them thought that their sister was ever anything but beautiful. In fact, they always thought she had been stunning. Apparently, that idea had not been shared by her. The lovely woman with the flashing green eyes had revealed a weakness that they had never known. She was vulnerable once, and for now, showing signs of that vulnerability. It was definitely still there, protected, but there.

Cynda had been searching for a story she could share with her sisters that would shed more light on the man that had been their daddy. She wondered if either of them remembered the hours they had spent jumping rope. How the jump rope was acquired was more important.

"Hey girls, do either of you remember the little grocery store on the hill?" Cynda said.

"Maybe," Marcy said, "What about it?"

"You know the one with the man who had a glass eye and sold rope by the foot," Cynda sang the words as if her use of discombobulated information would cause her sister to remember. She was certain Suzanne was too young to recall the store. In fact, the store had been torn down and a much larger one had built in its place at some point. She was not sure when.

"Yeah, I think I do now, more vividly than I first thought. It's coming back to me," she said shaking her head up and down, "Yes, the smell of singed hair, MINE. I remember backing up to that gas heater in the rear of the store and leaning back so far the heat singed my hair. It is a wonder that I did not catch my dress on fire," Marcy remarked, shaking her finger and wrinkling her nose as if she could still smell the odor. Cynda could almost smell the acrid odor herself.

Cynda, in perfect southern style began, "Well, Daddy would take us there ever so often to get a new jump rope. He would buy one long enough for two people to swing. Of course, we had to have at least three people to play."

The girls listened as their sister brought the story to life.

"Mr. Jack, I remember his name well, would remove the rope off of a big spool and measure it with his yellow wooden ruler. I can remember him asking Daddy to hold the end of the rope as he opened the ruler foot by foot. When he had measured the rope with the six feet of the ruler, he would get me to hold the place he had marked. I realize now he wanted to make me feel special by including me in the process, especially since I was the oldest child."

"I was a bit scared as I approached him because the glass eye seemed to fix its stare on me. I wanted the rope too bad to bolt and run; I would just close my eyes while I held on to the rope in his designated mark. He would finish the measurement. Then he took out his pocket knife, just like Daddy's. It had a pearl inset with two blades. He would cut the rope and hand it to me as if he were handing me the world. Come to think of it, it was the world. The world of jumping rope, before we jumped into adulthood," Cynda finished with a dramatic sigh.

Suzanne looked dreamily at her two sisters and said, "I do remember the two of you swinging that rope in a circular motion, one on each end, when someone came over to play. Then you all took turns, jumping until you missed, and then rotating out. I couldn't wait until I was big enough to join in."

"Well, the best part of the story was that Daddy would treat us to a YooHoo® chocolate drink and peanut butter crackers. I wish I had some right now!" Cynda continued.

"Now that's something I had forgotten, but it's coming back to me now," Marcy said with glee.

"Yep. And I remember that he liked to stop at the gas station in town. We could only go inside as long as he accompanied us. We did not dare go where the "men folk" gathered. That was taboo. If you didn't believe it, you could ask Aunt Sally. She would look at us down that overblown nose of hers and mimic like a parakeet what we had already heard. Mama would just roll her eyes and Daddy would suppress a smile. Aunt Sally would say something like this, 'You got to listen to me. Young ladies do not go cavorting around a gas station. It ain't no place for girls or boys for that matter. It's a man's world, I tell you. Listen to your Mama and your Daddy,' she would rant.

Cynda seemed to forget that she had asked her sisters to share their stories. It was as if a dam had been broken and there was no way to halt the steady stream of revelations spewing forth. They were thirsty for more.

"I have another story that would have 'set Aunt Sally on her ear' as Mama often said. My best guess is that it means 'to take heed'," Cynda said.

"There was a new soda fountain that opened in town. Rosemary and I wanted to go really bad. We both thought it would be so cool, since we were officially pre-teens. The only problem was that to get there, you had to walk through the parking lot of the gas station. We finally sucked it up and literally ran across the pavement like a couple of fools. Once we got inside, I can remember taking a deep breath inside that forbidden territory. No chaperones in sight, at least for the moment."

Marcy pictured her Aunt Sally making a grand entrance. Suzanne had the same thought.

"No sooner than we had ordered our Coca-Colas and fries, we were caught red-handed."

"Aunt Sally," Marcy murmured.

"No. It was Daddy and I was shaking in my boots. I knew I was in big trouble for crossing through that parking lot."

"What did he do?" Suzanne joined in.

"Nothing. Absolutely nothing. He sat down at the counter and ordered. In fact, he paid for our food without a word," Cynda said in a quiet tone.

"Did he reprimand you when you got home?" Marcy asked.

"No. I was devastated that I had let him down. I think he knew that was punishment enough. He never mentioned it."

"Daddy was really intuitive. He always seemed to know what my intentions were and he respected them. It was not too long after then that he died. I never went back to that soda fountain again. It went out of business pretty quickly and I was almost relieved. It reminded me too much of Daddy and his favor toward me."

Suzanne, who had felt cheated her whole life that her daddy had died so soon, caught a glimpse of a man bigger than life, at least to her. She said in honesty, "You were so lucky."

By this time, the wind had picked up and the threat of rain was eminent. The three gathered their belongings and quickly walked back to the cottage. The day had brought some sweet revelations of a daddy whose voice had long been silenced, but whose grace had sustained.

Chapter 20

It was seven a.m. and the practiced hand of a master pummeled the handle of the juicer repetitively. The apparatus had been lovingly wrapped and transported via one of the Louis Vuitton bags that Cynda had brought to the cottage. The remnants of half of a bag of orange halves lay on the Formica countertop ready for disposal.

Cynda had a good night's sleep and felt refreshed. She was dressed in her tangerine house coat with three quarter length sleeves, zipped to meet the mandarin collar. Her make-up was complete and the white turban accentuated the hollow cheekbones, but the green eyes portrayed a regal image.

She completed the task at hand and had a seat on the couch with no personality, a glass with the dancing flamingos in her hand, brimming with fresh orange juice. She savored each drink of the refreshing balm as she studied her surroundings. When her eyes met the mirrored wall, she only saw a shadow of herself, a grim reminder of her predicament. Again, her frequent recollections of her past began to permeate her mind, returning her to high school days.

Cynda had become more poised and mature. No longer did the slight crook of her nose appear to be her enemy as her piercing green eyes minimized its existence. She had an exotic look. Her heart-shaped face and high cheekbones were framed with long thick locks of auburn hair. She was a show stopper, and for those unkind young men who had teased her unmercifully in her younger years, they could only drool. She began to entertain the attention of the opposite sex.

Cynda did not date just one guy as most of her friends chose to do. She thought them shallow for wasting too much time on one person as they would certainly miss out on the fun of having lots of male attention. She had to admit that all of her flirtations left many of her male counterparts frustrated as several of them vied to be her one and only. She enjoyed the game and besides, it felt good to be the one on top, the one who had suffered so many injustices through what she considered her darker days, days of humiliation that only her father had helped to negate with his encouragement. She had become the victor then and her desire to be perfect had finally worked to her advantage. She took great pains in her personal appearance.

She breezed through the first three years of high school gaining more confidence as her extracurricular activities elevated her socially. She made the cheerleading squad in her senior year and was transformed in the eyes of her peers, as she had shirked the opportunity earlier. The thoughts of the teenage years that Cynda had once found so difficult now seemed like a piece of cake. They were not all bad; in fact, looking back she had rather enjoyed them.

The sound of her two sisters' footsteps on the stairs reminded Cynda that she was not alone. She turned her attention to them.

"Fresh juice is on the counter," she said.

The two looked at the mound of orange halves and the silver juicer that had been their mother's pride and joy.

"Where did that come from?" Suzanne asked.

"Don't answer Cynda. The contraband in the Louis has now made its appearance and I have a bruise on my leg to prove it," Marcy said as she pivoted on one foot for proof.

"When that bag slammed into my leg yesterday, I could not guess what you had in there. I had decided it was an iron hair dryer or something like that. Never would I have guessed it was Mama's juicer!" she continued.

"Well, I think it is awesome, Cynda, and who would have ever guessed you actually would use it? I thought you were just taking it for sentimental purposes when Mama died. I will be first to admit that I have never tasted juice as good as hers. Imagine how happy she would be if she could see us now," Suzanne said as she poured herself a glass.

"Marcy has to have her coffee first, but I am wasting no time."

Marcy poured herself a cup of coffee that had been on automatic brew and took a seat beside her sister on the couch.

"Go ahead and pour me a glass, Suzanne. This coffee is waking me up, but that juice is calling my name."

"Oh my goodness Cynda, the orange juice is divine! Are you sure Mama was not in the kitchen with you this morning?" Suzanne said.

Cynda smiled at her baby sister's effervescent morning demeanor. She appreciated it today as she was reminded that a compliment from her was always genuine.

"Thanks. Mama did some things really well and her juice was one of them. I make it often and think of her when I do. I pretend she is in the kitchen with me," Cynda said as she thought it odd of her to share that information.

"You know after Daddy died, when Mama decided to go to work, we had fresh juice only on the weekends or on her day off." Cynda said.

"I can't remember a time that she did not work while we were growing up," Suzanne recalled.

"Yes, and once Daddy was gone, I felt it was my responsibility to help out some myself. I know that he left us comfortable, but Mama wanted you all to have the best. I wanted to make some money so I could buy some extra things. Secretly, I just wanted to work at *Rich's* department store like Mama," Cynda added.

Over breakfast of fruit and English muffins, Cynda reminisced to them about working at *Rich's*. It was a time that she had cherished, even though the turn of events that led up to an early and failed marriage resulted from her meeting her first husband there.

It was May of Cynda's junior year of high school and she found herself dreaming of a perfect ending to her school career. She wanted to be dressed to the nines each and every day at school. Her senior year was beginning in three months and she wanted it to be memorable. She felt guilty for asking her mother for anything extra as she was doing all that she could do to raise her three girls by herself. Marcy would be starting high school in the fall and Suzanne was only three years behind her.

It was true that her mother had made many sacrifices as far as Cynda was concerned and she knew that. Her mother had taken the job at *Rich's* in downtown Atlanta, something that her father would have been totally against. She did it for the girls, she said, so that there would be no problem in them participating in extracurricular activities. Cynda suspected that it had been tougher to make ends meet as they had grown older and their needs had increased.

Now it was Cynda's turn to contribute, as she felt that she was the main reason her mother had taken a job in the first place. She had already thought it through of how she was going to broach the subject of working. Knowing how her mother felt about her working in high school, she was ready for her rebuttal.

Cynda heard her mother open and close the screen door that led to the living room. In her usual fashion, she gently tugged it shut as she lifted up on the handle. The door hinges needed adjusting, many repairs on the list of to do's that she had put aside to concentrate on her girls' needs.

Cynda raised her brows at her mother and said, "Mama, how long are you going to let that door go before you get it repaired?"

"It's okay, it just needs a little tender loving care when you open and close it," she said as she skirted the issue, "How was your day?"

Cynda replied, "It was fine, just winding down the school year; you know Mama, we are all just ready for the summer."

Her mother walked across the room and collapsed in the worn recliner that she had refused to get rid of since Lawrence had died. The chair was her comfort zone. There she felt solidarity with him, especially when she felt confrontation was at hand. Today she could sense that Cynda had an agenda. She said, "Okay, what is going on; is there something wrong? Are the girls okay?"

Cynda, who was nonchalantly looking at a *Better Homes and Gardens* magazine, flipped the pages, closed it, laid it on the couch beside her. She eyed her mother pensively, trying to decide if now was the right time to approach her with her idea and replied, "Nothing is wrong. The girls are in their rooms studying."

Her mother was not satisfied with her answer and said, "Cynda, you may as well spit it out. I know when you have something on your mind. You have never been able to hide your thoughts, especially when they are so intense, so out with it."

Cynda looked over at her mother and saw the tiredness in her eyes and knew she had to share her idea or her mother would be relentless in her pursuit of her.

She said, "Mama, I was thinking. You know how every summer *Rich's* hires some high school girls to work as clerks? I thought it would be great for me to get a summer job working there."

Her mother looked over at her and said with all of the resolve she could muster, "Cynda, you know how I feel about you working before you graduate from high school. It is possible that you will be working for the remainder of your life. I want you to enjoy your young adulthood without having that responsibility. Your father would have agreed."

Cynda replied in her most persuasive manner, "Mama, times have changed. I know that you work in order to give me, Marcy and Suzanne the extras you want us to have. I feel so guilty when I see you so tired like this. Please, will you consider allowing me to work just this summer, a few days each week? Marcy is old enough to take care of Suzanne and you and I could ride together on the bus into town."

Cynda continued in an effort to coerce her with flattery, "It would be an adventure, something we could talk about in later years. It would be our special time together. I am sure that you could have some pull in getting me hired. You know Miss Reed really seemed to like me that day I helped you with the fashion show. She even told me I had the makings of a model someday. I want to work in the lingerie department. You know how I have always loved pretty lingerie. Do you think there is an opening?"

"Oh Cynda, get those modeling thoughts out of your head. Modeling school costs a fortune and I don't like the idea of you putting yourself on display like that."

"For Heaven's sake Mama! I just want a summer job so that I can buy some really great clothes for my senior year of high school. Is that so wrong?"

Her mother just shook her head and felt her defeat was eminent. She touched her index finger to her lips and said, "I will think about it," knowing that Cynda had already won.

Cynda would have her way and her mother had recognized early on that her daughter would always be a challenge. She saw her perfectionist daughter exercising the one trait that went hand in hand with her perfectionism, control.

The next day Cynda got up a full hour before her mother, which was highly unusual for her as she coveted sleep. By the time her mother had showered and was downstairs making morning coffee, Cynda was close on her heels.

Cynda said, "I was thinking that maybe I could ride in town with you on the bus, since you have a short day. You know I can always catch a movie over at the Fox Theatre while you are working. Then...,"

Before she had a chance to finish, her mother interrupted and looked her square in the face, her brows lifted as she looked up from her reading glasses. Cynda knew that look and prepared herself for the response that surely would come.

"Cynda, you know how I feel about you going to that place alone; besides the girls need your supervision," her mother said, knowing full well that she almost ignored the girls these days, and them likewise.

Cynda had already practiced her response and blurted out her plan for the day without giving her mother a chance for rebuttal.

"Mama, I have it all planned out. The girls are going down to the pool. Cathy's mother will be there and you know she will not take her eyes off of them for one second. They will have her full attention, and if she has anything to do with it, she will be sitting within close enough range to hear their childish chatter. Really Mama, I am so glad you are not like that," she said, as she added that little tidbit of flattery to sweeten the pot of the plans she was about to divulge. Before her mother could even take a breath to respond, Cynda continued with her next line of persuasion.

"Clive has already agreed to meet us at the bus stop and ride in with us, and he is going to go to the Fox with me," she declared, as she knew that her mother's affection for Clive stopped short of her wanting him to be more to Cynda that just being a good friend.

Just as Lydia was about to digest the plan for the Fox Theatre, she was enlightened by Cynda of the real reason for the trip into town.

"After the movie, Clive and I are both going to apply for a job! Won't that be wonderful if we both get hired at *Rich's*? Clive is going to apply for the courtesy clerk to assist customers with their packages."

Her mother had already turned her back to her and was preparing herself a cup of coffee, a welcome reprieve from the persistent daughter that she had found harder and harder to manage. She allowed herself a few seconds of composure, turned and walked across the kitchen, feeling defeated, "If Lawrence were only here, this could be so much easier." But he wasn't and the business of raising three girls was getting harder and harder each day.

"Okay Cynda, you win, but there is no guarantee that either of you will get a job; but what the heck, it is worth a shot. I can't guarantee I can garner any help from Miss Reed. She takes her job very seriously and she has to be convinced you will be the right choice, not me."

That was all that Cynda needed to hear. She ran down the hallway to the rotary phone and began dialing the numbers, humming each time the dial clicked back into position. "This is going to be a great day," she thought, her confidence growing by the minute. "That Miss Reed will be convinced to hire me, before she even has a chance to consider anyone else. I will make a great first impression," she thought smugly.

Cynda did not feel so smug when she was escorted by Miss Reed into the Lingerie Department with her bringing up the rear. The spinster was ramrod straight, thin as a willow woman who wore a shirtwaist dress of starched pale blue poplin. The knife blade thin pleats marched around her waist and extended down to a semi-full skirt that covered her knees. Cynda presumed them to be as knobby as the sticklike limbs that protruded from the hem of her skirt that looked as they could not support even her tiny frame. When Miss Reed turned on her heel, she peered at her through her cat-eye glasses with an air of importance. Cynda felt the urge to disappear; instead she met the gaze with a warm smile and extended her hand to shake the birdlike limb that was offered to her.

Cynda had been right. She was hired by the time her mother finished her four-hour shift. She told herself that Miss Reed's decision had nothing to do with the fact that her mother was a highly respected employee. She was probably right as it was obvious that the spinster stood on principle and probably had no regard for playing favorites for anyone.

Miss Reed had played right into her hands as Cynda had seemed to dote on every fact that she disclosed about the Lingerie Department and its importance in the department store. According to her, the Lingerie Department was the anchor of the store; after all, if women were not properly fitted with foundations, their presence would be diminished in any social setting.

"Take the girdle for example," Miss Reed said, "Its importance can never be underestimated. Long ago, in the Victorian era, there was a word that was in most any refined lady's vocabulary, corsets. They were a must for any lady's attire, underneath their clothing and serving a most valiant purpose, stealing inches away from the waistline of many a lady, young and old. They were the heroes and enemies all rolled into one, somewhat like a multiple personality. One moment, a lady would be basking in the glory of compliments regarding her hourglass appearance, but without warning, she might swoon, hopefully landing on a fainting couch in close proximity, depleted of the oxygen that had been squeezed right out of her body." Cynda looked as if she might swoon as Miss Reed described the scene. It did not go without notice either. Score for Cynda.

Miss Reed continued, "Those were the days that no lady in this day and age would even consider living, much less visit in a nightmare," she said raising her eyebrows as she dipped her pointy chin toward her chest, looking at Cynda for agreement. Cynda played her part well as she shook her head as in utter disbelief.

Miss Reed continued her drama as if she were performing for the arts, "As time went on, corsets were modernized, but still quaint as they evolved into girdles, not quite as restricting, but nevertheless just as uncomfortable. Then garter belts and hose came into the picture. Women felt the power of liberation from the constricting apparatus of girdles and felt the freedom to finally breathe underneath their dresses. Alas, now pantyhose have made their debut, a welcome sign of the times, hot as they are in the summertime."

Miss Reed, still enjoying her own superior knowledge and Cynda's expression that indicated that she was mesmerized by the wealth of information, seized the opportunity to continue with her dissertation. "I have lived through the girdle era and owned a couple. I still like my girdle," she proclaimed. Cynda quietly wondered if Miss Reed wore a girdle today, and if so, the reason of her grayish pallor could readily be explained. What could not be explained in her mind was 'why' she would need one as thin as she was.

"And that brings us to one of the most important subjects at hand," Miss Reed finally said as she took a deep breath.

"Slips," she proclaimed, "Slips have long been an item in the female population's wardrobe. Even tiny baby girls wear slips underneath finely made dresses. Growing up, crinolines, fancy slips fashioned with layers of stiffened material, most often tulle, were welcomed by me and other little girls alike. They made our dresses full and fanciful, but again, the beautiful appearance had a price. The stiffened materials, more often than not, scratched the skin, making them uncomfortable. But we wore the slips because any other idea was simply not to be entertained, at least not for a very long time. Now slips are made of nylon –hot sticky nylon, clinging to the backs of the thigh area in summer heat. As a middle-aged woman, I find that slips are a must. A dress just does not fit right without a slip."

Cynda could not disagree more. Memories of the hated crinolines and now slips, items that she was sure would someday be reviled by the female gender, caused her to pause. As Miss Reed continued on with her dissertation of the importance of undergarments and of the qualities of a good slip, Cynda had repressed a smile as her thoughts settled on the situation she had recently found herself in.

Cynda's mind wandered to a recent incident in which she had chosen not to wear her slip to the corner market. She was tired of the nylon that stuck to her backside from the heat and the sweat that trickled down her legs. The long peasant style skirt was made of a fabric color and construction that did not allow transparency; her reasoning not to wear a slip.

Inside the market, she had bent over the drink box that was big enough to hold a human body. The thought crossed her mind to dive in. With her upper torso suspended into its compartment to retrieve a cold drink, she stopped mid-stream. Someone had tapped her on the shoulder.   There was no familiarity in the voice that said, "Excuse me. Ugh, your skirt!"

Suddenly, it came to her as crystal clear as Aunt Sally's fine glassware; her backside from the waist down was completely bared, exposing the only shield from the outside world, her panties. She unwittingly had tucked the hem into her underwear waistband.   Her world at that moment was filled with nothing, but males - mainly construction workers on their way to work.

Cynda pivoted her body with her head held high, the words ringing in her ears, "your skirt".   She then had her back to the drink box. Looking at her audience with a stone cold face, she performed the magical trick of pulling the bottom of her skirt from the waistband.   She wanted desperately to admonish them and quote her Aunt Sally, "Don't look at me like I have two heads" she would say. Instead she took the few steps to reach the counter to make her purchase with an air of poise and determination. She did not remember if she was courteous and generous enough to "thank" the man for his warning.

Cynda exited the building in a state of disarray, surely causing undisputable comic relief. Her shame was short lived because when she reached her safe haven, Aunt Sally's car, she realized that with one turn of the switch, she could put the car in reverse and drive away. She sat for just a few moments, laughing at herself and how that unknown man had become a hero, saving her from further embarrassment.   How had she so easily abandoned her friend, the slip, with its heroic attributes that could have saved her face or more appropriately, her rear?

Miss Reed might just be right, Cynda thought as she willed herself to pay attention to the continued litany of the value of the slip. She appeared to be fully engaged and began to turn her attention in earnest to what Miss Reed was saying.

"Now Cynda, our lingerie is to be handled with the care of a newborn baby. It is not in the same category as the five and dime and it deserves to be cherished!" Therefore, when we make a sale, we wrap it delicately in tissue paper and place it in a box."

As Miss Reed made this statement, she took a slip from a drawer and carefully laid it on the sales counter. Taking a piece of tissue paper, she demonstrated how to package a slip.

Cynda won the day with the simple test at hand. Miss Reed implored Cynda to re-package the slip in the same fashion, watching her vigilantly, arching her brows somewhat in disbelief, as her student repeated the exercise in great detail and perfection.

"Cynda, I believe you have yourself a job." Miss Reed declared as she put her hands on her shirtwaist dress that cinched her figure to a perfect hourglass.

Just as Miss Reed has made her declaration, Clive stopped in mid-stride as he approached the two of them, hesitating to enter the realm of the land of feminine mystery. He could not keep the grin from his face as he had just learned that he too had been hired for the summer as a courtesy clerk. The title sounded really important to Clive and he would take great pride in providing services to the customers, taking their packages for them to their cars. He could already hear the jingle of coins in his pockets as he knew that the tips could be quite generous.

Miss Reed dismissed Cynda with a nod of approval as Clive approached.

"Hi, Cynda!"

"Hello Clive. Don't worry, I am ready to leave now," she replied as she strode toward him, knowing how uncomfortable he would be entering the lingerie department. Her soft spot for Clive had grown over the years and she would avoid any embarrassment for him at all costs. He was, after all, her best friend.

It was written all over Clive's face and she knew he had some good news to share. She kept her own good news to herself as she quietly listened to him describe his new job.

"Cynda," he said breathlessly, "I got the job as courtesy clerk. There will be two of us, but we will rotate hours. You see, I will be assisting some really important people with their packages and you know what that means! I will be looking for some hefty tips. I might even get a chance to be recommended to be a doorman sometime. Now that would be sweet!"

"Well," Cynda said. "I will be working under the close supervision of the prudish Miss Reed assisting ladies with their selections of lingerie. She already likes the way I package slips and I am certain that I can win her over to allow me to train as a cashier."

Clive ran his fingers through his hair as he surveyed Cynda's demeanor. Cynda would be a great employee. She would take ownership in her duties and in his short observance of Miss Reed; it might not be so pretty if there was a bit of competition for sales. Cynda would be relentless in her perfection to do a great job and a force to be reckoned with in the *Rich's* lingerie department.

Avoiding the cashier topic, Clive diverted the conversation to their trip back home on the bus. Cynda's mother would be getting off from work in just a few minutes and they would be heading back to the suburbs.

"Think your mom will want to go down to *McCrory's* for a grilled cheese? I am really hungry."

"Sure, she should be ready to get off pretty soon. Let's go down the escalator to the shoe department."

"Cynda, did you ever believe that we could both be working at *Rich's*?"

"Of course, Clive, don't you have any faith in yourself?" Cynda said thoughtfully as she pondered her own confidence.

"Well, sure Cynda, but the two of us? It's pretty neat that both of us, being friends and all like that, well, that we both could land a job at the same place and be able to ride the bus together to work."

Cynda felt that same creepy feeling that she sometimes felt from Clive, as if there could be something more in this thing they called friendship. It certainly was not from her perspective, as Clive was the brother she had never had and that would always be his role, as far as she was concerned. The looks he gave her sometimes made her wonder how long their relationship could stay platonic as she feared his reluctance to be seriously interested in any one girl, a ploy to someday win her over. She would just not think of their friendship in that way. Clive was her rock and she did not want anything to stand in the way of their relationship. No complications.

"Oh my goodness, Cynda! How did you stand to work for that old bat? Do you mean to tell me that you were willing to work for someone that rigid? I just could not do it. I just could not do it," Marcy repeated upon hearing Cynda's description of Miss Reed.

"Simple. The idea of working for *Rich's* was a dream to me. I wanted to feel important. I really liked my job and I felt like the customers liked me. You know those old dyed in the wool ladies from around Atlanta would never consider buying their lingerie anywhere but *Rich's*. In fact, the delicate wrapping we used to put their purchases in their boxes was special – the tissue was as transparent as some of the lingerie itself. Even the wardrobes that held the peignoirs were made of solid mahogany and locked! Can you believe that one? I had to get permission to remove the key and open the doors," Cynda confided her importance.

"Wow! I guess I missed out on living through the girdle era. Talk about taking one's job seriously; that woman should have been working as a curator in a lingerie museum. The thought of her glorifying slips is beyond words. And you, baring your backside at a gas station? That must have been a sight to see," Suzanne hooted.

Before Cynda could respond, Marcy piped in and said, "So I was right. I thought all along that Clive had a thing for you. It was so obvious to see, even as young as I was, I could sense it in the way he looked at you. Poor Clive, he never had a chance and neither did I, with him that is."

Cynda was beginning to relish unlocking those memories that weren't so difficult after all, at least those younger years before her real trials and tribulations.

"Don't feel sorry for Clive. He deserved better than me. I was too much in love with the excitement of a new world, outside of the school room. Atlanta is a big city and I wanted to be a part of it. Working in *Rich's* was not enough. It sparked my appetite for the social scene of the big city. I met Brock and I was smitten. Clive tried to warn me. And we all know how that turned out."

Marcy and Suzanne exchanged knowing looks. They had been apprised of a tidbit of information that led up to their sister's first marriage, but they wanted to know more. After all, they had been too young to pay attention to her courtship with Brock. They both had wondered how Brock had met and romanced their older sister into marrying him so young. They knew he was suave and charming, still today. They also knew their sister had apparently fallen out of love with him.

Chapter 21

The weekend came and went with no other revelations from Cynda. On Sunday afternoon after lunch, the sisters loaded the *Hug Bug* with the few belongings that Cynda was taking back home with her. The three climbed into the car, but the mood was not nearly as lighthearted as it had been the previous Friday. Marcy had offered to drive her SUV, but Cynda declined, saying that she needed some hugs. The convertible top was up because a light rain had settled in.

The short drive back to Cynda's home was filled with idle chatter about the weather. When they arrived there, Dane hurried out to the Bug and greeted his wife with genuine adoration. The look on his face was obvious. He had really missed her. She returned Dane's affection in likewise fashion.

Marcy and Suzanne did not go into the house but promised to return for a visit on Tuesday. They wanted Cynda to have a chance to acclimate herself back to her own surroundings without their interruption, a day to herself.

Dane took Cynda's bags into her room. He noticed a pained look on her face and became concerned.

"Are you alright?" Dane said.

"I am fine, just a little bit tired. Will you forgive me if take a nap?" Cynda said, her energy waning.

Dane and Cynda had both been warned of the tremendous strain that chemo puts on the body. The days prior to the arrival of Cynda's sisters had been dicey as far as her energy level had been concerned. What amazed her though was it had not seemed to be an issue over the weekend. She had not pushed herself too much physically, but she had kept up with her sisters fairly well.

"Cynda, rest as much as you wish. You know that I am just a tinkle away," he said as he picked up the bell on the bedside table and gave it a ring. She smiled as he put it to rest back in its place and gave him a tender touch on the back of his hand.

"I'll let you know if I need anything. I hope you weren't too lonesome without me. I really appreciated your phone calls while I was gone,"

"You are my everything," he replied.

"And you are mine," she said without reservation.

Those practiced sentences were their trademark and had been for years. They came as natural as a drink of water. Now, Cynda could not help but wonder how deeply her husband really felt about her. Had she disappointed and disillusioned him with her unsolicited cancer?

Dane left the room and Cynda decided to unpack the suitcases before she lay down. The juicer and some of her cosmetics had been left in the care of her sisters. She made a mental note to pack some of her own towels when she returned the next weekend.

When Cynda was almost through unpacking, she extracted the healing oils from the zipped compartment of one of her bags. She placed them in the drawer out of sight. She had not told Dane about the oils.

When Cynda had met Dane many years ago, he made no secret to her that he was not a religious man. He was a believer in God but had no qualms about his aversion to church. His grandfather had been a Baptist minister and church had been a big part of his life growing up, so much so that he had rebelled against attending in his adult life.

Lydia Brooks had made sure of one thing. Her girls were raised in the Methodist Church in their community. It had been a big part of their lives. Cynda had raised her own daughter in the church and had always felt grounded in her religion.

It had been easy to stop going to church when she had met Dane. He had made it too easy. There were always big plans to fulfill on the weekend. Still, she had always felt the pull to be in God's house, and her personal relationship with Him had been kept private from Dane. She had not wanted to compromise their relationship by pushing religion down his throat. After all, had that not been what had turned him away from God in the beginning?

Cynda also had no idea what he would think about the healing oils. She had used them every day since her sisters had left them. She had also kept them under wraps while she was there with her sisters over the weekend. It would be her secret. The pull of slumber enveloped not only her body but also her mind. It was a grateful submission. When she woke, she felt sated and in a half dreaming state. She wanted to rebel against the memories that were surfacing but found it hard to escape them. Her thoughts returned to those sacred and life altering days of young love that had been swirling in her mind back on *Tybee* Island.

Cynda had not meant for it to happen. It certainly was beyond her control. She suddenly found herself in a world that she could not fathom, a world that ruled her thoughts and every move. Nothing could have prepared her for the giddy feeling that consumed her body and soul. She had fallen in love for the first time in her life and she was convinced it would be the last; after all, wasn't that what fairytales were made of, everlasting love?

Not only did Cynda find what she thought was a perfect summer job, she also found much, much more. It was her second day at work and she had just folded all of the slips to perfection and placed them in their designated drawers. On more than one occasion that morning, she had seen Miss Reed's eagle eye inspecting her handiwork. It was a task that she found to be discouraging as the slippery fabric had a mind of its own. Her frustration grew as she was determined to finish her task before her ten o'clock break. Clive would be meeting her for a quick soda in the breakroom and she looked forward to her respite.

Finishing the task at hand, she eyed the clock to be certain that she had accomplished her goal. She silently patted herself on the back as the second hand on the clock clipped away the seconds and her ticket to freedom. Not only did Cynda put herself into strict time management as a part of her perfectionism, but she also knew that Miss Reed was a willing partner in her need for success. The spinster would be watching the clock as well and would also be watching when Cynda returned from her break.

Cynda left her post and walked around the corner to find her way to the escalator to the second floor, looking for her redheaded companion to appear, who now stood six foot four. But someone else caught her attention and her eyes were fixated on the descending escalator as it carried the most beautiful man she had ever seen. He was tall and dark and his blue eyes pierced her heart from across the store. If they had been daggers, she would have be dead.

William Broderick Franklin, III felt Cynda's state and kept his eyes fixated on her, as he too was captivated by a pair of piercing green eyes and the most beautiful auburn hair he had ever seen. Cynda was frozen in her tracks and could not force herself to move, standing there as if her body had a mind of its own. She could not will it to even take a single step.

The escalator whisked the apparition to the bottom in hardly as much as four or five seconds, but to Cynda it was an eternity. She was sure the man had to be a ghost, for surely, no mortal could appear to be so handsome. The apparition seemingly floated over to her with his hands in his pockets and a smile that bared a perfect set of white teeth. It seemed to be contagious as she began to smile accordingly.

"Hello," he said.

"I am William Broderick Franklin, III. My friends call me Brock. It is a pleasure to meet you, Miss Brooks."

Cynda turned a shade of red and fumbled to find her name tag as she felt a bit of courage when she touched the silver shiny badge that proclaimed that she was an employee of *Rich's*. She eyed his badge that was shiny likewise, but its color was gold. She knew immediately that it meant he was her superior.

"Pleased to meet you, sir," Cynda replied.

Brock gave a toothy grin and threw his head back to burst into laughter. She suddenly became agitated at him and very defensive in her reply.

"That is no way to treat a lady, sir!" she almost shouted as she took a step back from his girth. Clive may be six foot four she thought, but this man was certainly as tall or perhaps taller.

"Please forgive me Miss Brooks; I mean no harm. I have just never been called sir before, and not from the likes of someone as beautiful as you. I'll take it as a compliment, but I much prefer Brock."

"Well, Mr. William Broderick Franklin, I don't know you well enough to call you anything, and for that matter, I am your subordinate. Shall we just shake hands and be on our way?" she said trying to hide her nervousness.

Cynda knew full well she was dying to know where in the store he worked and every detail about him. She was not about to give him any hint of the curiosity that was about to overtake her. She was finding it so hard to breathe, but relief was on the way in the form of a red headed bulk of a man.

Just at that moment Clive appeared out of nowhere and approached the two of them. He had a look of concern that showed on his face and she could feel his possessiveness surrounding the three of them. Suddenly the electricity in the air was almost audible.

123

"Hello, my name is Brock," the words from the man who now stood head to head with the arrival and extended his hand to Clive Fincher.

Clive returned the handshake in a like manner, making sure that his grip was well received as he shook the other man's hand vigorously.

"You must work in customer service," Clive observed as he released Brock's hand, eyeing his name badge.

"Well, you could say that. It's my job to see that customers are happy. I have been designated to walk around the store to troubleshoot problems, looking for anyone unhappy with their service or needing extra attention. It's a hobby of mine, this business of being an ambassador, building relationships and trust. I am working on my business degree. This is my fourth summer here, so I have been around the block a time or two," Brock said as he suddenly wondered why he was qualifying himself to these two obvious teenagers. He decided to display a more superior tactic with them as both seemed to expect nothing less from him.

"I must be about my business here as I am sure that you both must soon be getting back to your respective positions," Brock said. "It has been a pleasure to meet the two of you and I am sure that I will be seeing you both around," he said.

As a second thought, Brock asked them in his southern drawl, "What department do y'all work in?"

Clive was quick to give his answer, "Well, I work as a courtesy clerk and handle packages for our customers."

Cynda was reluctant to answer as she suddenly felt embarrassed by her position in the Lingerie Department. The color in her face was rising to a soft pink as she said, "I work with Miss Reed assisting ladies with foundations." She was sure that he knew the infamous Miss Reed as everyone surely did who worked at *Rich's*.

Brock hid the smug smile he had on his face as he imagined "Miss Brooks" cowering under the strict demeanor of her superior. It made him wonder what kind of girl could really be hiding under those lovely auburn locks. He suspected that she did not fit the bill as prudish. With a last thought, he asked, "By the way, Miss Brooks, what is your given name?"

Cynda replied in like fashion as he had enunciated his entire given name as if he were the king of England, "Lucinda Ophelia Brooks, but my friends call me Cynda."

"Boy, that's a mouthful," Brock said as he continued with his assessment of her declaration, "But why Cynda? I like it. It seems a bit more graceful than the more common nickname Lucy."

That statement struck a chord with Cynda and she found it hard to respond in a pleasant manner. She might not have liked for anyone to call her Lucy, but it was her daddy's pet name for her and she would not have anyone think that the name Lucy was anything less than gracious. She found herself tempering her words as she said in a somewhat condescending manner, "I changed my nickname from Lucy to Cynda. It was my choice. No one calls me Lucy anymore, at least not since my daddy died."

What had she just said? It had been years since Cynda had allowed even a hint of emotion to enter into any conversation, much less to a total stranger. What was she thinking? She looked at Clive with pleading and he read her emotions clearly.

"Let's get that Coke®, Cynda," Clive said as he gently guided her by the arm toward the escalator to the second floor.

Cynda looked over her shoulder to the mere mortal man who had quietly chipped away at her resolve to give her heart to no man. She did not realize until too late as she once again was pierced by the blue eyes. The daggers had found their unwilling target and pierced her heart. From that moment forward, she was changed. Her very being ceased to exist, and she held her breath as she caught another glimpse of William Broderick Franklin. She did not realize her endeavors were trumped as Brock superseded her efforts as he could not get the green eyed innocent out of his mind. He was there at her every turn, unbeknown to her.

There was another infatuated soul who did not miss the looks that both Brock and Cynda tried so hard to hide. Clive immediately took a disliking to Brock, and the uneasy feeling he had when he was around him was far more intuitive than Cynda would ever realize, at least not for many years to come.

Chapter 22

Marcy and Suzanne had a lazy Monday. Both of them got caught up on some of their correspondence. They were independently spending their day without their sister.

Suzanne found Marcy outside lounging in the sun. Her sunglasses hid her eyes and she was void of any expression. Maybe she was asleep. Suzanne went over and poured some of her bottle of water onto Marcy's stomach. She had on a tankini, but when in private she pulled it up and tucked it up just under her breasts. Since turning fifty, she had not felt it appropriate to show her midriff. It did not matter that she still had a pretty good figure. Marcy flinched and raised her right leg in reaction and began to chastise her sister.

"Okay little sis, there are other ways to get my attention. You can start by saying, 'Hello' and then waiting for a reply. What if I had been asleep?"

"Sorry," Suzanne said, ignoring her breach in manners.

"I just got off the phone with Audrey. I gave her an update on her mother and filled her in on our plan to get Cynda out of the house. Just so you know, I did not tell her that we have been trying to get closer to her by finding out more about her life; the one we never were a part of all of those years. Neither did I tell her about the healing oils. Too much information and I am not sure how she would feel about the oils anyway."

"So, how did the conversation end?" Marcy said.

"That is why I was in such a hurry to talk to you. When Audrey found out that her mother was spending the weekends with us here at the cottage, she wanted to come down and see her here. You know how she feels about Dane. There has never been any love lost for him. I get that, but that does not mean I agree."

"What did you tell her?" Marcy exclaimed as Suzanne now had her full attention over the dilemma.

"Of course, I beat around the bush. I told her that her mother was still very weak and needed to build her strength and that we felt bringing her out here would help. She agreed that she should not come until Cynda is stronger, but she is adamant that she come down for a week, maybe staying through two weekends," Suzanne indicated with exasperation.

"We can't just tell her 'no'. She would be hurt and I could never forgive myself if something happens, and we kept her from making peace with her mother," Suzanne continued.

"I know that it is painful for her to swallow her pride, but there comes a time when a person needs to grow up. Audrey needs to grow up," Marcy said emphatically.

"I know! I know! You also know that I have always had a soft spot for that girl. I was only fourteen when she was born. She has always been like a little sister to me."

At that moment, Suzanne looked over at her sister and said, "And I don't call her little sister. I don't want to get under her skin the way you do mine," she said as she turned her mouth down in a fake pout.

"What I did tell her was that she would have to wait until after this weekend. I told her that we would discuss it and get back with her soon. She told me that she needed to know rather quickly, so she could arrange to get off from work."

"There is one thing for sure," Marcy said, "Cynda will be thrilled to see her, but she has got to come around to accepting the choices Audrey has made in life. She can't live Audrey's life for her. Maybe we can accomplish that with subliminal messaging over the next few weeks."

Suzanne agreed with her sister; both knew they had their work cut out for them.

Chapter 23

Cynda and Dane had an uneventful week. Cynda could not help but turn her thoughts to the upcoming weekend with her sisters. They began their visits on Tuesday as planned, some days bringing in take-out and sharing with her. But the carefree hours the sisters spent the previous weekend could not compare to time spent at the pink stucco.

Dane kept the kitchen stocked with groceries and had continued his routine of cooking breakfast. He had his specialty meals that he prepared and for that Cynda was thankful. She was an excellent cook, but the kitchen had lost its charm for her at least for now. Maybe she would get her desire back to spend more time there. Maybe.

The days flew by quickly and soon it was the weekend again. On Friday afternoon, Marcy and Suzanne drove up in the SUV. Cynda had been waiting anxiously, even pacing a bit, trying not to let Dane see her eagerness. This intrusion on their existence had been an unexpected turn of events for the summer; for her, refreshing.

Cynda gave Dane a light kiss and a lingering hug as she headed for the SUV. This time she only had a small overnight bag that was easy for her to manage. She tried not to hide her disappointment as she had looked forward to riding in the *Hug Bug*. She had waited on that particular hug all week. Oh well. She was certain there would be a remedy to that as she would insist on a ride in the famed car soon.

It was not long before the three sisters arrived at the cottage and to freedom. They departed the SUV and made their way to the comfort of coolness in the humble abode. But, not before Cynda took an appraising look at the lonely little *Hug Bug* that seemed to wink at her as she paused her step on the walkway and touched the wreath with reverence as she passed the car.

Cynda noticed the outside of the cottage was much like the inside. It had eluded her notice on her past visits. It was well past the need for refurbishing. The cinder block siding painted white with yellow shutters and door might be charming, if a coat of fresh paint was applied. There was no other sign of color except for some pink oleander swaying in the ocean breeze. She decided that her assessment of the cottage exterior was unimportant as she made her way inside.

Cynda felt a sense of ownership as she entered the room with the dancing flamingo pillows. She had missed them and their novelty. It did not take her long to unpack her bag. She had left her clothes there and this time she added a few pieces of jewelry and a couple of outfits. When she stepped back into the living area, her sisters were busy in the kitchen preparing a salad for dinner.

"That looks like a mean salad. What are you serving with it?" she said.

"Oh, we thought we might grill a steak or some flounder. We have both. What do you think?" Marcy said as she shoved the lettuce core into the trash can.

"Sounds good to me. I could stir up some crab cakes if you girls would like," Cynda said to express her desire to be included.

"Are you sure you feel up to it?" Suzanne said.

"Of course, Suzanne, I am not an invalid, at least not yet!" Cynda said sharply.

"I didn't mean to imply that you were. It's just that we invited you here to relax and have fun, to rest." Suzanne said quietly.

Cynda did not miss the hurt in her sister's eyes and she was quick to rescue her feelings.

"I am sorry. It's been a tough week. Dane has been in the kitchen all week and I have just let him take over.

I've lost my desire. It just seems to feel right for me to be helping you girls. I want to be needed," she said with pleading in her eyes.

Marcy stepped back into the conversation and said, "Absolutely. I would kill for some of your crab cakes. I think that is an excellent idea. I just need to go down to the fish market and pick up some fresh crab. Make a list and I will get what you need."

"I have a better idea," Cynda said. "Let's all go. Even better let's ride in the Bug with the top down."

Within a few minutes, the three sisters were hopping in the aqua blue ride. Suzanne had taken the top down before they got in. The three were packed in the compact car like the sardines they enjoyed mimicking. Cynda rode in the back seat with her arms outstretched and holding on side to side.

The ride was short and sweet, but long enough for Cynda to surrender to the breeze and the lyrics of "Hang on Sloopy" blaring through the tiny radio. She was hanging on for dear life, literally, and decided in that moment she was just beginning to live.

The sisters unloaded the Bug and Cynda began to assemble her ingredients for the crab cakes.

"Oh no!" Cynda said as she surveyed the ingredients on the counter.

"What's wrong?" Suzanne said.

"We forgot to get onions."

"Not a problem," Suzanne replied, "Just look over there in the pantry.

Cynda crossed the room and opened the tiny door of the pantry and shut it quickly, letting out a shriek.

"On my goodness, what is wrong?" Suzanne raised her voice in alarm, hoping her sister had not seen a mouse. She despised the little varmints and would move out immediately if there was one in the pantry of all places.

"You didn't!" Cynda said as she opened the pantry again with both of her sisters creeping up behind her to take a look.

"What do mean?"

"There." Cynda said as she pointed.

Hanging on one of the shelves was an aluminum hanger with two clips on it. Fastened to the clips was the waistline of a pair of pantyhose. Cynda recognized that syrupy color as Cinnamon Toast. She remembered it from her days in *Rich's*. Dangling from the waist, the two legs were still attached and filled with famous *Vidalia Onions* from Vidalia, Georgia. Each onion was separated with knotting to keep them from touching one another.

"I haven't seen those stored in that fashion since Mama bought them in twenty-five pound bags, then separated them so they would not touch. I think they lasted for months." Cynda said, and then suddenly said, "I sure miss going to Luxomni when the onions came in season. Mama always had me a supply at her house when I visited to bring back down here," she continued quietly.

"Here are the scissors," Marcy said as she handed them to Cynda to release one of the onions from its trappings.

Suzanne started singing "Please Release Me, Let Me Go", once again lightening the mood with her comical use of song lyrics. Cynda deftly snipped the onion from its snare being careful not to disturb the adjoining one. Her mood had lightened. She paid homage to the prized onion as she carefully placed it on the counter. Marcy fully expected her to give last rites before she began to dice it for her crab cakes.

"I didn't know you felt so strongly about *Vidalia Onions*," Marcy said.

"Me either," Cynda said as she began to slice and dice them, "Not until I saw them trapped in those cinnamon toast legs, and thought about Mama and her allegiance to them."

"Cinnamon toast, where did you come up with that name?"

"Ain't that the tackiest color you have ever heard for pantyhose?" Cynda said using her Southern lingo for emphasis. She only used it for special occasions!

"And worse than that, it was the color I wore back in the day," Cynda continued laughingly, "In fact, it was the one recommended by the illustrious Miss Reed. I don't think she could have stood it, if she knew that pantyhose were being used to stockpile onions. Talk about knobby knees! Wait! I meant the onions, truly I did," Cynda said.

It was too late. That last remark was enough to start a chain reaction of laughter. It was just what they all needed, Suzanne thought as she held her sides. Cynda collapsed on the stool to regain her composure.

After a satisfying meal of Cynda's divine crab cakes and a delicious salad, the sisters settled in for a glass of wine in their pajamas in the decidedly unfashionable, but cozy living area. The conversation evolved into Cynda's expertise in the kitchen, as both sisters had always admired her cooking prowess.

"I don't get it," Suzanne said.

"I have no memory of Mama ever letting you in the kitchen before you married. How did you learn to cook so well, Cynda?"

"Oh, you just missed that part of our growing up. While Mama was working, I was experimenting some in the kitchen before she got home. You were just too busy being a little girl as you should have been," Cynda said.

"Well, I remember you burning a few things," Marcy interjected.

"I can't deny that. I remember one time I burned one of Mama's pots so bad that I had to throw it away. It took all afternoon to get that smell out of the house. I used a full can of Lysol®. I think she was so tired when she got home, she never even smelled the odor," Cynda admitted.

"I must admit the truth. There is one thing that my ex mother-in-law can do and that is cook, at least some things. The things that she cooked, she cooked very well and believe it or not, she taught me. I think it was her way of elevating my status in 'polite society' if she could broadcast my ability to cook gourmet dishes to her friends at the garden club. As if being a gourmet cook could do such a thing! I suppose she rationalized it so in her delusional mind."

"I certainly did not need her input into the finer things. I had my own ideas of how to decorate mine and Brock's home. I was no stranger to the Home Department at *Rich's*. When I was on break, I would sometimes go there and dream. While Brock and I were working there that first summer we met, he discovered that I was hanging out in the home department. He would slip up and scare me half to death. I would be lost in my dreaming state of how I would decorate my own home."

"Sounds romantic to me," Suzanne said.

"Yeah, I guess it was back then," Cynda said thoughtfully.

Cynda then began her story where she had left off the weekend before. She recanted in detail the first time she had laid eyes on Brock and the jolt of electricity that had rendered her almost speechless. She spared no details of how she fell head over heels for him. She also shared that her special bond with Clive was almost broken. Clive had been intuitive and she had been blind, she told them. It was a purging of her soul and a release of the overwhelming affection that she had not shared about her lost love, Brock.

The first summer that Cynda worked at *Rich's*, the weeks passed quicker than she could have imagined, and the days of her part-time job quickly drew to a close. Brock was determined to see her in the store every chance he got, and it did not take long for her to realize that he was just as infatuated with her as she was with him. Just an infatuation, she told herself. It had to be. She knew full well that her mother would not approve of her dating someone a full five years older than she, someone whom she discovered was almost through with college and about to attend law school. It was too much for Cynda to digest, but she reveled in the weekly flirtations. Flirtations. She was convinced they amounted to nothing. She was certain that when Brock went back to school, she would be an afterthought. In the meantime, it was fun and exciting.

Brock's visits to the Lingerie Department turned into quite a game. She would find Brock in the most bizarre places. Once he was hiding behind a mannequin garbed in a full peignoir set of pink ruffles. She could not stop laughing when the dummy went tumbling forward to land at Miss Reed's feet. He somehow explained his presence, and the sanctimonious Miss Reed acted as flustered as a schoolgirl. It was his mission to be as discreet as possible, but this time he had risked her wrath and won.

On one particular day, Miss Reed walked up behind Brock and nearly scared him witless. He quickly turned on the charm to her satisfaction by discussing the attributes of that same pink peignoir set and how much he thought his mother would like it. He even hinted that he was saving his money to purchase it for his mother's birthday. Miss Reed bought his story hook, line and sinker, seeing dollar signs in her commission. It was all that Cynda could do not to burst into laughter. He smoothly left the scene with a wink to Cynda and a nod of complacency. She shortly found herself searching for him on morning break. When she met him at the breakroom door, she could not contain her laughter anymore.

Their laughter died down to a soft chuckle as Clive found them together, obviously in a secret pact with one another, one that he knew he could not enter. He had warned her about Brock.

"Cynda, you know very well that Brock is too old for you," Clive had told her after the first few days of his first meeting him. He doubted Brock's sincerity and felt he must alert her, before she got hurt. Never mind that he had begun to be possessive. It was for her own good, or so he told her time and time again.

"Mind your own business," she said in a matter of fact tone one day, and Clive knew that she meant the topic was not up for discussion any longer. No matter how close the two of them were, she had closed the door on that subject and he dared not to open it.

What Cynda did not realize was that her Mama sensed there was more to the relationship between her and Brock. She had seen his kind before, and she knew he would be trouble for her daughter. Women were drawn to him like a moth to a flame. Anyone who could win the affection of Miss Reed was to be admired, but that also sent up a red flag as far as Lydia Brooks was concerned. She thought his innocent flirtations could certainly lead to more than Cynda could handle, so her mother kept her distance, but cautioned Cynda to never let her guard down.

It was the last day before Brock was supposed to go back to school at the University of Georgia. Fortunately for Cynda, she was scheduled to work. She dreaded the day as it was the end to what had been an exciting cat and mouse game. She would not be seeing Brock anymore. Just prior to her break, Miss Reed was called to the customer service office. Cynda was in charge of the department while she was gone. Suddenly, Brock appeared in the corner over by the dressing room. He signaled for her to come over, placing a finger across his lips. There was not a customer anywhere around, so she followed his direction.

When Cynda reached Brock, he grabbed her around the waist and pulled her into the dressing room closing the door behind him. Before she could say a word, he pressed his lips against hers with a kiss that seared her own and branded her body and soul. He held her that way for at least an eternity in her mind, before he let her go, breathless and limp. She had never been kissed before and she quickly took note of all of the thoughts racing through her mind. Not only had she kissed the man of her dreams and was at a loss for words, but maybe she might lose her job.

Cynda whispered to him frantically, "Do you realize what you're doing? If we get caught, we will both be fired and I will never be able to get a retail job again!"

Brock just looked at her and kissed her a second time, this time not as long and hard. It was short and sweet, like the wings of a butterfly, but its effect was just as powerful.

"Yes, I know what I am doing and it has been far too long in coming," he purred to her. "You know that you have wanted this as much as I have Cynda, so why not enjoy our last day together with just a little kiss to remember each other by?"

"But....but, I can't do this," she continued. "Miss Reed will be back any moment, and if I am not at the counter, I am doomed."

Brock said confidently, "She won't be back anytime soon. I guarantee you that. I had her called to the office about a dissatisfied customer. Lucky for us."

Cynda still felt uncomfortable and demanded to leave the dressing room, "I want to leave before someone else comes into the department."

Brock opened the door and surveyed the area to make sure the coast was clear. He signaled for her to leave the room. He kissed her once more on the cheek as she crept out of the tiny room. He followed. They found themselves standing next to the selection of slips that lay in the compartments. Ones like Cynda had packaged so perfectly to win her job for the summer. The summer that was filled with excitement and new experiences and most recently the sweetest experience she could ever know. She felt the hot sting of tears in her eyes, trying to hide their existence. She looked at Brock for one of the last times before he went away to school.

"Why did you do this to me William Broderick Franklin?" her heart cried as she said the words.

Sensing her anguish, Brock took her hands and said, "Until we meet again," and then he was gone, taking her heart with him.

Three hours later, when Cynda went to her locker to retrieve her belongings, she found a note from Brock that read:

Cynda, you have captured my imagination. Until we meet again. Brock.

"Until we meet again?" What is that supposed to mean?" she thought. She really wanted to hear, "I'll take you with me and we will live happily ever after," or something along that line.

Cynda had a dreamy look on her face as she recanted the very personal details of her love story. She looked at them wistfully before she continued. Marcy and Suzanne could not help but prod her for more information.

"It sounds so dreamy, especially then at your age," Suzanne said.

"Any age. I'd take a little of that sweetness any ole time," Marcy said in her most southern drawl.

Cynda gave them their money's worth with the dynamics of both her relationships with Brock and Clive.

Cynda's fun filled summer was over and what an experience. She muddled through the remaining days of her summer job without a thought of anything but Brock. On her last day of work, Miss Reed called her aside and asked if she would like to return during Christmas break. Her heart was screaming "no" as she could not imagine coming back to *Rich's* lingerie department without the appearances of Brock at the most inopportune times, his beautiful smile, and most of all his kiss. She could not bring herself to even look near the dressing room that had been the source of a revelation that even she could not have fathomed. She was in love and with someone she would never see again. The last man she had loved left her too and she had been determined in her resolve to allow no one new into her heart.

Cynda looked at Miss Reed and decided her answer would be yes. She would quietly suppress the pain of her new loss and would concentrate once again on what she could control. Cynda smiled and said, "Certainly, Miss Reed, it would be a pleasure to work for you during Christmas." Then it was over and she boarded the bus one last time with Clive in tow. At least, as long as she worked, she could sense Brock's presence. Her mother did not ask her any questions as she could sense the reluctance in Cynda to talk about her last day at work.

Clive was none too sad and especially glad that he and Cynda would be going back to school soon, back to their normal routine. Back to life without Brock; yes, this was going to be a great senior year for the two of them, of that he was sure. He was already eighteen and Cynda would be turning eighteen very soon. They were adults now and their senior year meant lots of good times. Clive's best friend would soon be sharing her confidences with him again, and he hoped much more. He hoped.

Cynda's eighteenth birthday came and went and was uneventful. She found herself fully involved in her classes and homework, yet there was a void. She went through the motions of living, but she realized that she wasn't really living. The hours after school were interminable. Cynda decided to do something that was beyond her realm of comfort. That is when she had decided to try out for cheerleading.

"Really, Cynda are you going to go through with this?" Clive said as he followed her up the sidewalk to her house.

"For once in your life, Clive, can you stop trying to be my daddy?" she replied.

The sting of her rejection felt like a pall had just descended over him; losing his step in midstream, he almost tripped. The revelation came to him as if someone had slapped him square in the face. He was no more to Cynda than just a friend and would never be, but he certainly was not her daddy. With quiet resolve he bit back the words that were on the tip of his tongue. Instead he replied, "You will make a great cheerleader."

Cynda did not miss the hurt in his eyes. She silently admonished herself and chose her next words very carefully before she responded to him.

"Clive you know that you have been my best friend through thick and thin. You have stood by me during my difficult days and I will always love you for that. I should not have compared your concern for me to anything but sincere friendship. You have kept all of my confidences and you know me better, perhaps even better than I know myself. I have shared everything with you," she declared knowing full well that her secret love for Brock was not a topic for discussion.

As soon as the words tumbled from her mouth, she felt a sense of guilt. How could she tell him how deeply she had been hurting and how lonely she felt? Not since her daddy had died had she felt complete and total helplessness. When she had made the decision to try out for cheerleading, it was to fill a void; after all she enjoyed football. She knew that she would have to become more social with the other girls on the squad, but shouldn't she start trying to be one of them now in her last year of school? She wouldn't have to give up her convictions of self-reliance and certainly not her best friend Clive.

Clive did not see it that way. She could read his expression and searched for words of reassurance.

"We will still have plenty of time to spend together, if I make the squad. Besides, I haven't made the squad yet. You know the vote is not just about a person's skills. It has a great deal to do with popularity. They sure do not advertise the fact that the prettiest girls always seem to make the squad, but somehow they do. I probably won't even make it, so stop worrying. Come on, let's eat some ice cream. I think Mama bought your favorite."

Clive paused for a moment before continuing on into the house. He knew full well that Cynda would make the team. When had she ever tried to do anything in her life without success? He remembered how she had won Miss Reed over with ease, not to mention Brock. He was right. Cynda made the squad.

Soon Clive's time with her became less and less. It was not that she shunned him; it was that the commitment was far more time consuming than she ever expected. Cynda practiced with a vengeance and screamed at the games with ferocity. She was determined to drive the demons of a lost love out of her mind and heart. Even with repeated urging from her new friends to date one of the guys, she resisted. They found it hard to understand and there was one who could not let a nagging feeling go.

Clive knew Cynda all too well. She seemed uncharacteristically happy and focused. He knew his chance of ever being any more to her than just a good friend was slim, but he could hope.

The days turned away from the autumn chill and moved full force into the approaching cold of winter. Christmas break was just around the corner and so was working at *Rich's*. Cynda wanted to hedge on her commitment, but she knew that her pledge to Miss Reed was as important as her word. She also knew that the memories of her last days with Brock had been suppressed, but would be fresh on her mind when she returned. All of her hard work to dismiss him from her mind would be in vain if she returned to her job. It was her cross to bear. There was one thing that she had to be thankful for when she returned. Clive would be returning with her. He had been contacted to resume his former position. Now that was one item on her agenda that she looked forward to doing, restoring their friendship. He had been there for her when her daddy had died and she was not going to let anything get in the way of their relationship. She was committed to rekindling their special friendship and purging herself of the guilt that hung in the balance.

The hour was getting late, but Cynda's sisters clung to her every word, terrified that she would close the door.

"Clive was the best," Marcy interrupted Cynda's story.

"Yes, and he was my rock, even though I know how deeply I disappointed him. I will always regret his obvious pain." She continued with her revelations.

Finally, the day came to return to *Rich's* and both Cynda and Clive boarded the bus. The feeling of solidarity with Clive was almost electric. Cynda had never felt the same about the holidays after her daddy had died, but today she could not dismiss the excitement as the bus traveled to their downtown destination. The air was crisp and it was hard not to get into the spirit of the holidays. As they approached the vibrant city life, she watched as people walked down the sidewalk with packages. Her eyes fixated on the *Rich's* Christmas tree that stood proudly atop the building and now in her vision as they approached the store. It rose in its austerity against the Atlanta skyline and for once, Cynda realized her love for the city had been born long ago.

Before her daddy had passed away, the yearly trek downtown on Thanksgiving night was a tradition. The lighting of the great tree on top of *Rich's* was paramount on that special day. She had forgotten how much she missed the ritual. It was going to be a great day at *Rich's* and it had begun on their ride into town on the bus. Cynda was sure of it. The crisp air carried a biting wind in its wings and it felt exhilarating.

After punching the clock for the first time since summer, Cynda found herself riding the escalator to the familiar surroundings that held a melancholy surrealism. She entered the hallowed walls of the Lingerie Department, eyeing the mahogany counter that shone from the tender loving care of Miss Reed's constant care. She polished the counter daily and the fruits of her labor were apparent.

Nothing has changed, Cynda observed. The counter remained the anchor of the department. She looked around to see the mirrored doors, knowing that when opened, the satin nightgowns and brassieres would be neatly folded. She saw the glass fronts on the drawers that held panties and garter belts and the crystal pulls that she had accessed many times.

Walking slowly around the department, Cynda found herself in the dressing area and suddenly felt her heart skip a beat and she took a deep breath. She quickly retreated from the area as the memories of Brock came flooding back to her, as if the kiss was only yesterday. She touched her mouth with the back of her hand, feeling a little queasy. Just as she was approaching the counter again, Miss Reed appeared out of nowhere and gave her a quick grin that looked as if it were etched out of a piece of stone.

"Well hello Cynda," she said without any real warmth, but with conviction in her voice she added, "It is great to have you here again. I sure hope you have not forgotten your touch. You know how much I admired the care you took with our foundations."

Suddenly, Miss Reed stopped still in her tracks. She surveyed Cynda's appearance looking at her as if she had metamorphosed into another being.

"Something is different about you. I can't put my finger on it right now, but I will. You have a different look about you, an air of confidence. Yes, that's it, confidence and maturity."

Cynda was not quite sure how to react. Yes, she had gained a great deal more of confidence. Her cheerleading stint was far more gratifying than she had imagined. Not only had she made some really good female friends, she had begun to form alliances with several of her male counterparts, even though she had refused to date anyone of them.

"Maybe it's my hair. It has grown and I have started rolling it on brush rollers and teasing it quite a bit on top and swirling it into a beehive. Actually, I have become pretty good at it. Mother gets me to style hers too," she said waiting to see how Miss Reed would react to her declaration, knowing how resistant she was to change. It was apparent in her dated hair style, which had been reported by other employees to be as old as the National Cash Register that remained in the department upon the spinster's request. She fancied that the cha ching actually gave Miss Reed a thrill every time she heard it, reminding her of the impending sale.

Miss Reed only looked at her quizzically and ignored the declaration. She began her morning ritual assessing the department and began to bark orders in her curt manner. Cynda turned at her command to dust the cases with a feather duster until their first customers arrived for the day.

Cynda did not allow the spinster to put a damper on her attitude. This was going to be a great day; how could it be otherwise? The excitement of the holidays was electric and the store decorations were like something out of a fairytale. She was glad to be a part of this great *Rich's* even for a few days. There was only one store that could compete and that was *Davison's* down the street. In her estimation, there was no competition. If there was one thing about her, Cynda had a fierce allegiance to any commitment she made, including her job.

It was true. Cynda had a definite air about her. She had walked through the store that morning with a new found confidence, holding her head high, and flashing a magnetic smile at the other employees. She could see out of the corner of her eye some of them whispering behind cupped hands. She did not think them rude, only curious in their appraisal of her. After all, her hairstyle alone was sure to be fodder for idle talk. The beehive was the rage and she wore it well. The auburn hair that swept across her brow only served to accentuate her green eyes.

Cynda was later walking toward the breakroom at her appointed time, once again to begin the ritual that she and Clive had begun in the summer. She rounded the corner and had the escalator in full view, somewhat distracted in her thoughts by a pair of piercing blue eyes, when she bumped right into someone. Feeling very agitated for the interruption, she looked up to find those haunting blue eyes staring down into hers. Was she looking at a ghost, she asked herself, but not before forgetting to breathe?

There was only one thing that kept her from running as far as her legs could take her from William Broderick Franklin. She realized too late that she had lost her balance and found herself in the untimely grasp of his large hands around both of her elbows. She tried to step back, but his grasp tightened, causing her demeanor to change from surprise to agitation. She continued in her efforts for his release, shaking her shoulders back and forth. She took a step back once she gained her balance.

Brock stretched his mouth into a lazy smile revealing his perfect white teeth, the ones that had intimately touched her own.

"Well, who do we have here?" he said and without giving her a chance to reply, he said, "Is this the same meek and mild girl who worked in the Lingerie Department last summer? Or is this a chameleon who has stolen the eyes of one that I have dreamed about every day since then?"

Cynda was trying desperately to regain her composure and at the same time, her anger was beginning to surface. She was finding it hard to contain herself as she stared back into his beautifully chiseled face, the one that had haunted her night and day. How dare he just appear into her life again? Had she not just spent the last three and a half months trying to erase any memory of him from her mind? And the note! She had convinced herself that he was just toying with her emotions.

At that moment she vowed that she would not respond to his shenanigans ever again. Shenanigans were the perfect word for his behavior. He had toyed with her heart and caused her to feel once more - to let her guard down. She would not allow him to do that to her again, under no circumstances. Clive was right. Brock had given him bad vibes and now she understood why. He was dangerous in his quest to win hearts and then calmly walk away as if he had won a tennis match.

Cynda tried to put the image of the note she had found months ago out of her mind as she searched for a response. Just then, Clive approached the two of them and her answer came easily, "This chameleon has a change to make. I am being summoned to the breakroom. See you around."

Before Brock had a chance to respond, Cynda turned on her heel and quickly made her move toward Clive and closed the gap between them. Clive gave Brock a cursory nod and grasped Cynda's elbow, the same one Brock had held just moments earlier. She could still feel his touch and was a bit perturbed with Clive for acting so possessively.

When Cynda reached the breakroom with Clive, she was battling to hide her mixed feelings of rage and pleasure of seeing Brock. She had not expected to ever see him again and certainly not under these circumstances. He should have been back at school. Why had he returned to *Rich's* to work during the break? She had never asked him exactly why he even worked at all. She had the impression that his parents were well off and who were footing the bill for his law school, were they not? It was expensive to go to college and the opportunity to extend schooling for a law degree even more so.

Cynda knew that college for her was not even in the realm of possibility. She could only hope to get her secretarial certificate and her sights were set on doing just that once she graduated. Her experience at *Rich's* would be a feather in her cap, as she hoped to work a retail job somewhere to help fund her endeavor. It was the least she could do to help her Mama she thought.

"Cynda, are you there," Clive said as he waved his hand back and forth in front of her face. Her expression was fixed as she stared out into space. Cynda returned her attention to Clive and put her thoughts aside to respond to him.

"How can you let him get to you that way?" Clive asked. "Is there something you have not told me?" he goaded her to answer.

"Of course not!" she said. "He just makes me so mad! You are right; he is all about himself and his good looks. I could care less about him; besides I was just shocked to see him here. I thought he was gone for good."

"Good looks?" Clive said. "So you think he is good looking. Now, I know the truth. You have been infatuated with him."

"Of course, his looks are undeniable."

"He has great teeth and nice eyes," she said not bothering to reveal her honest appraisal, "But that doesn't mean I am infatuated with him, not at all. You know that he is not my type. I have always stayed away from the likes of him and you know that Clive Fincher," she said emphasizing his entire name as she tried to convince him of her honesty.

Clive suspected there was more to her admonitions. He had known her far too long to believe there was not more information that she hesitated to disclose. Yes, there was something she had not told him and he would make it his business to find out. He would protect Cynda at all costs, even if it was from a broken heart. He would not have anyone take advantage of her. His commitment to their friendship was all encompassing, even at his own expense – especially if he could never have her for himself.

148

Brock

If Cynda had looked back, she would have seen Brock, frozen there for the few moments it took for the realization of rejection to take root in his brain. If she could have read his mind she would have realized a plan was developing. It was a new and exciting revelation for him as her rebuff spurred him on to more interesting thoughts.

It was true that Brock had his share of girls and had dated quite a few in his college career, but none too seriously. Now his college days were winding down and law school was looming on the horizon. He knew he had to be more serious in his studies and maybe, he thought, his choice of women. This green eyed minx presented a new kind of challenge for him. She had been receptive of his attentions and flirtations this past summer; yet there was a part of her that had remained aloof. He could sense it in her reluctance to kiss him on that last day they were together.

It did not go without his notice either that Cynda had changed. There was something different about her. She exuded a maturity in the way she held herself as she walked away, as if she owned the world. He vowed to find out what had changed her and he was curious to get to know this new woman better. Yes, that was it. She had become a woman in those few short months.

*Cynda was one that he would have to conquer and conquer he would. Maybe she would be worth the effort. When had he ever lost in his game of romancing? What difference did it make that she was five years younger than he? The sorority girls had begun to wear on his nerves, studying hard to get a degree, a M- R- S degree, he thought as he began his customary walk throughout the store. He smiled broadly at the customers, looking for any opportunity to spread the good will of **Rich's** .*

He planned to spread lots of good will this Christmas season in more ways than one. After all, wasn't that why he was hired?

The Christmas decorations and sounds of carols playing in the store suddenly became an elixir of sorts, one that Brock drank freely. He was sated and almost felt giddy as the green eyed chameleon that now occupied his thoughts was only an excuse away in the Lingerie Department. How convenient!

Cynda took a slow and deliberate swig of her wine and wondered if its potency was contributing to her loose lips. At that moment she did not care and continued to share her story.

When Cynda arrived at home that evening, she went directly to her room. There were three bedrooms in their modest brick home and she had been given her own room as soon as she had reached her teens. She flung herself across the pink chenille bedspread that her mother had saved to buy for her sixteenth birthday. The pink organza curtains were given to her last Christmas, replacing the white lace curtains that she had found so old fashioned. In a moment of anger, she had told her mother so, later regretting her outburst. Cynda knew her mother did the best that she could to give her and her sisters everything that she could afford.

Presently, the room offered her a comfortable and secure haven for her to ponder the circumstances of Brock's return. Had he been taunting her with the note that he had written her when he left last summer, assuming that she could not think of anyone else after that burning, searing kiss? Did he mean to brand her in a way that would make her only think of him as if he weren't just some summer fling? Well, he was wrong she told herself. All that he had done was to make her wish she had never met him. Her curiosity got the best of her.

Cynda opened her nightstand drawer to retrieve the note that she had secreted away from probing eyes. It was taped to the underside of the drawer. Rolling forward toward her grip on the drawer handle was the pill bottle that held the clay from her father's own hands. It was there. Always there, and she felt a measure of comfort in its presence. Her sisters never asked what was in the bottle, nor did either of them attempt to remove it from its place in the drawer. It was as if their curiosity had been satisfied just by knowing it existed. Her mother never asked either. She suspected her mother was aware that in that bottle, there was a bond that only Cynda was privy to possess.

Cynda placed the bottle on the night stand and carefully removed the additional contents in the drawer. She turned it over and peeled the note from the back of the drawer. The crisp white paper was folded in half and as she opened it, she read the words that had occupied her thoughts for many days and night, *Till we meet again.* Questioning herself for the thousandth time, she stared at the paper as if an explanation would appear.

The penmanship was precise and fluid with a final flair at the end of the sentence as if it was written with great care. Not one clue emerged from the words that she had studied over and over again. She did not dare allow herself to entertain the thought that he could be sincere, not one thought. She would remain firm in her belief that he could not have any feelings for her. It had taken months to convince herself of that fact. Just because he had made his unexpected appearance, she would not waver. No, not at all!

As she placed the pill bottle back in the drawer, her resolve was strengthened. It was a bleak reminder that her daddy was gone and the fear of loss was even greater than ever.

Brock

What Cynda did not know was that while she was trying to digest what had happened that day, Brock sped down Peachtree Road in his black sixty-two Chevrolet two door Coupe.   He had the window down, ignoring the December air that was not as cold as it could be in Atlanta, but brisk nonetheless.   He hoped the stinging cold would help to clear his head, as his thoughts were focused on one thing and one thing only, kissing those beautiful lips one more time.   He had told himself that over and over again as he made his regiment throughout the store.   Who was he fooling?   Those green eyes were more vibrant than he had remembered and what had she done to him as she walked away in defiance?

It was like a punch in the stomach as his initial thoughts of her being his conquest seemed to be somewhat farfetched.   He might find himself groveling to get her attention and that he was willing to do, if it meant another chance at winning her over.   Maybe, just maybe, she was the one he was looking to find, his challenge.

Brock was fast approaching Brookhaven,   the upscale community in which he had been reared. He took a quick turn on to the street that intersected with Peachtree Road and once again found himself driving down the quiet pathway that led him to his parent's home.   The circular drive was lined with neatly manicured hedges that formed a border between them and the street.   The red bows on all of the windows were a welcome and familiar sight.   He was home, but not ready for the onslaught of questions from his mother and father about his plans to attend law school.

*They were not in favor of his working at **Rich's** and felt it was a distraction for him.   They were right.   He had chosen to work there as a distraction during his breaks, but more so to avoid their never ending discussion of his future.   He also knew they had his best interest at heart and* *were well pleased that he had not made any real serious relationships with any of the girls he had met. There was plenty of time for that, they had expressed to him over and over again.*

It was obvious during dinner to Brock's parents that he was a little distracted. No matter how much his mother, who was the epitome of the pristine society she represented, tried to draw him into a conversation about law school, he resisted. His father retreated by acting more interested in his meal.

Brock excused himself after his meal was finished pleading fatigue. He slept that night, but it was a restless sleep that found him staring at two green eyes and a satisfied smile. He would wake to find himself eager to arrive at his job early, in hopes of getting a chance to see Cynda before she reported to the Lingerie Department.

Brock wanted to endear himself to her. It suddenly became the most important thing on his mind. His confidence was a little shaken as her dismissal of him yesterday had been rather earth shattering. The quiet community disappeared as the Chevy wound its way down Peachtree Road, its driver on a different path, the path to finding true love, something that Brock in his self-centered world, had never experienced.

From that day forward, Brock pursued Cynda with a vengeance. She ran into him at her every turn. Before long, he was asking her out.

As Cynda recanted her love story to her sisters, she skipped over some of the very private parts that almost made her blush, even now.

"I tried to resist, but Brock was so insistent in his pursuit of me. I kept telling myself, he was just playing a game. Finally, he asked me out, Cynda told her sisters.

Marcy looked at Cynda and said, "What a romantic story! You know that when we were younger Suzanne and

153

I both idolized Brock. In fact, until the day you two split, we never had a negative thought about him. He was our hero. Don't you remember that he always brought us ice cream on Sundays when you all came to see Mama? And once Mama got over you getting married so young, she loved him like a son. You know, she never did get over your split. She was not very verbal, but I could see it in her eyes, sadness I would say.

"But what I want to know is how did he propose?" Suzanne interrupted, trying to change the direction of the conversation, afraid Cynda would clam up.

Cynda let her guard down once more. She looked a little dreamy as she continued with her story.

"Mama was very intuitive about Brock's intentions. She saw the look in his eyes, she told me later. She thought he was too old for me, but as you well know she finally relented for me to go out with him. Once I started seeing Brock on the weekends, there was no stopping us. Of course, Mama would have died if she knew how much I was really seeing him. At least twice a week, I slipped out of the house around midnight."

"YOU!" Suzanne said incredulously.

"Yes, little old me. And it has taken me over thirty years to admit it. I just walked right out the front door. Mama always slept hard. I remember once trying to wake her up when I had a stomach ache. I thought I was going to have to call the rescue squad in to bring her back to life. She always slept like the dead."

"So, did he propose on one of those sneaky midnight rendezvous? Bet you money y'all were getting a little unnie-unda?" Marcy said, using one of their pet names while growing up.

"I said I would tell y'all about the proposal. I never said I would tell you all of my secrets. In fact, you might laugh when you hear about his first proposal."

"The first proposal," began Cynda.

"The first proposal?" interrupted Suzanne again.

"Yes, the first proposal was during the Christmas break when I saw Brock for the first time in months. He and I decided to ride the Pink Pig on our lunch break. We had first dibs on getting in the front of the line, since we were employees of *Rich's*."

"Oh my goodness! I have not thought of the Pink Pig in years. I remember," Marcy's face lit up like a Christmas tree, "Correct me if I am wrong, the original Pink Pig was a miniature train of sorts, which housed riders in its under belly and sported the face of a pig. It was suspended by some sort of cable and mounted on a rail!"

"Yes, riding it was like taking a tour in the clouds around the store of sheer Christmas wonder. The enchantment below was mesmerizing. The store was decorated in holiday splendor." Cynda added.

"You were lucky then. I remember the lines were long. It was obvious the lure of its magic extended far past Atlanta and its suburbs," Marcy nodded.

"Anyway, I guess the thrill of the moment went to Brock's head. When we got on the ride, we were given a trinket. Mine was a rub on tattoo. His was a ring. When the ride was almost over, he told me he loved me and gave me the ring, telling me he was going to marry me someday."

"And you took him seriously?" said Suzanne. "The Pink Pig! Yes, my memories are coming back now. I dreamed about the Pink Pig for nights before Christmas. I could not wait each year to ride it. You remember Mama made sure that we all got to ride it more than one time. Oh, the perks of mother being a *Rich's* employee. Speaking of perks, who would have ever thought about being proposed to in the belly of a pig? Maybe that was a bad omen, you know; he did turn out to be a swine," Suzanne continued without reservation, deciding to add her own twist to the conversation.

155

"Suzanne, can you be a little cruder?" Marcy admonished her.

"It is okay, Marcy. I reached the same conclusion long ago," Cynda said.

"Soooo, when was the second proposal?" Suzanne urged Cynda to continue.

"As I said before, we were dating on the weekends and slipping around a couple of times during the week. Brock was getting ready to graduate from college and his parents were pressing him to go to law school. He had no desire to get a law degree at that moment. He just wanted to start a career and get married."

"At the end of February, Brock took me to meet his parents. His father welcomed me with open arms. Good old Buie has always loved me as a daughter."

Buie was the nickname given to Brock's father when he was just a child. He was the second in the line of William Brodericks. Buie's mother had relented in giving him his father's name with the promise that she could give him a nickname. She chose Buie to honor her brother who had died at childbirth.

"He was always in my court. If you remember, Phyllis Franklin has never been a fan of mine. She tolerated me and I am certain at that time she thought I was the reason Brock might not fulfill "her dream" of him being a lawyer. I guess she kind of forgot that I gave up my dream of pursuing any kind of career all for the sake of love.

"Anyway, he asked his mother for his grandmother's ring right there on the spot. I was taken aback and really did not know how to react. Brock had told me that the ring would be his to give to his fiancé someday. I just did not know someday would be that day."

"Oh my goodness, what I would have given to have been there to see her face! I am sure that it was like a piece of stone; her perfectly chiseled face must have been on the verge of breaking. I can't believe she could have hidden that famous smirk of hers," Marcy said.

"I can't qualify that remark Marcy. I have always tried to put forth a positive attitude, especially to Audrey."

"Well, Audrey is not here! It's about time you unleash some of that pent up animosity. For heaven's sakes Cynda, she is a shrew!"

"Okay, the "shrew" got the ring out of the safe and refused to indicate to Brock that she understood the meaning of his request. She just dismissed us, pleading a headache."

"Wow, that must have been a slap in the face," Suzanne said.

"Not really. We were just too much in love to care. Brock had warned me about his mother and her worship of 'polite society'. Apparently, I was not 'polite society'."

"We left there and went to *Rich's*. Neither of us was employed there at the time. We rode the elevator to the top floor and slipped out to the roof escape. I was terrified and thrilled at the same time. With the Atlanta skyline surrounding us, Brock got on one knee and proposed. I was taken aback when I saw the ring. It was the most beautiful thing I had ever seen. It was more than I could have dreamed of in a million years. The emerald stone with diamonds encircling it made me feel like a princess."

"So you were," Suzanne said in a soft voice.

"You are still royalty, at least in our eyes, even if you no longer wear the ring. I am sure that you are saving it for Audrey if she gets married someday."

"The shrew asked for it back when Brock and I divorced, as if she had ownership of it. She had to have known that I would take care of it for Audrey."

157

"And what did you do?" Marcy chimed in an appalled manner.

"I gave it back to her, but when I did, I reminded her that the set of rules for 'polite society' must not apply to her. I told her that where I came from, being gracious reigned supreme."

"And we have our Aunt Sally to prove it," Suzanne said, knowing full well the facetiousness of her statement. "To tell the truth, if Aunt Sally had known about Phyllis' request for the ring, she might have demanded Phyllis give it back while packing heat.

That remark gave them all a chuckle.

Cynda said lightheartedly, "I can just imagine Aunt Sally knocking on the door of the Brookhaven fortress with her ever burning cigarette in hand demanding the ring. On second thought, she would have thrown the ring down on the pavement and squashed it with those black pointed toe shoes she always wore."

The three of them savored the memory of their beloved aunt that they all missed dearly.

Chapter 24

The evening was beginning to get late and Cynda begged for their forgiveness to retire. The sisters were left with a treasure trove of information. They quietly discussed all that they had learned about their mystery sister. Meanwhile, Cynda was restless in her own thoughts as sleep eluded her and she found the past invading her thoughts like a storm.

It had been an insult from the beginning when Phyllis Franklin had made it evident that she did not approve of the engagement. It was just another chip in Cynda's armor, the one she had fastidiously built around herself once her father had died. Being accepted by her peers was a piece of cake compared to the rejection her mother-in-law had exercised in her presence. The difference was that she had Brock in her court. Nonetheless, the wedding plans were set for June, as soon as she graduated from high school. It was a short engagement, but at the moment Cynda did not give it a second thought. She was in love and nothing could stop her.

Once Cynda's mother got over the shock of Brock and Cynda's engagement, she shared in the plans for a quiet and modest ceremony. Phyllis Franklin watched from the sidelines as her hopes for Brock to become a lawyer were dashed, at least for the moment. Cynda tried desperately to win the day with the "shrew", but to no avail.

Cynda and Brock got married at the First Methodist Church of Luxomni, a quaint and lovely church in Cynda's hometown. The wedding was held on a bright and brisk October day with her sisters in attendance. Clive agreed to walk her down the aisle with mixed emotions, but his adoration for her had won the day. He just wanted her to be happy. At least that is what he told himself.

Phyllis had been gracious with her gift of the wedding reception. It was held at the Piedmont Driving Club. It must have set Buie back a pretty penny, but he had always given in to the demands of his wife. It had been Buie who had paid off the house when she and Brock had gotten a divorce citing his reason as security for Audrey. Deep down, she knew that Buie's love for her was real and she was the daughter he never had, as he had told her that repeatedly. He had been the only reason she had been able to tolerate her mother-in-law during her marriage to Brock.

Cynda continued to toss and turn as she searched for pleasant memories of the time leading up to her wedding nuptials. The one that resonated the most was the shower held on the premises of *Rich's* in their famous Magnolia Room.

She lay there searching her memory for a visual. Then she remembered the wallpaper of magnolia blossoms and the elegant tables set for the occasion. It was the perfect venue for wedding and baby showers. Cynda and Brock received many lovely gifts from the 'polite society' of Brookhaven. Some of those were quite expensive.

She remembered it then like it was yesterday; it was the one gift that had meant more to her than anything. It had been wrapped in silver with pink ribbon. She knew immediately without opening it, the gift was from her mother. She also knew it had cost her mother a pretty penny. It was a tablecloth of white embroidered batiste, with a pink organza underlay, exquisite in its detail. The tiny label sewn along the hem on one side of the cloth read: *Made exclusively for Rich's – Switzerland.*

Cynda had used the cloth on many special occasions over the years and it was among her most treasured possessions. The significance of its origin was two-fold as a piece of her mother's heart had been given into buying the cloth from the department store and her own heart had been won at *Rich's*. The cloth was presently stored in her dining room buffet lovingly wrapped in tissue. It remained in perfect condition. Perfect she thought, unlike her failed marriage with Brock; then her thoughts turned sour.

Cynda decided not to allow the ugly to sully her recollections and changed her gears to nostalgia as she envisioned the tiny apartment on Morosgo Drive in Atlanta. It had been a happy haven for the two newlyweds. Brock had taken a job at the Federal Reserve Bank. She worked at a small dress shop over on Lindberg. It was the happiest time of their marriage.

Within a year, Brock announced to Cynda that he wanted to go back to school, law school. She knew full well who was behind his decision. He told her that his parents were willing to pay for the school and their rent, but he would have to go to school full time at Emory School of Law. When Cynda had protested that his decision had been made without consulting her, he was able to convince her it was the right thing for their future. As always, he was just as suave as he had been with Miss Reed, leaving her happily defeated.

The arrangement left Cynda feeling overwhelmed with responsibility. Even without having to pay the rent, they lived on a shoestring budget. She was always tired and felt inadequate as a wife. This went on for a three years and before she knew it, she was pregnant.

Brock had been more than thrilled when she had made the announcement. Buie had been ecstatic. Phyllis reacted as if she had been slapped in the face. The news had certainly not been in her plan. It was obvious that she was afraid that Brock would quit school to support the new baby. Cynda's mother wept with joy, but she expressed concern at the prospect of her daughter's unknown future.

Brock graduated from law school just a few short months after his daughter was born. Audrey Lucinda Franklin was born on the ides of March as the winds roared like a lion around Crawford Long Hospital in downtown Atlanta. A blanket of pink camellia blooms carpeted the ground just outside the main hospital entrance as a welcome mat for the young couple. A permanent smile was plastered on Brock's face. Cynda could see that he was totally and completely enamored with his new daughter and the wife who had brought her into the world.

If there was ever a time that Phyllis Franklin's face bore anything other than tolerance for her, Cynda caught a glimpse behind that façade the day Audrey was born. When she held her new granddaughter, Phyllis began to coo to her in a language that was old as time. She went on for a few minutes before she realized that she was being watched, almost forgetting where she was. She quickly stopped and seemed to search for something to say.

After a few minutes, Phyllis actually thanked Cynda for her granddaughter with kindness in her tone. She did not go as far as to offer concern for her welfare. Was she comfortable or did she need anything? Apparently Cynda had thought, she was only the vehicle which had produced the offspring of her son, her usefulness complete and a thank you very much was enough for Phyllis.

On the other hand, Cynda's mother arrived with a huge bouquet of jonquils and camellia blooms, much like the ones outside the hospital entrance. They were from her yard, gently cultivated and loved.

The young couple soon settled back into their apartment and a new routine with the new baby. As quickly as Brock had graduated from law school, he was taken on as a junior partner in a prestigious law firm in Atlanta. His father had called in some favors, Brock had told her. The partners were all fans who had graduated from the University of Georgia and they had welcomed him into their fold. Cynda took an extended maternity leave and planned to return to work three months after Audrey was born. Phyllis was not having it.

Buie paid Cynda a visit one day while Brock was at work. He told her that since Brock was drawing a salary, he would continue to pay their rent, so that she could stay home with the baby. She resisted as she never wanted to take handouts and more than that, she wanted independence. He reminded her how she had worked while Brock was in law school and the sacrifice she had made. It was easier for her to accept the offer when she thought of it that way.

Buie told her that he was convinced that the supplement to their income from him would be short-lived. He said that he knew that as Brock took on new clients and became established in the firm, he would make more money. Buie's main concern, he explained to her, was for Audrey's care. He and Phyllis felt like Cynda's place was to be home, and most importantly, to be a mother full time.

Cynda debated the decision. In her heart, she did want to be a full-time mother, but she was so afraid that she would lose her identity if she stayed home all of the time. And she really loved her job at the small boutique in Midtown. There would be no outlet for her as money would be tight and they could not afford to spend any extra on food or entertainment. In the end, when she consulted with Brock, the decision was made for her to stay home with their baby. She knew it had been the right one.

Presently, Cynda finally let go of the thoughts that she had buried deep inside and slipped into a fitful sleep. The storm subsided.

Chapter 25

Cynda woke early the next morning robbed of a restful night and immediately continued her thoughts of her life with Brock. She could not stop their invasion any more than she could stop their theft of her sleep.

Cynda reminisced in the joys of motherhood. Pretty soon after Audrey was born, the mundane tasks of taking care of her led to boredom. She absolutely adored the tiny little cherub that made her laugh and filled her moments with joy. However, she craved adult conversation. She drove out to her mother's house once a week, and that was her only outlet. Marcy was eighteen by then and Suzanne fifteen. Her sisters lived for the weekly visits and she likewise.

It was expected of Brock and Cynda to visit the Franklin compound every Sunday afternoon. Cynda had named it the fortress because almost everyone on one side of the street was either related in some shape, form, or fashion to Brock, or had known the Franklin family since birth. She dressed Audrey like a princess since her mother worked at *Rich's* and purchased clothing on sale and with a discount. Phyllis visited only high end boutiques in Buckhead for Audrey's clothes. She was on parade most of those afternoons in the neighborhood as she rested in her daddy's arms or sat perched on Phyllis' lap. Cynda was left barren of her charge for most of the day and found she liked to read *Southern Living* magazines. She perused their pages in search of living the gracious southern life. Secretly, she hoped that Phyllis observed her interest and elevated her opinion of Cynda's worthiness.

Except for Buie, Cynda felt totally ignored. He would take her out back and show her his garden of flowers. She bragged on his handiwork and he always beamed with pride. Of course Brock made idle conversation with her while they were visiting, but his focus was on showing off his daughter. And who could blame him? She was beautiful. Audrey had Brock's dark good looks and blue eyes. It had been too early to tell if they would change to green, but she was happy that they were blue and even happier that they stayed that way.

One Monday morning in the fall, Cynda woke up to see a *Mayflower* moving truck parked in front of their apartment complex. She realized that someone new was moving in right next door. The tenants had just vacated the apartment and she had been glad. Over and over again, Cynda had tried to be a good neighbor to the couple. They were quite reclusive and showed no interest in the Franklins. Not even when Audrey was born. Cynda had been hurt and could not fathom anyone ignoring her sweet baby.

Just as she was leaving to visit her mother, a tiny blonde woman about her age or a little older popped her head from around the screened door beside her. She held out her hand and introduced herself as Rumelle. Cynda took the small hand in her grasp and immediately felt a big heart attached to it. She was elated. From that point forward, Cynda's days of being bored ceased. Rumelle was a high energy woman with a bubbly personality that was contagious. She adored Audrey, as she had no children of her own, choosing to wait to start a family. The two women hit it off famously. They planned and cooked meals together and were at each other's apartment almost every day.

Rumelle's husband Jack was a nice enough fellow, but very quiet and low key. He and Brock were friendly enough to one another, but they did not seem to share the same interests. Brock was on the fast track to becoming a senior partner in the law firm and Jack worked as a salesman for pharmaceuticals. He was out of town quite a bit and Rumelle had a hard time being alone. Cynda and Brock invited her over at least one night a week for dinner. As the friendship grew, so did the friends' trust in confiding in one another.

Rumelle was born in North Georgia in the small college town of Dahlonega. She had attended college there and met her husband the first day of class. They had fallen madly in love with one another and married as soon as they both graduated. He had a hard time finding a job there and made the decision to move to Atlanta. Once he had gotten his position with the pharmaceutical company, they settled into the Midtown area for a short while. They decided to move a bit closer to his job and had landed on Morosco Drive. Rumelle was the best friend she had ever had, Cynda declared to herself. Cynda had found the vivacious Rumelle a breath of fresh air. She had loved her job, but the girls in the boutique had been rather stuffy and not near as much fun. Rumelle was full of stories of growing up in the North Georgia Mountains. Her accent was heavy and she had a southern drawl that bordered on a poor imitation of the south, but it was real!

Months went by and Audrey was almost two years old before Brock finally made senior associate in the firm. He began to talk of buying a house. Cynda was thrilled and at the same time she was sad to leave her friend Rumelle, her most trusted confidant in her lifetime, except for Clive. Cynda was even reluctant to share the decision about their impending move with her. She decided to wait until they found a house and the move was eminent.

Brock and Cynda looked for a few months to find a home in their price range. They wanted to stay in the Atlanta area, but the prices were pretty steep. They finally settled on a cape cod made of stone with a screened porch on the side of the house from the forties era. The quaint Decatur suburb of Atlanta was charming, still close enough to Brock's job to be economical.

The house had been kept in pristine condition with manicured flower beds of perennials with a profusion of color. It had a circular drive which added an irresistible charm to it. It looked like a dollhouse inside with hardwood floors and arched doorways. The stone fireplace was flanked with bookshelves on either side. The kitchen was small, but practical. A butler's pantry connected to the dining room. The window seats in the family room were an added bonus. Cynda could not wait to decorate it.

Cynda shared her news with Rumelle the following day and saw the disappointment in her eyes. She tried to feign excitement for her and did a pretty good job of it. She knew Rumelle's heart well enough to know that her feelings were not of jealousy, only disappointment.

Pretty soon Cynda was lulled back to sleep as her thoughts had waned into the pleasantness of the warm and wonderful friendship she had with Rumelle. She missed her terribly – even now. It would not be until ten o'clock in the morning before she awoke – still tormented.

Chapter 26

When Cynda graced their presence, her sisters had drunk their coffee, opting to wait for her to eat. The day began as a lazy morning for all, and a light rain settled in for the duration. The sisters ate a leisurely brunch that consisted of French toast and fruit. It was one of Suzanne's favorite Saturday morning meals. She had become quite efficient in the preparation, and the presentation was quite appealing with its powdered sugar, topped with strawberries. Cynda opted for a lighter fare, toasting an English muffin and putting the juicer into action once again, this time with pink grapefruit. Cynda took a deep and satisfying drink of the juice and spoke in the thoughtful manner that she had used as of late.

"I hope you girls slept well last night. I got myself into trouble by stirring up all those old memories. They kept boiling like a pot of water until well into the morning hours. I just could not stop them. I woke early and then went back to sleep. It was like I was watching a movie of my life playing before me with all of the drama in 3D."

"But they were good memories, weren't they? I mean the story of you meeting Brock, and the engagement is something you only see in the movies," Suzanne said.

"Sure, and those early years of our marriage were the best. We coasted along quite nicely, I must admit, with the help of Buie and Phyllis. That's because she insisted that he get his law degree. I will always wonder if he had not advanced so quickly in the firm and let his ego get the best of him, what would have happened to us. He has eternally had the gift of gab and a silver tongue."

"Of course, his success made Phyllis wildly happy. She had something to brag about at her garden club. I guess she has never let on to those unsuspecting members that Buie really had the green thumb in her family."

"By the way, of course you girls remember my friend Rumelle who lived in the apartment over on Morosgo? She was a thorn in Phyllis' side."

"Sure, I remember her," Marcy said.

"Barely," said Suzanne. "Wasn't she the one whom Audrey adored and thought was her aunt?"

"Jealous," said Marcy. "I didn't like the competition and she spent much more time with her than we did. I wanted to be the favorite aunt because Suzanne was more like a sister to Audrey."

"Well, I never knew you felt that way! Why didn't you tell me? I could have assured you both that Audrey thought you both hung the moon and the stars. Remember, absence makes the heart grow fonder. She certainly loved Rumelle, but no more so than you two. Always has and always will. You might say I am a little jealous sometimes when I think how close y'all are with her," Cynda said in a matter of fact, but pleasant tone.

Suzanne recognized that the conversation was treading on dangerous ground and re-directed it.

"Back to Rumelle, what on earth could Phyllis have against that sweet girl?"

"Why her accent, of course! Rumelle was born and raised in the North Georgia Mountains and her strong accent was an abomination as far as Phyllis was concerned. In her tunnel vision, she equated Rumelle's speech as ignorant. Forget that Rumelle had a four-year degree in Language Arts from North Georgia College."

"I wish you could have heard her screeching like a hoot owl when Audrey said ain't for the first time. I still say ain't when I feel like it. You know, when I am with you two. Nothing got under Phyllis' skin any more than when I started churning out the ain't word. Boy, did I turn it on when I felt like needling her. Instant headache for her; for me, instant peace and tranquility."

169

"Cynda, I did not know you had it in you!" Marcy cheered.

"Sometimes, my patience wore just a little thin and the very thought of her 'polite society' mantra would push me over the edge, especially where Rumelle was concerned."

"Want to hear a story that would have had Phyllis standing on her ear?" Cynda said with a little smirk.

"We are all ears," Suzanne almost whispered.

"First let me tell you that Rumelle was thrilled for Brock and me when we bought our first house. By the same token she was very sad to see us move away; after all, we had spent time with one another daily for about two years. She became distant those last few weeks and I thought she was taking our moving much too hard. I was having a tough time equally as well."

"Finally, a few days before we were to move, I confronted Rumelle about her feelings. I thought she was a little jealous and I did everything I could to include her in the process and assure her I would just be a few miles away."

"Rumelle broke down and told me the real reason she had been so aloof. She had found out that Jack was having some sort of affair. She did not have many details, but she knew that he had not been truthful about the length of some of his business trips. It appeared that he extended the trips by making a stop in downtown Atlanta for a night or two before coming home."

"At first, I did not believe that Jack was capable of cheating on Rumelle. He just did not seem the type. She had found some receipts, and the evidence was pretty damaging. I couldn't leave my best friend in a lurch. She needed me and I just could not walk away. The week before we were to move, I formulated a plan. I wanted to help her settle her suspicions once and for all."

"I think I see where this is going. You wanted to help her catch him red handed. Am I right?" Marcy said.

"You got it. Atlanta is a big city, but it only takes one little stone to slay a giant. I guess you could say I was a little stone."

"We had to plan the surveillance at just the right moment. So, we had to wait until Jack was out of town. We did not have to wait long, as he routinely traveled several times a month. He was due back in Atlanta on a Thursday. Rumelle had snooped around in Jack's briefcase and found that his flight was returning on Wednesday. She also found reservations for the Hyatt Regency downtown for that same night. When she showed me the information, I knew we had to take drastic steps to get to the truth."

"Don't tell me the two of you tried to confront him right there at the hotel!" Marcy stared in disbelief.

"No. It gets better," Cynda said with a knowing smile.

"You do remember that Rumelle was quiet and soft spoken and would not hurt a fly. She was convinced that she was right and I wanted to prove her wrong. Really, I did. I wanted nothing more than to find out not only was she wrong, but that she was just dead wrong. I knew the only way to find out for sure was to go to the *Hyatt Regency* and see for ourselves."

"How did you pull that one off?" said Suzanne.

"Yeah, what about Audrey and where did you tell Brock you were going?" Marcy said while trying to get a visual in her mind of her sister being involved in a cheating investigation.

"Actually it was pretty easy. I just told Brock that Rumelle and I were going out for one last dinner before we moved, you know, a girls night out. He was happy enough to keep Audrey. There was only one thing. We wanted to use a car that would not be recognizable by Jack, just in case."

"With Brock's permission, we drove over to his parent's house and swapped my car for the sixty-two Chevy that he kept covered there. We told them that it was just a little fun added to our final hoorah before Brock and I moved. Of course Buie was thrilled to be a part of taking the cover off the car and cranking it up and revving up the engine. Phyllis just stood in the doorway watching us as if one of us was the plague. I knew of course her distaste was for Rumelle, but I was a rung higher on her social ladder, only because I was the mother of Audrey."

"I would like to have been a fly on the wall," said Suzanne, and then quickly added, "Well, a fly on the dashboard of that Chevy."

"You would have been blown into oblivion. We rolled the windows down as we turned that baby out onto Peachtree Road," Cynda said loving to use the lingo that easily rolled from her tongue in her sisters' presence. The lingo that was born in the outskirts of the city of Atlanta and previously practiced at the drop of a hat had been carefully tucked away. It spewed now like a geyser on the incredulous ears of her audience."

"We did not care that the pollen was swirling around our heads and penetrating our nostrils in an invisible cloud of dust. We didn't even care that our hair was whipping in our faces and projected us into heathen imagery. We were on a mission of truth or dare. And the dare was mine because as it turned out, Rumelle became faint of heart."

"What happened to your plan?" Marcy said.

"All Rumelle had to do was to go up to the hotel desk and pretend she had left her key in the room. Once she had the key, it was her confirmation that Jack was indeed checked in there. Long story short, she chickened out."

"So what was your role?" Suzanne asked.

"Well, I was going to wait in the valet parking area for her, but she froze. We changed roles and Rumelle slid into the driver's seat."

"I put a baseball cap on my head and some large sunglasses over my eyes. When I stepped inside the lobby, I removed the glasses and walked right up to the desk. I played it off really well. I told the clerk that I was Mrs. Jack Stonewall. I told him my husband had gone out for a business dinner and that I had accidentally left my key in the room. Once he identified the room that Jack was staying in, he handed me the key, just like that. I had even memorized his driver's license number just in case I needed to verify my relationship to him. Back then, keys had room numbers on them. That little plan sure would not have worked in this day and time."

"So you just left, not knowing if there was someone with him?" Suzanne looked as if the story had lost its appeal.

"No. I had an adrenaline rush once I got the key. I took it up to the fifth floor and found the room. I knocked and walked down the hall quickly and turned my back as if I was going into another room. Nothing happened. I did it again for extra measure, still no one answered the door."

"I returned to the door a third time and with my heart in my throat, I turned the key and slowly walked in the room. Jack's sports coat was hanging on the back of a chair with his name tag on it. Bingo, I had hit the jackpot. It was obvious he was not alone and I saw two rather large suitcases that definitely belonged to a woman. One was a yellow Samsonite suitcase that was big enough to hold an entire wardrobe. The other was a chuchu bag. Remember those?"

"Yes, but what was a grown woman doing with a chuchu bag? Those were popular when I was a teenager," Suzanne asked in disbelief.

"Who knows? All I knew was that I needed to get out of there fast, but I needed some real proof to show Rumelle what I had found."

"Without thinking, I grabbed the bags and left the room within seconds of entering it. I took the elevator down and walked out the front door as if I owned the place."

"Oh, my God Cynda, what were you thinking when you took that luggage? That was breaking and entering, theft by taking. Can we say you could have been arrested? Were you?" Suzanne looked incredulous.

"No. Of course not."

"It was a struggle to put the bags in the back seat. Remember the Chevy was a two door. Once I got them in there, I flipped the bucket seat back in place and jumped into the passenger side and directed Rumelle to get out of there as soon as possible."

"Rumelle just started driving and I knew she was a basket case once she saw the luggage that did not belong to Jack. We drove down Peachtree Street deeper into the city, and then turned onto Ponce de Leon Avenue. We saw the Krispy Kreme Doughnuts and Rumelle turned in on a dime. She was shaking so badly that I thought we were going to need some heat turned on in the car. Now that would have been a first in the month of June."

"Don't tell me you girls went in to the Krispy Kreme. I know how much you love those doughnuts; surely you could not even think of putting one of those greasy torpedoes in your stomach!" Marcy said as if it would have been an abomination. She secretly craved them herself and made clandestine trips to the store, sometimes late at night.

"For the first time in my life, I was oblivious to Krispy Kreme doughnut haven. My thoughts were solely on the luggage. Without thinking, I had taken it as proof and a little part of me was thinking of revenge. I thought it would be good enough for Jack's paramour to come back and find her things gone. Little did I know what we would find packed in those babies. It was like opening a whore's bag of tricks right in the parking lot. Under the green and red florescent lights of doughnut heaven, Rumelle's hell was revealed. I still can't pass a Krispy Kreme without having flashbacks."

"You don't mean the woman was a lady of the night, do you?" Marcy was flabbergasted.

"Please, Marcy, cut the southern gracious stuff when it comes to a whore; she certainly could not be described as anything with the name of 'lady' in it. I am sure her name was to the tune of 'Brownie Bite or Lemon Chiffon,' based on her hair color! But, if it will make you feel better, hussy, she was just a hussy. Besides, Aunt Sally would have made no bones about the terminology."

"Okay, cut to the chase. What did Rumelle say when she saw what was in the bag?" said Suzanne.

"At first she was so angry she could not even speak. Imagine how she felt. She was being betrayed by a man who apparently thought a hussy with a whip was more exciting than she was. Forget the assorted pairs of platform shoes. There were some things in that bag neither one of us could identify. Rumelle gained her composure and asked quietly for me to drive her back to pick up my car to go home. At that point, I thought she had found a measure of calm. I was wrong."

"When we were well on our way down Ponce de Leon Avenue, Rumelle began to reach in the back seat. Before I knew it, she rolled her window down and started chunking piece after piece of the paraphernalia out the window. She was careful to avoid any law enforcement. She began to laugh in an almost unnatural way. Then, she looked at me and I saw a flicker of my old friend's persona break through and I just started laughing with her. We both laughed till we cried and I wet my pants. My stomach rebelled from the spasms of laughter and I almost threw up. Imagine if we had actually eaten some Krispy Kreme Doughnuts. We would have barfed all the way home."

"What did you do with the luggage?" Marcy said.

"Oh we hopped out and left it at a bus stop, hoping someone who needed it would find it. Then, we composed ourselves and drove back to the compound and switched cars without even disturbing the Franklins. I had guilty written all over my face; in fact, it probably read, 'impolite society' on my forehead with a red flashing bulb on my nose. No, I avoided that meeting which would have been one of the biggest mistakes of my life."

"Really Cynda? How could Phyllis possibly know what you had done?" Marcy questioned.

"Don't ever underestimate that woman. As soon as the light of day chased away the night, she was examining that car from bumper to bumper."

"How could you possibly know that?" Suzanne said.

"Easy. When Brock and I went over to the compound that following Sunday, she called me aside. I was at a loss for words when she produced a sexy platform shoe of red patent leather with a rhinestone buckle."

"I was so angry that I did not qualify an explanation to her. She did not deserve it. I just laughed it off and jokingly said, 'Looks like Brock has been having a little fun.'"

"She knew full well that Brock had not driven the car in months. I knew she thought the worst. But I was not going to allow her to think any less of Rumelle than she already did. I certainly was not going to share the sordid story of Jack's infidelity. From that point forward, I think she thought she had the upper hand with me."

"And you didn't care, did you?" Suzanne said with a satisfied look.

"Not really. I knew that any explanation I had to offer would be questionable in her 'polite society' mind. She really was not worth it. I owed my allegiance to someone who was worth it, Rumelle, my friend."

Marcy and Suzanne both saw a conviction in their sister that they had never seen before. To their knowledge, Cynda had never had that many close friends. Apparently, the ones she did have had her complete devotion. They had always felt that allegiance from her, but not on the level they had just witnessed when she told her story.

There were no other extraordinary revelations, certainly none with the magnitude of her escapade with Rumelle. Cynda did not question why the direction of their conversations had evolved into her story of Rumelle's dilemma or her heroics to help her friend in a time of need. What she did do was to question why she had shared so much of her past with them. It was as if she were compelled to do so by some unknown force.

Chapter 27

Cynda returned to her home after lunch on Sunday. The force that had compelled her to share her past continued to control her thoughts. It seemed to dominate her every waking moment. It followed her every step she took in her home inside and out. As she sat on the screened porch for her quiet time without Dane, she thought about the last twenty years.

Since leaving the family at such a young age and later moving to Wilmington Island, it suddenly occurred to her that her sisters never got to know the real Cynda. Marcy was forty and Suzanne thirty-seven when she had moved to the area. Prior to that, Cynda was totally involved in her life with Brock and somewhat reluctantly, 'polite society'. Cynda's two visits a year were limited in the time she was able to spend with them. She had flown their mother down quite often and kept a close relationship with her before her death. Her mother was the keeper of her past and the revelations of her failed marriage. Apparently, she had taken them to her grave as she now realized her sisters were totally in the dark about her life.

On Monday, Marcy and Suzanne decided to spend the day at the beach. On the weekends when Cynda was there, they limited their time by the water in deference to her condition. It was also apparent that Cynda seemed uninterested in the beach. They did not make a big deal out of it; they just found other things to keep them occupied. Each of them had taken part in preparing meals that had solidified their camaraderie. They complimented one another in their individual skills.

Suzanne had waited until she and her sister were on the beach to broach the subject of Audrey. Audrey had called once again to discuss the idea of her impending visit.

"Marcy, what do you think of Audrey coming down the last weekend that we are here?"

"Why? Has she called you again?" Marcy said.

"Of course. You know we talk at least once a week. She deserves an answer. We just can't keep putting her off. It's not fair."

"Well, it's not fair to Cynda either if she is blind sighted by Audrey making an appearance. Look, Suzanne, Cynda has just started opening up to us. I think it is so important to her well-being and healing if her mental state is strong. I just get the feeling that there is much more to her life's story than we know. How I wish she had not been so private all of these years! Having said that, I think we are making progress. In fact, our idea to get her to open up to us seems more like her idea," Marcy responded and then continued, "When she gets started on one of her stories, she goes on and on. Frankly, I want to know what is underneath those green eyes. She gets a faraway look in them and seems to leave us sometimes when we are talking. No matter what the outcome is as far as she is concerned, it is important that we all come to a level of understanding of how much we all mean to one another. That includes Audrey. Don't get me wrong, I believe Cynda can be healed, but I also believe she has to believe that as well."

"Can we just tell Audrey she can come down the last weekend? Even if we have to cancel, she can make preparations. I don't know the answer, but we have to try and act as mediators in this situation."

"I agree Suzanne. I just think it may be too much for Cynda to handle right now. You know as well as I do, Cynda will not even share her medical condition with us. We know that her chemo is finished, at least for now. Dane did tell me that she goes back for a CAT scan just after we leave to go back to Atlanta. Did I tell you that?"

"You did and that is why we need to make sure we have at least one healing ceremony. I am keeping my fingers crossed that she is using the healing oils on her own. We just have to believe. You know that is part of the reason the oils work."

"I know. I know," Marcy said as she looked out at the waves cresting and then breaking on their journey to shore. The water nipped at their feet, then retreated as it left a lacy film of foam in its wake. Its redundancy was a beckon of peace and tranquility; but sometimes powerful storms were a disruption, inevitably bringing a lasting peace. Right now their sister was in a powerful storm that threatened to take her life. Marcy picked up the myriad of bubbles in her hand and watched as they dissipated, wishing for the same outcome for her sister. She wanted the disease to go away and leave her sister in peace. No matter what the outcome was for Cynda and whether the oils worked, she prayed for peace. She wanted to believe just as much as Suzanne.

At the pink stucco, another kind of storm was brewing in Cynda's mind. Cynda had gotten settled into her room that same evening. Her thoughts began to wander back to the turbulent times that led up to the time when she and Brock were no longer man and wife. Her mother-in-law seemed to relish in the situation after the initial breakup. She did however keep herself in check; Cynda was sure of the reasoning. There was Audrey.

Phyllis adored Audrey and she stopped short of completely alienating Cynda for fear of offending her and retaliation. In that regard, Cynda had one up on her former mother-in-law. Phyllis had nothing to worry about though. She had made up her mind that she would never keep Audrey from her grandparents. In fact, while she was growing up, Audrey had a standing appointment with her grandmother. It had worked then to Cynda's advantage by giving her a most needed break. She was glad to share her daughter with her grandparents as the weight of being a single mom became taxing, especially when Audrey tested her. As she grew older, that could be almost daily.

Cynda resigned herself to finding something pleasant to think about or she would never get any sleep. She tried to think of the upcoming week ahead which would include July Fourth. Instead, all paths led back to the unsettling thoughts that swirled below the surface of her mind. She had dragons to slay.

Chapter 28

Cynda had an uneventful week with Dane and a quiet Fourth of July celebration with the girls. He was kind and considerate and she seemed to sense an improvement in his treatment of her. He no longer seemed as distant as he had been before she began spending the weekends with her sisters. She was already dreading the end to the visits, she thought. There were only a couple left before they returned to Atlanta.

Suzanne and Marcy joined the two on the Fourth of July for a cookout. It had been a while since Cynda had indulged in red meat, but she decided to eat a hamburger and she relished it. The four of them relaxed by the pool and enjoyed the traditional fare of fresh corn and season fruit as sides. Marcy surprised them all with her contribution of fresh peach ice cream. There was no time to make it, but she had found it at one of the touristy venues in the downtown area of *Tybee*. Cynda had not had any homemade peach ice cream since she had left Atlanta.

Cynda reminded them of her loss by emphasizing her passion for the treat by saying, "Now I know why I have been in the pits," as she tasted the coveted ice cream and used a double-entendre.

"Score one for Cynda," Suzanne said as she made an imaginary mark in the air.

Cynda continued, "I was missing some peach ice cream. Mama would have us turn that darn ice cream churn crank for what seemed like forever."

Marcy said, "Yeah, remember we each took turns sitting on top of the churn to keep it from turning over? Mama made a cushion out of folded towels she put on top of it to keep us from freezing our 'bohunkus' off."

"Bohunkus?" Dane said as he twisted his spoon into his cup and displayed a frown.

"Another word from the Brooks dictionary. Aunt Sally gave it her blessing and we obliged her by using it as often as possible," Cynda said as she snickered, "In fact, our use of the word may have set a world record." She licked the peach ice cream from the end of her spoon as she held it into an upright position. She sounded as if she were making a world changing announcement. Her audience seemed happy to be apprised of such a revelation, especially coming from Cynda, except for Dane who looked annoyed.

When dinner was finished, the sisters boarded Dane's boat and he commandeered it through the canal to see the fireworks. It had always been the custom of Dane and Cynda to join in the parade, decorating their boats with lights and waving the American flag. They had decided not to register their craft this year and now Cydna was having regrets. She was quiet and melancholy as the vessel plunged through the waters surrounded by other vessels afloat with patriotic themes.

Her thoughts had been on Rumelle for the last few days. Rumelle, her one true friend. They had shared several Fourth of July celebrations together, with and without husbands. She recalled that the days in Atlanta after the escapade down Peachtree Street had been chaotic. Cynda was busy packing to move. Rumelle was packing to leave Jack. It was rather ironic the way it had all turned out.

Rumelle had confronted Jack about his infidelity and he had professed his undying love to her. He had made no excuse about his choice of women to spend time with. In fact, he alluded to the idea that it was a physical liaison only and there was no love. Rumelle thought the revelation was almost worse. She had been appalled and asked him to leave so they could have some time apart. She decided immediately to move back to North Georgia.

If there was one thing that Cynda knew for certain, Rumelle had loved her husband without reserve. The petite blonde was as beautiful a woman as any man could wish for. Cynda had learned over the years that infidelity had nothing to do with beauty. It all seemed to center around a need having nothing to do with sex. Instead, it was a need to fulfill a void that even the participant did not understand.

Rumelle eventually divorced Jack because she could never trust him again. Cynda had been crushed when Rumelle had moved back to North Georgia as their visits became fewer and fewer. Rumelle had been part of her world for so long and the best friend she had ever had. How long had it been since she had seen her dear friend she asked herself? Even now, they only corresponded a few times a year, one more regret of her growing list of many. It was no time to reach out to her now she thought. She still loved her friend but did not want her pity.

Marcy and Suzanne stretched out on the bough of the boat making idle conversation with Dane about the celebration. "The Star Spangled Banner" was blaring from a much larger vessel in the parade of boats that swam before their eyes in glorious splendor. The fireworks show soon followed with bursts of color over the bay and bursts of pride filling the occupants of the boat. It was not long before the well-orchestrated profusion of light in a myriad of colors proclaimed the grand finale. It signaled an end to the fanfare, and the stillness of the night was only interrupted by the constant rippling of waves against the boat. Cynda felt an emptiness that she could not fathom as the boat powered its sleek presence into the night before them. She was too fragile to join the others on the bough. Instead she released the uneasy feelings that surrounded her and instead, reveled in the glory of the night. She allowed her thoughts to return to the present.

Cynda watched as her sisters seemed to be at ease with Dane. On the other hand, his body language spoke otherwise. Did he feel threatened by their presence, she wondered? Afraid they would influence or change her? Or that they could sense the discord between them?

Cynda knew it was not a conscious effort he had made to create the discourse; it had just happened. He was afraid and he did not know what to do. His perfect wife had made his existence complete. Now her own existence was being threatened. Come to think of it, Cynda thought, Dane's was too, at least the only one he knew.

Chapter 29

There was a change in plans the following Friday. Marcy and Suzanne picked Cynda up late in the evening and they went to Fannie Pink's Oyster House for dinner. They had wanted to take Cynda out to her favorite restaurant. Her appetite had been improving over the last couple of weeks, especially since her last round of chemo had been completed before they had arrived in town.

Fannie Pink's Oyster House was nothing more than a shack filled with eclectic signs on the walls, picnic tables with oil cloth scattered throughout and some of the best seafood known to man. Cynda's opinion of the seafood was shared by many as the wait time to be seated prompted them to an early arrival.

The wait staff sat the ladies in Cynda's favorite spot as soon as they arrived. The atmosphere was charged with live music and fun; the enthusiasm was contagious. Cynda seemed to have her own agenda and the tables were turned on her sisters as the topic of conversation centered on them. The years apart had left many questions in Cynda's mind about their lives. Little did they realize she wanted to know what she missed by not being a part of their lives as much as they did about hers. Yes, the tables were turned. The subject of vacations came up. Suzanne recanted one.

"I've got a vacation memory that was a script straight from the twilight zone. We spent the night on the way down to Daytona Beach and got up early to finish our three-hour drive. Just after we started down I-95, the Blue Goose ran hot. We managed to get off at the next exit and to a gas station. Lucky for us, it was one of those old fashioned stations that employed a mechanic," Suzanne recanted.

"Oh my goodness, Suzanne, do you always name your cars?" Cynda said looking perplexed.

"No, just old ones. We had recently bought a used Pontiac that looked great on the outside, but little did we know, some of its insides were in need of a transplant. It blew a head gasket and I blew one too before we got out of that god-forsaken town we were stuck in for two and a half days."

"When we were told by the mechanic that the repairs could not be completed until the next afternoon, we realized that we had to find a place to stay overnight. Unfortunately, the town was so small that we had to be driven fifteen miles to the next town, courtesy of the owner's wife. We loaded up in her gold Lincoln Continental and checked into the Best Guest that afternoon."

"We checked out the next day at eleven a.m. and waited in the lobby of the Best Guest for our 'chauffeur' to arrive. Did I mention that she was a rather large woman who looked as if she could whip any man into shape? I was a little skeptical until she opened her mouth to spill out a string of southernisms. Her 'honey this and baby that' was the only comfort I had in the disastrous situation."

"Once we were delivered back to the gas station in the gold roadster, we settled into the gas station. It must have radiated a heat index well above 100 degrees. We soon learned that the mechanic was not quite through with his work. So, I sat in the station which was equivalent to half the size of a boxcar with no air conditioner. The kids were soon overdosed on crackers, soft drinks, candy and chewing gum. They entertained themselves for the three hours by opening and closing the drink box, begging for more snacks and ignoring the smacks on their bottoms when they got out of control. Stephen could not stop pacing outside. I could not stop the rivers of sweat that ran rampant down my entire body. I even pretended to search for a soda in the drink box, just to get a breath of cool air."

"And that was not the end. We had to return in that gold tank of a car, roomier than the gas station, I might add. The Best Guest which has become a legend in our family was our home for one more night. I had learned to hate it in a short twenty-four hours. At that point, we were on our fourth day of travel to that grand Daytona Beach of which you all know we sisters hold in great esteem."

"Do you actually remember that last vacation we took there with Mama and Daddy?" Cynda said in quiet reverence.

"How could we forget?" said Marcy duplicating her tone.

"One of the worst parts of that trip was the ride down through all those small Georgia towns. I was green with car sickness, sitting in the front seat of that 1955 Bel Air Chevrolet. It was two-tone yellow and white. Daddy was so proud of that car," Cynda said as she shook her head from side to side.

"I can remember the day he brought it home. I was outside on the porch and he drove up so quietly, I almost jumped out of my skin when he hopped out and shut the door. He put his finger over his lips to shush me as he slipped past me into the house. He returned with Mama sandwiched against his chest with his hands covering her eyes. When he pulled them away, she shrieked and covered her mouth in delight. The words he said still ring in my ears, 'It purrs like a kitten, a yellow tabby one, I say.'"

Both of her sisters looked at her as if she had gifted them with a magnificent prize.

"The only saving grace that made the ride worthwhile was the pecan log roll at the famous Stuckey's in Eastman, Georgia. I know y'all can't forget that part of the trip," she continued.

Once again, her affinity to southern lingo came readily off of her tongue. "Y'all" was one word in her southern lingo that she felt was vital to the 'Brooks' dictionary, one that she refused to extract from her vocabulary. She decided long ago to fiercely hold on to the word, using it when she felt the need to hold on to her southern identity, regardless of what Dane thought about it.

"Well, I was only five," Suzanne said quietly yearning for more memories.

"Oh, I loved those log rolls just as much as you did. In fact, I would watch until you finished eating yours, reserving mine, secretly having a private thrill that I still had some left and you did not," Marcy said.

"Did you really think I was fooled? Let me name a few of your antics. I watched as you nibbled the ears off your Easter bunny and then slipped it back into the wrapper, sipped slowly on your bottled Coca Cola® AND ate your bag of chips, one mocking chip at a time. No, you did not have me fooled," Cynda said lowering her chin and raising one eyebrow.

"Well, being older you got everything first. I just wanted to have something you didn't have, even if was just a little old earless bunny that I nibbled on for days. Don't get me wrong. I loved your hand-me-downs as much as I loved you. And if you had asked for it, I would have given you my mutilated bunny," Marcy said with an engaging smile.

In a childlike manner as if she had been left out of the entire conversation, Suzanne said, "I can remember Daddy throwing me up in the air time after time in the swimming pool that summer. It is probably one of the only things I do remember. I can barely recall his face, but it was smiling," Suzanne said.

The direction of the conversation turned back to the destination on that last vacation.

"I can still see that cluster of cinder block cottages when we drove up and the red flashing VACANCY sign hanging on the office door. You know Daddy never made reservations. We all just piled in the car in the middle of the night with little warning from him. He had Mama on standby and gave the green light just hours before he was ready to leave. She told me that she kept all of our clothes washed and ready to pack the minute he mentioned the possibility of going to the beach. She forgave him that, since he ran his own business, and it was hard to leave town," Cynda confessed to them.

"You know he must have loathed driving in the daytime with a carload of hormones. At least some of us slept part of the way," Cynda continued nodding toward her younger sisters.

"Well, I can't for the life of me understand why we never had a reservation before we left town." Marcy questioned further.

"Mama always said Daddy flew by the seat of his pants. I guess that was a fine example. We cruised up and down on the cheap side of A1A in Daytona scoping out the VACANCY signs; then Mama and Daddy would inspect the rooms before they made a commitment. The only requirement for lodging was that we all wanted to have a pool with a sliding board, of course."

"I remember that the pool was centered in that white cluster of cottages with a most beautiful curved sliding board. I did not care about anything but the road to that slippery slope of exhilarating madness. I must have slid down that board a hundred times that summer," Cynda said smiling as if she were still there.

Cynda then redirected the conversation back to Suzanne's story and said apologetically, "Sorry for the interruption of your saga. So, half of your vacation was spent in the Twilight Zone; how awful!"

"Oh, it did not end there. After we checked in, we spent a half day on the beach. It rained for the next two days and we finally just packed up and left. We never went back there again. I think I prefer to remember Daytona as the last trip we all took with Daddy."

The feelings were mutual as the three sat there in the haze of *Fanny Pink's* nostalgic splendor. It was one of the few sister moments that was shared in unison. They each clung to the remnants of a vacation with their daddy in its treasured brilliance. That last vacation was held together in a cluster of cinder blocks and memories of a man they called Daddy.

It was the beginning of a weekend that would cement the sisters' relationship into a cohesive bond. They continued to reach into their past and reminisced throughout the following days.

The next morning, the three sat around the breakfast table. Cynda poured her coffee from her cup into the saucer it rested on to cool.

"Well, there has been a long time since I saw anyone do that," Marcy said.

"In fact, Aunt Sally was known for her 'saucer sipping' if I remember correctly," she continued.

"Yes, and Mama detested it when she did it. She told her that she was setting a bad example for us," I remember her telling Aunt Sally," Cynda said.

"Guess Aunt Sally was right. I have been 'saucer sipping' all of my adult life and I haven't burned my tongue yet. Of course, I do it in private. Dane would be appalled."

"Well you are in good company now. We won't tell. I am sure that Aunt Sally would be tooting her horn right now if she could see you following in her footsteps," Marcy said.

"Now I wouldn't go that far. You know she wore a size ten shoe," Cynda winked.

"I still remember what a bitter weed she was to everyone," Marcy said.

"Bitter weed?" said Suzanne, "What is that supposed to mean?

Cynda immediately knew what she meant.

"I think I can explain that one," Cynda said.

Cynda had given that topic a great deal of thought over the years. She reflected on her remark before she started to explain. She had always vowed and was determined not to become one of them. She hated to preface her explanation with her first sentence, but she felt compelled to do so.

"If I live long enough, I vow that I will not be like those bitter and angry women who succumb to the dreaded disease, the one that saps its victim of the joys of life. The disease hovers over them, waiting for any opportunity to seize their very being. I will not be a bitter weed," she proclaimed as she simultaneously wondered if she had already succumbed. She went on to explain, "Those ones who began their downward spiral, more often than not, after the fifty mark; women who suddenly realized that after assessing themselves, life had left them floundering and subsequently, angry."

"In looking back, I realize that the bitter weeds I have witnessed in my lifetime all shared one common bond. Disappointment."

Cynda finished her sentence and then paused to think. Her sisters did not respond as they seemed to be processing her last words. She was thoughtful for the next few minutes.

The realization hit her hard, as if she had been slapped in the face, as she too had recently spewed venom at Dane with her angry words, like a poisonous reptile. And the venom was just as lethal, falling on its prey, leaving the victim speechless and at a loss for words. Then another thought hit her like a ton of bricks. She too was disappointed, but at what? She did not have a reason to be bitter. Her life had made a ninety degree turn when she had met Dane, had it not?

Cynda had told herself over and over again; fulfillment, measured in expectations of others, results in disappointment. It was her motto as she had learned not to expect too much from the world around her, much less than her own family.

No. This could not be happening to her. She would not allow herself to fall into the abyss as women like her Aunt Sally had surely done. She would put up a good fight and in doing so, she would begin an examination from the beginning, looking at her life with a magnifying glass, deeper into her core. She would not allow her own dissension into bitterness. She would search for her once vibrant self, before it was too late. She did not want to leave this earth as being a 'bitter weed' as her legacy.

Cynda then spoke with finality to her sisters as she was sharing the most important words she could muster to help overcome state of a startling reality.

"The weeds I speak of were women, once young and innocent and untarnished by life's disappointments, including Aunt Sally. I am sure of that. Promise me that y'all do not want make the same mistake as she did," she said as her own words resonated a truth she had not expected on this day.

When Cynda returned to the living area after taking a nap, she found her sisters preparing and packing a late lunch.

"Hope you feel like taking a trip to the beach. We thought we would go down by the Back River beach area for a change. You know *Little Tybee* is just across the way and the view is so beautiful. If you don't, *Hug Bug* is at your service. I can leave you the key," Suzanne proclaimed hopefully.

Cynda became thoughtful as she had not been on that area of *Tybee* in what seemed forever. "I think I will go for a little while, and yes, *Hug Bug* must be missing me as much as I am missing him. By the way, is *Hug Bug* a him? I have forgotten to ask," Cynda replied.

"I guess you could say that; his hugs are more strong and powerful than a woman's. And when the wind whispers in your ear, it's gruff and demanding, just like a man," Suzanne said satisfied with her playful analogy of manliness.

"Well, that was a rather logical analysis of manhood. Are you always so analytical in your assessments of the opposite sex?" Cynda questioned.

"Actually, in my early twenties is when I started using analogies of song titles, it began with men. I preferred to compare men to songs that were on the charts during an event in my life. My first real breakup was to the tune of 'Everybody Plays the Fool Sometime' to the realization of 'I Can See Clearly Now'. So now I use song titles for life in general," Suzanne answered in earnest.

Cynda thought about the answer as the three of them loaded the *Hug Bug*, top down and ready for the beach. To her calculations, Suzanne had been about twenty when she and Brock had divorced. It was almost as if she had read Cynda's mindless thoughts back then. Those very songs had always struck a chord when she randomly allowed herself to visit that dark time when her marriage ended. The words to both "Everybody Plays the Fool

Sometime" and "I Can See Clearly Now" were etched into her own memories of Brock that rarely had a chance to surface, at least if she could help it.

The three sisters lounged on the beach in quiet reverence, each lost in their own thoughts. Marcy and Suzanne had discreetly discussed bringing up the subject of Audrey when they arrived there. They had to try to get some resolution between mother and daughter if that was all they accomplished this summer.

The subject of Audrey would have them treading on thin ice as Cynda had just started opening up to them. Neither one was willing to risk the tentative relationship that was now beginning to solidify into something special. They both agreed to learn more about Cynda and Dane's past relationship with Audrey and why there was so much animosity among the three. Audrey had certainly not given them much to go on over the years. She always seemed to be protecting her mother, yet persecuting Dane.

Cynda was lost in her own thoughts, unable to shake the memories of Brock and the songs that were associated with him. She forced herself to focus on Dane by thinking about her first meeting with him and a song that was associated with that time in their lives. It was not hard. Dane was twenty years older than Cynda and had a penchant for the forties music that she had found so antiquated. She, on the other hand, liked all types of music, even some country.

The song that would eclipse any other when she and Dane met was "You Light up My Life". The style crossed generations and gave both of them hope of a life together. Cynda who had lost all hope had met a man whose hope was in finding someone to take care of him for the rest of his life, she was to learn, literally. She was willing and had no regrets.

Their love had been ageless. Cynda had met him while he was a client at a securities firm she worked at in downtown Atlanta. It was a chance meeting. She was assigned to his account when one of the other account executives was out on leave. Their attraction had been instant. She had tried hard to fight her feelings, telling herself over and over again that he was too old. She rationalized the attraction. Could she have been looking for a father figure?

After her disappointing marriage to Brock, she had dated off and on for seven years. Dating had not been a focus in her life. She had spent all of her time and energy on Audrey, making her top priority. She had thrown herself into a routine that focused on work and her daughter. The two had moved back to Luxomni to a quiet neighborhood in a small economical two-bedroom house with a neat yard and nice neighbors.

Sweet Rumelle, she thought. Her visits had been often at first back then, and she was her rock during the transition to being a divorced mother. The years ticked by and Rumelle had remarried and had a family of her own. Audrey had adored Rumelle and that adoration never ceased. As far as she knew, the two still kept in touch. Cynda had to admit to herself that she had been remiss in her communication with her old friend. It was a conscious effort that she made not to taint the sweetness of their bond unnecessarily. No. She had not wanted to share details of her illness; after all, maybe just maybe she would be healed, she thought.

"I was just thinking," Cynda said as she resumed her earlier conversation of the significance of songs.

"Dane and I had a favorite song. It was 'You Light Up My Life'. That was the song that we played on our first date. The lyrics spoke to both of us. He was a shining light in my pitiful existence," she said wistfully.

Marcy quickly saw this as an opportunity to talk about the early years with Dane and hopefully the dynamics of why Audrey's relationship with him had turned sour. Had it always been that way, she wondered? She was determined to find out.

"Speaking of Dane, that was some whirlwind romance. Suzanne and I were so busy with our lives; we had no idea you were even dating, much less contemplating getting married again. Plus, you were so secretive," Marcy said in a matter of fact tone.

"That was because I was so careful not to let plans for our new life together overshadow Audrey's high school graduation and her move to Savannah College of Art and Design. She worked so hard to be her own person, even though Phyllis worked just as hard to persuade her to take a different course in life. I will have to applaud my daughter for that. Not once have I ever spoken a negative word about Phyllis or Brock to her, for that matter as hard as it was not to do."

"But your move to Savannah was so sudden. We were all surprised that you left your roots so quickly and so far away, but we expected you to move back when Audrey finished school," Marcy said knowing she was treading on dangerous waters.

"I didn't exactly follow her to Savannah you know. Who would have ever dreamed that Dane had ties to Savannah with his Wilmington Island home. He was on the verge of retiring when we met. It was the perfect scenario. I could be close enough to Audrey without totally interfering in her life too much. It was the only way I could allow her to make such a drastic move."

"Listen, I made a vow to myself when Brock and I split that Audrey was my number one priority. Of course you know I moved back to Luxomni because I wanted Audrey to be closer to Mama, and I truly needed her, too. I don't know what I would have done if I had not had Mama to help with that child. You remember that Phyllis did everything she could to convince me to allow Audrey to attend a private school in Atlanta. Of course, that would mean her living there with her and Buie. I was not having it."

"You will also recall that Brock was involved in her life, but on the fringes. He was happy enough to see her on his own turf, Phyllis' turf that is. The weekends that she spent with her daddy had to be shared with Phyllis and Buie. I really did not mind Buie's influence, but Phyllis was another story. If you will remember, Audrey rebelled against me during those teenage years. I will always believe Phyllis had a hand in that. I could never put my finger on it, but after she turned sixteen, it was almost as if she hated me at times."

"Enough of that; I sacrificed for Audrey. Actually, it was not much of a sacrifice. I was happy those years before I met Dane. Audrey fulfilled my life in a wonderful way even through our difficult times. But as her graduation approached, I began to feel anxious, even a little scared. It was like you said Suzanne. The empty nest syndrome, though I did not have a husband, much less a *Hug Bug* to comfort me. Then I met Dane."

Suzanne looked at her sister and felt a pang of regret that she had not shared with Cynda about the things that Audrey had shared with her in confidentiality back then. She knew full well what had disturbed Audrey during those difficult years. She had always blamed her mother for the divorce. Even Suzanne could not defend her own sister because as far as she knew, Cynda had just decided that she did not want to be married to Brock. She was not so sure about that anymore.

She and Marcy had been so wrapped up in their own lives then, but were thankful when Cynda met Dane.

She realized now that her older sister needed them and had been right under their noses. No wonder she had been so guarded about her seemingly full but empty life. Cynda had been so secretive about her breakup with Brock. They expected no less when she met and married Dane in just a few short months. And just like that, she was gone.

"I am so glad that Dane came into your life, Cynda, just sad that we were not there for you during your tough times. I guess we were pretty selfish," Suzanne said with pleading eyes.

"I was a tough old bird back then and still am, if I am given the chance. You girls were just getting settled with your husbands and families. Suzanne's children were so much younger than Audrey. I did not want to burden you with my problems. I knew that Mama had been devastated when Brock and I split. He had charmed Mama just like he had charmed me," Cynda said.

"So when did he lose his charm? I thought you and Brock were the dreamiest couple. Now that I know the details of your engagement, I can't imagine you just falling out of love with someone that perfectly romantic," Marcy said, trying her best to get to the truth of the breakup.

Cynda pursed her lips as if to suppress the truth that threatened to escape and shook her head back and forth. She said, "Sometimes perfect is your enemy." Cynda then quickly changed the subject back to Dane and her move to Savannah.

"Dane already had the house down here and I knew that Audrey would not be running back and forth from Savannah to Atlanta very often. After all, it is a four to five hour drive depending on the traffic. So I decided to take the plunge. Dane was quite agreeable to live in Savannah and spend time up there as often as we wanted to do. I knew he would be happier here and I have always hated the

Atlanta traffic. It was a pretty easy decision. My only regret was the time I missed spending with Mama. I don't think she ever got over losing Audrey and me at the same time. I flew her down here as often as she would come, but it was not the same."

"Speaking of Audrey, what really happened between her and Dane? I know her side of the story. Something about Dane not really liking her and being jealous of her relationship with you," Suzanne asked.

"You know Audrey. Always drama. I spoiled her rotten and gave her the world. What I did not give her, Phyllis and Brock competed with one another to give her more. You both saw that for yourselves when we lived in Atlanta."

"Back then when Brock remarried, the gravy train for Audrey began to dwindle somewhat, even though he continued to do plenty on the sly. You know Prissy Crissy wasn't having it. Oh, no. No one was going to infringe on the fringe benefits of being married to a successful lawyer. Once Audrey reached eighteen, child support stopped and she was given an allowance for college, beyond books, tuition and housing. I suppose Crissy could buy a few more designer handbags and shoes each month in one of those posh boutiques she loved to frequent once that happened."

"Brock had always been more than generous with his alimony. He agreed to ten years of it much to Phyllis' chagrin. The agreement was to stop if I got remarried. Of course, by the time I met and married Dane, there were two years left. Phyllis must have danced a jig to that revelation. I was glad to be off that gravy train myself, and just lucky that Dane came along and we fell in love. I could finally wash my hands of the old money of the 'polite society'."

It did not go unnoticed that Cynda received alimony for ten years when she was the one who wanted out of the marriage. That made no sense to either one of her eager listeners, but both refrained from questioning her.

Cynda continued with her explanation, "Audrey saw Dane as her new gravy train. When she visited, she was a slob and expected me to wait on her hand and foot. Dane refused to coddle her and demanded that she clean up behind herself. Apparently she abused her allowance from Brock in Savannah and was always coming up short. Phyllis was not as generous either. She probably thought that if she restrained her monetary support, Audrey would pack up and move back to Atlanta. That did not happen, so Audrey started pumping me for funds. I had a budget for her also and I refused to budge. So, she blamed Dane."

"The relationship with Dane went from bad to worse. Throughout all of her visits for the last twenty years, we have always ended up in some disagreement. Dane and Audrey tolerate one another and that is that," Cynda concluded with finality.

Neither Marcy nor Suzanne pushed the issue any further. The darkening skies gave them a reason to change the direction of the conversation to the impending weather.

"I think we had better pack up and go back to the cottage," Suzanne said, "I can walk back really quickly and bring the *Hug Bug* closer."

"That sounds like a good idea," Marcy said.

"I will pack things up while you are gone."

Suzanne was back in record time and soon the three of them were sandwiched in the Bug, but not before huge raindrops began to hit with a vengeance on their unprotected heads and bodies. The sisters reveled in the refreshing deluge of pin prickles and for Cynda, it felt as her soul was being washed as well. They began to laugh as Suzanne accelerated the Bug to escape the rain. The car leaped and then shuttered as the clutch was released. They were jerked forward and then backward against their seats, causing them to break out into hilarious hysteria. They began to pantomime the motions to head dancing.

Suddenly as soon as the rain began, it stopped. The three drenched women broke into song, with Cynda in the lead and her fellow partners to follow "I Can See Clearly Now". Cynda again felt another cleansing moment as the words to the song flowed freely from her mouth.

Chapter 30

When Cynda awoke early on Sunday morning, she pondered the days after her breakup with Brock. The blinding rain the evening before reminded her of another day long ago, another day of cleansing. A trip alone to the beach had begun her healing in a way that she could not have imagined. *Tybee*, Sweet *Tybee*. Bittersweet *Tybee*.

It was there on the coast of Georgia, on quaint *Tybee* Island that Cynda had found refuge. It had been nine long months since the fateful day in September when her world had turned upside down. Her divorce had been devastating and her sense of security had suffered, both mentally and financially. She needed the break and a break from Audrey too. She had poured all of her love and affection into her daughter since the divorce, so much so that she did not have to think, to feel, only to exist.

It was on the beach that Cynda watched as the ocean waves crested, collapsing into a sea of foam that rushed toward the shore on a mission of triumph, only to be defeated as the pull of the current demanded surrender. The days behind and now the days before her were much like the mighty ocean as she experienced a gamut of emotions and final capitulation to her own defeat. She looked at the mighty sea and compared herself to its repetitive motion. Since Brock had been gone, she had daily found herself rising up into a wall of courage. Then intermittently, the release of emotions would ambush her into a slow submission to the pain and anger that choked her resolve and pulled her back from the safety of the shore.

In the distance, Cynda looked for hope and encouragement from the ships that sailed into port in their mightiness. She thought of the days that they must have been at sea, when the sleek and powerful vessels sliced through the water, as though it were their playground. She wondered if their crews were weary of endless days of mundane tasks and the monotony of ocean scenery or if they relished the challenge that would take them to their final destination.

Cynda wanted to be like the ships, mighty and powerful and unafraid of the future. But she was afraid. Not since her father had died had Cynda been so lost, so desperate for control; after all, perfection demands control, she thought. And that is how it had been since the day that she told Brock goodbye. She yearned for the life that had been so perfectly controlled. She wanted the mundane, the routine, the car pools, swim lessons and date nights. More than anything she could now imagine, she wanted to trust again. How had she been so blind? Never again would she be so trusting that she would lose control of her judgment.

Cynda directed her attention to the flight of seagulls overhead and the impending rain clouds that promised a swift and steady rain. She debated leaving the beach, but chose instead to stay; after all, she had her umbrella.

The rain suddenly began with a fierceness that surprised Cynda, so much so that she struggled to contain the umbrella, her only source of shelter. The wind whipped wildly about her and was stinging as the pellets forced their way under the covering. She worked desperately to secure the covering to her chair with the elasticized attachment. It took a few minutes as the battle to succeed appeared fruitless. She was ready to give up, when suddenly her efforts were rewarded as the attachment snapped in place. Cynda sank into her beach chair, her task complete, her energy spent. The fierce rain continued to pelt her legs, as the covering could not prevent the rain from blowing underneath. Her upper body remained protected.

She sat underneath the umbrella wrapped in her towel and waited for the rain to cease. It did. The rain stopped as quickly as it came, along with the wind. Within a few minutes, the sun championed its way through the clouds and began to shine again. It was as though it had not rained at all. A large ship was moving out to sea, seamlessly moving at a steady and determined pace.

Suddenly, her spirits lifted as if the deluge had washed away some of the pain and the sea offered her hope of moving forward. She could almost hear its whisper. In that moment she felt liberated and reveled in her new found sense of encouragement. Yes, she had thought, the beach is just what I needed.

The remainder of the day was spent by the sea and Cynda allowed herself to think, to feel and to exist again. She began to plan what she would do with her life in the future, and that did not include any man. She would be independent and vowed to rely on no one.

Cynda remembered strolling along the edge of the ocean as she walked back to her cottage. As she approached the cluster of cottages, she surveyed the white fencing in front of her own cottage, which was in need of paint and repair. The fencing mirrored the unkempt appearance. It had been all that she could afford.

Unlike the cluster of cinder block cottages from her last childhood vacation with her daddy, there was no pool or sliding board. No one to catch her as she playfully shrieked while soaring down the slide. No one to wrap their strong arms around her. Yet, her resolve had been born on that cloud ridden day.

Her thoughts caused her to pause and reflect on her surroundings in a way that became entrenched in her memory. She noticed the screen door was covered by an iron and metal replica of an egret surrounded by marsh reeds. The paint was faded and chipping away on the egret's body, the rust bleeding through. However, inside the two-room abode was tidy and inviting. The linoleum floors were kept clean and waxed. In addition to the living area and kitchen combination, there was a small bedroom and bath. The maple bed was covered with a white chenille bedspread with blue and yellow interspersed throughout. The window in the bedroom was void of a curtain, as a shade served to cover the window. Thank goodness the smell of pine cleaner had faded as Cynda's stay of three days included multiple sprays of perfume in frequent intervals. She had refused to allow the maid service to clean the bath, opting only for a fresh supply of linens.

Cynda found herself peering into the sink in the bathroom that hung from the wall. She stared down at the rust stain that surrounded the drain. She carefully placed the sink stopper in the drain opening to fill the sink with water. A chain was attached to it, but free from the anchor used to secure it. She turned the water on and watched as it filled the basin, directing her attention away from the mirror. It was a habit of hers. Looking at herself would cause her an examination that she avoided. It was something she had done for quite some time.

Cynda lifted her eyes to the mirror that was attached to a medicine cabinet. The green eyes stared back at her past the pretentious nose. She spoke to the mirror in a voice that surprised even her, "I will survive. Not only will I survive, I will prevail. This will be the last time that I will settle for less than I am worthy. The next lodging I stay in will be beautiful and luxurious." With that she dipped the clean white cloth into the water, lathering it with soap. She scrubbed her face as if purging herself of a fiend, leaving her with a mask of red, of which she soon soothed with cream. She would stay inside on this last night, opting to eat a sandwich from the provisions she had placed in the refrigerator when she had arrived.

A sweet sensation had come over Cynda as she clung to the thoughts of her final evening. She watched a rerun of *The Lawrence Walk Show* and fell asleep to the crooning of the Lennon Sisters' "Wish Upon a Star". When she awoke, it was time to pack her things and head back to Atlanta, back to a new beginning.

How ironic that Cynda would end up living within a few short miles of her Sweet *Tybee* Island? Yes, she thought now, that beach trip had been a cleansing trip for sure. She was beginning to realize that her time with her sisters was also cleansing, something that now seemed as essential as breathing. She reached into the drawer beside her bed for the vial of oil. Cynda prayed a most reverent prayer of healing and applied the oils to her temples. She had not missed one day of the ritual. It was her secret. She knew now that there were more secrets to be revealed. Her confidence fortified, she began to dress for the day.

Cynda found the juicer and had three glasses of orange juice squeezed and chilled by the time her sisters arrived for their morning breakfast. Unbeknown to her, they had been having their own thoughts about the conversation of the previous evening. Before going down to breakfast, they were in a quiet discussion.

Chapter 31

Marcy and Suzanne had some ideas of their own about Cynda's mysterious breakup with Brock. Once they woke up and were out of earshot of their sister, they whispered to one another. Both had their doubts of the true reason their sister had seemingly fallen out of love with him.

"I just know there is more to the breakup of Cynda and Brock. I find it hard to believe that she just fell out of love with him. Furthermore, Audrey has resented her all of these years for the divorce. And once Dane came into the picture, that resentment grew even more," Suzanne whispered.

"You are right. You know that when they moved out to Decatur, they were so happy. When we went to visit them, I left dreaming that my marriage would be that perfect someday. Their house was so adorable and she had furnished it like a magazine. It just does not make sense," Marcy answered.

"Yeah, and I almost forgot the lake house. They did not have it for very long, maybe for a year or two before they divorced. I remember when Mama told me they had bought it. She said that Cynda had been ecstatic and could not wait to decorate it," Suzanne reminded her sister.

"In fact, the one and only time that Steve and I went up there to visit, it was just darling. We were just married and so impressed. She had worked so hard to make it homey and I got the impression it was her pride and joy. I did not get that same vibe from Brock. I thought Cynda was stepping up in the world. It's just like the house never existed," Suzanne said.

"Phillip and I went on one or two occasions. She wanted to have a family gathering there with all of us and Mama. That never happened as you well know. In fact, she has never mentioned the house to me either, not once since their divorce. I got the idea from Mama that Brock sold the lake house and the proceeds helped to pay for Cynda's house out in Luxomni. It is awfully strange that something that was that important to her has never been mentioned but just in passing. Maybe that lake house was their downfall. Just maybe, it was too much of a burden. Perhaps Brock did not want it as much as Cynda. Who knows? We are just guessing," Suzanne concluded.

"I believe in my heart if we could get to the truth about what caused the breakup, Audrey and Cynda could heal their relationship. Speaking of healing, when are we going to talk to her about the healing ceremony? Do you think she has used the oils?" Marcy questioned.

"Who knows? We will find a way to approach that subject. Right now I do know one thing for sure; you are right. We have to get more information about Brock and Cynda's divorce," Suzanne agreed.

"Let's go down to breakfast, before she starts wondering why we have not come down."

When the two sisters found their juice waiting for them, they were reminded once again of how special their mother had been. They were beginning to see that Cynda had developed many of those traits. She was a wonderful cook just like their Mama. Not only that, she was a wonderful hostess. It was difficult to see their sister as only the shadow of the person she had once been. Before her illness, she would have had a gourmet breakfast awaiting them when they got up. It wasn't as if they expected such royal treatment; it was that they missed the Cynda who was hidden underneath the burden of her sickness, the only one they had really known.

"I propose a toast," Cynda said as the three of them sat down at the table to drink their juice.

"Here's to sisterhood," she proposed.

"To sisterhood," they all agreed as they tapped their glasses together.

The pleasant mood of the morning prevailed throughout the remainder of the day. However, neither Marcy nor Suzanne found an opportunity to broach the subject of "the breakup". In fact, the conversation was geared more toward the sisters' limited memories together during their childhood.

"I just want to know one thing, Cynda," said Marcy, "How did you ever survive that perm Mama had you to get when you were twelve? I lived in fear that she was going to do the same thing to me. And, I was scared to ask you about it. I thought you looked funny at first, until I realized that you were pretty upset. I thought you might not ever come out of your room."

"Let's just say headbands saved my life," Cynda replied with a small smile.

The sisters concluded their weekend with stories about their childhood before Cynda deserted their ranks. They had begged for tales about their daddy since he had been a part of her life for longer than theirs.

Cynda had resisted telling the story of the red Georgia clay. It was her only link to her daddy that belonged uniquely to her. She treasured the memory and nurtured it in her thoughts with care. She relived it on occasions for comfort. Her daddy had encouraged her to be strong and persevere, no matter what, even when her perfection could not conquer the arrogance of human nature.

Chapter 32

Cynda returned home for the week with a song in her heart, literally. The words to "I Can See Clearly Now" kept playing in her mind like a broken record. She had a new found energy. She was sleeping late, but when she woke she was ready to face her day.

Dane had fallen into his new routine without her, but seemed anxious to share more time with her when she returned. They piddled together in the yard, planting a few new annuals for the fall season. He appeared to be happy that she was spending time with him during his chores, even if she was just watching.

Cynda observed the man she had married twenty years ago as he was weeding the flower bed. He had been such a young and vibrant man at the age of sixty. The years had not been unkind to her husband. He was still very handsome. His neatly trimmed mustache and beard framed a finely chiseled face. The steely blue eyes remained a constant. She had always been a sucker for blue eyes, she thought. Dane's frame was still fairly lean and firm. He had taken very good care of himself. His golf and tennis games had been good for his physical stature.

What Cynda could not ascertain were the thoughts that were hidden behind the wall that he had built when she had become ill. He had of course professed his love and support for her when the truth of her disease had been discovered. For the most part, he had been very supportive, aside from his emotional withdrawal.

She began to dissect his support during her illness. How ironic, this business of healing. Had Cynda not been to the best doctors both inside and outside of Atlanta? Had Dane not spent thousands of dollars on specialized clinics, hoping that she could be cured? The perfect husband with all of his money; what did it matter? But it did matter, because she was not ready to give up, especially not now as her relationship with her sisters had begun to flourish. In fact, she had decided that the time spent with her sisters had been a healing balm for both her and Dane. She was beginning to wonder what she would do when the two of them returned to Atlanta in a couple of weeks. Only two more weekends with them. She would make the best of them. Cynda was almost giddy with anticipation for the next weekend.

While Cynda was contemplating her much anticipated return to the cottage, her sisters were contemplating the dilemma of Audrey.

"We have just got to get Cynda to open up this weekend," Suzanne said.

"You're telling me," Marcy said and then continued.

"Haven't I said it over and over again? We have to be blunt with her."

"I don't think that pressuring her is the answer. If we gently extract some more information from her without her realizing our intention, we can win her confidence. So far, it has worked," Suzanne said.

"Yes, but we are running out of time. After this weekend Audrey is expecting to come and try to make amends with her mother."

"I don't see how this is all going to work out. I can see Cynda getting angry with us for attempting to reconcile her relationship with Audrey. I know that Audrey is in so much agony over her mother's illness. She feels guilty and helpless at the same time," Suzanne shared with her.

"That's all more the reason; we have to get to the bottom of the problem. This is too important. Mama would never forgive us if we didn't try to help Cynda through this. I don't think Cynda even realizes how much Audrey is hurting. How can she not communicate with her? I never hear her speak of her. What does Audrey say?" Marcy implored.

"She says they talk about three or four times a month, but not on a regular basis. The conversation is always the same, just small talk, and no talk of the cancer. Cynda apparently will not share very much with her, choosing to ignore the subject. Audrey is beside herself with worry," Suzanne said.

Chapter 33

The week flew by and before Cynda could blink, it was Friday. She and Dane had enjoyed one another's company more than ever. She could sense his relief in her new found energy.

Dane prepared their breakfast and had cleaned the kitchen before Cynda had even gotten up. When she entered what had always been her domain, she immediately noticed there were a few crumbs he had missed on the countertops. The dishcloth was lying in a crumble in the sink. She found her plate warming in the oven, retrieved it and strolled out onto the patio. For the first time in her life, she turned and left the kitchen in disarray, at least by her standards. For the first time in her life she was beginning to realize, it did not matter.

When her sisters picked her up in the *Hug Bug*, they were casually dressed in shorts, flip-flops and t-shirts. To their surprise, Cynda did not have on her usual long sleeve blouse and slacks. She did not even have a cosmetic case in her hand.

Cynda kissed and hugged Dane lovingly before she turned to wave hello to the girls. She had been sitting outside on the curbing around the flower bed watching Dane deadhead blooms.

When Cynda approached the car with only a large purse in her hand, Marcy said, "Aren't you forgetting something?"

"As a matter of fact, I'm not," Cynda said cheerfully.

"I have all I need in this purse."

The sisters looked at one another and said together, "That's a first!"

"Jinx, you owe me a Coke®!" both of them said, again together, each hoping to beat the other to the phrase.

"Well, it's been a couple of decades since I have heard that phrase," Cynda laughed, "Audrey and her buddies always said 'punch bug' when two of them repeated a sentence."

Suzanne thought about asking her if she had talked to Audrey in the past week. Instead she thought twice about it and zipped her lip.

"Well, I like the idea of getting a Coke® right now. If you wouldn't mind Suzanne, I like the idea of driving this little *Hug Bug* of yours even better," Cynda said as she waited for a reply.

"Absolutely," Suzanne said as she swung the tiny door open and then settled herself in the back seat.

"By the way, I forgot to ask, can you drive a stick?"

"I was driving a stick when you were still in grade school; of course I can. Clive let me drive his truck on the dirt road over by the water tower before I even turned sixteen," Cynda said as she balanced a pair of large round sunglasses on her nose.

With a flick of her wrist, she threw the gear in reverse and backed down the drive, choking and jerking as she eased the clutch out less than smoothly. Once she changed the gear to drive, her technique changed and proved to be less questionable. They were on their way, but to where?

Cynda turned the Bug to the left, instead of in the direction of *Tybee* Island and pushed the accelerator to full throttle. Pretty soon, the three of them were speeding down the four-lane highway exceeding the speed limit.

Neither Marcy nor Suzanne said a word when the direction to the cottage changed. They remained quiet until the hands of the speedometer hovered around sixty miles per hour.

"Okay sister, don't you think you had better slow down before you get a ticket?" Marcy said as she was

215

clinging to the hair that was threatening to obstruct her vision.

Suzanne was enjoying the dizzying ride, since she never rode in the back seat. She felt elated and free as she too struggled to keep her hair from its blinding course across her face.

Cynda immediately released the pressure on the accelerator and slowed the car to an acceptable speed and shouted into the wind, "Sorry, I got a little carried away!"

"By the way, where are we headed?" Marcy shouted in like fashion.

"Shopping."

Suzanne leaned forward and said, "What are we shopping for?"

"I need some new clothes. I am tired of looking like the bag lady. Everything I own is too big," Cynda said as she slowed the car down to turn onto Skidaway Road.

Pretty soon the sisters were turning into a strip mall that had a row of shops with colorful awnings. The shops were flanked with pots of flowers and rows of tables with umbrellas. The scene beckoned the sisters like a moth to a flame.

The three unloaded from the car like a group of schoolgirls out for the day. Cynda took the lead and they entered a t-shirt shop. Marcy and Suzanne gave one another questioning looks. They had never seen their sister wear a t-shirt, at least not as an adult. Cynda rifled through the shirts and found a soft pink shirt that had a script that read, "Wishing". She held the shirt up and showed it to her sisters.

"Look, it has a little car with a surfboard on top! I think it was meant for me, don't you?"

Suzanne answered rather quickly and said, "Hey that's my shirt! I'm the one with the little car."

"Well, I've adopted the Bug for today. I would buy a surfboard if we didn't have to put the top down for our adventure," Cynda laughed.

After selecting a couple other shirts with like slogans in different colors, she found some capris made of soft jersey. The shop also sold flip-flops and she was able to find a couple of pairs.

"Nothing like one stop shopping," Cynda said as she placed the items on the counter."

"Dane would never allow me to stop in this shop. He said I was too classy," Cynda said under her breath as she paid for her purchases. The three of them left the shop and placed the packages in the trunk. Cynda looked like the cat that swallowed a rat.

Instead of getting into the car, she said, "I have always wanted to stop here and hang out a little while. There is a little restaurant that sells chili dogs over there," she said as she pointed to the building.

"What do you think? I have missed the Varsity in Atlanta. It's been a long time," she said as she made a little puppy dog face.

"You don't have to beg me. I am sure they can't compete with the Varsity's famous chili dogs, but it's worth a shot. My stomach has been yearning for some good old fashioned grease," Suzanne said as she rubbed her stomach in a circular motion.

The sisters ordered chili dogs, chips and drinks. They sat underneath one of the umbrellas and all came to the same conclusion. The Varsity was number one, but these dogs were running a close second.

"To think that I have lived here for twenty years with this right under my nose," Cynda said as she relished the last bite. "Of course I would have to sneak to get one. Dane abhors hotdogs; thinks they are horrible. I am so glad we came here today. When you two are gone, I have something to look forward to."

Marcy and Suzanne were beginning to wonder about their perfectionist sister who always seemed to be in control. It appeared that Dane had his hand on some of those controls. They both wondered if she had given up on some of the simple things that made life worth living. Maybe that castle she lived in was more like a fortress.

The sisters remained in the little utopia for a few leisurely hours, reluctantly leaving after visiting more of the shops. It had been a pleasant surprise, the impromptu trip to the quaint little area. The colorful awnings were flapping in the wind waving their goodbye as the little *Hug Bug* left the area at a much slower pace than its arrival.

Cynda changed her speed to a slow and leisurely pace as she navigated the little Bug to the cottage, taking the scenic route. The three of them did not talk much, lost in their own nostalgic thoughts, wishing there had been more of the camaraderie while growing up. Cynda had always been so distant, but the tides seemed to be changing and none too soon.

The little bug slid into the parking space in its temporary home. It sputtered its last breath for the day with three sisters longing for more. Cynda begged their pardons to take a nap when they arrived. She took her bounty and her purse to the 'enchanted room'; yes, that was what Suzanne had called it when she moved in and it stuck with her. She removed her new clothes from the bag and inspected them, satisfied with her selections. She would leave them at the cottage when she returned home on Sunday. Dane would not understand their significance, her link to the past.

Chapter 34

When Cynda joined her sisters in the kitchen, preparations were already in progress for dinner. She stepped into their steady rhythm clothed in the pink t-shirt and capris. She had no problem falling into the shared task of preparing the meal. Undoubtedly, cooking was her forte. Cynda decided to take a back seat for once and took directions in her part of prepping the meal. It felt good. When she opened the broccoli to put it into the salad they were making, the odor transcended decency.

"For a moment there, I thought Clive had arrived in a cloud of gas," Cynda wrinkled her nose in distaste.
"Clive?"
"What made you think of him?" Marcy said as she recalled the object of her childhood affections.
"Oh, he was notorious for passing gas. In seventh grade, we almost had to evacuate the agriculture building. When he sat on one of the radiator heater vents and showed no mercy, he passed gas for a full five minutes, you know one of those machine gun numbers. Pow, puh puh pow pow pow!"
Suzanne and Marcy both snickered at her rendition of Clive's outburst.
"Besides the agriculture department, there were a couple of classrooms located in that building. I was unlucky enough to be in that class with him. It was so cold outside; some of us were allowed to step in the hallway until the smell evaporated. Bobbie Jean Hill threw up all over her new blue scarf as she was holding it over her nose."
"Well, that little story destroys any romantic notions that I ever had about Clive," Marcy said wrinkling her nose.

"He did grow up and out of those shenanigans once we became close friends. I miss Clive. You know when he came back from Vietnam, he was never the same. I tried to stay in touch with him, but he was so aloof, not the same Clive. Finally, I gave up."

"So sad, I never was able to tell him how very right he was about Brock. I really wanted to, but I decided not to burden him. He seemed to have enough to worry about."

"That is sad to hear. Did he ever marry?" Marcy said as she wondered what Cynda's statement meant.

"Yes, I did hear that he married some girl from the Southside of Atlanta when we went to our ten-year reunion. That was the last I heard of him."

"That must have been fun, your ten-year reunion that is. Wasn't that about the time that you and Brock split up?" Suzanne said as she joined the conversation.

"A treasure trove of fun. Thankfully, it was just before Brock and I parted ways. I would not have shown my face for those cows to moo over. You know I was never a favorite of the girls in my class. I blame myself somewhat for that because I know that I remained aloof. It wasn't that I didn't want friends. I guess I just didn't know how. To be frank, I was just more comfortable with guys. That is why Clive and I were such good friends."

"I can just imagine them all chewing their cud when they heard the news about Brock and me."

"I didn't know you had such much animosity for your classmates. Comparing the girls to cows just doesn't seem to be in your character, especially coming from 'polite society'," Suzanne teased her.

"If you are talking about my stint in Brookhaven, you know I never really transitioned into that society. And if you get right down to it, Phyllis was never fooled. She was constantly reminding me of what was expected of a young lady of 'polite society'."

"Well, that must have been pleasant. What were you supposed to do and how were you supposed to act?" Suzanne said fascinated with the premise.

"In 'polite society', one must never be seen outside the home without one's makeup done and hair perfectly coiffed," Cynda patted her hair and mocked her own words.

Suzanne giggled thinking of Phyllis. No wonder Audrey always joked about her grandmother. In fact, her motions when she imitated her grandmother were the very cookie cutter of what her mother had just done.

"I daresay Phyllis would have gone into cardiac arrest if she had met Bertha Snodgrass at Turner's Drugs in downtown Luxomni on Saturday morning. Her constitution could not have handled that one. You know Miss Bertha had no qualms about showing up with curlers in her hair if the notion struck her. I always wondered if that is why she never married," Cynda added thoughtfully.

"Mama told me that she heard Miss Bertha was engaged once. Supposedly, her fiancé ran off with someone he met at the Snake Show at the county fairgrounds," Cynda went on to say as she lifted her brow.

"Maybe that was her way of fending off the men...you know, curlers in the hair," Suzanne said.

"Maybe so, but those brogans she wore were pretty disturbing," Cynda made a face as she spoke.

"She might have been hurt so bad that she really did not care if she ever attracted anyone," Suzanne continued, "That is so sad if true."

"What is sad is that when I moved down here to Savannah and on to Wilmington Island, I fell into the web of 'polite society' that I had fought so hard to resist in Atlanta," Cynda said quietly.

"I do not have Phyllis constantly reminding me to do this and do that; I have Dane. Unlike Brock, my present husband expects 'polite society' behavior from me. Who would have guessed? Foolishness is what Brock called it. I can tip my hat to him on that account."

"Of course I have always wanted to please Dane, a little different from the demands of a mother-in-law. Just to be perfect for him. Not really hard to do when my own perfectionism has controlled my life," Cynda said as a matter of fact.

Wow, that was profound Marcy thought! Suzanne seemed to mirror her thoughts as she raised her brows in Marcy's direction. Neither one of the sisters knew quite how to respond to that admonition. They certainly had seen her perfectionism, but never knew how much it really controlled her life – and the essence of her being.

The evening progressed into much less dramatic dialogue and into topics like the current events and the weather.

Chapter 35

Cynda could not shake the nagging memories that she had suppressed during the day. She had a restless night when she retired, as she continued to think about her marriage to Brock. She had put her memories of him in a neat and tidy box in the attic of her mind, stored there with items that she found hard to depart with. Of course, she could not just throw them away, she told herself. They were part of her and who she had become.

Rumelle was the one and only that she had told the truth to about her divorce, other than her mother. Rumelle had seen her raw with emotion and stripped of her pride. The one person, who on some level that could understand her when no one else could, was her sweet friend Rumelle.

She had been ashamed to reveal the truth to her family then; ashamed that she had sacrificed her life to marry a man who betrayed her in the worst possible way. She who had always been a perfectionist and exercised control to that end. Losing Brock had been losing control of her very existence. He had robbed her of her perfect life. She had been a loving wife to him and a wonderful mother to Audrey. She had entertained his friends, kept a lovely home and had always been there for him in every way.

Where had she failed? She had asked herself during those dark days. What good was trying to be perfect if you could not even measure up no matter how hard you tried? During those troubling times, she could not overcome those feelings of low self-esteem she had fought so hard to suppress from her childhood. And her precious lake house had been the accomplice of Brock's heartless deed. If it had a soul, she knew the lake house would have grieved as deeply as she had when he used it so callously to destroy her world.

It had been a lark that Cynda and Brock had bought the lake house. They had been riding around one Sunday afternoon and discovered it. Located on the outskirts of Athens on beautiful Lake Oconee, it proved to be a perfect investment for them. They could use it when they attended Georgia games, and best of all, it was on the water. They both loved the water. It was no surprise when Brock had arrived home with the paperwork for the purchase. She had been thrilled. It would be their getaway. Audrey was getting older and enjoyed time away from her parents.

It sickened her to think how hard she had worked on the lake house to please Brock. He wanted to hire someone to do some of the work, but she insisted on using her own manual labor. She stripped wallpaper, painted and scrubbed her heart out, a labor of love in itself. The act of physical labor had been rewarding, unlike anything she had ever felt before.

The two would go up on the weekends to work on the house. Her zeal for the restorations was contagious and Brock seemed to enjoy it as much as she. Cynda wore ragged jean shorts and t-shirts, and he likewise. She felt more in her comfort zone than she had in years. They were both relaxed and loving in the world that had become their escape from day to day activities. Each and every time they went to the lake, she felt their marriage bonds deepen even stronger.

Brock's work had become more demanding and the lake house seemed to become a passion for him as well. Cynda of course was just as passionate in her quest to make their little getaway something special. There were times when living life in the shadows of the city with the mundane tasks of keeping a home bored her to tears. Never tiring of being a mother, Cynda soon learned that as Audrey grew older, she needed her mother less and less. The lake house was Cynda's second child.

Thinking of a second child now made her sad; back then she had been devastated. She had miscarried a couple of times after Audrey was born. Both she and Brock had decided not to try again. Cynda could not stand the idea of losing another baby and resigned herself to being the best mother she could be to Audrey. Brock knew how much the getaway meant to her, a place to fill the void.

That is why the betrayal had almost ripped her heart out. She could not speak of it to her mother until much later after the divorce, and never to her sisters. She did not want their pity. She had thought it was much easier for them to think she had wanted out, that she did not want to be married anymore. It appeased her need to be perfect.

Had it been easier, or had she just wanted her family to continue to see her as perfect? The never failing at anything, always getting what she wanted; the man of her dreams, a beautiful home and daughter, perfect Cynda. Maybe she told herself now; she had just wanted to pretend to herself that her perfect life had ended of her own choosing. Had she ever really faced the truth, or had she forced it into the recesses of her mind, never accepting reality? Did it really matter now, she thought? Maybe it was time that her sisters knew the truth, she told herself. Maybe it was time she faced the truth.

At that moment the questions that swirled in her mind like a storm were robbing her from precious rest. She continued to analyze the past until the pull of slumber overtook her senses.

Saturday morning brought a deluge of thunderstorms. It was almost an omen of the day to come as it descended on the three women in a kaleidoscope of truths. They unknowingly waited blindly for the real storm to show its face, all unaware of its cleansing power. Cynda appeared to be agitated and distant at breakfast. Afterwards, she planted herself on the "couch with no personality" and covered herself with an afghan, flipping channels on the television. The sisters joined her and they all agreed to watch reruns of their favorite shows for the remainder of the day.

After dinner, they were perusing magazines and making small talk. Cynda seemed distant and joined in occasionally commenting on the subject at hand. It was as if fate intervened and truth ensued. Marcy was looking at a magazine that had beach destinations and homes for sale.

"Wow, I wish Phillip and I could afford a second home, maybe one to refurbish."

Cynda's attention was immediately directed to her sister and she said, "Spare yourself the pain. I worked on the lake house like it was my baby and when it was gone, it left a hole in my heart," her voice tempered with anguish.

Marcy was afraid to ask, but decided to press her sister for answers, "I am so sorry. I know you spent a great deal of time there. It must have really hurt when y'all sold it."

"Not near as bad as the hurt I endured the last time that I stepped foot on that property," Cynda said quietly and reverently.

Suzanne and Marcy were at full attention and waited expectantly for her to reveal why she had been so hurt. The story was unleashed with all the painful and sordid details that had been pent up inside for a lifetime. As she began telling her story, no details were spared. The pain was etched in her face as she shared the particulars of the timeline and the events that led her on the road to regret.

Chapter 36

September in Atlanta had a way of teasing its inhabitants into believing that summer would never end as far as the temperature was concerned. Many of those hot days lasted well into September. A cool and brisk morning was often snuffed out by a hot and humid afternoon, as once again summer reared its relentless head to suppress any thought of relief from the sweltering heat.

It was on one of those fine September Saturdays that began with a chill in the air, enough to lull the senses and the senseless into believing that a football game in nearby Athens, Georgia would be absent of the hot and humid air that threatened asphyxiation. Brock was one of those senseless die-hard football fans who lived and breathed to swelter "between the hedges" in Sanford Stadium, cheering his team to hopeful victory. No matter, he was the victor of hours of a camaraderie that precluded anything that essentially happened on the field. Those famous hedges that surrounded the field held more than wins and losses. They held the hopes, dreams and reality for some whose lives would be forever changed by being a part of the "Bulldog Nation". For many, football was a way of life. For Brock, it was as essential as breathing.

It was a tradition for most of the female fans of football and who swore their allegiance to their alma mater to "dress to the nines" on game day. Cynda was no exception, hers vicariously, but no less faithful. Anyway, Brock was a graduate of the University of Georgia and she was his wife and that should count for something, she had always thought.

Cynda had magnanimously given her ticket to one of Brock's buddies who was in town for the weekend. It had not taken much cajoling from Brock to convince her to give up her ticket, especially since her friend Judy would not be there to tailgate, as she was in the last stages of pregnancy. The sheer agony of last week's game, although a win, was fresh on her mind. She remembered the perspiration that had formed its sheen of torture on hers and the faces of the well styled females who carefully dabbed themselves with tissues to keep their makeup intact. She often wondered even then if it really mattered, the business of being the perfect wife-fan. Cynda sometimes felt as if Brock paraded her in front of his friends like a steer at auction. The pink tinge of sunburn on her face from the last Saturday and the memory of the sweat running between her breasts made her cringe. Once the game was over, it had taken all of the energy she had left after hours of cheering, to strip the panty girdle that was molded to her body. She had removed it in the car, lying in a semi-prone position, gasping for air as she peeled it from her unforgiving hips. Once home, it had lain in the bathroom floor indefinitely, before she was able to pick it up and unroll it to its original form. At best, it was far superior to the girdles that Miss Reed had touted. She remembered staring at it when she dropped it into the washing machine and wondering if it were really worth the sacrifice. The torment of that girdle alone was enough for her to pretend to Brock that she was making a great sacrifice to relinquish her ticket. Yes, she would play the martyr and why not she had thought. Who knew when a woman might need a little clout, some power in persuasion?

Cynda thought about the lake house and wondered how she and Brock would balance time at the lake and football. When they had bought it, all they could think of doing was escaping to the water. They never attended many "away" games, so it should work out beautifully. Lost in thought about how wonderful life seemed to be going for her, Cynda became conscious of the sound of Audrey's voice in the background.

"Please, Mama, please, can we go see MeeMee?" Audrey said.

Brock had just left for the ballgame. The thought of spending a nice leisurely day enjoying the last rays of summer sun and reading a book was the only thing that appealed to Cynda at that point.

She was thoughtful for a minute, but knew what her answer would be. She looked at Audrey with her big blue eyes and sheepish grin and saw Brock. She could not ever say no to her. Her capitulation to defeat to those very eyes that mirrored her father's had always been her downfall. She surrendered as she waved her dishrag into the air.

"Go change your clothes," Cynda had told Audrey as she stared pensively at the breakfast dishes wishing they would just go away. "I need to clean the kitchen before we leave. Call MeeMee and tell her we are coming." Cynda knew that her mother would be thrilled, especially if the call came from Audrey.

After about an hour, mother and daughter climbed into the 1970 Pontiac Malibu. The car was two years old when Brock had bought it for her a few months ago, but she loved it like it was brand new. Cynda decided to roll the windows down and allow the sweltering humid breeze to tickle the fancy of their moment of companionship. It was a habit of hers, whenever the weather permitted, to tempt the fate of good judgment. She knew they would arrive windblown and crispy around the edges, but intoxicated with the sheer pleasure of drinking in the outside world.

It was always comforting and a little exhilarating to return home. Home, now that was a heartening word. Cynda reflected a little bit on the small brick structure that housed so many memories, both wonderful and painfully bittersweet. Behind its walls lay the foundation of the Brooks family, layers of pride and dignity, with an icing of graciousness of Southern tradition; yes, that was one way to describe her Mama.

Cynda considered herself lucky that she lived only a half hour away from her childhood home. When she needed her soul restored, she sometimes found herself driving there. If for only a couple of hours to breathe the untainted air of rigorous agendas and to avoid the suffocation of rigidity of her daily tasks. The effort was worth it. And then she would find her mother there to give her opinions, welcome or not. It was a constant in her life, her childhood home. Today she felt good that she had made the decision to surrender to its strength and charm. Today would be a good day, a time to recharge.

As much as Cynda loved the hustle and bustle of Decatur, the quaint little town of Luxomni whispered its message of welcome each time she entered the city limits. There was only one red light and a couple of turns that completed her arrival, once she entered the hallowed ground of her childhood. There would always be a piece of her heart in Luxomni.

She pulled into the driveway at eleven o'clock and could hardly put the car in park before Audrey hopped out to run inside. Cynda observed the enthusiasm for her MeeMee that was unequaled in its honest adoration, compared to anything she herself had ever experienced. She was content at that moment to bask in the ripples of its contagious magic.

Cynda had never had that kind of relationship as her grandparents were all dead and gone before she was born. How odd that must have been for her parents, never to have that connection of "home" once they were married. She had never really given it much thought until now. The reassurance of her good fortune lay heavy in the air.

Her mother had missed the encouragement and advice of her own mother when raising her girls. However, there were plenty of generational traditions ingrained in her soul before the loss. Of course there was always Aunt Sally, but she knew her Mama had taken that guidance with a "grain of salt".

Not once after Cynda married did her mother fail to mention her own mother's sage advice each and every time she visited. It had been explained to Cynda that it was her duty as matriarch to impart words of wisdom from the hierarchy of her past, a true southern practice in her mind. It did not matter if Cynda asked for the so called wisdom. Her mother would always impress upon her how important it was for her to listen and that was that! Deep in those thoughts, she exited the car, and in doing so, she decided to make a concerted effort to heed more of her mother's advice and at the least, placate her a little more.

The subject of her contemplation was found immersed within the hallowed walls of the kitchen. The word that immediately entered Cynda's thoughts was "tending". Mama had always "tended" to something. Whether it was her meal, her home or her three girls, she always "tended" to something or someone. At the moment, she was competing with the steam that was rising rapidly from one of the pots and was losing. Her face was flush and damp with perspiration. The situation did not deter her from "tending" to her daughter's business. She greeted her with a reprimand, "Audrey should not be allowed to wear that lipstick." Cynda ignored the statement and hugged her in silence.

It was becoming more evident that Audrey had a mind of her own. She was like a little colt, running and dancing, kicking up her heels in defiance of the mare that had born her. Cynda decidedly chose to ignore the lipstick and choose her battles carefully. Recently, the child had been a little rebellious in following the rules that her mother and father had put in place. Audrey did not want to go to bed on time and was found more than once with her light on, reading well after ten o'clock. It certainly was not harmful. Reading was a wonderful habit and she certainly did not want to discourage it, but rules were rules.

It was sometimes hard to exercise control over Audrey and it had been becoming more and more difficult. Brock was no help. He allowed her to do what she wanted to do. He lamented often that Audrey was his princess and that Cynda was his queen. She knew that where Brock and Audrey were concerned, it was a losing battle and wondered if her mother had felt the same about her and her relationship with her own father. Brock and Audrey's relationship was so special and she certainly did not wish to intrude on it, especially since she had experienced that kind of bond firsthand.

Cynda changed the subject by commenting on the heavenly smells that filled the kitchen. She looked around to find that the table had already been set. She filled the glasses with ice as her mother was finalizing the finishing touches of the meal that she had prepared. Cynda would miss the tailgating today, but what her mother had cooked would surely surpass its offerings by a mile.

The food at the tailgate was always phenomenal, since everyone competed to bring the best dish. Today there was no competition. Her mother had won hands down and Cynda was basking in the decadence of pure ecstasy of southern food haven. Feeling glad that Athens was miles away, she took a swig of the elixir of sweet tea that complimented the meal like a lovesick man's pontification of his own virtues. The euphoric feeling permeated her being like an addict's fix. It wasn't just the food; it was the sanctity of her Mama's presence that comforted her very soul. There must have been some perception in her bones of what lay ahead, for she would need all of the strength she could muster the next day.

Cynda thought now when looking back, it was more like the last meal before being led to the firing squad. The next day she wanted to block out reality's grip that sucked the breath from her lungs. She wanted to hit rewind to the day before to exist again in the nourishment of her Mama's presence.

Brock had planned to spend the night with some of his fraternity brothers, so after lunch Cynda was in no hurry to return to Decatur. She relaxed for the afternoon, even sitting in the sun for a little while watching her mother work in her flowerbed. When it was time to go, she could not find her purse. Once again, it had been innocently hidden. She knew the culprit. It was Audrey of course. One of her ploys to prolong their stay. Cynda demanded her to give it up, so Audrey moved to her second line of defense to keep from leaving. She begged to spend the night with her MeeMee.

Cynda knew she would be lonely without Audrey but decided to give in. It was a weakness she had about the grandparent relationship. In Cynda's mind, there were some things only a grandparent could give a child, time without their parents. She did not want to deprive Audrey of that special gift so with unselfish reluctance she consented. She had always given the same courtesy to Phyllis and Buie.

Cynda leaned over to roll up the window on the passenger side of the Malibu as she prepared to leave her mother's home. She felt a little melancholy and wondered if she should stay but decided to leave Audrey and her mother to enjoy each other's company without her. It wasn't long before the evening sun hid its radiance, dropping down behind the tree line ahead on the roadway. Cynda could feel a crispness in the air and reluctantly rolled up her window. She turned on the radio to the sounds of Otis Redding's "Sitting on the Dock of the Bay" cranking out its soulful melody. She sang as loud as she could with abandon, knowing that she could not carry a tune. As her mother would say, *you can't carry a tune in a bucket.* She smiled as the string of words from the song paraded across her mind with her mother's old school phrase attached as their caboose. All was right with her world.

The song ended and she felt an unfathomable sense of dread. The feeling of gloom began to descend over her like a pall. Suddenly she wished she had gone with Brock. On the other hand, her good sense pleaded the injustice. They both needed their own space sometimes. She knew he needed time with his friends and the game had been a great way for him to catch up. He worked so hard and deserved a break.

Cynda began to put her day in perspective and admitted that it had been priceless. She chased away the feelings of dread and focused on the next day. It was a chance for her to sleep in the next morning and maybe read a little, something she never got to do. She decided she would skip church for once. Raising Audrey in the church was a commitment she had made and had been an integral part of her own life; for Brock, it was not as important.

When Cynda got up the next morning, she immediately made some coffee. It was odd that she had not heard from Brock the night before but she brushed it off. He was busy being his social self and forgetting to call her was not an issue. She had just finished her coffee and was going to take a shower when the phone rang. It was the social butterfly. He sounded like he too had just gotten up. His greeting was nothing out of the ordinary as he said to her, "Hey babe, how are you doing this morning? Sorry I did not call last night. Jake and I were just talking and the time got away from me. I hated to call so late."

The sound of Brock's voice always made her heart skip a beat and this day was no different. She immediately responded with fondness in her voice and told him that she had been pretty tired. She went on to tell him about her visit with her mother. In fact, she said, "Audrey stayed and spent the night. We can pick her up when you get home."

Cynda crossed her fingers and held her breath just a little as she knew that Brock did not like it when he got home and Audrey was not there. It did not seem to faze him at all. He actually ignored the statement about Audrey; instead he said, "Since I am so close to the lake house, I think I will go over and check on things. You know, they are talking about frost this week. In fact, I might just spend another night and drive into work from there in the morning, if you don't mind."

Cynda did mind and suddenly felt jilted a little. She started wishing again that she had gone with him to the game and felt resentment welling in her chest. It would have been a good chance to have some private time without Audrey she thought. Instead, Cynda gave him the nod as always. She rarely disagreed with his decisions. Feeling silly, she quickly said, "There are things that need my attention around the house." Then, nonchalantly she added, "Call me later and try not to miss me too much."

When Cynda hung up the phone, she could not shake the feeling of wishing she was there with Brock. She even thought about driving down to surprise him. Opting to clean the house, her focus changed to the task ahead. She worked tirelessly and into the late afternoon, then decided it was time to drive out to pick up Audrey.

Brock's office was located in the back of the house close to the kitchen. Cynda was finishing her housework and decided to step into the office to call her mother to let her know that she would be there soon. There was a light blinking on the answering machine and she decided to retrieve the message, in case it was something important that Brock needed to know before work the next day. The voice on the recording paralyzed her in her steps. She could not breathe as the raspy sound spit through the air and ripped her world into tiny shreds of confetti that fell about her feet in a pool of despair. The splintering of a glass rendered her helpless as it shattered into a million pieces. It had fallen from her hand as she too was free-falling in an unstoppable plunge into urgent despair.

The words came in a sickeningly sweet tenor, "Heyy, Brock, its Paula. Just touching base to see if our plans haven't changed. I realize that you will not know when the game will end tomorrow, but I will be waiting at the lake house for you. Let me know if there is anything I need to pick up."

Cynda stood frozen in her tracks. She felt like someone had just punched her in the stomach. Her crumpled stature lost its strength as she sank down in the desk chair, pushing the button again to be sure that she had heard what her mind told her could not be true. Her heart sank as her head fell against the back of the chair. She closed her eyes, attempting to squeeze the images of infidelity from her certainty. The elephant on her chest was tap dancing in a slow and painful rhythm as breathing seemed to cease.

After a few minutes, she opened her eyes and affixed them on the answering machine. She stared at it as if it were a demon, taking her fist and hitting her tormentor over and over again as if she could purge the damning words from its depth.

Anger overtook her very being and thoughts for the next few minutes, and a plan formulated that left her blind with anticipation. She wanted immediate satisfaction. She had never been one to avoid a confrontation, at least not since that day in seventh grade when she had sent Clive Fincher away with his tail tucked between his legs.

Cynda's mind met the truth square in the face. The "heyy voice" was not attached to anything tangible and she had to see for herself the low-life that owned it. She would not wait to be belittled by the likes of a homewrecker and insincerely coddled by a husband that apparently did not love and respect her.

Her first mission was to take care of Audrey. She called her mother once she gathered her wits that took a deep breath of courage. After seven rings, Cynda was preparing to hang up the phone. The voice was clearly out of breath, and for a moment, she took a nosedive of panic. Cynda practically jumped through the phone line as she asked in the calmest voice she could muster, "What took you so long to answer the phone?" Then the answer came in the sweetest voice that stilled her beating heart. Her mother said, "We were just digging in the dirt a little, fixin' to put some pansies in the ground".

Cynda was so relieved to hear the sound of calm and steady that her knees almost buckled. She told her mother that she was getting ready to pick up Audrey when Brock called to say he was going to the lake house. She could almost feel the itch of her nose at it grew in the lie she told her. "Brock needs me to drive down to help him with a few things there," she said. Cynda tried to sound nonchalant when next she hit her mother with the biggie, "Do you mind if Audrey could spend another night?"

Without hesitation, her mother immediately agreed for her to stay, but Cynda could hear in her voice that she was hedging. "Is it okay for Audrey to miss school?" she asked.

Cynda assured her it would be fine and went as far as to tell her that Audrey was well ahead of the other students in her class. At that moment, she did not know that to be true and could feel her nose itching even more. She then said with absolute honesty, "Besides, can her teachers compete with your instruction? Just because Phyllis Franklin is in the garden club does not mean she belongs there. Your green thumb would put her in the shade, literally. Audrey will be getting a hands-on experience in science and biology that will be priceless."

Lydia Brooks absolutely loved praise, but she was no stranger to deceit. After all, she had raised three girls without a father. Cynda was certain that her mother gave pause to what she was saying and knew something must be wrong but decided not to press the issue by further defending her actions.

Once her mother agreed, Cynda was thankful that she always kept extra clothes for Audrey there. She suspected that her mother got as much of a thrill out of telling Audrey that she would be spending another night as Audrey did hearing the news. At that moment, Cynda was almost glad of her recent defiant nature; skipping school would be right up Audrey's alley. The die was set, but she needed to hear her baby's voice. She needed to feel grounded, before she took the plunge into the unknown. "Put her on the phone," she told her mother.

Audrey quickly took the phone from her grandmother. Cynda could remember so well her daughter squealing with happiness, when she also told her that she was spending another night. "Thank you, thank you, *so* much!" she practically sung into the phone, but you know I will miss you and Daddy. Tell him I love him and I love you, too." Her words cut Cynda like a knife. Still, she knew that Audrey was elated to stay with her MeeMee, but smart enough to try to cajole her into thinking that she was a little disappointed that she was not going to come home that night.

Cynda sighed as she heard the words that meant more today than ever. She needed Audrey right now, but she needed an immediate closure to the nightmare that she had woken up to on this brisk September day, one that she would never forget.

Cynda's delayed response was genuine as she responded, "I love you too sweetie, but just this one special time. Bye sweetheart. See you soon," Cynda almost crooned to Audrey.

That sweet little innocent could always get to her, even when she rebelled. Ordinarily, she would have never allowed Audrey to spend the night when school was in session. Audrey had begged on more than one occasion to do so with a firm "no" from Cynda. It would be the first of many times that she would choose the easy way out with Audrey; this time though it suited her own purpose. Audrey is an innocent in the whole damn mess, she thought.

Cynda clung to the final words to her daughter, as she knew that her world had been shattered, unless she had been living a horrible dream for the past few minutes. The assurance of Audrey's happiness was a priority at that moment and Cynda had to hold on to it for dear life. The only assurance Brock would have of the outcome of his folly remained to be seen. Cynda thought with conviction that the determination of his guilt was eminent and obviously settled. The handwriting was on the wall; she just had to read it for herself.

Cynda hung up the phone and took a quick shower. She dressed carefully and meticulously as she prepared to meet her adversary. She was anxious to encounter the husband stealer who obviously could not have an ounce of class. This "Paula" would certainly not be expecting her and she wanted the homewrecker to see exactly how class really looked. Her mother had always said, "You can't make a silk purse out of a sow's ear." Cynda now appreciated those pieces of wisdom from the hierarchy of her ancestral tree, delivered regularly from her mother. They were beginning to make plenty of sense.

Cynda did not have many clothes, but what she did have were chic and she wore them like a model. She opened her lingerie drawer to find the girdle she had tolerated at last week's ballgame. It was a grim reminder that only one week ago her life seemed to be a story book. The thought of smothering her body from mid-thigh to just above the waist in a shroud of rubbery Playtex® took her breath. It was utterly symbolic of the way she felt at that moment, bereft of air. This was one time that the sacrifice fit the crime, for surely wearing a girdle was a crime wasn't it, she thought.

She put on her best pants suit and pumps. Her auburn hair was swept back in a fashionable ponytail with a tortoiseshell clasp. She applied her make-up with care and looked in the mirror at her green eyes. She studied them as if they held the answers to her pain. How many times had Brock looked into those same green eyes, met with his own eyes of flashing blue, and caused her heart to skip a beat? He used them as a weapon against her, time and time again. This time she would not succumb to any excuse he had to offer.

Cynda took one last look at her image in the full length mirror in the foyer as she grabbed her purse and keys. In that moment, she could feel her courage resonate from deep within her being, remembering a day long ago, when she had been triumphant over Clive Fincher whose mockery was born from his own low self-esteem. Today, her adversary was quite the opposite, he was born with self-confidence, and that was what had attracted her to him. It was time to meet the opposition, she decided, and with finality she shut the cottage door behind her.

Cynda pulled the Malibu into the Gulf station on the corner of Ponce and Piedmont practically on two wheels. The attendant approached as she quickly rolled the window down in a circular motion. He wiped his greasy hands on a blue cloth and the smell of oil took her by surprise for just a moment. The faded blue shirt he wore had his name embroidered on the pocket. *Hank* was pulling double duty as gas attendant and mechanic. His teeth were a dull yellow color, needing some attention from a toothbrush, but nonetheless, he smiled with a big cheeky grin that made her feel at ease. "Fill her up please," Cynda said as she dug into the brown alligator purse that had been her pride and joy just a few short days ago. She had longed to have one of her own and practically salivated over its rough and exotic appeal. The excitement she had felt when she finally got it out of layaway, after sixty days, appeared ludicrous now. She had not wanted to ask Brock for the money for the purchase; instead she used her allowance to pay for it in installments. What had seemed to be important then was now quickly taking last place after her new found discovery.

"Check your oil, ma'am?" the attendant asked as he leaned over to give the finishing touches to her windshield wash he was performing, his toothy grin a bit too close for comfort. Her initial assessment of him began to fade as she started to analyze her feelings of trust for anyone.

"Yes, go ahead," Cynda replied as she absent mindedly answered, even though Brock had just had the oil changed the week before. He was good at that, taking care of cars that is, she thought. Again, her mind began to wander.

Good old Brock, the good old boy that was always taking care of everything. He made sure that they lived in a comfortable home and was a wonderful provider. His expectations of her included nothing more than what he called her wifely duties.

She thought he must be really proud of himself and how clever he had been; she was sure of that. He had always thought of himself very shrewd and prided himself on his ability to win his clients over. He was a people magnet, there was no doubt. Is that what had happened? Had his magnetic personality attracted homewrecker Paula or had she used her pathetic little southern drawl dripping with imitation sugar to trap him? Had she seen the golden boy image at work, the one on the fast track to success? She shook her head to clear her mind.

Cynda then stared at the speck of dirt left on the window by the attendant, as if the action would make it go away. "Sixteen dollars and forty-nine cents," the attendant repeated for the second time as Cynda's head moved slowly toward the voice that brought her back to reality.

"Oh, sorry sir, I was just daydreaming," Cynda murmured as she handed him the crisp twenty-dollar bill that she had been saving for their summer vacation.

Cynda gave herself a cynical snicker as the attendant walked away to get her change, reminding herself that "daydreaming" was hardly the appropriate terminology for her thoughts. Her thoughts were more like a reassessment of her life and the man who now had become a stranger. All of their dreams were beginning to pass before her very eyes and her life as she had known it appeared to be a farce. Just where did the truth begin and end, she thought. The scenarios would plague her for the next couple of hours as she drove without pause, allowing the endless interruptions to control her mind. Where had she gone wrong? Why had she trusted so blindly? Their marriage and her complete trust of her husband had taken some time to evolve. She had been afraid in the beginning of their marriage and had finally let her guard down as he had peeled away layer after layer of the deep fears for her to love again, after losing her father.

The images of Brock and this Paula, whoever she was, were spiraling out of control as she drove closer and closer to the lake house. Cynda started to imagine Brock's horror as he discovered that she knew the secret life he had been hiding and for God knows how long. She knew that he would look at her with those big blue eyes, eyes that would beg for forgiveness. Those eyes would not be her downfall, she promised herself again and again on that long trip. As for the so called homewrecker Paula, Cynda would enjoy making her squirm. What did Paula have that she did not?

Cynda finally turned down the long dirt road that led to the lake house. She was holding her breath and had to mentally tell herself to breathe again. The driveway was short and the view of the house was hidden. She remained relentless in her mission as her foot gave one last thrust on the pedal of the accelerator, the act that would bring her face to face with betrayal.

When Cynda arrived at her destination, there were no vehicles to be found. In fact, there was only stillness. All of her pent up anxiety had reached a pinnacle which could no longer be suppressed as she put the car into park. She took in all the air that her lungs could sustain and dropped her head to her open palms, releasing her breath in one long sigh. Then, she lifted her head and stared out into the setting sun and freed an agonizing scream from the depths of soul that shocked and startled her. Then large sorrowful tears began to flow like a river and she whimpered like a newborn puppy at the release that liberated her. It had been a long time, since she had allowed herself to feel the pain of loss. She knew that this loss was just as devastating as it had been sixteen years ago when her father had left the earth. This time it was the death of trust.

Once again, her muddled thoughts evaluated the length of time it had taken for her to fully love without fear of losing. She had kept a quiet reserve about her that Brock had often teased her about, saying she was aloof. When Audrey was born, the tenderness he showed their daughter began to chip away at her armor and after years, she thought she had finally been set free in his kingdom. She silently questioned that judgment.

Cynda did not know how long she sat there, but darkness had fallen like a blanket of finality around her. She knew that Brock had to be coming back soon and she quickly formulated a plan.

The small garage at the rear of the lake house was rarely used and could easily hide the Malibu from view when Brock approached the house. Cynda put the car in reverse, backing it up in the grass, thankful for the darkness that would hide her tracks. She pulled the car into the garage and put it into park. Cognizant that Brock could arrive any minute, she began to gather her alligator purse and her courage. Suddenly, she felt compelled to hurry inside.

The night air was refreshingly cool and Cynda freely drank from its reservoir. The cicadas hummed in unison as the tree frogs seemed to compete, a sound that ordinarily would make her hesitate in reflection of their song. Instead, she ran up the stone steps at the back of the house, only to find the screen door latched. She clenched her fists and hurriedly ran back down the steps, angry at the obstacle that was now costing her precious time. Time was a commodity for her now and she did not wish to spend any of it unwisely as her plan began to unfold.

Cynda reached the front steps and soon was on the front porch as she took the steps two at a time. The door was locked. She dug into her alligator purse and damned it as she found her fingers taking too long to find the key to the house. Seconds seemed like hours as her fingers finally felt the shape of the small Coke® bottle keychain that she had placed the lake house key on. It slid into the lock and she pressed the latch. Cynda sighed with relief as it released and the door swung open. How many times, she wondered, had she gone through those very motions thrilled with anticipation? Today, she felt it was almost sacrilege to enter with intentions of the discovery of deceit.

Cynda shut the heavy door that resisted slightly as its frame shuddered from years of repetitive closures. The resistance held her attention and in her haste, she did not lock it back. She did not dare to turn on a light, but stood patiently as her eyes became accustomed to the dark.

Cynda felt her way around the house, touching and then feeling all the memories of the prior months. She relished the cover of darkness that prevented her from considering her surroundings awash with treachery. She felt numb as it seemed to magnify the surreal.

The numbness could not thwart the sanctity of the intimacy that was born within the walls of the house. In those very walls that had made her feel secure in Brock's love, she had totally let go of her fears of losing; she now felt lost. Aside from that, she knew that her need to be perfect had been a lifetime struggle. Brock had been a part of aiding her to liberate herself from its power in this hallowed place. She had finally let her guard down, convinced that their special place had been his gift to assure her of *forever*. Her lack of trust had not been his fault. In fact, he had slowly, but steadily worked to erode her defenses. Now he was her adversary.

Cynda slipped quietly down the hall to the bedroom that they shared. She found that the bed was made and was relieved at the reprieve. The thought of the sight of the two of them made her shiver. She ran her hand across the crocheted bedspread that her grandmother had made and became angry at the image of infidelity beneath the labor of love from her grandmother's hands, hands she had never seen. She suddenly ripped the spread from the bed and clutched it to her chest, sinking to the floor in quiet defeat.

245

Cynda did not know how long she had been sitting in the dark corner of the bedroom. She had willed herself to think of Audrey, trying to banish the thoughts of the moments to come. In the distant corners of her mind, she heard the sound of the front door opening and closing. The dead bolt lock clicked, signaling the beginning of the end.

She heard another click that sounded like the den lamp being turned on. It was an eternity before Cynda heard the familiar sound of a squeaky cabinet door in the kitchen open then shut. The refrigerator door heaved and the sound of ice clinking in a glass rang in her ears. She strained to hear voices but heard only the silence of apprehension. Brock must be alone, she thought. She heard the water running in the kitchen sink and then nothing. The sound of steps walking across the living area gripped her like a vise. The fear in the pit of her stomach caused her to swallow. The owner of the footsteps stopped its stride. The clunk of the recliner footrest resounded in a thunderous roar. It was confirmation to her that she must decide to confront or to wait in ambush. Before she had time to make her decision, she heard another sound.

The rotary phone was just beside the recliner and she recognized the purring of its dial as it was being turned. She strained to listen. Brock should be calling her right about now, she remembered. Good. He would not be hearing her voice on the other end of the line. She hoped that he wondered where she was when she did not answer. Good old reliable Cynda, always there for him, always the perfect wife.

Instead of the silence as she had expected when he heard nothing but ringing in his ear, Brock started talking.

"Hi, I was hoping you would answer. I wasn't sure if you would be home yet."

Silence. Cynda tensed to hear his next sentence and wondered if she could decipher what was being said on the other end of the line.

"Yes, I went down to the corner café and got a bite to eat. Thought I would just relax a few minutes before I call Cynda. I sure dread that phone call. I would almost feel better if she were a little angry with me. It might make it a little easier."

Silence again.

"I know Paula, but it is not that easy. It is not just one life that we are affecting; it is two and I would move hell and high water to keep from hurting Audrey. She is the innocent in this."

"How dare he?" Cynda thought. "What was her role in this game of betrayal?" Her unfortunate role at this moment was wife and mother of his child.

Cynda's thoughts returned to the conversation at hand as she heard Brock say, "By the way, didn't I lock the front door when we left?"

Paula must have said that she had not noticed, since Brock answered, "I guess I am losing it. All of this slipping around we are doing is affecting my game." He gave a little chuckle and then added with some self-satisfaction, "Speaking of games, I am already missing those long passes you kept throwing me. I liked your pretty little pink panties."

If Cynda had any trouble breathing before now, she felt as if she might asphyxiate. She felt the elephant on her chest once again. She clutched the bedspread tightly for comfort, willing it to conjure the images of the grandmother she had never known. She wanted and needed someone, something, earthly or otherwise to intercede.

The earthly nor otherwise did not make an appearance. Her heart was pounding so hard in her chest; the thought occurred to her that it might burst. At that moment, she decided to confront him and ditch the idea of ambush. Just when she stood to make her way to the den, she heard him telling Paula goodbye.

"Bye sweetie. I will talk to you soon. I better give Cynda a call before she starts to wonder if something is wrong."

The sound of the rotary dial began to click again until all of the digits were completed. It was a few minutes before Brock finally hung up the phone. He mumbled something unintelligibly to himself and then she heard him push the foot rest back against the chair. The sound of footsteps approaching the bedroom suddenly gave Cynda the resolve she needed to confront her betrayer.

Brock stepped in the bedroom and she knew he immediately sensed her presence. If she had been in his skin, she would have felt a slow and encompassing chill run down his spine and the prickle of the hairs on the back of his head. He flipped the light on, without even a thought or explanation and said, "I knew I locked that door."

There was a long pause when Cynda finished her story. Marcy and Suzanne had sat on the edge of their seats almost trembling with loathing. They were at a loss for words, both suspended in the drama of the past. It had unfolded for them in its sordid details.

Cynda looked at them both and said, "Now you know the truth. I was not unhappy. In fact, I was so in love with Brock after ten years; I kept telling myself it wasn't true as I took that trip to the lake house. Even as I heard the words he spoke to her, I still did not want to believe them. By the time I drove back home, I was a basket case.

"You forgot to tell us what you said to him," Marcy said, wanting to know more.

"Absolutely nothing. I walked past him, cradling the bedspread in my arms. Thank God for Grandmother's spread and the courage it gave me. I don't think I could have made it past his pleading eyes without it. I never looked at him, not even when he called after me."

"Thank goodness I remembered my purse somehow. It was tucked under my arm; otherwise I would have had to go back into the house. Once I got out the front door, I literally ran to the car as if I were being chased by demons. It was not until I started down the drive that I realized that Brock was running behind the car. I guess he thought I would just run outside and crumble before his eyes."

"Did you stop?" Marcy said in wonder.

"Just long enough to allow him to go around to the driver's side of the car; when I rolled my window down I told him, 'Just going to pick up some pink panties for Pink Panty Paula'. And oh by the way, don't bother to come home'. I left him standing there looking like a little boy who had just had his toy taken from him."

"Oh my goodness, I guess you slapped him in the face with that little tidbit. I am sure he had no idea how much you could hear when he was talking to HER," Suzanne commented.

"Not exactly a slap. When I accelerated, if there had been any asphalt, I would have laid some rubber. Instead, when I looked in my rear view, I saw Brock dodging rocks and eating dust. It was the only satisfaction I managed to gain. I just wish Pink Panty Paula had been there to get the same dose of retribution, if you can call it that."

"What did you do then? I mean, how could you drive back home in that state of mind?" Marcy wondered out loud.

"I prayed for guidance and somehow made it home. I crashed into bed and slept from exhaustion. The next day I drove by rote to Mama's house to pick up Audrey. I could not wait to wrap her in my arms and feel her precious unadulterated love. Once I got there, I pleaded a headache to Mama and told her I needed to get back home. I am not sure she believed me. At that point, Audrey had been there for two nights, so she did not put up a fight to go home. Besides, she knew that missing another day of school was out of the question."

"Well, what did you tell Audrey when she discovered that her daddy was not coming home?" Marcy asked.

"I lied to Audrey. I told her that he was on a business trip. It was all I could do to get her ready for school and drive her there the next day. When I got back home, I climbed back into the bed and covered myself with grandmother's bedspread. I stayed there until it was time to pick her up. That routine went on for a week."

"When Brock did not come home for a couple of days, Audrey sensed something was wrong. I had to tell her something, so I told her that Brock and I needed some time apart. She was not happy."

"Brock and I communicated on the phone and one face to face meeting the following week. I made up my mind to never play second to anyone. There was nothing left to say. He knew that the ultimate sin had been committed and that no amount of persuasion would change my mind. He conceded without a fight, but made sure to cover all his bases. I was too broken to care."

"I finally admitted to Audrey that her mother and daddy had decided it would be best if they did not live together anymore. Brock did not have the guts to face her with me."

Marcy took that comment to the trash dump and rephrased it, "You mean balls. Brock did not have balls to tell his daughter what an asshole he was – you mean. You did grow up in the same neighborhood that we did."

"Yes, but times were different. I was just a few years older than ya'll, but if you cussed, and I mean cussed not cursed, you were just a step away from being a tramp.

And if you smoked cigarettes in the smoking room at the theatre, you were on the road to hell. Remember, I got married and left the area before I was tempted by some of those influences. Lucky me."

"Don't feel too short-changed. Neither of us could wait to escape that small town atmosphere, but live to return to its charm," Suzanne added.

Cynda went on to explain the repercussions after she informed Audrey of the situation. "I told her it would not change how much we loved her. She had to be so confused because she had never seen us raise our voices to one another."

"I did not want pity from anyone. I was ashamed that I had made a choice to marry right out of high school to the first one that came along and showed me love. I thought I had the perfect life and it came tumbling down."

"I felt like such a failure. I had always tried to be so perfect and be in control of everything."

"But why did you let everyone think that you wanted out and did not love Brock anymore? Could you not have let us in on your little secret?" Marcy said.

"I did it for Brock" replied Cynda.

"For Brock?" Suzanne asked incredulously.

"Yes, I covered the whole thing up. He was moving up fast in the firm. The partners were old school with very traditional values. The senior partners would not have been happy with him and from a client standpoint; it could have been very detrimental. You know, the 'polite society' that guarded their own, secrets that is, might have been appalled. He convinced me it was for the best for me financially to keep mum, once he saw that I would not stay in the marriage after his infidelity. It was a financial decision for me, nothing more. He agreed to ten years of alimony, or if and when I married, it would cease. Yes, I would say he covered all his bases."

"I am sure that Phyllis was complicit in covering up

Brock's dirty little secret," Suzanne said.

"Yes, of course, but that is another story," Cynda said, but not revealing any details.

"I guess what I am trying to understand in this whole breakup is why you have lied to Audrey all of these years. Why not tell her the truth when she was old enough to handle it? Why did you have to be the bad guy?"

"I did not want Audrey to be disenchanted with men. I wanted her to trust. I wanted her to meet her knight in shining armor without reservations, to accept true love."

"Like you?" Suzanne said quietly.

"I guess you could say that. Brock was my knight in shining armor and I lived a fairytale for ten years. Not everyone will be like Brock and turn into a dragon."

Marcy and Suzanne both realized that in trying to protect Audrey from being disillusioned, Cynda had caused the reverse to happen. Instead of accepting love, Audrey was afraid that she might turn out like her mother and fall out of love. Audrey had not been able to stay in a relationship for any length of time. "Best laid plans come undone," Marcy said using one of their mother's repetitive chants from her ancestral tree.

Suzanne considered her sister's woeful tale. She decided to comment on the sacred words of advice of their beloved mother. She tempered her statement a little when she said, "How I wish that you had been more honest with Mama. She was so insightful. She may have regurgitated those clichés and tidbits of advice, but her wisdom was priceless. Just hearing you speak of that day in such great detail makes me feel sad because I am certain her support would have helped you more than you could ever know," she said wistfully.

Cynda continued, "I finally did, but not until years later with the promise that she would never tell anyone."

Both of her sisters were shocked at her declaration.

Cynda said, "But Mama did help in ways that she never realized by just being Mama. She solidified my courage back then. The details of that time spent with Mama and Audrey the day before my world shattered was my saving grace. I could block out the sordid events at the lake house to keep from falling from the edge of my sanity by concentrating on my comfort zone."

"I played the events that led up to my discovery over and over again in my mind. However, I soothed myself with thoughts of Mama and her love for us all. I will never forget the meal that she served and maybe, just maybe, a premonition."

"That Sunday when I stepped into the house, the smells were pure heavenly. The menu was my favorite; roasted chicken and gravy, peas and cornbread, and of course sweet iced tea," Cynda smiled as if the remembrance transcended time. She concluded with lighthearted assertion, "I was not watching what I ate that day. The only thing I was watching was whether Mama saw me take more than one helping." Then she solemnly said, "It would be a long time after that before I would appreciate any meal, much less Mama's simple gift of devotion," then adding "Mama was standing in the kitchen with her back to me and I remember seeing myself in a few years, but not without Brock. At that moment, how could I have known? It was almost a premonition."

"Her hair was sprinkled with gray, the only sign that Mama was aging. It dawned on me then, the monumental task Mama had before her when raising three girls without our daddy. Alone, the sound of that made me cringe."

"I had not ever thought of how lost Mama must have felt when Daddy died. I was too devastated to think of anyone but me back then. I was not the strong older sister, helping to comfort you girls as much as I should have been. As the days turned into months, you girls seemed to adjust.

I was just barely existing, going blindly through my days of school and activities, never really living, just surviving. Of course I put on a good act. Everyone thought I was this savvy chick that the guys just loved to be around. However, I felt like I never really lived until I met Brock. Then when our marriage was over, I shared a common bond with Mama; alone is not a good feeling."

Cynda continued with the particulars of the time she had spent with their Mama over the years.

"Mama never asked me about that day, but a mother's intuition supersedes a veil of falsehood. I have learned that the hard way with my own daughter. Mama was always very careful not to press me about Brock and I never gave her any reason to think he had done anything wrong, at least not until I married Dane. You know she loved him like a son and I did not want to destroy that image. My one regret is that Mama should have been told the truth sooner."

Marcy and Suzanne were reliving with her the moments that were obviously tender to her heart, and their feelings were mutual. They were deeply touched at her raw emotion. The sound of breath being sucked into the small army of her allegiance was all that could be heard in the room.

In the following moments, the silence was welcomed by Cynda's audience as she retreated to the refrigerator to retrieve a bottle of water. She left the two in a stunned reflection of her words and desperate to understand her decision to take responsibility for the divorce.

Cynda's special relationship with their father had been no secret. Marcy remembered being a little jealous, but decided the reason their relationship had been so special was because Cynda was older. She was content to wait for "her time". Of course it never came and there were times she had felt cheated. She had never considered how cheated Cynda had felt when their father had died. It had happened at such a vulnerable time for her. Over the years she had even admitted to herself that she held a little resentment toward her older sister. Today, the resentment was dissipating like the fog that hung over a waking city that dared its presence to persist. Likewise, the secret of their sister that had been surrounded in its own heady fog for years now rose from obscurity no longer shrouded in mystery.

Chapter 37

Brock

  Cynda would never be privy to the swirl of events that took place at the compound in Brookhaven the following Sunday.

  If Cynda could have been in Brock's head, she would have witnessed the drama of his defeat playing out there. He had pleaded for Cynda not to leave him, but he had seen the handwriting on the wall. No amount of begging would ever change her mind. The hurt in her eyes was burned into his memory and he was sure that it would never leave. It was not what he had wanted, certainly not to end their marriage. His silver tongue of which had always been his weapon had become tied as he saw his efforts to save their marriage prove fruitless and he had quietly surrendered, to his shame. His declaration of love could only hang suspended under a suspicious shroud of a lie.

  What had he done, he asked himself? He had destroyed his marriage and the mother of his beautiful daughter was about to walk out of his life. His first true love. It was hard enough to face Cynda; on the other hand, his mother was an adversary to be reckoned with. Brock choked. His pride superseded any defense of Cynda that may have been offered. Yes, he was a coward and he acknowledged it, at least to himself.

  He had convinced Cynda that the divorce should be on the grounds of irreconcilable differences. That is exactly what he told his parents. He was too much of a coward to put his reputation out there for his mother to rip to shreds privately, even if she would never divulge his indiscretion publicly.

Phyllis

When Cynda did not show up with Audrey and Brock on Sunday, Phyllis knew something was wrong. She felt it in her bones, brittle as they were. Brock's lame excuse was that Cynda had a headache. She could see right through that ruse. Before the afternoon was over, a nervous Brock called Phyllis and Buie aside to share a revelation. Cynda and he had agreed to get a divorce. What he did not share was the real reason for the breakup. Irreconcilable differences? Well, she would see about that. Brock had worked too long and hard to achieve his status.

One thing she could say for Cynda, was she had adapted fairly well as the wife of her son. At least she had never had a reason to doubt her devotion to her son or granddaughter, except for that one nasty time.

She thought back to that little incident when Cynda had gone out on the town with that ignorant neighbor. It was the only indiscretion that she had ever witnessed. Who in the world would have a name such as Rumelle? That name itself made her shudder. Thank goodness Atlanta was a big city. If there had been any rumors of that rendezvous, they had been stifled. She felt sure that if the taint of impropriety had presented itself, one of her friends from the 'polite society' would have found it their duty to inform her. That had not happened.

Phyllis kept the shoe that she had found in Brock's car the night that Cynda and Rumelle had driven it. The shoe was a reminder to her of the fragility of success, Brock's success. One misstep from him or any family member could damage his career. The red shoe with its glittering strap was just a little piece of insurance, just in case she ever needed it. Phyllis' warning to Cynda after she found the shoe was crystal clear. Brock was a successful lawyer. She reiterated that one wrong move and

257

his success could be shattered into a thousand pieces. She had seen the look of contempt in Cynda's eyes. But she had not heard an excuse uttered or seen any remorse for her apparent actions when she had confronted her after the incident.

The next day Phyllis could not dismiss the feeling in her bones that ached daily in arthritic torture. How many times had the old timers made the comment, "I can feel it in my bones"? The encompassing fears of the prospect of her son's divorce made her cringe. In fact, she was certain that the reason had something to do with Cynda's probable infidelity. Did she not have the proof of a previous indiscretion hidden in her cedar chest? She decided she had to hear the reason from Cynda firsthand.

Phyllis dressed in a pale yellow pantsuit with matching shoes. She tied a white sweater loosely over her shoulders. Her hair was cut in a short bob. It was still a raven black color with a little gray in it. Her crystal blue eyes shone from the depths of puffiness that she had unsuccessfully tried to cover. She had not slept.

Driving down Ponce de Leon Avenue, Phyllis failed to observe the magnificence of the tapestry of stately homes. They were shrouded in the old money of Atlanta and dripped with the jewels of opulent lighting that reflected the majesty of their presence. Perfect landscapes, brick and stone walls that projected an air of superiority flanked the road before them. Some had iron gates that reeked of the prosperity of its proprietors. The royalty was carelessly dismissed as her focus did not waver in her mission.

Phyllis questioned her rationale in making the trip out to Decatur to confront Cynda. She began to think about the daughter-in-law of whom she had actually become very fond.

Cynda had essentially begun to fit the mold of the wife of a successful lawyer. She was very gracious and her talents in entertaining were commendable. She was a wonderful cook and her knack for decorating was admirable. On many occasions Phyllis had heard praises of Cynda at her Garden Club. Even as far out as Decatur, the word had spread of the successful hostess.

Phyllis herself had not gone without noticing the lovely and gracious way that Cynda had entertained. It had only been just a few short weeks since that she had given a lovely shower for her youngest sister, Suzanne. Phyllis had been so impressed. It was these thoughts that convinced her that she would be welcomed with the same graciousness in the moments to come. She had metamorphosed into a lovely young lady.

Her thoughts turned to Rumelle. She wondered if Rumelle was still "hanging around" her son's family. That was the inappropriate term she had used to describe her relationship with Cynda. It was at the shower when Phyllis had asked if she and her daughter-in-law had much time to connect. She had used the term "hanging around" in the same context with "ain't". She likened her to a juvenile on adulthood's horizon, refusing to accept impending maturity. Proper English was the backbone of being accepted into 'polite society' and she had reminded herself to "remind" Cynda once again of her friend's impropriety.

Thankfully she thought, Rumelle had moved back to North Georgia, so the distance alone precluded many visits. It was bad enough that she and Cynda were friends. Phyllis just could not stand the thought of her being around her granddaughter. Her butchering of the English language was just reprehensible and that accent! She had tried to warn both Brock and Cynda of her influence on Audrey. Her insinuations had been met with irritation. Brock had even taken up for use of 'slang'. On one

259

occasion Cynda made it clear the subject was closed. That was before the rendezvous to Atlanta. After that, she listened with no response.

Phyllis turned into the circular driveway that led to her son's home. The pea gravel was reminiscent of the southern homes of long ago. The lawn was scattered with a kaleidoscope of reds and golds. Underneath, there lay a carpet of lush green grass, even for late September. The white house had black shutters that mirrored the period of its cottage structure.

The short walkway was flanked with hearty shades of pink and purple caladiums that formed a backdrop for green foliage mixed with white and periwinkle blooms. It was quite a presentation. The walkway was of red brick pavers that led up to a cheery portico with small columns that supported the roof. The door was a watermelon red with an arched window inset above eye level.

The scene was picturesque and was quite welcoming. But on this day, Phyllis felt the tightening of her stomach muscles as she put her aging Mercedes in park. The pea gravel tugged at her shoe heels as she walked slowly to the front door and she was relieved to touch the walkway. She tapped the brass knocker lightly several times, almost hoping there would be no response. The door opened before the thought had barely entered her brain.

Chapter 38

Cynda felt heady with relief that she had finally told her sisters the truth of her breakup with Brock. She had excused herself to rest again. Instead, she remembered her victorious battle with Phyllis that would change their relationship forever. Cynda recalled the Monday after her absence for the weekly visit to the compound. She had been home all morning cleaning house. She knew that the arrival of her mother-in-law was eminent. She knew.

The doorbell rang. Cynda answered after removing her apron, spotting Phyllis' car in the drive.

"Well, hello Phyllis. What took you so long?" Cynda said as she pulled the door back in a sweeping motion.

"Do come in," she continued.

Phyllis shook the remainder of the clinging pea gravel on the doormat before she entered the house.

"Do you mind if we talk?" Phyllis said hopefully.

"Of course not; I would have expected no less from you. I know that this has come as a shock. I felt like Brock owed it to you to explain the situation himself," Cynda said as the two of them retreated to the living area to sit down.

"Well, he did give me his explanation, but I would have rather heard it from the both of you. For the life of me, I just can't understand how you two have just decided that you do not want to be married anymore. What about Audrey, doesn't she deserve more?" Phyllis answered, the tone of her voice beginning to sound accusatory.

"Is that what he told you?" Cynda said incredulously.

Phyllis felt a slow chill run up her spine as she heard Cynda's words.

"I should have known he didn't have the guts to tell you the truth. It is a little technique he uses when his cowardice emerges, lying that is. He doesn't do it very often, but he felt forced to lie to you many times throughout our marriage; you know, just little white lies. He did it to gain your sympathy to avoid the wrath," Cynda could not resist getting her digs in on her mother-in-law.

Cynda continued, "My Mama always said, 'Don't make me lie." In other words, don't make a person's life so miserable with your criticism, they will avoid honesty. In Brock's pitiful defense, I understand his cowardice."

Phyllis paled at her words.

Before she had a chance to respond, Cynda poured the words over her mother-in-law's self-righteous constitution like molasses dripping over a stack of pancakes, painstakingly slow. She recanted her story of discovery not sparing the sordid details, enjoying the facial expressions that accompanied the truth.

"The ultimate deception was to use the lake house for his little rendezvous. It was our little paradise and he sullied it with his Pink Pantied Paula," she choked out the stinging words as they ricocheted back to her painfully. Her voice quivered as she blurted out the conclusion of his infidelity, "I can't live with a cheater and a liar," Cynda said feeling the betrayal all over again.

Now he had betrayed her once again, to his mother no less. She felt defeated. It was more than she could stand at the moment. Taking a few deep breaths, she fought back the tears that she had kept at bay upon seeing Phyllis for the first time since she had discovered Brock at the lake. She had cried a river and thought there were no more tears left.

Phyllis mimicked Cynda's demeanor, struggling to compose herself as she took a deep breath before responding to the devastating news about her son. It was certainly not the news she had expected to hear. She fully expected the shoe to be on the other foot.

"I-I don't know what to say. This is not what I expected to hear. I just thought you both wanted the divorce. Maybe that you were tired of being married and playing the devoted wife. At least that was the idea that I got from Brock, when he seemed so evasive," Phyllis said.

"Or, that I was so tired of my domestic life and needed a little spice, like going to downtown Atlanta in a pair of platform shoes for some excitement? Is that what you thought? Well, you thought wrong," Cynda said as her voice trailed into a whisper.

Phyllis felt the color in her cheeks rising and she began to squirm slightly as she then lifted her chin to meet screaming green eyes. Their depths showed no trace of the total despair that Cynda was feeling.

"The thought had not entered my mind," Phyllis said with false sincerity.

"Please tell me this 'Pink Pantied Paula' as you call her is not some little piece of tail with no breeding, if you know what I mean. My son would never stoop that low," she continued her shoulders rising as she was heaving to breathe.

Cynda felt the bile rise in her throat as she steadied herself in her chair.

"No breeding, maybe someone like me, someone whose background did not include your 'polite society' on their resume."

"C'mon Cynda. You know that I have grown quite fond of you. I have never said one derogatory word to you or about you. You have made Brock a lovely wife and a loving mother for Audrey," Phyllis said with as much sincerity as she was capable of giving.

"No. Your BREEDING has kept you from expressing your disapproval of our marriage with words, but your actions have been to the contrary. Well, it's a little too late to let me in on your 'high opinion' of me that seems to have changed like a chameleon," Cynda responded.

Phyllis could see that the conversation was going nowhere. The tit for tat was getting a bit tiresome for her. Now that she had been apprised of Brock's infidelity, she was more concerned about the scandal than anything. She did have that one little piece of evidence against Cynda if she had to use it.

"You know, it would be in yours and Brock's best interest to keep his infidelity quiet. I hope that you have not shared my son's indiscretion publicly."

"Like mother, like son. The apple doesn't fall far from the tree. You, like Brock, seem only to be concerned for the scandal and status in your 'polite society' club. Your concern for me and Audrey seems to have taken a backseat. I see the chameleon is changing colors again."

Phyllis bristled at the implication of her insincerity towards Audrey. She would protect her at all costs from anything or anyone. Even from her son's shame to his family.

"Please Cynda, for Audrey's sake; spare her the humiliation of what her father has done. It is bad enough that you have chosen not to look the other way and seek divorce. I have kept your little secret these past years. I am not above telling Brock about your own indiscretion in Atlanta."

She faltered for a moment then added, "I still have the proof."

Cynda sat there for a few moments trying to digest the words that had just been flung at her. She did not know which insult made her angrier. The idea that she should turn the other way when her husband was having an affair at their lake house, of all places, or her insinuation of Cynda's alleged impropriety. The declaration that she had just made about the proof of her supposed indiscretion was a joke. If she were not so furious, she would probably break out into a fit of laughter.

Did she really think that threatening to tell Brock about the damned shoe would force her hand to be quiet? Cynda would not give Phyllis any satisfaction by trying to defend her actions, certainly not at this late date. Nor would she throw the only true friend she had ever had under the bus, just to appease the high handed woman who had been the bane of her existence. Let her think what she wanted to think. She would anyway. It did not matter anymore. Brock would never believe the real story at this point. It would give him justification for his own actions. She preferred to play the martyr to him for that had been her decided role. No reason to muddy the waters now.

"I think it is time for you to leave Phyllis," Cynda said with all the resolve she could muster.

She got up from her chair and showed Phyllis to the door without another word, wondering if her dismissal would have been acceptable in 'polite society'. Maybe Cynda should have offered her a cup of tea with her dose of reality she had thought.

Phyllis Franklin did not look back as she exited the open door, nor did she extend a farewell. Her earlier assessment of the picturesque lawn and house turned ugly. The surroundings had evolved from welcoming to taunting. The pea gravel was no more forgiving than her daughter-in-law. It found its way into one of her yellow shoes, sending tortuous shoots of pain through her foot.

She limped until she reached the sanctuary of her car. The culprit of her pain spilled onto the driveway as she emptied her shoe. How ironic she thought that it was a shoe that was the source of her current pain, both mentally and physically. She eased down the driveway careful not to disturb the substance of its foundation that had already proven to be her enemy.

Chapter 39

That last meeting with Phyllis had finally convinced Cynda that she had made a mistake in marrying Brock. She had always thought she could conquer the obstacles by playing the role of dutiful wife and courting the 'polite society' with her charm. In fact, she was almost complacent in her success. Sure, she knew that Phyllis seemed to be wary of her achievement, never giving her credit where credit was due. However, that had not mattered. She had Brock in her corner.

Brock had been her champion against his mother. With that knowledge she would prevail, at least that was what she had thought. She knew now that she had been wrong. Brock had not only betrayed her; he had thrown her to the wolves, at least to a she wolf.

Then there was Audrey. Cynda could not destroy the image that she had of her father, especially at such a young and tender age. Neither could she reveal to Audrey the ugliness of her own grandmother. She knew that Audrey would see Phyllis for the shallow and unkind person who portrayed herself as just the opposite someday for herself. As far as Brock was concerned, Audrey's opinion of him would remain to be seen. Cynda knew that Brock loved his daughter dearly and his infidelity did not make him a bad father, just a selfish one.

The day came when Audrey rebelled against her father. It was when he decided to marry Prissy Crissy, the name that she had assigned her future stepmother. She refused to be a part of the wedding. She was fifteen and had become willful and defiant to both Cynda and Brock.

Phyllis had been thrilled about the nuptials, of that Cynda was sure. Crissy's father was a prominent judge in Atlanta. Once again Phyllis had gone to Brock's defense, begging Audrey to change her mind and to no avail.

Phyllis had found herself on the receiving end of one of her tirades when Audrey flatly refused to be a part of 'the circus', her terminology for the ceremony.

Of course, Cynda was convinced that Phyllis blamed her for the insolent behavior. Audrey had gotten wise and could see right through her grandmother. She did not relent in her decision. Buie intervened on Audrey's behalf, for she was his pride and joy. There was one person that Phyllis Franklin could not ramrod once he made up his mind, no matter how she tried to coddle him and get him on her side. It was Buie. He simply refused to listen to her reasoning.

Cynda knew the real reason Audrey had been so adamant about the wedding. She continued to harbor a secret hope that her parents would get back together someday. She knew because she found a note written to that effect. It seemed she kept the hope alive for several years after the divorce, and the news of Brock's impending marriage must have been devastating. Audrey would not discuss it with her and Cynda did not press the issue.

Brock had no patience for Audrey's insolence. His precious daughter who thought he hung the moon had turned her back on his future happiness. The sad part was he could not understand why. Cynda certainly did not share with him the contents of the note their daughter had written. Score one for her.

Cynda's relationship had been amicable with Brock over the years for Audrey's sake. Quite often she dropped Audrey off at Phyllis and Buie's house for visitation. It had been easier for her that way. Back then she wanted to avoid those blue eyes that haunted her at all cost!

Thanks to Cynda there had never been a hint of scandal. Paula had apparently faded into the woodwork and Cynda was surprised it had taken him so long to find someone new. She had certainly not looked for anyone else. The healing process had been long and tedious. Her love for him had died a slow and painful death. Sometimes, she wondered if she had ever really healed. She could not answer that question, even now.

Cynda had certainly moved on with her life when she had married Dane. The hurt that she had buried deep inside sometimes felt tender after all of these years. Maybe this purging she had been doing over the last few weeks was good for her soul. Tomorrow she would deliver the goods. Her sisters deserved to know what a coward she had really been as far as Phyllis was concerned. She could not let them think that her refusal to expose Brock's indiscretion to everyone was totally of her own volition. Tomorrow.

Cynda drifted into a fitful sleep, her thoughts plaguing her as she tried desperately to dispel them from her mind. Meanwhile her sisters had found solidarity in Suzanne's bedroom upstairs as they discussed the revelations of the day.

"I just can't believe Cynda's logic in not ratting out that sneak!" Suzanne said in a hushed tone.

"Me either. She tried so hard to protect Audrey from disillusionment. It just backfired! She cannot even stay in a relationship for very long," Marcy whispered in exasperation.

"It is obvious that she is afraid that she will fall out of love and make the same mistake her mother made," Marcy continued.

"What makes matters worse is that I know Lane has asked her to marry him over and over again. She just can't make a commitment. They love each other, I have no doubt. I just hate to see her spending the rest of her life alone. He is not going to wait forever, and she is not getting any younger," Suzanne responded.

Marcy with her usual assertive personality vowed, "Well, we have got to do something. Audrey has got to hear the truth AND it can't come from us!"

"Exactly, and we have got to tell Cynda that Audrey is coming up next weekend. No surprises. She will just have to get over Audrey not coming to her house this one time. We can't get any resolution with Dane in the mix. That's another situation that needs some attention."

"Yeah, let's not open that can of worms," Suzanne agreed as she wiggled her fingers in the air.

"I guess we will have to be happy just doing our best. We sure cannot work miracles before we leave. Maybe once Audrey learns the truth about her mother's decision to protect her father, she will soften her attitude toward Dane and realize her mother deserves some happiness," Marcy sighed and yawned at her departure, "Neither one of us will be good for anything tomorrow, if we don't get some sleep," she said as she slid off the bed and into her animal print mules. "Goodnight," she said, as she disappeared through the door.

Suzanne responded likewise, but her thoughts were stirred in a way that she had not imagined they would be. The strong and beautiful Cynda was no longer an enigma; she was a mortal with hopes, fears and hidden disappointments that had surfaced before their eyes. She pulled the kohl black sleep mask over her eyes in a desperate attempt to aid her dissent into slumber.

Chapter 40

Marcy and Suzanne were already plotting in the kitchen the next morning when Cynda sailed through the door. They both stared at her wondering if she were an illusion. Suzanne remarked, "Faster than the speed of light!"

Cynda finished the sentence in cosmic fashion, "And Kryptonite Radiation! Just call me superwoman. I could not sleep very well last night. In fact, I hardly slept at all," Cynda chimed.

That seemed hard to believe as she virtually zoomed into the kitchen. Both Marcy and Suzanne wished they could attain that kind of energy with no sleep. It was if she was on some kind of high. Was it possible that she had taken too many painkillers? That subject had not been open for discussion. "Mum" had been the word as far as her giving up any details of her illness or her treatments. Maybe she had just dropped a hint.

"Well, you are mighty chipper this morning for someone who has had no sleep," Marcy said as she stirred cheese into the sin of southern grits.

"I made your favorite. Cheese grits. I hope you are hungry," she continued.

"Sounds great," Cynda said as she settled herself on one of the barstools.

"By the way," Cynda continued, "I have a confession to make. I left out the big reason that I did not rat Brock out. I think it is only fair for me to tell you the entire story of why I protected Brock's reputation. I was trying to protect someone else," she said.

"Who was that?" Suzanne said as she lowered her chin and looked up at Cynda under arched brows.

"Me," Cynda answered.

"You, but what did you do?"

"Nothing really. My rationale at the time seems so senseless now. I just wanted to protect the image that Brock had always had of me. I craved to be perfect in his eyes and I had always tried so hard to make him proud. You see, the only thing I had not been honest with him about was my involvement in Rumelle's little escapade. I was the one who committed a crime when she chickened out! I lived in fear of being arrested for a very long time. That would have been as bad as Brock's infidelity being revealed, probably worse!"

"But years had passed when Brock started his shenanigans. Weren't you satisfied by then that you would not be discovered?" Suzanne questioned.

"Yes, but there was one person who held the information about the incident close to her finagling heart," Cynda said with resolve.

"Let me guess – 'Miss Polite Society' herself!" Marcy joined the conversation.

Cynda then told her sisters about the visit from Phyllis after she had discovered Brock with Paula.

"Well, my respect for Brock has just been lowered about five notches. I always felt sorry for him after your divorce. I thought he was the one to be pitied. I just can't believe he did not have the balls to tell his mother the truth!" Marcy cried not flinching in her terminology.

"Well, I rather enjoyed telling her myself. You should have seen her face when I gave her the blow by blow details; it was unforgettable. I fully expected the blood that drained from her face to run right out onto her pale yellow pantsuit," Cynda said wryly.

Suzanne could not suppress her laugh. In fact, it was just the thing they all needed to take the edge off of the disturbing conversation and then she added her appraisal.

"The very idea that she would threaten to disclose your suspected infidelity to Brock is classic for her. I sure would like to know what she did with that shoe. I guarantee she hid it somewhere in the house. Maybe she took it out every once in a while, trying to live vicariously."

Cynda snickered at the idea and said, "I have to admit I rather enjoyed the idea of her thinking the worst of me. She felt it her duty to protect my so called secret from 'polite society' and from her darling Brock. At least until she thought it was to her advantage to tell him."

With sardonic laughter Cynda continued, "I should have known she would try to use it as leverage against me. I wasn't the least bit worried because I was innocent. But as it turned out, Brock would have been eager to latch on to that piece of information, justifying his own betrayal. I knew he would choose to believe her story, to satisfy his own guilt. Shamefully, even then I continued to crave his respect and approval."

It was still hard for Marcy and Suzanne to believe that their sister had been so entrenched in the idea that Brock deserved her loyalty after his infidelity. Marcy found it even harder to believe that she allowed Phyllis to threaten her in such a way. She made a declaration of unity in her statement, "Phyllis may be the grandmother to your daughter and I have always given her the utmost respect. I will have to revisit my rules of graciousness where she is concerned. Let's put it this way, she sure showed her true colors that day. I wonder how long it took for her to choose the color she wore, yellow, yellow bellied coward."

Cynda looked at her sister and thought she had watched too many westerns reeking of that jargon. She went on to explain.

"Brock and I had already agreed to dissolve the marriage as irreconcilable. Nothing she said had any effect on my decision not to tell anyone what the real reason was for our divorce. Shamefully, I allowed her to think her threat about the shoe influenced me. I still cannot reconcile the idea that she had actually thought I should turn my head the other way of his infidelity. That may be the way they do it in 'polite society' to maintain their financial security. That is where I drew the line.

"Good for you!" Suzanne said emphatically.

"So there you have it. Phyllis won the battle and I lost, trying to hold on to the illusion that it was more important for me to be perfect in Brock's eyes than to be true to myself," Cynda sighed with relief.

Suzanne reached over and squeezed her sister's hand and said, "Don't beat yourself up. We all have done things of which we are not proud. You did what you thought was the right thing to do at the time. Your intentions were gallant," she said then thinking she did not have the heart to tell her the negative impact it had made on Audrey.

How ironic Suzanne thought. Cynda had made the ultimate sacrifice to protect her daughter. She had bartered her own reputation to keep the image of Brock as unsullied in Audrey's eyes. She had wanted Audrey to find her own knight in shining armor without being afraid of betrayal. Soon, she would have to face the folly of her effort. Maybe it would not be too late.

Quiet settled around the kitchen and the reality of Cynda's past life surrounded them like a shroud. Suddenly Cynda burst into uncontrollable laughter. The sight of her perching atop the barstool in her coral colored housecoat shaking all over was mystifying. She laughed until she had tears in her eyes. Her sisters stood there transfixed as they tried to decide how to react. She stopped as suddenly as she started and became very still.

"Why do I feel so happy and free? It's like all the pretenses of life have caught up with me and found me out. Instead of being upset, I feel liberated!"

Cynda looked up at them with childlike eyes, eyes that begged for approval. She climbed down from the barstool and went over to the 'couch with no personality'. She said, "I can't change how I handled my divorce with Brock. What I can change is my relationship with Audrey. I have to tell her the truth," she said assuredly.

"You know your daughter loves you as deeply as any daughter can love a mother," Suzanne said quickly.

"I guess, but why can't she show me, make some concessions to the situation? I know that she and Dane do not see eye to eye, but I am in the middle. Doesn't that count for something? Dane is willing to call for a truce if she will just come around," Cynda said with tears welling in her eyes that she quickly wiped away.

"Cynda, I don't think the root of the problem is Dane. In fact, if she finds out the truth about her father, I believe it will temper her heart towards him. Maybe she will stop comparing her 'perfect' father to him."

"When she does hear the truth, I pray that she will forgive me and my actions. Hopefully she will understand I only tried to protect her."

"Please don't take offense when I say this Cynda, but your decision left your daughter confused and afraid. Afraid to love and have a meaningful relationship, afraid to trust," Suzanne said.

"I have given her everything. I have always been there for her," Cynda said defensively.

Now that was the pot calling the kettle black, Suzanne thought. Cynda in her need to control every situation intervened where Dane and Audrey were concerned. Audrey had told Suzanne on many occasions that her mother blamed her for the bad blood between the two because she was so "spoiled".

Cynda appeared to turn a blind eye to her own shortcomings as far as her daughter was concerned. Her own need to control and demand perfection had a direct effect on Audrey. Audrey had shared with Suzanne how difficult meeting her mother's expectations had been. It was apparent now that she had lived a lie trying valiantly to protect her daughter, a pretty valiant sacrifice. In the grand scheme of things, that had been a mistake – one that had cost her dearly in the grand scheme of things.

"Your demand for perfection from your daughter as well as yourself has contributed to the problem also. You have tried to fix things for everyone all of your life. When you are truthful with Audrey, I think the problems will work themselves out," Suzanne said in a hushed tone.

"The truth is, I may not have enough time," Cynda looked at both of her sisters with frankness.

Marcy and Suzanne were at a loss for words. Suzanne spoke first choosing not to address Cynda's illness. Instead she focused on the issue of Audrey.

"Cynda, Audrey wants to come down next weekend. We told her to come. She's looking forward to seeing you."

"So, I guess you planned this behind my back. Why haven't you already told me?" Cynda said with hurt in her eyes.

"We did want to tell you. To be honest, we were waiting for the right moment," Suzanne sputtered.

"Oh, is that it? So you think now is the right time. Now that I have bared my soul to y'all."

"You just said that you had to be honest with Audrey," Suzanne pleaded.

"Think about it this way Cynda. Here at the cottage, you are on neutral ground. There will not be any tension between Audrey and Dane to worry about," Marcy intervened.

"I guess you are right. We have to start somewhere. It may as well be here. What day is she coming?"

"Marcy is picking her up at the airport Thursday night. And don't worry, we will find a way to give the two of you some space when she comes," Suzanne said reassuringly.

"If you don't mind, I think I need to get my things together to go home."

Marcy and Suzanne were at a loss for words. The plans had been laid out before their sister. The ball was in her court and they both fervently wanted them to work. So far, Pandora's box had revealed a lifetime of secrets and personal discoveries.

When Cynda returned with her belongings, she had her purse and the clothes she had purchased. Her cosmetic bag was in her hand. She had on one of the t-shirts and a pair of the pants from her new wardrobe. Cynda smiled brightly and said, "Suzanne, if you don't mind, I would like to borrow the *Hug Bug* this week."

Suzanne was so taken aback. She was still wondering why Cynda had changed her mind about taking her new clothes back home. After all, she had expressed Dane's disapproval of them if she wore them.

When Suzanne did not answer right away Cynda said, "If you don't want me to, it's okay."

Suzanne answered quickly, "Oh no, it is fine! I just was wondering why you decided to take your new clothes. I thought you were leaving them here."

"I've changed my mind. I am going to start living for a change."

Suzanne reached in her purse and gave Cynda her car keys. There was an awkward silence.

"I thought if you girls didn't mind, I would come over on Thursday afternoon. I would like to be here when Audrey arrives."

"Of course, you do not have to leave now. You can stay all week if you would like," Marcy said.

"No. There are some things I need to take care of at home. Besides, Dane will not know what to do with himself."

Cynda gave her sisters hugs, but this time, instead of the customary squeeze, she hugged each one with a renewed tenderness.

She quickly walked to the *Hug Bug*, and dropped her belongings on the back seat and climbed into the driver's side, closing the door gently behind her. As soon as she heard the purr of the engine, she closed her eyes and felt a liberating calm coursing through her veins.

The ride was long and sweet. She stopped and filled the car up with gas just before getting on Interstate 95. Then she drove for miles and allowed her thoughts to control her being. She suddenly realized she had driven much further than she intended, but she kept on driving. She realized that in the last few weeks, she had lived a lifetime of memories.

Even before she had become ill, Cynda had begun to access her life after turning fifty. The sands of time became boulders that crashed and fell, turning days into weeks and weeks to years and the first thing that she knew, the mid-life had arrived. It arrived in austere reality, impossible to ignore.

In retrospect, she had seen the clock turning faster. Her forties had slipped away like a summer afternoon turning to nightfall with the sound of a thousand crickets, reminding the listener another day had been spent. Cynda had heard it all, hundreds of times, her mother reciting the chants of old timers in a sing, sing song of how the days would get shorter the older that one became. She had believed them, but never quite grasping their intent. It was a subtle warning. And then when she arrived at the chasm of her mid-life, she began assessing her being. Just who was she and what had she done to make her arrival monumental? For was it really monumental at all? Had she made a difference in the world that she had lived, created and existed in for a sum of fifty plus years? That would remain to be seen, for she had finally begun to slowly dissect her mistakes even before her sisters had arrived and forced her hand.

Those closest to Cynda's heart, Audrey and Dane, had been on her mind for quite some time. It was time to free herself from the bondage of the past and to be a more wise and insightful person. She looked forward to redeeming herself to Audrey and was hopeful of the outcome. There was just one other person that she had to face.

Chapter 41

An idea had formulated in Cynda's mind as she continued on her ride. She exited Interstate 95 and began to follow US 17 with a vengeance, ignoring the marshes and the beauty she usually drank with pleasure. She picked up her cell phone. Dane had no idea that she had left her sisters a few hours ago. She dialed his number and waited.

"Hello Cynda," Dane answered.

"Hi Dane, just wanted to let you know I've decided to spend the night with the girls if that is okay."

Dane answered hesitantly, "Sure, but I was looking forward to seeing you. I've missed you."

"Me too Dane, but the time with the girls is winding down and I am beginning to dread them going back to Atlanta. It's just this one time. After next weekend, they will be gone back to their homes and you will have me for good."

"Sure Cynda, I don't mean to be selfish."

"Good. I'll see you tomorrow after lunch."

Cynda hung up the phone and remembered her mother had told her little white lies were acceptable, if it kept from hurting someone. This was the time to use that tactic she told herself. She certainly could not tell him that she was going to see Brock.

Dane hung up the phone, somewhat with relief. He loved Cynda dearly, but the past months had been trying. He had to admit to himself that he was at a loss as how to be supportive of a person who was dying. He knew he had pushed her away. But he did not mean it, did he? Accepting her illness was something he had not been able to do. It was easier to pretend that it wasn't true. And the anger. How did someone deal with the anger without directing it at the victim? He was at a loss for answers. All that he knew was that the distance from Cynda made everything easier. He admitted to himself how grateful he was that he had the reprieve the last few weekends. What would he do when her sisters were gone? That was a question that could only be answered by time. He walked in the kitchen and poured himself a drink and contemplated.

Cynda dialed a second number. It was to speak with Buie. He answered on the second ring. Thank goodness. He must not be on the golf course today.

"Hi, Buie. How are you?" Cynda said cheerfully.

"Well, hello Cynda, nice to hear from you. Is something wrong?" he asked hesitantly.

"Oh, no. I was calling to see if Brock might be in town?" she said crossing her fingers and hoping he was not.

"No, I am afraid not. He and Crissy went down to Amelia Island for the week. Have you not tried to call him on his cell phone?"

"Actually, I deleted some of my contacts by accident," she said, hating the lie.

Buie took a few minutes to retrieve the number for Cynda and she pretended to take the information. She thanked him for his help and told him she missed him. He hesitated to ask her how she was doing.

"I hope you are doing well," he said.

"Actually, I am doing better than I have been in a very long time," she said earnestly.

"That sounds great. Don't be a stranger," he said with relief.

Those were the words he had used since the day she had left Brock. He never failed to end their conversations with those fond words that now touched her heart more deeply than ever.

"Not a danger," she said reverently.

Cynda was relieved that she had guessed right. There was no way possible to drive all the way to Atlanta.

She was on a roll now and Brock had made her mission much easier, unwittingly, meeting her half way.

She was almost to the end of close to a three-hour journey. She stopped at a roadside center to freshen up. She removed some more new clothes from the back seat and took them in the restroom. After relieving herself, she freshened up and then changed into a new outfit. She chose the pink t-shirt and the soft jersey capris.

The woman in the mirror stared back at her as she applied a fresh coat of make-up. She was pale and gaunt, but there was a gleam in her green eyes that peered up from underneath one of the colorful scarves that had become typical of her wardrobe. *Hug Bug* welcomed her with open arms as Cynda returned to the sanctity of its berth. She was in good company.

Brock and Crissy had purchased the Amelia Island, Florida home and he had taken a partial retirement. According to Audrey, they traveled down to the coast pretty often. The five hours that separated Brock for almost twenty years had made Cynda feel safe and comfortable. She resented that he had a home only three hours away from her; even at that distance she had felt smothered by his mere presence. She wanted her marriage to him a lifetime ago to remain just that, a lifetime ago. The idea of him living just across the Georgia line made her cringe. But today, she had some unfinished business.

Chapter 42

When Cynda pulled up to the posh gated community of cluster homes, she panicked. She had not thought of how she was going to enter the community without a code. The security guard that stepped out of the gatehouse was short and stocky. Cynda was undecided if the guard was a he or a she and the nametag did not help. It read 'Pat'. She had hoped the guard would be a male and she could use her feminine wiles on him.

An idea suddenly popped in her mind when the guard asked, "Your name please."

Cynda replied, as she crossed her fingers, hoping that the guard did not know her daughter, "Audrey, Audrey Franklin," she said.

After the guard checked the computer, the husky voice still did not reveal the gender of the guard upon the reply, "Is Mr. Franklin expecting you? There are no notes on the screen."

"I want to surprise him. I drove all the way from Atlanta." The guard gave her an appraising look and decided to let her through the gate.

Cynda gave a sigh of relief as she drove through the gate, hoping beyond hope that Brock would be home. The hell with Crissy. She would just have to deal with it.

She drove down the street of well-appointed houses with perfectly manicured lawns, maintained courtesy of a hefty fee; she was certain of that. Brock had never so much as cut a blade of grass in his lifetime.

A brand new 2000 red Mercedes convertible sat in the driveway at 1800 Heron Drive. She surmised it was Crissy's latest purchase. Audrey never failed to share information about Brock and Crissy's most recent acquisitions, even though Cynda had told her that she was not interested in hearing about them. Sometimes, she thought that Audrey rather enjoyed taunting her.

Cynda chose to park the *Hug Bug* on the street. She put the car in park and rubbed her sweaty palms on her pants. Then she removed the scarf from her head and took one last look in the rearview mirror. She wanted Brock to see the imperfect Cynda, no pretenses.

It was dusk when Cynda rang the doorbell. A series of barking began and she could hear the pitter patter of doggy paws approaching the door. She could see someone scoop a dog up, through the glass pane. The door swung open to reveal the face of a woman, suspended in time. She still teased her blond hair on the top of her head in helmet fashion, with bangs. The length of her hair touched her collar that formed a continuous flip around the back of her head. Cynda suppressed a laugh wondering where her headband was. She was face to face with Crissy. Crissy could not hide the shock in her eyes as it took a moment for her to recognize Cynda.

She turned and called out to Brock, "Brock honey, you have a visitor."

She just stood there and stared for a moment until Brock walked up behind her. The still handsome Brock who had aged so gracefully looked as if he had seen a ghost.

"I'll just leave you two alone," Crissy said as she turned and walked down the hallway, the uni-roll bouncing and the still yapping pooch under her arm.

"Come in Cynda. Is there something wrong? Is Audrey okay? Please tell me there is nothing wrong with Audrey."

"Audrey is fine. Actually, I am quite fine myself," Cynda intimated his disregard for her.

"Sorry, I didn't mean to ignore your well-being, I am just so shocked you are here. I - I just thought the only reason you would come here would be in regards to Audrey."

"Like I said, I am fine."

Brock found that hard to believe as he had made a brief assessment of her physical state and could only guess her medical condition. He guided her into the sitting room adjacent to the hallway.

"Please have a seat," Brock signaled to her as she entered the room.

The room was gauche in its furnishings. All of the seating was covered in white upholstery and smothered with animal print cushions. There was a large white fur rug in front of the marble fireplace. The mirrored end tables had matching lamps of molded peacocks as their base and tacky shades with feathers around their bottoms. She did not know whether to sit or perch.

Cynda rested herself lightly on one of the overstuffed chairs, fearing it would swallow her up in the jungle of its depth. Brock sat across from her and she met his blue eyes for the first time in a long time. They looked tired and seemed to have lost their sparkle.

"What brings you here Cynda?" Brock said.

"It's Audrey," she said pausing for a moment.

"I thought you said she was okay," he said as he shook his head with confusion.

"She is physically, but not emotionally. It's because of me," she hesitated again.

"What have you done?"

"It is not what I have done, but what you did to me."

"Our marriage ended years ago, Cynda. This is old news," Brock tried not to sound as perturbed as he felt. "What is Audrey up to now? Is she trying to gain some sympathy now by crying foul after all these years? I know you two aren't on the best of terms. I had hoped your relationship would improve since..." Brock stuttered and could not bring himself to say the words.

"We have not even discussed this," Cynda said ignoring his insinuation about her illness. I have been doing some soul searching for the last few months and have come to some realization about mistakes I can't undo, but I can sure try to make amends to our daughter for my complicity in preserving a false image of you."

She continued, "You betrayed me in the worst kind of way, Brock. I would have moved heaven and earth for you and Audrey. I dedicated my life for you both. I was the perfect wife and followed the rules of 'polite society' to please your mother because I thought it would make your life easier. I gave you my all."

"Do you think for one minute that I did not realize your dedication?" Brock interrupted.

Cynda raised her hand and said, "Hear me out, Brock. You need to understand what I did to Audrey on your behalf, one of the biggest mistakes I could have ever made."

She continued, "I did not keep your dirty little secret just to protect your good name. I just wanted our pure and innocent little daughter to believe in fairytales, like the one I had always told her, yours and mine. I did not want to take away that illusion of a white knight in shining armor that would love and protect her forever. I took the blame for our failed marriage on your behalf," she said emphatically.

"I also had my pride and I never wanted you to see me as nothing, but perfect. I wanted you to remember our marriage as perfect just as much. I thought if you did, you would never be able to forgive yourself."

He looked at her with sincerity in his eyes, the ones that had haunted her from the first time they met. He said, "I haven't...I mean ever been able to forgive myself. Cynda, you were perfect. I was the one who ruined it all."

"Yes. But there was one thing that you did not know. It could have changed your opinion of me, and at that time I would not allow that to happen. It may have given you some justification for what you did."

Now Cynda had his attention. He sat up a little straighter and asked, "Justification?"

She shared her story about the night that she and Rumelle had gone into Atlanta to confront Jack. She told him about her role in the discovery of Jack's own infidelity. Then, the fear of being arrested, smearing his name. She even giggled a little as she relived the stint of throwing clothing out on Ponce de Leon Avenue. Then she told him about the shoe that Phyllis had found.

"She threatened me when she saw me, after she found the shoe. I was so mad that I would not explain, nor would I throw Rumelle under the bus. You know how Phyllis has always felt about Rumelle. Her unfounded opinion of her is shameful. I decided not to tell you because I thought you would be so angry with me. That was a mistake. I could never have believed that she would use it against me to her advantage years later." Cynda then told him about the visit from Phyllis once she found out they were getting a divorce.

"After her visit, I was sure that you would have believed her, therefore giving you justification for your infidelity and worst of all lowering your opinion of me. My need to be perfect in your eyes blinded me from anything, especially where you were concerned."

Brock listened to her story and realized that every word she said was true, even the part about his using it as an excuse for his own betrayal. He knew that his arrogance in his younger days had been his downfall. But, he failed to see how Cynda's silence had affected Audrey so adversely. He just thought Audrey had been spoiled by both him and Cynda and his parents and he said as much.

"You can't blame yourself for Audrey's inability to find her way. We've all spoiled her. Even Lane has danced to her tune for years now without commitment," Brock reasoned.

"That is just it, Brock. She can't commit. She is afraid that she will fall out of love, just like me. The unfortunate side of this story is that it took years for me to get over you. But I did," she said as she looked directly into the blue eyes that had haunted her for far more years than she cared to remember.

"If it is any consolation to you Cynda, I have never thought of you as any less than perfect," Brock said as he stared deep into those green eyes that had not changed.

Cynda rose from the chair, her frail body accentuated by the absence of hair, but looking regal as she reached out her hand to take Brock's hand. She did not miss the pity in his eyes when he accepted it.

"This has been a long time coming. I have only recently discovered my mistake. It has taken a lot of soul searching to realize the injustice of it all. All I have to do now is make it right, if possible, with Audrey. Hopefully, she will understand my motives."

Brock stuttered as he said, "How are you really doing Cynda? I mean, your illness. Are you getting better?"

Cynda thought for a moment and said, "Yes, I am healing."

Without ceremony, Cynda dismissed herself to the front door as Brock followed. She saw Prissy Crissy out of the corner of her eye as she stepped back, obviously eavesdropping. She smiled to herself as she wondered if Brock had ever admitted to Crissy his infidelity or if his cowardice was still intact. Not her problem.

Brock

Brock watched as his first true love left his presence with her dignity in hand, just as she had over twenty-five years ago, on a cool September day at the lake. He felt a loss now that suddenly consumed him and left him empty.

For the first time in his life, he felt an overwhelming desire to do the right thing with no ulterior motive. His own cowardice had caused his ex-wife and daughter untold heartache. He admitted to himself that he had just seen one of the strongest women he had ever known, walk away with a pride and dignity he could only desire. Both were traits that had eluded him in his quest to climb the ladder of success.

At that moment, Brock made the decision to make it right with Audrey. He owed Cynda that much. It was not her place to tell Audrey what he had done. It was his.

Brock walked down the hallway to the comfort of his family room, but did not feel so comfortable.

"Crissy, I need to fly to Atlanta first thing in the morning. Can you make arrangements?"

"Sure Brock," Crissy acted puzzled then continued, "Is there something wrong?"

"As a matter of fact there is. Something has been wrong for about twenty-five years"

He did not give any further explanation and Crissy did not force the issue. He turned and walked out of the room as she sat on the outside of his self-discovery.

Cynda drove to a local bed and breakfast that she had found on the Internet when she had stopped to freshen up. She preferred the personal touch that they offered and felt safer there. She decided to call her sisters and let them know her location.

Suzanne did not question her motives, nor did Cynda offer her any explanation. She assured her that she would let Marcy know of her whereabouts. Cynda did apologize for taking the *Hug Bug* so far away.

Thank goodness for her toilet articles and new clothing. It had made it easier to carry out her plan she thought. When Cynda finally settled down, she allowed herself to engage in the reality of what she had just done. It was an invigorating freedom of which she had not ever known. There were only a few days left before she would reveal her motives for protecting Brock to her daughter. She hoped it was not too late.

Chapter 43

Cynda arrived home in the *Hug Bug* shortly after noon the next day. Dane walked out to the vehicle with a look of puzzlement on his face.

"I could have come out to pick you up," he said as she exited the car in her new casual clothing.

"I asked Suzanne to borrow the *Hug Bug* for the week."

"Really? Your Mercedes needs its engine exercised if you need to drive. Besides, I can take you anywhere you need to go or you can take the Lincoln."

"The *Hug Bug* is my therapy! I guess I have been bit just like Suzanne. She told me, 'You feel a big hug when you drive it, like your best friend is with you'!"

Dane was beginning to feel a little bit slighted with this sister club, and now an antique car was competing for attention. He suddenly realized how different Cynda looked. She was wearing clothes he had never seen her wear, a t-shirt and pants out of a similar material. She wore flip flops that were a florescent green.

"Wow, you certainly look different. I don't think I have ever seen you wear a t-shirt before. You look nice," he added hesitantly.

Cynda could sense the insincerity in his voice, but she just blew it off.

"Yes, Dane, I am pretty comfortable. It feels good not to be restricted."

"Of course. That outfit will be comfy around the house, but I am sure you will change when or if you leave." he said in an effort to drive his point home.

"As a matter of fact Dane, if I feel like wearing this out, I will," she answered defiantly.

Not wanting to cause any further friction, he agreed but added a stipulation by saying, "I just meant to the grocery or to the club, you know, anywhere our friends might see you."

"I can't promise what I will wear if and when I decide to get out Dane. I am over living the perfect life for the 'polite society'. I just want to live," she said as she reached for her bag.

Cynda disappeared into the house as Dane watched the apparition shut the door. Where was Cynda, he asked himself?

Cynda went into the guest room. Its presence emanated perfection. She suddenly decided to make her belongings more accessible. The tissues she had hidden in the drawer of the nightstand were placed in full view. She began to unload the cosmetics onto the dressing table, leaving them on the surface for easy access. There. That was a start. She felt exonerated from her own restrictive rules. Next she would work on Dane. He would just have to understand that the minute details of living did not require constant organization.

Cynda took a nap and woke up feeling rested enough to challenge herself in the kitchen. When she arrived there, Dane was preparing fish in a dry-rub.

"That looks good; do we have any asparagus? I thought I might roast some in the oven."

"Sure, the asparagus is in the frig. I bought some of your favorite veggies, hoping you would have an appetite."

"Yes, I am pretty hungry," Cynda said as she surveyed the offerings.

"By the way, Audrey is coming in to town this weekend," she said as she munched on a carrot.

"*So* – does that mean you will be staying here?" Dane said with alarm in his voice.

"In fact, no, we will all be staying out on *Tybee* Island. I am going Thursday night if you don't mind.

Dane's mixed emotions about the prospect of Cynda spending so much time with her sisters surfaced. He felt somewhat abandoned, but at the same time, he felt relief. Once again he re-examined his overwhelming guilt. He told himself that it was not his fault that he could not handle her illness, and the secret anger he harbored for the woman he loved. After all, she could not help it. The potential finality of her illness had caused his self-imposed exclusion from reality. It was easier to pretend it did not exist.

Audrey did exist, however and he really did hope for reconciliation with her mother, but his anger got the best of him when he responded.

"Looks like your focus has been diverted from your husband; where do I fit into this picture?"

"I am sorry Dane, but I have done a lot of soul searching these past few weeks. I have to make things right with Audrey and I intend to start this weekend. I've made mistakes where she is concerned and I have to make amends."

Dane's anger continued to rise. As far as Audrey was concerned, he had lost his patience.

"There you go again, blaming yourself for her lack of respect of you, and me for that matter. She is a spoiled brat and you know it! She needs to grow up," Dane almost shouted. He wiped away the spittle that had accumulated around his angry mouth.

"I will admit she is spoiled Dane. I am guilty. Brock is guilty and heaven knows Phyllis and Buie have helped to make it impossible for her to take any responsibility. But, I have made one major mistake with her and that is not being honest. That I intend to rectify," Cynda said without elaborating on her reasoning for dishonesty.

"I cannot see how anything you attempt to rectify will make a difference at this late date," Dane said quietly.

"I certainly do not expect any change in the way she feels about me," he continued.

"Well, I have to try to make things right, Dane, and maybe, just maybe it will make a difference for you," Cynda finished.

Dane just looked at Cynda, turned and picked up the plate of fish, and went outside to put it on the grill. Cynda watched him leave and thought about his slow smoldering anger that was aimed at her. She had admitted to herself time and time again that he could not handle her illness. She did not want his pity, but she certainly did not want his anger.

Chapter 44

Cynda could hardly contain herself when it was time to leave for the cottage on Thursday evening. Her relationship with Dane during the week had been strained, but amicable since the confrontation on Monday. She knew he would be fine as he had developed a routine while she was gone, including going to the club with friends. She tried to act nonchalant when she gave Dane a final kiss goodbye, for the weekend. However, when she stepped into the *Hug Bug*, her flushed face told quite a different story. She was giddy with anticipation. The back seat was already packed with her clothes, along with some memorabilia. She also had some decorative items packed.

Cynda backed the *Hug Bug* down the driveway, this time smoothly as she released the clutch like a pro. She smiled to herself as she felt a rush of accomplishment. Her short trips during the week had helped to hone her skills.

It took only a few minutes to arrive at the cottage. She felt a lump in her throat as the *Hug Bug* crept up the driveway. Suzanne appeared at the door as soon as she arrived.

"I have been watching for you," Suzanne exclaimed as she hurriedly ran out to the car and hastily removed the items.

"Marcy has already left from the airport, but she said traffic is horrendous," Suzanne went on to say.

"I know I am early, but I am so anxious to see Audrey," Cynda said nervously as she followed Suzanne into the cottage with her arms full of shopping bags.

"I figured as much, that is why I have been watching for you. By the way, what do you have in those?" Suzanne said as she pointed to the bags.

"Oh, just a few little things to make the cottage feel a little cozier," Cynda said as she dropped the contents from her arms down in front of the couch.

She pulled two beautiful pillows with a splash of colorful flowers from the bag. She placed them on the couch. Then she removed a throw in a muted jacquard weave, which pulled the colors from the pillows and placed it willy-nilly beside them. The effect was striking. Suddenly the 'couch with no personality' was screaming with individuality.

"Oh my gosh Cynda! The 'couch with no personality' has turned from an ugly duckling to a beautiful swan. You are too much. You can't just leave those pillows and the throw here when we start home on Monday morning. You have to take them back home with you."

"Oh no I don't! It's my going away present to the cottage. After all, it has been a big part of my ticket to freedom."

"Well, I am sure the owners will be pleased with your contribution. How very generous of you."

"Just a little token of appreciation. I thought we could all enjoy the change."

Cynda dismissed herself to her bedroom to put away her things. As soon as the door was closed, she stopped mid stride and studied the room that Suzanne had called *Enchanted.*

Cynda was going to miss this room and the safe haven of its presence. It too had arms, she had discovered. It was only a few short miles from her home. But it had become a refuge; a place to explore the secrets that she had kept hidden in what seemed like a lifetime. Now she was free of their bondage. And to think it was here on *Tybee,* her sweet *Tybee,* the place that had given her the courage to move on with her life so long ago, and now the courage to truly heal.

Cynda placed her belongings in the closet. She took one of the smaller bags over to her bed. She reached it to remove the Waterford bell that she used at home to summon Dane. She put it on the bedside table. Then she placed the healing oils in the drawer beneath.

Cynda stared at the bell on the table. She needed it to solidify her new-found strength. It was a reminder of the divide between her and Dane. She realized now that she had moved to the guest room to make it easier for him. It was not because she was uncomfortable in the room with him. She needed him more than she had ever needed anyone in her life. But she had seen the handwriting on the wall, the fear in his eyes. He was weak. She was strong. He still depended on her strength even in her time of trouble. This weekend she needed to be reminded of her strength, she told herself because she would need all of it.

When Cynda joined Suzanne in the living area, she was pleased to see her relaxing on the couch with its new persona.

"I guess we could start some dinner," Cynda said as she sat beside her.

"Marcy and I talked. We thought it would be a good idea to go out to celebrate."

"Celebrate?"

"Yes, your liberation," Suzanne said as she gave a tight little smile.

"Liberation from what?" Cynda quizzed her.

"Your old life, your bondage to perfection to avoid the truth."

"And from Brock," Cynda said.

"I have been dying to ask. What did you say to Brock? Did you tell him the truth; I mean everything?"

"I did," Cynda said with conviction.

"It was long overdue and the funny thing is, instead of feeling ashamed, I was triumphant. I was not humiliated by my appearance as I bore my hairless soul to his astonishment. For once, the humiliation was his own. It felt good."

Suzanne suddenly reached over to Cynda and hugged her shamelessly. The tears rose in both of their eyes and each swallowed the lump that formed in their throats, trying desperately not to cry. It was fruitless, as their release was simultaneous in heart wrenching sobs. It was a cleansing that was long overdue. Neither one spoke, but the release was enough. The two gathered their wits.

"Cynda, let's dry our eyes and put ourselves back together before Marcy and Audrey arrive. I promise not to do that to you again."

"I needed it and maybe before I saw Audrey. It has been a few months, too long."

Chapter 45

When Marcy and Audrey arrived, it was after seven. Cynda watched as the mini-me stepped from the car. She was flawless, contrary to the opinion she had of herself. She was graceful with her father's finely chiseled nose and a pair of green eyes that mirrored her mother's. Audrey's tall and slender body was youthful even at thirty-three. She spotted her mother standing at the door and rushed to embrace her. Instead, she gently hugged her frail body and squeezed her eyes to keep the tears at bay that were forming. Nevertheless, she could not hide her horror when she saw her mother's frailty. Cynda reciprocated her greeting with genuine enthusiasm, relieving some of Audrey's distress.

Marcy looked for something to break the tension in the air. She immediately noticed the couch and commented on its new look.

"Looks like we've got a new personality in the room," she said admiringly.

Audrey looked confused and Suzanne quickly explained why the couch had a new persona.

"Leave it Mom to make things perfect," Audrey said in a lighthearted tone that stung Cynda for a moment.

Cynda rebounded instead and said, "I made you and you are pretty perfect."

Audrey laughed and said shamelessly, "Pretty fair assessment, if I do say so myself."

The rhetoric of compliments was ripe in creating a comradeship that precluded a pleasant evening. The four went to dinner at *Beachside Break* that was one of Audrey's favorites when she visited. They discussed everything but Cynda's illness or Audrey's sudden visit.

Cynda observed her daughter during the meal. She seemed to be more relaxed and supportive of any of

299

Cynda's responses. Gone was the combative nature she had last seen in her. She was witnessing a more kind and thoughtful person.

The evening came to a close and the four arrived back at the cottage, all tired from a long day. Suzanne had decided to move in with Marcy for the weekend, so that Audrey could have her privacy. It was a bit awkward for all of them as they each went to their respective rooms to sleep, after agreeing to retire early. Cynda watched as the little girl she had nurtured into adulthood ascended the steps. She will always be my little girl, she thought. Each of them had their own thoughts of what the weekend would bring.

Cynda woke from a peaceful sleep the next morning, something that she had not experienced in months. She wanted to be the first in the kitchen, so she hurriedly dressed.

After gathering the items, she needed to make French toast, Cynda placed them on the countertop. She removed the juicer from underneath the counter and began the process of extracting the juice, orange of course. She was surprised to look up and see Audrey fully dressed and coming down the stairs.

"Is that a ghost I see there? It could not possibly be my Audrey who loves her sleep more than anything."

Audrey did not respond to the comment as her attention was focused on the motion of Cynda's arm.

"Oh my goodness Mom! That was MeMe's juicer. I did not know you had it! I loved it when she made me juice," Audrey smiled with great pleasure.

"Well, I know I can never fill her shoes, but I can at least try to carry on a few of her traditions."

"Mom, you could never fill MeMe's shoes. You know she wore a size nine and you barely wear a seven!"

Audrey answered with a laugh as she grabbed a glass of the freshly squeezed juice.

"Mmm," Audrey said as she turned the glass up and drained half the glass in one swoop.

"Slow down there, Missy; you know this juice is a commodity and there are no orange trees in the neighborhood."

Audrey knew her mother would move heaven and earth to get more oranges if the juice ran out and her daughter wanted more. Ignoring her comment, she saw the ingredients for the French toast and said, "You're making my favorite, French Toast," she said thoughtfully.

Cynda had already decided to make the toast as sort of a peace offering. After last night, she did not see the need, but she was taking no chances. She had also decided her plan of action for the day.

"I have an idea Audrey. Let's take a ride in the *Hug Bug* this morning after breakfast," she said as she began to prepare the toast.

"Sure," Audrey said, "Where were you thinking of going?" she said in a less than convincing manner.

Audrey was wondering if her mother had something up her sleeve that had something to do with Dane. She had no intention of seeing him this weekend. She had more important dragons to slay.

"Just for a nice ride," Cynda said, "We might even stop for a quick bite to eat. I don't think Marcy or Suzanne would mind. They know we have not had any time together for a while. What do you say?"

"Of course," Audrey said with more conviction and relief that Dane would not be in the picture.

The smell of French toast had wafted its way up the stairs, and a pair of sisters descended still dressed in their pajamas.

"Well we didn't get the notice. Is this the new protocol, dressing for breakfast? Besides Cynda, when did you become the breakfast chef; that is our job," Suzanne said in a lighthearted manner when she stepped into the kitchen.

"Well we have a special guest and no one can cook French toast like me," Cynda said as a matter of fact.

No one begged to differ. Instead, they all silently agreed to her statement.

"I am starving," Suzanne said as she grabbed a plate once Audrey had filled hers.

"You don't have to convince me," Marcy finally said as she followed suit.

As soon as the four had settled into light conversation over breakfast, Cynda announced that she and Audrey were going to take a ride in the *Hug Bug,* if it was okay with Suzanne.

"Absolutely," Suzanne said.

"In fact," Marcy said, "We both need to start putting away some of our things for the trip home. I need to wash some clothes and pack some of the things into the car that we will not need."

Cynda knew her sisters well enough that the excuses they used were just a ruse to encourage the outing. If the truth were told, Audrey probably suspected the same. The sisters insisted on cleaning the dishes and shooed mother and daughter out of the door.

Once again Cynda felt the freedom that the *Hug Bug* brought while she navigated through the island and over the causeway toward Savannah. She also felt truth looming over her in a possessive grip waiting to be released. She hoped and prayed its release would surround the two in solidarity.

Cynda found her way back down Skidaway Road. Her destination once again was the little strip mall that she and her sisters had frequented the weekend before. The fringe on its colorful canopies was swaying in the wind.

This time she was on a different mission. Her mouth was dry and her tongue was thick with the truth that she hoped and prayed would tear down the barriers that had choked the life out of her relationship with her daughter. She held onto the reflections of her precious daughter before the tumultuous times of her teenage years when maturity had snuffed out her innocence. Before the belief in her mother's motives for divorce were clouded.

Audrey on the other hand was anxious for the climax of the long awaited revelation for quite another reason. She could not deal with the situation fast enough, after her father had revealed the truth to her.

"Let's go into the little t-shirt shop over there," her mother said, thinking it would calm her nerves to focus on shopping for a few minutes.

"Mom, I'm not a child anymore. I have a few t-shirts, but I don't exactly shop for them."

"Not for you. I want to look around. I really like the t-shirts with cute slogans. The messages are all positive. I have even purchased a few."

Audrey was quite taken aback and responded as much.

"Wow Mom, that's a big change," Audrey announced, wondering how Dane liked his 'trophy wife' wearing clothes beneath her status.

"You could say that," her mother answered noncommittally.

Mother and daughter made small talk as they rummaged through the wares at the shop. They made their selections and paid for their purchases.

Cynda had thought the act of shopping together and focusing on their purchases would take away some of the anxiety she was feeling. Instead of taking the edge off, her anxiety began to suffocate her ability to concentrate. They left the shop and browsed through several of the other ones on the strip.　She found herself wandering mindlessly and making small talk.

Cynda looked at her watch when they left the last store and suggested, "How long has it been since you have had a chili dog?"

"It's been a while, Mom.　You know I'm trying to watch my figure."

"Right over there is a chili dog shop that comes to a close second to the Varsity.　Don't think I have forgotten your passion for the dogs."

Audrey's reluctance quickly changed and she agreed to partake in the treat that she denied herself in Atlanta.

"Why not Mom; I think this should be our day to throw caution to the wind."

"I have been doing a lot of that lately," Cynda said as she thought of the days of renewal that had brought her to this juncture.

Mother and daughter sat underneath the umbrella of tropical foliage. In unison, they battled the chili that errantly spilled over the sides of the hotdog buns, wiping their chins of its rusty hue. It was a moment of solidarity that conquered an unseen divide, giving Cynda the courage that she needed to speak. Unaware of Audrey's visit with her father, Cynda's apprehension caused her to blurt out a question about Audrey's personal life.

"So, how are you and Lane doing?" Cynda said, treading lightly as she knew that Audrey was aware of her feelings about them living together.

"Oh Mom, nothing has changed; he still wants me to marry him."

"And?"

"That's a big AND."

"Why Audrey, what is the big AND? You are not getting any younger."

Audrey held her breath and waited. She had heard the truth from her father, but she wanted to hear it from her mother, the one who had tried so valiantly to protect her. She decided to give her mother a little help.

"I want to know for sure that he is the one, Mom. I don't want to make the same mistake you did."

"The only mistake I have made Audrey is not being honest with you. You need to know the truth, as late as it is coming. I have to confess something to you. But first, I want to tell you a story that I have never shared with anyone else."

"It is important for you to know how I became the person I am today. I think I was born driven and craved to be perfect. Your grandfather and I had a very special bond and he was intuitive unlike anyone I have ever known. I hung on his every word. We were like two peas in a pod."

Audrey saw the softening in her mother's eyes and the faraway look as the past came up to swallow her with tenacity. She knew her mother had been close to her daddy and waited on the precipice of her mother's words to pull her into the awe of their power.

"Just a few short months before his death, your grandfather shared some wisdom with me. He tried desperately to warn me of always trying to be perfect. He wanted me to have courage, even when I could not control the world around me with my own perfection. He wanted me to know that even when others did not believe in me, I had not failed, as long as I had the courage to believe in myself."

Cynda then told her daughter of the healing clay that her father had used to heal his nose. She relived the moment that had been suspended in time and tucked away in reverence.

"I will never forget his words. 'Keep this to remember the secret of the healing power of the red clay of your Georgia home. Keep it to know that God will heal a broken heart and that you will always be perfect in his eyes and my eyes too. You must believe in yourself,' he told me on that night long ago."

"His words helped me to overcome the bullies in my life and I did believe in myself. I gained confidence over the next few months after that, but once he was gone I forgot some very important things. I forgot that I could not always be in control of anyone or anything, much less my own self. Trying to always be perfect is a curse."

"I just wish now that I remembered the part about a broken heart being healed. I failed to trust God. I resurrected the powers of perfection to control my very life when I married your father. I thought that being perfect in the eyes of a mere mortal man was more important than my own happiness."

Audrey listened as her mother continued to bare her very soul. She spoke of her perfection as being an affliction. Audrey felt sorry for the pain it had obviously caused her. Her father's admittance of guilt could never have conveyed the power of her mother's own words at this moment.

"I loved your father from the moment I set eyes on him in *Rich's*. He took my breath from my very soul. The idea that I could fall in love with someone so deeply scared me to death. I was so young and I had built a wall around me when my daddy was gone. As I said, my overwhelming need to be perfect and in control intensified once he died. I was terrified of loving and losing. At first, even after your father and I married, it took me a while to let my guard down. Then you were born and the completeness of our love overwhelmed me. I loved your daddy unconditionally and gave him my heart and my very soul. We laughed; we cried and built a beautiful life for ten years together. Then when we bought the lake house, it created a secret world of our own that was our escape. It was our cocoon, our secret world," Cynda said as her eyes filled with moisture.

"It was the only place I had your daddy all to myself. There was no competition from his work and least of all the 'polite society' did not exist. Phyllis' shadow did not reach as far as the lake, but something more sinister did. It was the betrayal of your father. It was bad enough that he cheated on me. But to do it at the lake house was like taking my soul. Once I found out that he had been there with a woman, I never went back again. Just like that, my perfect world was gone, and I was gone too; I ceased to exist for a very long time."

As each and every word flowed from Cynda's mouth, the hurt erupted like a fresh wound that bled as freely as her words. She began to cry with a deep moaning sob that came from within her, captured for a lifetime. Cynda realized in that moment that she was finally free of the pain that had festered, and then stifled her very soul. She finally had true release.

Audrey witnessed the raw emotions of love erupt from her mother on a level she could have never imagined.

Cynda lifted her sobbing face to her daughter and said, "I am sorry Audrey. I only wanted to protect you. I never wanted to destroy the image you had of your father and have you be embittered toward men. I wanted you to find love in its purest form and hold on for dear life without the waters being muddied. I could never have realized my decision had the opposite effect, your fear of falling out of love."

Audrey reached over and took her mother's hands in hers and said, "Daddy finally did the right thing. He told me the truth. For what it is worth, I think the shame of what he has done to both of us has haunted him for all of his life. I only have pity for him. He will never have the dignity and pride that you have carried all of your life;

although your own perfection and control over everything stifled me at times."

"Losing control over my perfect life did a number on me, Audrey. Instead of learning a lesson from it, I worked harder at trying to be perfect and expected the same from those around me. You see, trying to be perfect actually controls the person itself. I am just a big mess," she said sighing in defeat.

"I have looked up to you always Mom. You have nothing to be ashamed of."

"Well, there is one more thing," Cynda said.

"If it's about the escape with Rumelle, Daddy already told me. I think it makes you a hero and I don't care if Grandmother believes it or not."

"What do you mean?"

"I went straight to Grandmother once Daddy met with me and told her the whole thing. I shamed her for threatening you too, even though it doesn't matter anymore. I told her that Rumelle had more class in her little finger than she or her 'polite society' could ever dream about. Then, I demanded that she give me the shoe."

"YOU did?"

"I did and she tried to pretend she did not have it. She finally pulled it out of her cedar chest and handed it to me," pleading one of her famous headaches.

"I told her I was going to find a pair of shoes that looked just like it and wear them on my wedding day."

Cynda started laughing uncontrollably as she envisioned her daughter lifting her dress at the altar to reveal red platform shoes. She could just see the horror plastered on Phyllis' face. The release was classic as Audrey joined in and both laughed until tears formed in the corners of their eyes.

All of a sudden Cynda stopped laughing and said, "Your wedding day? Did I just hear you say 'your wedding day'?"

Audrey grinned as she revealed the engagement ring that she had carefully hidden.

"I was waiting for the right moment. Once Daddy told me the truth, I did some soul searching. You have been right; I am not sure that Lane would have waited forever. How he has put up with me, I do not know. I am just thankful he has stayed around."

The ride home held a plethora of emotions that were experienced by both mother and daughter. The wind blew so ferociously through the confines of the little Bug that they gave up trying to have a conversation. Instead, they both savored the quiet moments of their newfound harmony.

The *Hug Bug* settled its tiny aqua blue frame into the parking space in front of the cottage. It was well after two o'clock when it took its last breath of the day. Neither mother nor daughter wanted their time to end, but both were full with hope and renewal. The pink wreath on the front of the little car touted the royalty of its occupants, at least according to Suzanne. Cynda smiled at the notion when she walked past the *Hug Bug* and questioned her worthiness of that title.

The remainder of the afternoon was filled with harmonious laughter and the bonds of sisterhood grew stronger. The pall of sickness was swept into the corner as it had been on each and every weekend that the sisters were together. Especially this weekend it had no place in those hallowed walls that held mother, daughter and sister alike, in a union of hope and healing.

Chapter 46

Sunday came much too soon. It was the last day, not only for the sisters at the cottage, but Audrey would be leaving the next morning also. Cynda decided to stay one more night to savor every moment with her family. The day was spent discussing Audrey's plans for her upcoming wedding. She wanted to have a very small and private ceremony. With her mother's health in mind, she and Lane had decided to set a date as soon as possible. Audrey did not give any indication to her mother as to her reasoning other than the fact that she and Lane were anxious to be married. They all agreed that their mother and Audrey's grandmother would have been thrilled for her. It was a bittersweet day of reminiscing for all of them. It was a day they had all hoped and prayed would come.

It was no secret among them that Phyllis would be "chomping at the bit" to get involved with the plans.

"Mama, you must know Grandmother wants to have a reception for us at the Piedmont Driving Club. I am adamant that it is not going to happen, especially now that I know the truth about Daddy's shame."

Cynda thought for a moment and said to her daughter in complete honesty.

"Audrey, I fell in love with the beautiful and lovely Lady Atlanta as a young woman. Its grace and charm has never ceased to amaze me. The Piedmont Driving Club is one of her most gracious children. It would be a privilege for me to see you honored there."

Audrey was taken aback. Her allegiance to her mother's wishes was uppermost in her priorities for wedding plans.

"But Mama, I thought it would bring back painful memories for you there," she said softly.

"Not anymore. I am past that now. I know now that I can't just shut out everything that has been dear to me in my lifetime, because of someone else's mistake."

Audrey looked at the mother she had loved and rebelled against for most of her life. She saw a strong woman whom she admired more than anyone she had ever known.

"I will only do it for you," she said, reaching out to squeeze her mother's hand.

"Don't ever forget that Phyllis is your Grandmother and she loves you very much. I love you very much, but do it for yourself, no one else. Don't ever lose your sense of who you are, a beautiful and accomplished woman of whom I am very proud."

Audrey hugged her mother and fought back the tears as she struggled to gain her composure. Cynda felt a rush of motherly protection for her daughter and sought to soothe her daughter's raw emotions that were surfacing. She realized that Audrey's happiness was being overshadowed by her illness. She was determined to finish their time together as one to be remembered with happiness.

"How about some of that ice cream we talked about earlier?" Audrey took her cue and excused herself to run some errands. Marcy was waiting for the chance to get up the nerve to ask about the healing oils when Audrey left the cottage.

"I wondered if you have been using the healing oils Cynda," Marcy said. Before there was an answer, she continued, "We could pray with you and rub the oils into your temples."

Cynda felt a divide from across the room. She had been private about her use of the oils and was not ready to disclose her own conclusion. In fact, her privacy remained her shield, at least until she knew the outcome of her chemo, the shield that sustained her in her fight for her life.

"Let's talk about something else. I have my scan on Tuesday and a consult on Thursday. I don't want to ruin this important time with Audrey."

"I'm sorry," Marcy stuttered, "We will be leaving tomorrow and I had hoped…I mean, just promise me you will think about using the oils."

Cynda regarded her sister and then Suzanne who gave her an expectant look. She could see the hope in their eyes.

"I promise," Cynda said with certainty.

Silence hung in the air and for a long moment, the fruits of their efforts seemed lost. Then Cynda reassured them with her words.

"These weeks have been a renewal for me. I have my daughter back and I have realized the love we have for one another is just an extension of Daddy and Mama. I have missed them so much and forgot to appreciate the pieces they left behind, all of us."

As the older sister, I have failed you both. I was the keeper of our childhood and selfishly, I did not share the memories once Mama and Daddy were gone. I held them close to my heart and hoarded them, especially the memories of Daddy. It seemed as if I had shared them, they would no longer be mine. I hope that you can forgive me for that. I hope you will share the memories with your families. The three of us are their legacy, and it is up to us to instill that into them."

Marcy and Suzanne both fought back the tears that were forming in their eyes, not wishing to put a damper on the last few hours with their sister.

Audrey broke the cloud of sadness when she arrived from the store with the ice cream and ingredients for dinner. They continued to discuss wedding plans for

Audrey. When it was time to go to bed Cynda made a request.

"Audrey, what do think about sleeping with me? You know I have the 'enchanted' room with dancing flamingos as my bedfellows. One more guest won't make a difference," she said laughingly.

"Sounds good to me," Audrey said almost shyly.

The ladies made their sojourn to bed rather early as they all had a long day. Cynda and Audrey lay in the bed with only darkness and renewal between them. The loss for words was unimportant to either. They lay hand in hand, mother and daughter, filled with contentment. The euphoria held them in its grip long after the stars had settled in their universe, and the triumph of motherhood and sisterhood touted a new song of victory.

There was a cover of fog in the early morning hours as the inhabitants of the cottage rose for the last time in the shroud of renewal. The next few hours were filled with last minute details of packing. By the time the ladies were ready to make their final check of their belongings, the sun had poked its lovely face above the palms and was beaming down on hope.

Cynda carefully placed her mother's juicer in the padded bag in which she had first brought it to the cottage. She handed it to Marcy and said to her, "You are the keeper now, since you are next to the oldest."

Marcy took the juicer and disregarded the hidden meaning of her sister's words, just as she did the fact that in a few hours she and Suzanne would be on their way back to Atlanta. She took the bag with its contents and held it with care as she could not bear to refuse Cynda.

"I am only taking this, since I do know that you have one of those newfangled ones that cost an arm and a leg," she said lightheartedly.

Suzanne held back the tears and made her way out to the *Hug Bug*. The sheen of morning dew was covering the seats as they had forgotten to put the top up on the car. Suddenly she had an idea. She had planned to drive her car back to Atlanta. Instead she loaded her things into Marcy's SUV.

When the others came out for the last time, Suzanne announced that she would not be taking the *Hug Bug* home.

"I want to leave the *Hug Bug* for you so that when we are gone, you will have plenty of hugs. Besides, it was meant for royalty."

"I can't let you do that, "Cynda said.

"Just watch me," Suzanne replied

"But, what will you do when you need it? I know you will miss it desperately."

"I will be fine. It will give me a reason to come back soon. Besides, I have to return to work and won't be driving it as much."

It was time for goodbyes for all of them as each promised to keep in touch. There was no effort made to control the tears that flowed freely as the four stood together and the sun rose to its magnificence.

The menacing truth of Cynda's illness lay in reptilian fashion ready to strike, if anyone of them dared to call its name. And no one did. Sisterhood restored was enough at that moment.

Cynda watched as the SUV carrying her sisters and her only child disappeared out of her sight. She had become weaker and weaker over the last week or so and had tried hard to mask her discomfort. Now she sank into the depths of the Adirondack chair that sat neatly outside the cottage door. She could not bring herself to think about returning home, even though she was anxious to see Dane. She thought it was more important to gather her thoughts of what had transpired over the last few weeks with her sisters and as of late, her daughter. She searched for the word or words that could describe how she felt at that very moment. It was a renewal and a rebirth. She felt as unencumbered at that moment as she had ever felt in her life.

Cynda studied the *Hug Bug* briefly before she decided to climb in. The seats had dried compliments of the morning sun, but she did not care if they had not. Some of the anguish she felt when her family had left began to dissipate.

As she rode through the Wilmington Island community that she called home, she felt whole again. She could feel the love emanating from the very seats of the car. Suzanne was right. The keeper of their childhood was on a mission, to be healed completely. She knew as she always had that the 'desire to overcome' played a big part of success in fighting an illness. She embraced its fierceness now as never before.

It was time to face the monster that she had kept at bay. It would soon rear its ugly head. Tomorrow she had her scan and the results would not be revealed until Thursday. In the meantime, she had today.

Chapter 47

When Cynda arrived home, Dane was in the garage tinkering around. He walked out into the driveway, the look of disapproval on his face when he saw the Bug. He did not remark. Instead, he gave her a mechanical hug and a kiss. She knew that he was disturbed about her time with Audrey, somehow feeling left out. He had always been jealous of their relationship as if somehow, the relationship of mother and daughter had taken sides against him. Dane was back to his distant self.

"I had a great few days with Audrey and we were able to patch things up," she said hopeful of his support.

Before he had a chance to respond she said, "She is getting married Dane. Lane gave her an engagement ring."

"Well it's about time she grew up and showed some responsibility instead of depending on everyone else."

"I did not ask for your opinion of her lifestyle. I only hoped to get your approval. I should have known you were too selfish to put aside your own petty feelings. Could you not just do that this one time for me Dane?

Dane looked at her pensively and began to say something. The wind reached out with its gnarly fingers and ripped the words that stood between them and silenced them before they were born. Cynda turned and went into the house. He could unload her things, she thought. Suddenly she was very tired. She lay down on the bed and found sleep quickly, surrendering to its sweet reprieve.

That evening passed with unspoken words. Dane and Cynda resorted to the usual small talk. They watched the news and ate a light dinner in the living room. The room was comfortable and did not demand any intimacy, as they ate on trays, sitting on their respective chairs.

How will I ever get through this next week in this state Cynda thought? Dane was no help and her army of support had just left for Atlanta. She did not and could not ask them to stay. This was her private battle to fight. She may have told them about her past with Brock, but Dane was another story.

How could she share with them his rejection? Cynda knew he could not help himself. He was a lost soul and she did not have the strength to try to save him. Yet, he still demanded her perfection. Her manner of dress when she went in public was now a bone of contention with him. The Hug *Bug* was unacceptable. He did not want her to drive it, even knowing how much she enjoyed the thrill of it.

Cynda knew that life as she had known it with Dane was over, no matter the outcome of her illness. She could never go back in to the club and pretend she was someone she really wasn't. She would dress in whatever clothes made her feel comfortable, and if she never got into her Mercedes again, so be it. Right now the *Bug* was at her disposal and to hell with his 'polite society' and any 'Phyllis' who stood in her way. In fact, where were they? Where were the polite and genteel women from the club and neighborhood now that she was ill?

In the beginning they had been there for her, but one by one as months had gone by the wayside, they seemed to have capitulated into resignation of her destiny. Their concern had been reduced to phone calls, and for some, probably sudden relief when they learned her sisters were coming into town.

After dinner, Dane escaped into slumber in his chair with the remote in hand; it teetered on its demise threatening to fall to the floor. Cynda moved quietly to ease it from his hand and then stepped outside for some fresh air. It must have been the magic of its whisper that led her to the *Hug Bug*. She effortlessly slipped into the sanctuary of the Bug and reclined the front seat. She closed her eyes as the night was filled with the shattering sound of cicadas, and escaped to another time where the sound of crickets was humming a much gentler tune.

It was the summer of Cynda's tenth year and her family was on a fishing trip. She waited patiently as her father baited her hook. The worm wiggled back and forth even after its middle was pierced and looped around to cover its trappings. She remembered feeling sorry for the worm and turning her head in distaste. But she resigned herself to the necessity in order to catch her prey. If she had any remorse for the worm, it was lost on the excitement of reeling in a fish. The excitement of her father's praise when she reeled the fish in far exceeded the act of fishing.

She wondered now if those small acts of approval from her father had laid the foundation of her preconceptions of the male gender. Or was it her need for perfection? She certainly had put a lot of store in his admiration. And when he was gone, she was lost and she held onto the things that were the very essence of him. One of those was his approval.

Her need for Brock's approval had cost her dearly. Now Dane's disapproval of her rejection of living the rest of her life pretentiously could threaten alienation from him. Had he not essentially done that already she asked herself? The man whom she had always thought was strong had been reduced to a weakling by her disease. She told herself once more, she would have to go it alone.

Thinking of her father's death, she realized something. The moments that take your heart to the limits of hurt and pain, to a level that can only be tolerated by sheer perseverance can only make you stronger. That is how she had survived all of her life. That is how she would survive now, no matter the outcome.

Morning came and Dane was already dressed for the doctor's appointment. He was down on the dock with his coffee. He had left Cynda a plate of breakfast on the table and she found that she could not eat. She drank a cup of black coffee and settled on the screened porch to contemplate her day. It would be long and tedious; the business with Dane was in the forefront of her mind. Her scan was secondary at the moment. She knew the results would not be discussed until her appointment on Thursday. In the meantime, she would live by her new standards.

Dane walked back from the dock to find Cynda sitting in what he called her "lounging" clothes. She sensed his disappointment, but he did not address her attire. Instead he greeted her warmly.

"Good Morning, hope you slept well last night."

"Good Morning," Cynda said feigning pleasantry.

"I left you in your chair last night. I did not have the heart to wake you since you were sleeping so hard. I thought you might find waking up on your own easier," she said trying to make light of the task before her.

"I hardly remember going to bed," he told her.

"Are you about ready to leave?"

"Yes, just give me a few minutes to finish my coffee."

And so they sat, making small talk and avoiding the elephant in the room; an unspoken truce was formed, a companionship that precluded a very real and life threatening outcome.

Dane had chosen his battle on the clothes, but when Cynda started toward the *Hug Bug*, she realized that he drew the line.

"I refuse to ride in that excuse for a car."

"Fine, but you can follow me in yours, if you see fit," Cynda retorted as she slid into the *Hug Bug*.

She waited as Dane got into the Mercedes to follow her to her appointment. The victory was small, but she felt elated as she steered the car into the direction that would take her to the first step in determining her fate. She needed to feel victorious at that moment, instead of the numbing fear that she had tamed for the past few weeks during her sisters' visits.

Chapter 48

Thursday came all too soon for Cynda. On this day she conceded to Dane's wishes of driving the Mercedes. It was not a battle she cared to fight. Cynda and Dane sat in the doctor's office waiting room in a suspended world that had no place in normalcy. What could be normal about finding out your very fate of living or dying, she asked herself? Their conversation was pretentious at the very least.

When the two were called back to the office of the doctor, Cynda's legs turned to rubber as she stood to take her first step toward the truth. Her mouth was as dry as cotton and she swallowed hard to relieve the lump in her throat. The two sat across from the doctor's desk with only reality between them. His words needed no explanation. They were as cut and dried as the faux floral arrangement that sat on his credenza.

"I am sorry to tell you this. The cancer has spread and is out of control. We could administer more chemotherapy, but I am afraid it would be useless. It is your choice, but if it were me, I would not put myself through it. You can have some quality of life left. It is your choice."

The words seemed to lay stagnant in the air, but then slowly drifted across the room to reach their ears and the undeniable certainty of their meaning. Cynda watched the doctor immediately drop his eyes to avoid the two pairs of pleading ones across his desk. He perused her chart as if he were studying it to find an answer that he knew was not really there.

"Tell me how long," Cynda screamed silently, but instead she mouthed the words.

"Three to six months at best. I suggest you get your personal affairs in order and we will make you as comfortable as possible."

You could have cut the tension with a knife. Dane paled as the words pierced the air with finality. Cynda became numb with the realization that her fears had been realized. Without further discussion and no counsel from Dane, she looked at the doctor and said, "No more chemo."

The doctor nodded his head in agreement and shifted his gaze down to her file. It resembled the three-inch Atlanta phone book that she had used to boost Audrey in her chair when she was little. He started making notes and issuing prescriptions for her. He also emphasized a regimen of plenty of rest and some exercise if she was able.

The doctor appeared to go through the motions of his delivery as if by rote. Cynda wondered how many times he had shared news of this kind with his patients and how deeply it affected him. She decided it was more often than not and felt a stab of pity for him in his chosen field.

The moment of contemplation ended rather quickly as she found Dane leading her by the elbow. The two thanked the doctor for his efforts and moved trancelike through the motions of leaving the practice and driving home.

The remainder of the day was like a blur. There wasn't any conversation, just silence. Each of them wanted to speak, but could not find the words. Cynda wanted to be alone to wrap herself in a cocoon of misery, and she was sure that Dane wanted to run away as fast as he could.

"Dane, I think I'll rest this afternoon," Cynda implored as she looked at him.

He answered in a relieved manner, "Sure, you need to rest. I think I will take the boat out for a few hours."

She knew that the boat was his escape anytime he needed to think. Today, she was sure it was from reality.

Chapter 49

In Atlanta, Marcy called Suzanne numerous times to see if she had heard from their sister. Their conversation mimicked the same one they had on the day they had left Cynda to head home. They discussed their fears of the outcome of Cynda's scan, but agreed to stay positive. They had also regretted their unsuccessful efforts to use the healing oils on her. The trip had been bittersweet as they realized 'the keeper of their childhood' had unlocked many memories that had been foreign to them.

It was late evening and Marcy continued to wait on pins and needles for the phone call from Cynda for the results of her cat scan. Marcy had kept herself occupied with mundane tasks to fill her day. She could not shake the feeling of dread that gripped her. Finally, she went to bed.

The phone rang with a piercing sound that shook Marcy's being. The sound was exaggerated as it made its way to her ears just as she had drifted into slumber. She looked at the clock and realized it was after ten p.m.

"Hello," Marcy practically shouted as she answered.

"Hi Marcy, this is Cynda."

"Sorry for calling so late, but I wanted to let you know about my test results. First, I want you to know that I have been healed."

Marcy gasped, and put her hand across her mouth to cover the sound before Cynda continued.

"Not physically, I am sorry to say, but more importantly, my soul. Please listen before you respond. Thanks for being a big part of that healing. I could not have done it without you and Suzanne.

By the way, I used the healing oils from the day you girls brought them to me. I have prayed for God's healing power and he has answered. He has opened my eyes to the sisterhood I neglected to embrace and restored the trust my daughter had lost in me. Yes, dear sister, I have been healed in a way that I never thought possible. For that I am grateful. I know it is not the healing that we had all hoped for; no one wanted it more than I did. But, it is enough. I am at peace. I am finally free from my own perfection."

"Thanks for being the 'keeper of our childhood'," Marcy whispered as she managed to choke the words out in her state of shock.

"The Keeper will pass that torch on to you, but for now she is signing off," Cynda replied matter of fact.

"Goodnight," Marcy said quickly to avoid choking on the emotions that were bringing her to tears of dread. She did not dare ask Cynda any more details of her visit to the doctor. Instead, she concentrated on the mission she and Suzanne had made to her sister's territory. They had accomplished much in the past few weeks; of that she was certain. She would call Suzanne in the morning and tell her of the wonderful news of Cynda's spiritual healing and the fearful outcome of her future. She did not sleep until the morning hours and only in intervals of submission.

For Dane, there had been no words that evening. He was lost in pain and fear. He drank excessively until he passed out. At dusk, Cynda had not turned the lights on, preferring the darkness to the intrusion of certainty. She was spent with emotion and had finally made the phone call to her sister. Sleep overcame her as she lay in the room that had become her personal prison. When Cynda woke in the wee hours the numbness prevailed, but the revelations of the last few weeks occupied her mind, keeping the fear of her future at bay.

Once again, it was as if she were drawn to the *Hug Bug*. She slipped her robe on and silently moved through the house to the door that would lead her to the sanctity of the tiny car. She touched the hood as if the feel of it would prove its existence to be on a human level. She then touched the convertible roof with tenderness. Its persona was tangible to her and it was important for her to embrace it accordingly.

Cynda clutched the keys in her hand so tightly that she realized that they were making indentions in her palm. She opened the door and slipped into the driver's seat. She let the roof down with the automatic lever; then she slumped forward against her hands that clutched the steering wheel.

When her head touched her hands, she was reminded of another day in which she had dropped her head against another steering wheel in despair. It was the dissent into the loss of her way of life. That day at the lake she had lost hope and cheated herself out of years of really living. Now she realized that the act of living was all that she could hope for in the way she handled her situation. Cynda did not wail and cry as she had done on that day long ago. Instead she reached within her soul and breathed in the rush of peacefulness. She contemplated the renewed and special relationship with her sisters and was sorry for its absence over the years. The relationship with Audrey was on its road to recovery.

Cynda had to admit to herself that she had suppressed her joy of the discovery of the deep healing that had been taking place. It was as if she had done so to use it as a secret weapon to ward off impending bad news. She now focused on the deep wounds within her that had slowly eaten at her humanity over the course of her life. They had been conquered and were now the scars that would strengthen her. Most importantly, she had exorcised the ghosts that had plagued her very soul.

Cynda had finally let Brock go and the suppressed notion that she still needed his approval. Admittedly, his presence had loomed over her marriage with Dane. She had to face it. Certainly, her love for him had died a slow and painful death even before she had met Dane. But its carcass lay on the surface of her subconscious waiting for her to finally put it to rest. She had finally realized the closure had set in motion a freedom she had denied herself for a lifetime.

It occurred to Cynda that her healing now surpassed anything that a body could conquer. Her broken spirit that had lain dormant below the surface as she went through the motions of life was now renewed. Her emotions ran wild and she abruptly felt giddy. Yes, she said to herself, the words that she had shared with Marcy earlier about her healing were not just an appeasement for her sister to hear. They were real and they were true; indeed, she was healed!

Cynda threw her head back against the seat and allowed the tears to flow freely and silently. They brought her to a level of acceptance and perseverance. She freed herself of the confines of the *Hug Bug* and gently touched her hand to her lips. She kissed it and touched it again with tenderness, tracing her hand along its side.

Cynda quickly went to her bedroom and walked over to dressing table and sat on the stool. She allowed herself the privilege of taking it slow and easy, with no audience, just herself and the mirror; no one demanding perfection, not even Cynda. She studied the picture that had been stuck into the corner of the oval mirror. Cynda had placed it there like a dreamy teenager foraging a personal place in the world. It was of the *Hug Bug*. She reached out and traced her hand around it as if to bring it to life.

Next, she pulled the glass handle on the bottom drawer and it opened to reveal an array of scarves in all colors. She reached to the back of the drawer and searched until her hand found the pill bottle. She cradled the bottle to her chest and closed her eyes, resolved in her mission.

Cynda sat there for a long time, just staring at herself in the mirror. She no longer saw the gaunt face that had haunted her each time she had looked into it. Instead she saw the glittering green eyes that had never lost their sparkle. They looked back at her, perfect in their shape and vibrancy; yes, they were perfect. They had served her well. She took comfort in knowing that she would always be remembered for them, both from Dane and her family.

She walked past the sleeping Dane. He lay there in his recliner with his arms crossed over his chest. She thought it rather ironic. He was lying there in his perfect robe and bedroom shoes to match. Underneath, the collar of his pajamas betrayed more perfection; his perfectly trimmed beard and mustache completed the flawless picture. Cynda paused to stare at him for a moment. There it was, the end to the picture of perfection, a hair from Dane's mustache dancing wildly as he snored, mocking him in silence. He took in each and every breath as if it were a battle. She slid past him quietly, finding her way through the shadows as they loomed over her.

Cynda opened the sliding glass door with familiar ease. She walked over to the pool and into the fading moonlight that was now her accomplice. The shadows it cast were eerily comforting. She stripped her gown and stepped into the water, clutching the pill bottle in her hand. She lowered herself onto the steps and sat down, the water rippling away in tiny waves; she still clutched the bottle. She looked down at her breasts as they begin to take on a life of their own and floated easily away from the confines of her chest. She acknowledged her acceptance of her breasts, the imperfections of their form. They were floating freely, as she would be soon, no restrictions.

Cynda thought of her father now. She closed her eyes and softly said her name, Lucy. The name sounded foreign but was like music to her ears. She was Lucy again, self-assured, confident. She was whole, healed and no longer searching for perfection, but embracing her freedom from the demons that had controlled her very soul.

Lucy took the bottle from underneath the water and brought it up to stare at it. She slowly removed the cap and emptied the contents into her hand. It was time. She looked at the ball of clay that had now turned into a hard substance, no longer soft and pliable. She touched it to her heart and then put her tightly held fist into the water. She held it there for a couple of minutes. She then pulled her hand from the water and watched as her fingers unfurled to reveal the lump, remnants of the Georgia clay, no longer a perfect ball, but a myriad of particles absent of perfection. Lucinda Ophelia Brooks had been healed and Lucy was found.

Surrender

It had been eleven months since Cynda had been given her death sentence and she had beaten the odds by almost five. It was no small measure as she knew her strength came from the healing of her soul.

In her now weakened state, she lay on the black wrought iron chaise that had become her ally. Marcy had found a cushion with fabric made of dancing pink flamingos and brought it to her to use for her comfort. The chaise was her happy place.

The remnants of spring had slowly turned to summer and the tapestry of color met her half-closed eyes. Plants surrounded the pool in pots that were bursting with blooms. The air was still and she strained to listen to the gentle sloshing of the water as it kissed the side of the pool, like the first kiss of a lover's unrequited love; soft and gentle. The memory of her own first kiss blazed like a flame for a moment and then, into a dying ember. The mahogany door in the *Rich's* dressing room was closed. It had been all that had stood between her and the ecstasy of being propelled into her first true love, the sweetness of its memory fleeting from her mind.

Those memories had been unduly resurrected as she had recently witnessed her daughter's wedding vows in a quiet ceremony in Atlanta. The after party was held at the Piedmont Driving Club a week later, much to Phyllis' satisfaction. The well-orchestrated event had been her swan song and had surely been recorded in the hallowed books of 'polite society'. For once in her life, Cynda had taken a backseat and allowed Phyllis full rein. It wasn't worth the fight, she had decided. Audrey had followed suit in her decision as well. Prissy Crissy's involvement had been on the fringes as there had been no sign of animal prints or faux fur making an appearance at the reception, except on her person. Apparently, Phyllis had seen enough of that slant at the shower she had thrown for Audrey. Brock had been low key and gracious in his role as father of the bride.

Cynda studied the pink polish on her fingernails that Suzanne had so carefully painted. She had always known that her love for Brock had been real, and finally she was at peace with the idea that it only lasted for ten years, a lifetime ago. Her thoughts again turned to that first tender kiss that she had shared with him. The days and years afterward had been idyllic-something from out of a movie. She had finally resigned herself to savor the memory. There were people in this world, she thought that may never experience even one moment of what she had had with Brock so long ago. She was at peace. She thought of the evidence of their lovemaking and knew without a doubt that it had been genuine. If not, how could she have had such a wonderful daughter? Cynda no longer allowed herself to visit those dark days that followed her broken marriage for the light of her healing had obliterated them.

Cynda heard a noise from within the house. Dane was somewhere in there, still fighting his own battles. He had secreted her away so many years ago and had loved her in the best way he knew how. She had been his trophy. It had been enough, Cynda had reasoned.

Cynda prayed for him daily and secretly rubbed the healing oils into his temples as he lay in his recliner at night. He could not accept the inevitable and she knew he was terribly afraid. Only he had the keys to unlock the peace that eluded him. She could not do that for him.

Marcy and Suzanne had returned for an undetermined length of time. Audrey would be arriving soon. They had thanked her repeatedly for being the 'keeper of their childhood'. She smiled as she thought of the little *Hug Bug* that sat in her driveway, for now. She could see it out the window while in her bedroom. It held the camaraderie of sisterhood in its tiny cubicle, but had been large enough to embrace its occupants in a final healing.

Cynda's eyes felt heavy and she felt the pull of peace and tranquility tugging at her soul, absent of human matter. Reaching for the open arms of the ONE true love that had been her constant forever, she closed her eyes and embraced eternity.